THE RHYTHM SECTION

Mark Burnell

The carder was a stout skinhead in a Reebok track-suit who carried a canvas satchel stuffed with prostitutes' advertising cards. Along Baker Street, he moved from phone-box to phone-box, sticking the cards to the glass with Blu-Tack. Keith Proctor watched him from a distance before approaching him. He showed him the scrap of card he'd been given by one of her friends and asked the man if he knew who she was. It cost fifty pounds to persuade the carder to talk. Yes, he knew who she was. No, she wasn't one of his. He'd heard a rumour she was working in Soho.

On the fragment of dirty yellow card there was a photograph of a woman offering her breasts, plumping them between her hands. The bottom half of the card – the half with the phone number – was missing.

An hour later, Proctor hurried along Shaftesbury Avenue. The falling drizzle was so fine it hung in the air like mist but its wetness penetrated everything. Those who were heading across Cambridge Circus towards the Palace Theatre for the evening's performance of *Les Misérables* looked suitably miserable, shoulders curved and heads bowed against the damp chill. The traffic on the Charing Cross Road was solid.

HarperCollins*Publishers*

MARK BURNELL

THE
RHYTHM
SECTION

HarperCollins*Publishers*

HarperCollins*Publishers*
77–85 Fulham Palace Road,
Hammersmith, London W6 8JB

www.**fir**eand**water**.com

This paperback edition 2000

First Published in Great Britain by
HarperCollins*Publishers* 1999

Copyright © Mark Burnell 1999

The Author asserts the moral right to
be identified as the author of this work

ISBN 978-0-00-651337-7

Set in PostScript Linotype Meridien by
Rowland Phototypesetting Ltd, Bury St Edmunds

To my parents,
with love and thanks for your ceaseless support.

ACKNOWLEDGEMENTS

Of all those who have helped me during the writing of this book, I would particularly like to thank Julian Warren for his technical assistance. I would also like to thank Susan Watt for making editing such a painless process.

I am especially indebted to Toby Eady for reasons too numerous to list here. Suffice to say that I regard this book as something of a joint venture.

Character is destiny.
George Eliot/Mill On The Floss

Let's make us medicine of our great revenge,
to cure this deadly grief.
William Shakespeare/Macbeth

Outside, the temperature has reached −52°C. Inside, it's a constant 23°C. Outside, there is speed. Inside, there is stillness. Outside, the air pressure is consistent with an altitude of thirty-seven thousand feet. Inside, the air pressure is equivalent to an altitude of six thousand five hundred feet. Made from aluminium and assembled near Seattle, the dividing line between these two mutually hostile environments is just two millimetres thick.

Martin Douglas had his eyes closed but he was not asleep. The occupant of seat 49C, a resident of Manhattan and a native of Uniondale, New York, Douglas focused on his breathing and tried to ignore the tension that was his invisible co-passenger on every flight he took. The airline's classical music channel piped Mahler through his headphones. The music took the edge off the drone of the engines, masking the tiny changes in pitch, every one of which usually accelerated Douglas' pulse. Now, however, with soothing music in his ears and with the fatigue that follows relentless anxiety starting to set in, he was almost relaxed. His eyelids were heavy when he half-opened them. An in-flight movie was flickering on the TV screens above the aisles but most of the passengers around him were asleep. He envied them. On the far side of the cabin he noticed a couple of cones of brightness falling from reading lights embedded in the ceiling. He closed his eyes again.

When the explosion occurred, North Eastern Airlines flight NE027 was flying over the Atlantic, bound for London's

1

Heathrow Airport from New York's JFK. Including flight crew and cabin crew, there were three hundred and eighty-eight people on board the twenty-six-year-old Boeing 747.

First Officer Elliot Sweitzer was drinking coffee. Larry Cooke, the engineer, was returning to his seat after a brief walk to stretch his legs. The lights on the flight deck were dimmed. Outside, it was a beautiful clear night. A brilliant moon cast silver light on to the gentle ocean below. The stars glittered above the aircraft. To the east and to the north, the sky was plum purple with a hint of bloody red along the curved horizon.

The countless hours spent in a 747 simulator combined with years of actual flying experience counted for nothing in preparing the pilots for the physical shock of the blast. Sweitzer's coffee cup flew free of his grasp and shattered on the instruments in front of him. Cooke's seat-belt was not properly fastened and he was hurled into the back of Sweitzer's seat. He heard his collar-bone snap.

Instantly, the flight deck was filled with mist as the howl of decompression began. Captain Lewis Marriot reacted first. Attaching an oxygen mask to his face, he began to absorb the terrifying information that surrounded him. 'Rapid depressurization drill!' He turned to his co-pilot. 'Elliot, are you all right?'

Sweitzer was fumbling with his mask. 'Okay ... I'm okay ...'

'You fly it,' Marriot commanded him, before turning to check on Cooke. 'Larry?'

There was blood on Cooke's forehead. His left arm was entirely numb. He could feel the break in the collarbone against his shirt. Gingerly, he hauled himself back into his seat and attached his own oxygen mask. 'I'll be ... fine ...'

'Then talk to me.'

On the panel in front of Cooke the loss of cabin pressure

was indicated by a red flashing light. A siren began to wail. Cooke pressed the light to silence it. 'I got a master warning for loss of cabin pressure.'

Sweitzer said, 'We need to get to a lower altitude.'

Marriot nodded. 'Set flight level change. Close thrust. Activate speed brake.'

A yellow light began to flash in front of Cooke. 'I've got a hydraulics master caution.' He pressed the light to reset it. Two seconds later, it went off again. 'We've lost one set of hydraulics.' The 747–200 was fitted with three different hydraulics systems. 'I also got a fuel imbalance warning.' A red master warning light came on, accompanied by the ringing of a bell. '*Fire!*'

Sweitzer said, 'The auto-pilot's in trouble. I'm getting a vibration.'

Marriot looked at Cooke. 'Engine fire check list. What's it on?'

'Two.'

Under Cooke's supervision, Marriot closed the number two engine, shut off the fuel control switch, and then pulled the number two fire handle to close the hydraulics and fuel valves. Then he twisted the handle to activate the fire extinguishers.

'We're losing the auto-pilot. The second set of hydraulics is going.'

'Deactivate the auto-pilot, Elliot.'

Sweitzer nodded. 'We're going to have to slow her down. There's too much vibration.'

'Just keep her steady and make the turn. We're heading for Gander.'

Gander, in Newfoundland, was the closest runway to them.

Sweitzer was struggling with the control column. '*God, she's sluggish!*'

The fire bell sounded again in conjunction with a master warning light. Cooke said, 'We need the second shot with the fire extinguisher. It's still burning.'

'I think we've got a rudder problem and maybe a jammed stabilizer. The trim's shot to hell.'

Marriot turned the radio to VHF 1215, the emergency frequency. 'Mayday, Mayday, Mayday! This is North Eastern Zero Two Seven. We are in emergency descent. We have structural damage. We have an engine fire, not extinguished.'

The violent deceleration hurled everyone forwards. Those whose seat-belts were unfastened were ejected from their seats. Martin Douglas was lifted from his but the belt cut across the top of his thighs and restrained him. His head hit the seat in front. The blow knocked him senseless and his body was immediately snapped back against his own seat.

He was only unconscious for three seconds. Despite being dazed, Douglas knew that his nose was broken. The back of the seat in front had crushed it and ripped the skin in several directions. Blood was seeping from the star-shaped gash but it was not slithering down his face. It was not staining his shirt or splattering his lap. Instead, it was being sucked off his skin. A sticky stream of crimson drops was hurtling forwards, flying over the seats in front, borne on the rushing air.

Further forward, part of the cabin floor had collapsed. Broken seats were wrenched from their moorings and sucked into the night. A tornado tore through the fuselage, ripping clothes from bodies, bodies from seats, hand-luggage from floors and overhead lockers. All of this debris was inhaled by some enormous invisible force towards the front of the 747. The majority of those who could were screaming, but their pitiful shrieks were lost in the roar of decompression. Others were unconscious. Or already dead.

The pain in his ears was agonizing, a consequence of the colossal percussive clap and the violent change in air pressure. But compared to the fear, his pain was a minor irritation. The terror constricted his throat, his stomach, his chest. As the aircraft began to descend, Douglas instinctively pushed against the arm-rests, raising himself upwards, stretching himself, as if to counteract, in whatever minuscule way possible, the 747's descent. The entire aircraft was vibrating uncontrollably. To Douglas, it seemed that this was Hell and that whatever was to follow could be no worse.

The boy who had been asleep in seat 49B was no longer there. His belt had been fastened but not securely enough. The girl by the window was either unconscious or dead. Her hair was drawn forwards, masking her face, but there was a thick smudge of her blood on the window's blind. It looked black.

Oxygen masks fell from the ceiling and were drawn towards the source of depressurization. Douglas reached for one, retrieved it by the plastic tube and yanked it towards him, placing it over his nose and mouth. Breathing through the mask proved to be harder than fixing it to his face; his lungs seemed to be shutting down, each breath becoming shallower than the one before, the time between them shrinking. Small white stars were exploding in his eyes.

He allowed himself to look around. It was dark in the cabin but of those he could see, he was one of the few who was still conscious. Even as a nervous flyer, he had never imagined that any fear could be so acute, that his worst nightmare made real would be quite so surgical in the way that it sliced him apart.

The fire bell sounded again. Cooke didn't know where to start. Every light was ablaze. He guessed – because he didn't want to admit to himself that he knew – that the fire, which was still raging, was burning through the third and last of their hydraulics systems. The aircraft's descent was transforming into a plunge.

He gripped Marriot's shoulder. 'The fire's spreading. You better make the call.'

Marriot checked the 1215 frequency. 'Mayday, Mayday, Mayday! This is North Eastern Zero Two Seven. We are in emergency descent. We are going down. We have an uncontrolled fire on board. We have a complete hydraulics failure. We cannot complete our turn for Gander. This is our last call. Our position is fifty-four north, forty west. We will try to –'

Martin Douglas was on the verge of hyperventilating, a condition that would have been welcome. To pass out would have been a merciful relief. There was smoke in the cabin.

He had been in a car crash once. Travelling at over seventy miles an hour on a road that cut through a forest in Vermont, he had hit a patch of black ice. His car had skidded sideways and veered on to the wrong side of the road. Fortunately, there had been no oncoming traffic. Unfortunately, there had been pine trees lining the road. He'd had time to think, then – a few moments to anticipate the collision, to feel fear, to contemplate death as a serious possibility. This was different. Death was not a serious possibility. It was an inevitability. The aircraft was falling like a rock. Essentially, he knew that he was already dead.

When his breathing could become no shallower or quicker, he stopped. For a second. And then took a deep breath. With it, the accumulated tension flooded out of him. He felt it drain from his head, through his chest and stomach, down his legs and out through the soles of his feet and into the frame of the disintegrating 747.

And for one moment in his life, Martin Douglas was at peace inside an aircraft.

6

1

LISA'S
WORLD

1

She's a chemical blonde.

The carder was a stout skinhead in a Reebok track-suit who carried a canvas satchel stuffed with prostitutes' advertising cards. Along Baker Street, he moved from phone-box to phone-box, sticking the cards to the glass with Blu-Tack. Keith Proctor watched him from a distance before approaching him. He showed him the scrap of card he'd been given by one of her friends and asked the man if he knew who she was. It cost fifty pounds to persuade the carder to talk. Yes, he knew who she was. No, she wasn't one of his. He'd heard a rumour she was working in Soho.

On the fragment of dirty yellow card there was a photograph of a woman offering her breasts, plumping them between her hands. The bottom half of the card – the half with the phone number – was missing.

An hour later, Proctor hurried along Shaftesbury Avenue. The falling drizzle was so fine it hung in the air like mist but its wetness penetrated everything. Those who were heading across Cambridge Circus towards the Palace Theatre for the evening's performance of *Les Misérables* looked suitably miserable, shoulders curved and heads bowed against the damp chill. The traffic on the Charing Cross Road was solid. Red tail lights shivered in puddles.

There was a cluster of four old-fashioned phone-boxes on Cambridge Circus. Proctor waited for five minutes for one of them to become free. As the heavy door swung behind him, muting the sound outside, he realized someone had been smoking in the phone-box. The smell of stale cigarettes was unpleasant but Proctor found himself grudgingly grateful for it since it mostly masked the under-lying stench of urine.

Three sides of the phone-box were covered by prosti-tutes' advertising cards. Proctor let his eyes roam over the selection. Some were photos, in colour or black and white, others were drawings. Some merely contained text, usually printed although, in a few cases, they had been scrawled by hand. They offered straight sex, oral sex, anal sex. They were redheads, blondes and brunettes. They were older women and they were teenagers. To the top of the phone-box, they were stacked like goods on a supermarket shelf. Black, Asian, Oriental, Scandinavian, Proctor saw specific nationalities singled out; 'busty Dutch girl – only 21', 'Brazilian transsexual – new in town', 'Aussie babe for fun and games', 'German nymphomaniac, 19 – nothing refused'. One card proclaimed: 'Mature woman – and proud of it! Forty-four's not just my chest size – it's my age!'

Proctor took the torn yellow card out of his pocket and scanned those in the phone-box. He made a match high to his left. The one on the wall was complete, the phone number running along the bottom half. He forced a twenty-pence piece into the slot and dialled.

A woman answered, her voice more weary than seductive.

'I . . . I'm in a phone-box,' Proctor stammered. 'On . . . on Cambridge Circus.'

'We're in Brewer Street. Do you know it?'

'Yes.'

'The girl we've got on today is a real stunner. She's called Lisa and she's a blonde with a gorgeous figure and lovely long legs. She's a genuine eighteen-year-old and her measurements are . . .'

Proctor felt deadened by the pitch.

'It's thirty pounds for a massage with hand-relief and her prices go up to eighty pounds for the full personal service. What was it you were looking for, darling?'

He had no answer at the ready. 'I . . . I'm not sure . . .'

'Well, why don't you discuss it with the young lady in person?'

'What?'

'You can decide when you get here. When were you thinking of coming round?'

'I don't know. When would be . . . ?'

'She's free now.' Like a door-to-door salesman, she gave Proctor no time to think. 'It'll only take you five minutes to get here. Do you want the address?'

There were Christmas decorations draped across the roads and hanging from street lamps. They filled the windows of pubs and restaurants. Their crass brightness matched the gaudy lights of the sex shops. Proctor passed a young homeless couple, who were huddling in a shallow doorway, trying to keep dry, if not warm. They were sharing a can of Special Brew.

The address was opposite the Raymond Revuebar, between an Asian mini-market and a store peddling pornographic videos. The woman answered the intercom. 'Top of the stairs.'

The hall was cramped and poorly lit. Broken bicycles and discarded furniture had been stored beneath the fragile staircase. Proctor felt a tightness in his stomach as he started to climb the stairs. On each landing there were either two or three front doors. None of them matched. Most were dilapidated, their hinges barely clinging to their rotting frames, rendering their locks redundant. On the third floor, though, he passed a new door. It was painted black and it was clear that a whole section of wall had been removed and rebuilt to accommodate it. It had three, gleaming, heavy-duty steel locks.

The door at the top of the staircase was held open by an obese woman in her fifties with tinted glasses. She wore Nike trainers, a pair of stretched grey leggings and a violet jersey, sleeves rolled up to the elbows. The flat was a converted attic. In a small sitting room, a large television dominated. On a broken beige sofa there was an open pizza carton; half the pizza was still in it. The woman steered Proctor into the room at the end.

'You want something to drink, darling?'

'No.'

'All right, then. You wait here. She'll be with you in a minute.'

She closed the door and Proctor was alone. There was a king-sized mattress on a low wooden frame. The bedcover was dark green. On the mantelpiece, on the table in the far corner and on the two boxes that passed for bedside tables, there were old bottles of wine with candles protruding from their necks. On top of a chest of drawers there was a blue glass bowl with several dozen condoms in it. The room was hot and reeked of baby oil and cigarettes. Proctor walked over to the window, the naked floorboards creaking beneath his feet. Pulsing lights from the street tinted curtains so flimsy that he could almost see through them. He parted them and looked down upon the congested road below.

'Looking for someone?'

He hadn't heard her open the door. He turned round. She wore a crimson satin gown and when she turned to close the door, Proctor noticed a large dragon running down the back of it. The gown was open and beneath it, she wore black underwear, a suspender-belt and a pair of high-heeled shoes. Her hair was blonde – *chemically blonde* – but her dark roots were showing. It was shoulder-length and, even in the relative gloom, looked as though it could have been cleaner.

No trick of the light, however, could disguise her paleness, her thinness or her weariness. She had a frame for a fuller figure but she didn't have the flesh for it. When she moved, her open gown parted further and, from across the room, Proctor could see her ribs corrugating her skin. Her face was made-up – peach cheeks, bloody lips and heavy eye-liner – but the rest of her body was utterly white, and when she smiled she only succeeded in looking tired. 'My name's Lisa. What's yours?'

He ignored the question. 'You don't look like you do on the card.'

She shrugged. 'I don't want to be walking down the street seeing myself in every phone-box I pass. And I don't want people pointing at me because they've recognized me from my picture, do I?'

'I guess not.'

She kept her distance and put a hand on her hip, revealing a little more of herself. 'So, what do you want?'

Proctor's hand was in his coat pocket. He felt the torn yellow card. 'I just want to talk.'

Her cheap smile faded. 'I don't charge less than thirty for anything. And for that, you get a massage and hand-relief.'

'What's your name?'

'I told you. Lisa.'

'Is that your real name?'

'Maybe.'

'Is that a yes or a no?'

'What's it to you?'

'I'd just like to know, that's all.'

She paused for a moment. 'Tell you what, why don't you tell me? Who do you think I am? Lisa, or someone else?'

'I think you're someone else.'

'Really?' She smiled again but it failed to soften the hardness in her gaze. 'Who?'

'I think your real name might be . . . Stephanie.' Not even a flinch. Proctor was disappointed. '*Are* you Stephanie?'

'That depends.'

'On what?'

'On your money. If I don't see some, I'm nobody. If you just want to talk, that's fine but it'll still cost you thirty. I don't do anything for free.'

Proctor reached for his wallet. 'Thirty?'

She nodded. 'Thirty. And for thirty, I'll be Stephanie, or Lisa, or whoever you want.'

Proctor held three tens just out of her grasp. 'Will you be yourself?'

She said nothing until he handed her the notes. And then, as she was folding them in half, she asked, 'What are you doing here? What do you really want?'

'The truth.'

'I'm a prostitute, not a priest. There's no truth here. Not from me, not from you.' When Proctor frowned at this, she added: 'When you get home this evening, are you going to tell your wife you went to see a hooker? That you paid her money?'

'I'm not married.'

'Your girlfriend, then. Anyone ...' Proctor didn't need to say anything. 'I thought not. So don't come here and talk to me about the truth.'

Not only was her tone changing, so was her accent; south London was being displaced by something less readily identifiable. Just as her opening remarks had been laced with a dose of sleazy tease, now she was cold and direct.

Proctor was equally blunt. 'I think your real name is Stephanie Patrick.'

This time, he knew he was right. The surname betrayed her and she froze, if only for a fraction of a second. He saw her try to shrug it off but he also saw that she knew he'd seen it.

'I'm right, aren't I?'

For the first time, she looked openly hostile. 'Who are you?'

'Your name *is* Stephanie Patrick, isn't it?'

She looked down at the money in her fist and said, 'Let me give this to the maid and then we'll talk. Okay?'

It took Proctor a couple of seconds to realize that the 'maid' was the fat woman who had admitted him to the flat. 'Okay.'

14

Lisa – for that was who she still seemed to be – turned away and left him alone in the room. When she returned, a couple of minutes later, she had transformed into a man who was six-foot-four and built like a weight-lifter. He had no neck, his huge shaven head merging with the grotesque bulges of his shoulder muscles. His white T-shirt was so tight it could have been body-paint.

He didn't need to raise his voice when he pointed at Proctor and murmured, 'You. Outside. Now.'

Proctor rolled over, vaguely aware of the soggy rubbish that was squashed beneath his body. The drizzle fell softly on to his stinging face. One eye was closing. Through the other, he saw two walls of blackened brick converging as they rose. He was in an alley of some sort and it stank.

The beating had been short, brutal and depressingly efficient; the administrator was clearly no novice. After a final kick to the ribs, he'd hissed a blunt warning: 'If I ever see you here again, I'll tear your fucking balls off. And that's just for starters. Now piss off out of here.'

With that, a door had slammed shut and Proctor had been by himself, lying on a bed of rotting rubbish. For a while, he made no attempt to move. He lay on his back, his arms wrapped around his burning ribs. He tasted blood in his mouth.

He looked up and saw smudges of buttery light seeping from cracks in drawn curtains. And from a partially-opened window, he heard Bing Crosby crooning on a radio.

I'm dreaming of a White Christmas . . .

2

Proctor saw her before she saw him. He was standing in a restaurant doorway, trying to keep dry. The drizzle of the previous night had matured into real rain. When he glimpsed her, she was heading his way, so he retreated from view. Inside the restaurant, staff were preparing for lunch, placing tall wine glasses and small dishes of chilled butter on tables draped in starched white cloth.

He waited until she was close. 'Lisa?'

She stopped but it took a moment for her to recognize him beneath his mask of bruises. Proctor raised his hands in surrender. 'I don't want any trouble. I just want to talk.'

She looked as though she would run. 'Leave me alone,' she hissed.

'Please. It's important.'

He saw the hardness in her gaze again. 'Which part don't you understand? Or maybe you just enjoy getting your head kicked in.'

'No, I don't. That's why I waited for you here and not in Brewer Street.'

'How'd you know I'd come this way?'

He shrugged. 'I didn't. But I guessed you didn't live there so you'd be coming from somewhere else. And then I guessed you'd come on the Underground, not a bus. And since this is on the shortest route between the nearest station and Brewer Street . . .'

'Smart,' she said, flatly. 'But I could've come another way. I often do.'

'You could've. But you didn't.'

According to Proctor's information, Stephanie Patrick was twenty-two. The woman in front of him looked at least ten years older than that. Her dyed blonde hair was dishevelled and with her make-up removed, her face was as colourless as the rest of her. Except for the dark smudges around both eyes. But now, in the morning, they were natural, not cosmetic.

She wore a tatty, black, leather bomber-jacket over a grey sweatshirt. Her jeans were frayed at the knees and down the thighs; given the weather, this seemed more like a financial statement than one of fashion. Her blue canvas trainers were soaked.

'How long have you been here?' she asked him.

'Since nine-thirty.'

She glanced at her plastic watch. It was after eleven. 'You must be cold.'

'And wet. And in pain.'

He saw a hint of a smile.

'I can imagine. He's not known for his subtlety. Just for his thoroughness.' She examined Proctor's face. 'You look like shit.'

Proctor hadn't slept. When the paracetamol had failed, he'd resorted to alcoholic painkiller, which had also failed. And not being a seasoned drinker, the experience had left him with a hangover to compound his misery. His body was peppered with bruises, his left eye was badly swollen, his ribs ached with every breath and his right ankle, which had been twisted on the stairs, was aflame.

'Look, if you're not going to talk to me, fine. But let me ask you one question. Are you or are you not Stephanie Patrick, daughter of Dr Andrew Patrick and Monica Patrick?'

He needed to hear the answer that he already knew. She took her time.

'First, who are you?'

'My name is Keith Proctor.'

'Why are you asking me these things?'

'It's part of my job.'

'Which is what?'

17

'I'm a journalist.' Predictably, she grew yet more defensive, her posture betraying her silence. Proctor said, 'Your parents were on the North Eastern Airlines flight that crashed into the Atlantic two years ago. So were your sister and your younger brother.'

He watched her run through the phrases in her mind before she chose one. 'I've got nothing to say to you. Leave me alone. Leave *it* alone.'

'Believe me, I'd like to. But I can't.'

'Why not?'

'Because it wasn't an accident.'

The bait was cast and she considered it for a moment. Before ignoring it. 'I don't believe you.'

'I don't expect you to. Not yet. Not until you've given me a chance.' She shook her head but Proctor persisted. 'I need a cup of coffee, Miss Patrick. Will you let me buy you one, too? I'll pay for your time.'

'People pay me for my body, not my time.'

'They pay for both. Come on. Just one cup of coffee.'

Bar Bruno, on the corner of Wardour Street and Peter Street, was half-full. It offered fried breakfasts all day. There was a large Coke vending machine just inside the door. Behind a long glass counter, sandwich fillings were displayed in dishes. The table-tops looked like wood but weren't. The banquettes were covered in shiny green plastic.

They ordered coffee and sat at the back where there were fewer people. Stephanie wriggled out of her leather jacket and dumped it beside her. Proctor's eyes were immediately drawn to her wrists. Both were seriously bruised. She looked as if she was wearing purple handcuffs. They hadn't been there the previous night; he was sure he would have noticed. She saw him looking at them.

'What happened?' he asked.

'Nothing,' she snapped.

'It doesn't look like nothing.'

'You're a fine one to talk. Have you looked in a mirror this morning?'

'Unfortunately, yes.'

Momentarily angry, she thrust both wrists in front of Proctor's face for closer inspection. 'You want to know what this is? It's an occasional occupational hazard, that's what it is.' Then she was calm and stirring sugar into her milky coffee, before changing the subject. 'Have you got any cigarettes on you?'

'I don't smoke.'

'I didn't think so, but you never know until you ask.' Proctor watched her produce a packet of her own from her jacket pocket. She lit one and dropped the dead match on her saucer. 'So, you're a journalist.'

'Yes.'

'You don't look like one.'

'I didn't realize there was a look.'

'I'm not saying there is. I'm talking about the way *you* look. Good haircut, nice suit, expensive shoes and clear skin – apart from the bruises, of course. You look like you take care of yourself.'

'I try to.'

'Who do you work for?'

'I'm freelance. But I used to work for *The Independent* and then the *Financial Times*.'

'Impressive.'

'Not to you, I shouldn't think.'

Stephanie took a sip of coffee. 'You haven't a clue what I think.'

More than anything, she looked nervous, despite the aggression in her small talk. She fidgeted incessantly and her eyes never settled on anything. Proctor took a sip of his own coffee and grimaced.

'Your parents were murdered,' he said for effect. She seemed oblivious, as though she hadn't even heard him. 'Along with everyone else on that flight.'

'That's not true. There was an investigation – '

19

'Faulty electrics in the belly of the aircraft which produced a spark igniting aviation fuel fumes, causing the first of two catastrophic explosions? I read the FAA and CAA findings like everyone else. And until recently, I believed them. Everyone believed them. And, as a consequence of that, some of the electrical systems on some of the older 747s were changed. Problem addressed, problem solved. Except it wasn't. The problem's still out there, walking around with a pulse, a brain and a name.'

Her look said it all. *You're either crazy or you're stupid.* Proctor leaned forward and lowered his voice. 'It was a bomb that destroyed that aircraft. It wasn't an accident.'

He waited for the reaction; a gasp of shock, or a denial, or something else. Instead, he got nothing. Stephanie picked at her fingernails and he noticed how dirty they were. And cracked. Her fingertips looked raw.

'How much money have you got on you?' she asked.

'What?'

'Cash. How much have you got on you?'

'I don't know.'

She looked up to meet his eyes. 'I need money and you said you'd pay me.'

Proctor was at sea. 'Look, I'm trying to explain to you –'

'I know. But I need this money now.'

'Aren't you interested?'

'Are you going to give it to me or not? Because if you're not, I'm leaving.'

'I paid you thirty last night and look what it bought me.'

She stood up and picked up her jacket.

To buy himself time, Proctor reached for his wallet again. 'There was a bomb on that flight. The authorities know this but they're keeping it secret.'

Stephanie sounded bored. 'You reckon?'

'They even know who planted it.'

'Right.' Her eyes were on the wallet.

'He's alive and he's here, in London. But they're making no attempt to apprehend him.'

She held out her hand. 'Whatever you say.'

Proctor gave her two twenties. 'I don't get it. This is your family we're talking about, not mine.'

'Forty? I need a hundred. Seventy-five, at least.'

Proctor gave a cough of bitter laughter. 'For what? *Your time?* Do me a favour . . .'

'Bastard.'

He reached across the table and grabbed a purple wrist. She winced but he didn't loosen his grip. With his other hand, he pressed a business card on to the two twenties and then closed her cold fingers over it. 'Why don't you go home and think about it, and then give me a call?'

She stared him down with a face as full of hatred as any he had ever seen. 'Let go of me.'

I am difficult. I always have been and I always will be. I'm not proud of it but I'm not ashamed of it, either. It's just the way I am, it's my nature. In the past, I was aggressively difficult – sometimes out of pure malice – but these days, I would say that I am difficult in a more defensive way. It's a form of protection.

Proctor was wrong when he accused me of not listening. I listen to everything. I just don't absorb much. I am like a stone; a product of molten heat turned cold and hard. Yes, we were talking about my family. But the four that are dead cannot be retrieved – nor, for that matter, can the one that still lives – and that is all there is to it.

So as I walk along Wardour Street leaving Bar Bruno behind me, I don't think about Keith Proctor. I am not interested in his conspiracy theories. I think about the hours ahead and those who will come to see me. The regulars and the strangers. And the one who left these bands of bruising around both my wrists last night. I doubt a man like Proctor could understand how I accept that and then return the following day to run the risk of receiving the same treatment. Or something even worse. The truth is, it's not so hard. Not any more. I live alone inside a fortress of my own construction. Physical pain means nothing to me.

I am sure there are analysts out there who would enjoy

21

studying me. Of course, they would be frustrated by me since I would refuse to speak to them. Nobody is allowed inside. That is how I survive. I am two different people; the protected, vulnerable soul within the walls and the indestructible, empty soul on the outside. When I am on track, this is how I live; but when I am derailed, it's a different story.

It's not easy being two different people at once. The pressure never ceases. Unless you have experienced it, you cannot know. So sometimes, when the borders blur, I fall apart. When I am cold and hard, I have to be in total control of myself – even in the worst situations. If I lose the slightest fraction of that control, I effectively lose it all. And then I crash. Spectacularly. Alcohol and narcotics are what I resort to in my pursuit of utter oblivion. When I come round from one bout of drinking or drug-taking, I immediately embark upon the next. It's critical that I allow no time for sober thought because it's during these prolonged lows that I see myself as others see me. Then the guilt, the shame and the self-disgust set in. In these moments, the hatred I feel for myself is too much to bear and it scares me to consider the options. So I'll ignore the taste of vomit in my mouth and reach for the vodka bottle again. And I'll keep going until I wake up and find the phase has passed and that I am as hard as stone once more.

Those analysts would probably say that my situation is, in part, a consequence of circumstance. And, in part, they might be right. But the greater truth is this: my situation is a product of choice. I chose this life. I could have had any life I wanted. I'm certainly intelligent enough. In fact, immodest as it sounds, I can't remember the last time I encountered an intellectual equal. Most of the time, though, I pretend I'm stupid so as to avoid unnecessary trouble; in this business, nobody likes a smart mouth. They prefer a willing mouth.

So, of all the options available to me two years ago, this is the one I chose, which begs the obvious question: why? And the honest answer is, I don't remember any more.

3

It was the smoker's cough that woke her, a ghastly rib-rattling hack that repeated itself for the first hour of every morning. Stephanie was glad that it wasn't hers. Then she remembered that it belonged to Steve Mitchell, Anne's husband, and this reminded her of where she was. On their sofa, in their cramped sitting room.

Headswim brought on a wave of nausea. She swallowed. Her throat was dry, her skull ached, her nose was blocked. Anne and Steve were arguing in their bedroom, shouting between the coughs. The radio was on, loud enough to compete with them. Stephanie tried to ignore the noise and the smell of burned toast. How many consecutive hangovers was this? How long was it since Keith Proctor had bought her coffee? Four days? Five?

She struggled to her feet and tiptoed to the window. The Denton Estate in Chalk Farm, on the corner of Prince of Wales Road and Malden Crescent, had one high-rise build-ing with several smaller buildings crawling around its ankles. It was a cheerless place, an ugly marriage of vertical and horizontal construction, in possession of one saving grace. The high-rise, where Steve and Anne Mitchell had their small eighth-floor flat, was a grim tower of red brick, but the view to the south was spectacular, worthy of any Park Lane penthouse. Stephanie absorbed it slowly, pan-ning over Primrose Hill, Regent's Park, Telecom Tower and the city beyond.

She went to the bathroom and locked herself in. She sat on the edge of the avocado bath, clutching the sink, wondering whether she was going to throw up. Last night, there had been gin, then some hideous fluid that passed for wine – possibly Turkish – before other drinks, the quantities and identities of which were now a mystery. She had no recollection of returning to Chalk Farm. But she did remember the foreign businessmen at the hotel in King's Cross and how they had plied her with alcohol and yapped at her in a language that made no sense. With their droopy moustaches, their hairy backs, their pot-bellies, their gold medallions and their cheap polyester suits, they offered no surprises. Stephanie was regrettably familiar with the type.

At least it had only been alcohol. On the night after her second encounter with Proctor, she'd gone to see Barry Green and traded Proctor's money for heroin. She'd asked Green to inject it into her – a service he sometimes provided for his regular customers – but he'd refused.

'No punter likes to shag a slag with puncture points in her arm.'

'What do you care?'

'Plenty, as it happens. I don't want to have to explain to Dean West why I put one of his girls out of action.'

'I don't belong to Dean West. I don't belong to anybody.'

Green always found it hard to deny those who waved cash at him and so Stephanie got her heroin, smoking it instead of injecting it. As she had anticipated – indeed, as she secretly demanded – it was too much for her system; she threw up and passed out. When she came round, she was on a stained, damp mattress in a dimly lit store-room on the premises adjacent to Green's ticketing agency. She was surrounded by cans of chopped tomatoes, bags of rice, drums of vegetable oil. She smelt the vomit on her jacket and the stench made her retch.

Green was standing over her. 'That's the last time, Steph, you got that? Any more and you're gonna develop a habit. Are you listening to me?' He bent down and slapped her face three times before wiping her saliva off the palm of his hand on to her leg. 'You already do enough damage to yourself. You don't need this.'

24

'You're right,' she'd croaked. 'I don't need any of this.'

Anne Mitchell made Stephanie another cup of coffee. There was barely room for both of them in the kitchen. They sat at the small table, a tower of dirty plates between them; on the top one, tomato sauce had hardened to a crust. The gas boiler on the wall grumbled intermittently.

'Steph, we need to talk.'

Stephanie had sensed this moment coming since Steve had gone to work. He was a plumber, which seemed unfortunately ironic considering his numerous infidelities. Whether Anne was fully aware of the extent to which he was unfaithful was unclear to Stephanie, but she knew he cheated on her and that she tolerated it because it was better than the alternative. Anne had been a prostitute when Stephanie first came to London and believed, for no good reason, that without Steve she was destined to become one again. He was still ignorant of her history and, in her mind, Anne had convinced herself that his infidelity was the price she should pay for concealing her past from him.

'It's Steve,' she said, staring into her mug.

'That's what it sounded like.'

'I'm sorry. Did you hear?'

'Just the volume. Not the content.'

Anne had been pretty once; fine-featured with strawberry-blonde hair and freckles on her cheeks. Ten years ago, her regular clients had taken her away for weekends and bought her gifts. But when Stephanie had first met her, just two years ago, and shortly before she met Steve, she was selling herself cheaply and indiscriminately, and still not making enough. Now, she just looked exhausted, fifteen years older than she really was, suffering from too little sleep and too much worry.

'You said a night, maybe two. It's almost a week now and –'

'It's okay.'

Anne scratched a sore on her forearm. 'If it was up to me, you could stay as long as you like. But you know how he is.'

Stephanie knew exactly how he was. Steve might not have known she was a prostitute but he regarded her as one, or as something equally deserving of his contempt. He never overlooked an opportunity to grope Stephanie, or to press himself against her. On one occasion, when she'd been in the bathroom, he'd barged in and locked the door behind him. Anne had been asleep on the other side of the flimsy partition wall, which was why he'd whispered his instruction to Stephanie, as he dropped his trousers: 'On your knees.'

Similarly, she'd whispered her reply. 'You put that anywhere near my mouth and you're going to end up with a dick so short you'll need a bionic eye to find it. Now put it away and get out.'

Since that incident, Steve had been increasingly hostile towards Stephanie. Consequently, her visits to Chalk Farm had become less frequent. Stephanie never stayed anywhere for long. It was nine months since she'd paid rent for a room of her own, in a flat for five that was home to eleven. Since then, she had rotated from one sofa to the next, stretching the charity of her ever-decreasing number of friends on each occasion.

'How long have I got?'

'You can stay tonight.'

Anne's expression suggested that it would be better for her if Stephanie didn't.

Stephanie sat in the last carriage, where a bored guard amused himself by hanging his head out of the door every time the train pulled away from the platform, reeling it in just before the tunnel. The Northern Line was running slow. It took half an hour to get to Leicester Square from Chalk Farm.

Stephanie preferred Soho in the morning, when it was quieter, when street-cleaners and dustmen were the ones who congested the pavements, not tourists and drunks. She stopped for a cup of coffee in a café and recognized three prostitutes at a table. None of them appeared to recognize her. She sat at the counter with her back to them. In her experience, friendships and solidarity were scarce among prostitutes. In a world mostly populated by transients, one hooker's client was another's missed opportunity, so there was little room for sentiment.

She overheard their conversation. They were talking about a Swedish hooker who had been gang-raped after stripping at a drunken stag night. Stephanie had recognized one of the girls at the table in particular. She called herself Claire. She was a seventeen-year-old from Chester, or Hereford, or Carlisle, or any one of a hundred other English towns that offered total disenchantment to the teenagers who grew up in them. Claire had come to London at fourteen and had been selling herself ever since. The previous year, she had spent three months in hospital after a drunken vacuum-cleaner salesman from Liverpool had beaten her to a pulp and left her for dead in a sleazy hotel off Oxford Street. She had deep, livid scars around her eyes and Stephanie knew that the reason she grew her hair long was to disguise the burns her attacker had left at the nape of her neck.

They were commenting on the Swede's injuries with the indifference of accountants discussing tax rebate. Claire was as outwardly unmoved as the other two. As unpleasant as the facts were, they were not uncommon; if you were on the game long enough, you were bound to encounter violence. Stephanie was no exception. It was a risk run daily, a risk run hourly.

When working, Stephanie usually arrived in the West End during the late morning, from wherever she had spent the night, and then killed a few hours before being 'on-call'. Most often, she watched TV with Joan, her 'maid'.

27

They drank coffee, smoked cigarettes and read the tabloids. At some point, she might eat – this was usually the only period of the day that Stephanie considered food – rolling all her meals into one. Sometimes she went to McDonald's or Burger King, or sometimes she bought tourist fodder; grease-laden fish and chips or huge, triangular slices of pizza with lukewarm synthetic toppings and bases like damp cardboard. On other days, she visited the few friends she had made in the area; a nearby Bangladeshi news-agent, a Japanese girl from Osaka named Aki, or Clive, a diminutive Glaswegian who had a stall in the Berwick Street market and who allowed her to take a free piece of fruit from him each time she passed. When her mood was wrong, she drank before work, most often at the Coach and Horses, or else at The Ship.

As a rule, the later the hour, the rougher the trade so, given a choice, Stephanie preferred to stop working by ten. Generally, however, she found herself working later than that. And whatever the final hour, she was exhausted when it was over, even on a quiet night. Even on a blank night. Staying emotionally frozen bled all her mental stamina.

Stephanie drained her cup, left the three girls in the café – they were still discussing the attack on the unfortunate Swede – and walked to Brewer Street. She climbed the stairs and noticed that the reinforced door on the third-floor landing was open. A familiar voice came from within.

'In here, Steph.'

Dean West. She felt her body tense and took a moment to compose herself before entering. West was drinking from a can of Red Bull. He wore a burgundy leather coat, a black polo-neck, black jeans and a pair of Doc Martens. As usual, Stephanie found her own eyes drawn to his eyes, which bulged out of his head like a frog's, and to his teeth, which were a disaster. His mouth was too small for them; a dental crowd in an oral crush, a collage of chipped yellow chaos.

'How was last night? Some hotel in King's Cross, right?'

28

She nodded. 'But there were two of them when I got there. Bulgarians, I think. Or Romanians.'

'So? Twice the money.'

'They wouldn't pay twice.'

'What?'

'They didn't speak English. They thought they'd already paid for both of them.'

'I don't care what they fucking thought. Money up front. That's the rule. *Always*.'

'Not this time.'

His anger deepening, West's brow furrowed. 'What the fuck's wrong with you? We used to get on, you and me. I thought you was smarter than the others but now I ain't so sure. What was the one thing I always said? *Money up front!* How many times d'you have to be told?'

'I got the money up front.' Stephanie handed West his cut. 'For one.'

He began to count it. 'Ain't my fault you didn't collect right. I want my piece of the second. And before you start, I don't care if it comes out of your cut.'

'They were both drunk when I arrived. They wanted me drunk too. Given the mood they were in, I thought it was best to go along with them. So I did everything they wanted and then I drank them under the table. That was when I lifted these.' Stephanie produced two wallets from her pocket and tossed them to West. 'You can take your cut for the second one out of there.'

West's bloodless lips stretched into a smile as he examined the wallets. 'Credit cards? Diners, Visa *and* Mastercard. Nice. What've we got in the other one? Visa and Amex Gold. Very tasty. Barry'll be well chuffed.' Barry Green, occasional vendor of drugs to Stephanie, also had a line in reprocessing credit cards, using a Korean machine that altered PIN codes on the magnetic strips. West's good humour vanished as quickly as it had materialized. 'But only sixty quid in cash? How much are you charging these days, Steph?'

29

'The usual.'

'And after that they only had sixty quid between them?'

'I wouldn't know. I haven't counted it.'

'Bollocks. You've trousered a little for yourself, ain't you?'

A total of three hundred and fifty-five pounds. All she'd left them with were their coins. 'They must have blown what they had on all that cheap wine they were throwing down my neck.'

'Don't try to be funny, Steph. And don't try to pull a fast one on me, neither. Now cough it up.'

'Just what Detective McKinnon was always saying to me. I've still got his number somewhere, you know.'

Superficially, West's anger dissipated but, internally, he was seething and they both knew it. 'Don't push your luck, Steph. One day, it's gonna run out.'

'I know. And so will yours. We're both on borrowed time.'

Dean West raped me once. I say 'raped' because that is how it appears to me now but, at the time, I was less sure. Anne Mitchell was the one who introduced me to him. She was still a prostitute in those days, working for West, and I think she did it purely to please him although she said it was in my best interest. She told me that for a small percentage of my earnings he would provide protection for me and that, anyway, without his authority, I wouldn't be allowed to operate in this area. That was a lie. So were most of the things that Anne said in those days. But I don't hold that against her. She was no different to anyone else in this business, no different to me.

It occurred here, in Brewer Street, in the very room in which I am currently standing. In fact, I am looking at West right now and I am wondering if he is also thinking about it. It seems a lifetime ago. Or rather, it seems like another life altogether. Not mine, but someone else's. I barely recognize the Stephanie who features in my memories. If I was ever really her, I no longer am.

As I entered this room on that morning, he was polite in an old-fashioned way. Courteously, he held out a chair for me to sit in. This, I later learned, was typical of West. One moment he's charm itself, the next he's a savage. I have never discovered whether this is genuine or whether it's something he has cultivated but, either way, it's part of his legend. What is beyond dispute is that West has always enjoyed his reputation as a man not to be crossed. He's thirty-five years old and has spent twelve of his last nineteen years in custody.

To look at him, you would never think he was so vicious. There is nothing in his physique that suggests menace. He is not particularly tall – five-nine, I should think – and he's very thin with fine features; he has hands as delicate and long-fingered as a female pianist's. His lank, light-brown hair falls limply from a centre parting, giving a rather effeminate appearance. In a crowd, he is invisible. But when the rage is in him, the bulging eyes threaten to pop out of their sockets, the pale skin becomes so bloodless it almost looks blue and he radiates a feeling that is unmistakable: pure evil.

There is no bluff with West. Everyone knows it. If he says he'll play noughts and crosses on your face with a pair of scissors, you know he will because if you know anything about him, you'll know that he's done it before. When I first entered this room, about two years ago, I never even noticed the screwdriver on the table next to where I was sitting.

At first, he told me how sexy I was, how I was going to make so much money. He told me that if there was anything I needed all I had to do was ask him. Then he came round from the other side of the desk, picked up the screwdriver and stood behind me, before stooping to whisper in my ear, 'I want to see what you've got. And then I'm gonna try you out. Now get your clothes off.'

He never threatened me verbally, or with the screwdriver. He didn't have to. And the fact that he didn't somehow persuaded me at the time – and for some time after – that it wasn't really rape. Now I know that it was because my compliance was automatic and was based on the certainty that, one way or the other, West would have sex with me. There was no choice in the matter.

31

Compliance was self-preservation. And this was before I knew of his fearsome reputation. I could feel the menace and I knew it was genuine. I think he would have preferred me to protest, or even to struggle, just to provide him with some justification for violence. But I didn't. Instead, I stripped and let him take me as he wanted. It was mechanical, brutal and painful but I never let it show.

This disappointed him. So over the following fortnight, he forced me to have sex with him on a dozen occasions. Each time, he was rougher than before, determined to provoke some reaction from me, but I never gave him that satisfaction. My icy composure remained intact, each humiliation only serving to strengthen me. Every time he finished, I held his gaze in mine and we'd both know whose victory it was. With every attempt to break me, West unmanned himself a little more.

I see now how stupid this was. Sooner or later, his patience would have snapped and I would have paid a fearful price for his humiliation. Fortunately, it never came to that.

An East End heroin peddler named Gary Crowther fell out with Barry Green over some money that Crowther owed. As a favour to Green, Dean West agreed to teach Crowther a painful lesson, choosing to deal with him personally. Unfortunately, Crowther had come off a Kawasaki on the M25 the previous year. The accident had left him with multiple skull fractures and had required two operations on the brain to save his life. West's first punch knocked Crowther unconscious and he never recovered. What should have been a mere warning ended up as murder.

I never saw the blow that killed Crowther – by all accounts, it was more of a slap than a punch – but I did glimpse the unconscious body through a partially-opened door. Just for a second, but a second is all it takes.

I was the only witness that West couldn't trust. Those who dumped the unconscious Crowther in Docklands were West's closest men. They were never going to be a problem. But considering how he had treated me, West had every reason to be nervous.

Most of all, I remember the confusion in his face because I

don't think I've seen it since. He was truly scared. He knew that if he was convicted, he was looking at a life sentence. As for me, he wasn't sure whether to try to sweet-talk me or whether to resort to violence. As it was, he did neither because I made up my mind before he made up his. I said to him, 'If I was never here, you're never going to touch me again. Do you understand?'

Dumbfounded, he'd simply nodded.

'Let me hear you say it.'

'I understand.'

Since then, I've kept silent and West has kept his word and Detective McKinnon – the officer who headed the investigation – has remained frustrated.

As for the rape – or should I say, the first rape? – I have analysed it constantly since it happened. I cannot pretend it was the brutal assault it could have been – the type that makes the news, the type that leaves a mutilated corpse in its wake – but it was a horror to be endured nevertheless. Having been endured, however, I think the experience has been strangely empowering. Primarily, having survived such an ordeal, it taught me that I could survive such an ordeal.

I began to be able to see myself as West saw me – as a thing, not a person – and this has enabled me to divide myself in two so that there is a part of me that nobody can reach, no matter what abuses they visit upon my body. This has allowed me to do what I do, to cope with the repulsive acts I perform for my repellent clients. It's allowed me to live with the threat of violence without it driving me crazy.

West still makes me nervous and my hold over him is tenuous. There is no guarantee that I won't become a victim of his violence at some point. As the months have passed and the Crowther incident has receded, West has become more intolerant of me. Thinly-veiled threats are starting to seep into our conversations. I've seen the way he looks at me and I know he'd like to try to break me again, even though he says I am no longer attractive, that I'm disgusting to him.

It is true that I don't look good these days. I've lost so much weight. My skin has no real colour, except for the red blotches.

*My eyes look permanently bruised but aren't and my gums are
always bleeding.*

*Perhaps the most humiliating thing that has happened to me
in this, the most humiliating of trades, is that I've been forced
to lower my prices. Anne once said to me, just as she was on her
way out of the business and I was on my way in, 'You don't know
what true degradation is until you have to discount yourself, only
to find out it makes no difference.'*

I am not in that position yet. But I am not far away.

I am twenty-two years old.

Joan was peeling the wrapper off her third packet of
Benson & Hedges of the day. 'You're shaking.'

It was true. Stephanie's hands were trembling. 'I'm tired,
that's all.'

For Anne's sake, she hadn't returned to Chalk Farm, so
the next two nights had been spent upon the lumpy sofa
currently occupied by Joan's sprawling bulk. Uncomfortable nights they had been, too; once the heating cut out,
it had been freezing, so she'd curled herself into a ball and
pulled two coats around her to keep warm. Then she'd
sucked at the gin bottle until she'd passed out, managing
three hours' sleep the first night and two the second. Now
she was paying the price for it.

Shrouded in smoke, Joan was chewing peanuts while
flicking through the TV channels with the remote. On the
floor, next to her overflowing ashtray, there were three
phones, waiting for business. None of them was ringing.
She said, 'He's ready when you are.'

'What's he like?'

'Big bloke. I think he's had a few.' She glanced at Stephanie through her tinted lenses and shook her head. 'Better
pull yourself together, girl. You don't look a million
dollars.'

Joan looked like a beached whale. In Lycra. Stephanie
said, 'Who among us does?'

She poured herself half a mug of gin, stole one of Joan's

cigarettes, and went to the bathroom. She washed her face, the cold water bringing temporary refreshment, before applying foundation and mascara. When she looked this bad, Stephanie always tried to draw attention to her mouth and to her eyes, which were deep brown beneath long, thick lashes. The lipstick she selected was a bloodier red than usual. No matter how emaciated the rest of her became, her fleshy lips looked as ripe as they ever had.

She changed back into her lacy black underwear and fastened her suspender-belt. There were mauve smudges on her thighs, souvenirs from anonymous fingers that had pressed into her too eagerly. The bruises around her wrists had faded to a band of pale yellow that was barely noticeable.

She drained the gin, took a final drag from the cigarette and rinsed out her mouth with Listerine. Then she took a deep breath and tried to clear her mind. But when she caught her reflection in the mirror, the feeling returned; the fear of the stranger, the fear of fear itself. It was in her stomach, which was cold and cramping, and in her throat, which was arid and tight.

To the cadaverous face in the glass, she whispered a terse instruction. 'No. Not now.'

'Hi, I'm Lisa. What's your name?'

He thought about it, presumably choosing something new. 'Grant.'

Joan was right about his size. Not only was he tall, but he was massive. An ample gut hung over the top of black trousers that looked painfully tight. Stephanie never knew that Ralph Lauren shirts came in such a gargantuan size. His sleeves were rolled up to the elbow, exposing thick forearms, each of which sported a large tattoo. His hair was buzz-cropped and a band of gold hung from his left ear. But the watch on his wrist was a Rolex. He looked as if he was in another man's things. He looked like an impostor. Then again, they nearly always did.

'What are you looking for?'

He shrugged. 'Dunno.'

Stephanie put her hand on her hip, as she always did at this moment, allowing her gown to fall further open. In the right mood, it felt like a tempting tease. Today, it felt cold and sad. She watched his eyes roll down her body. 'I start at thirty and go up to eighty. For thirty, you get a massage and hand-relief. For eighty, you get the full personal service.'

'Sex?'

She wanted to snap but managed to restrain herself, forcing a smile instead. 'Unless you can think of something *more* personal.'

Grant frowned. 'What?'

Stephanie saw the fog of alcohol clouding his eyes. 'So, what do you want?'

'The full . . . thing . . . service . . .'

'That's eighty.'

'Okay.' When he nodded, his entire body swayed.

'Why don't we get the money out of the way now?'

'Later.'

'I think now would be better.'

'Half now, half after?'

'No. Everything now. It's better this way.'

His mouth flapped open, as though he were about to protest, but no sound emerged. So he stuffed a hand into his pocket and pulled out a fistful of fives and tens. As he came close, she smelt the alcohol on his breath and the body odour that is peculiar to sweat. With fat, pink fingers, he sorted through the grubby notes and handed them to her.

She counted quickly. 'There's only seventy here.'

'It's all I got.'

'It's not enough. Not for sex. Perhaps there's something else you'd like?'

He grinned stupidly. 'Come on,' he slurred. 'Ten quid. That's all it is . . .'

'Yeah, I know. Ten quid too little.'

'It's my birthday on Saturday.'

Stephanie was aware of her irritation rising to the surface, the blood flushing her skin. 'So come back then. And make sure you bring your wallet.'

Her change in tone seemed to have a sobering effect upon him. He straightened. 'What do I get for seventy?'

The words seemed to echo in her skull. *What do I get for seventy?* The question was not new, nor was the contempt in the voice. Yet Stephanie had suspected there might come a moment like this. For several days, she had known something was wrong, but she had refused to accept it. Initially, she'd tried to ignore it, to convince herself she was imagining it. Later, as she felt the cancer of anxiety spreading within her, she had tried to crush it with reason. And when that had failed, she'd tried to blot it out chemically.

It had nothing to do with Grant. It could have been anyone. *What do I get for seventy?*

'You don't.'

Grant looked perplexed. 'What?'

'I'm sorry.'

'You said you went from thirty up to eighty. Now what do I get for seventy?'

'You don't understand. I'm not doing anything. Not for seventy, not for eighty, not for one hundred and eighty.' She thrust his money back at him. 'Here. Take it.'

He swiped her hand away, the notes fluttering to the floor. 'I don't want it. I want –'

'I know what you want. But you can't have it.'

He took one step towards her and it was enough. Her right hand had already reached behind her and found what she knew would be there; on the table, by the bowl – an old champagne bottle, half a candle protruding from the top, its neck coated in dribbles of cold wax.

She swung her arm with all the might she could muster, creating a perfect arc. The glass exploded against the side of his face. Splinters showered on to the naked floorboards. Stephanie watched the lights go out in Grant's eyes. He managed to raise a hand to his lacerated cheek but he was not aware of it. He lurched one way and then the other, before collapsing. The floor shook beneath the impact of his body.

It took Joan ten seconds to waddle through the door. She looked at the body on the floor and then at Stephanie, who was crouched over him, still clutching a fragment of the bottle's neck in a way that suggested she might yet drive it into him.

Joan put a hand to her mouth. Stephanie turned to look at her, not a trace of an emotion on her face. Through her fingers, Joan muttered, 'Oh shit, what've you done?'

Stephanie walked past her without a word and headed for the room next door. She shrugged off her gown and picked up her coat. Joan followed her into the room. 'What're we gonna do with him?'

Stephanie looked for the small rucksack that contained her worldly belongings. She opened it, checked nothing was missing and then fastened the straps. Then she started to put on her coat.

'West's gonna go fucking mental,' Joan said. 'We've got to get this wanker out of here.'

Stephanie looked at her. 'If I were you, *I'd* get out of here. Right now. That's what I'm going to do.'

'You can't just walk out. He's downstairs, for God's sake. For all we know, he could've heard it. He could be on his way up here right now.'

'Exactly. And when he finds out about this, how do you think he's going to react? Do you think he's going to look for an explanation? Or do you think he's going to look for someone to take it out on?'

Joan's expression darkened. 'Well, it won't be me, love. I ain't the one that done it.'

'Fine. That's your decision. But it's not mine.'

'I ain't going. And you ain't, neither.'

Joan reached for the phone. Stephanie grabbed her bag and ran.

Whoever answered the phone on the third floor took their time. The door was still shut when Stephanie passed it. The heels on her shoes slowed her on the uneven stairs but she reached the ground floor and was halfway to the front door when she heard the shout from above, followed by the multiple thump of descending boots.

She knew she had to lose them immediately. If her pursuers saw her, they'd catch her. She turned right and then right again, out of Brewer Street and into Wardour Street, before taking the first left into Old Compton Street and another first left into Dean Street. She never dared look back.

It wasn't yet ten in the evening. The area was busy, which was a blessing. She turned right at Carlisle Street and only stopped running when that led into Soho Square.

The distance covered wasn't great but her lungs were pleading for mercy. She slowed to an unsteady walk. It was then that she noticed that her coat was still only half-buttoned, which explained some of the astonished looks she'd seen on the faces that had blurred past her. Black underwear and a suspender-belt were all she had on beneath the coat. And given her appearance, she suddenly realized that if her hunters were asking pedestrians for the direction she'd taken, she'd be the freshest thing in the memory of just about everyone she'd passed.

She fastened the remaining buttons to the throat and forced herself into another run. She'd known she was unfit, but she'd never guessed that her physical decline had become so acute. For the moment, fear compensated but she knew it wouldn't last.

She took Soho Street out of the Square and then crossed Oxford Street before turning round for the first time. There were no obvious signs that she was being followed. She headed up Rathbone Place and turned right into Percy Street. Her mind was starting to function again. The immediate danger appeared to have been averted but there was a more sinister threat ahead. If her pursuers returned to Brewer Street empty-handed, West would use his network to try to locate her. The word would go out and the search would be on. When that happened, anybody she passed on the street would be a potential danger.

She wondered how long she had and where she should go. Chalk Farm was out of the question. In fact, anyone she knew was out of the question; it was too risky to involve them. Which was why she chose Proctor. She felt nothing for him.

At the junction with the Tottenham Court Road, she turned left and headed north. She found a working BT phone-box outside the National Bank of Greece. She dialled and luck was with her.

'It's Stephanie Patrick.'

If surprise had a sound, it was to be found in Proctor's silence.

She said, 'Can we meet?'

He was trying to gather himself. 'I guess . . . sure. Sure. When?'

'Now.'

'Now? Er, that's not very convenient. I'm busy. Working –'

'I'm in trouble. I need help. And I need it right now.'

4

I am drinking a *cup of coffee in the McDonald's on the corner of Warren Street and the Tottenham Court Road. I keep my head bowed, aware of the strange looks that I am attracting from some of the other patrons. I should be standing in the entrance to the Underground station across the street, but it's cold outside. I'll return there when it's time to be collected.*

I am trying not to think about the man I hit or the situation in which I find myself. Instead, I am thinking about the trigger.

I am wondering what it is like to be in a plane crash. To be going down and to be conscious of it. To know that you are doomed. What does that feel like? What does it sound like? These are matters that I've considered on too many occasions to count. The images creep up on me in the night. I see Sarah, my sister, her hair on fire. David, my younger brother, looks at the stump on his shoulder from where his arm used to hang. And my parents are ash, instantly incinerated and scattered on the wind.

These are the things that wake me at night. They're the reason I drink myself to sleep. That's where they belong – in the sleeping world. But tonight, they crossed over.

I looked at Grant – whoever he really was – and I thought about what we were going to do. For seventy pounds – not even eighty – since I would have discounted myself in the end. Except, it never came to that. Instead, I imagined my parents were in the room too, with David on one side, Sarah on the other, the smell of charred flesh everywhere, the floor slippery with their blood. I saw myself on all fours, Grant drunkenly ploughing into me from behind, my family watching, their total disappointment evident through their hideous wounds.

It has never happened before. I have never seen them when I've been selling myself. Some instinct has always blocked them

41

– and anything I have ever cared about – from my mind. But lately, there has been something wrong. I've felt it building within me, a pressure in search of release. And now I know the cause.

Proctor. Proctor and his far-fetched conspiracy theories. He has resurrected the ghosts. He is to blame.

Outside, on the Euston Road, running over the underpass, there is a construction of concrete with a metal grille set into it. Perhaps it is some kind of ventilation unit. I don't know. Anyway, beneath the grille, there is some graffiti which I noticed before coming in here.

It says: NO ONE IS INNOCENT.

Proctor was driving a small, rusting Fiat. Stephanie had imagined he'd be in the latest BMW or Audi, something sleek and German. He leaned over and opened the passenger door. Stephanie stepped out of the entrance to Warren Street Underground station and crossed the pavement.

'You're twenty minutes late.'

'The car wouldn't start.'

She looked at it disdainfully. 'You don't say.'

Proctor's surprise was self-evident. 'For someone in trouble, you've got a crappy way of saying thank you.' When she failed to speak, he said, 'Are you getting in the car, or not?'

'I don't know.'

'*You don't know?* I thought you needed a place to stay.'

'I need a *safe* place to stay.'

The wind blew newspaper along the pavement. She shivered.

Proctor nodded slowly. 'I won't harm you –' She looked unconvinced. '– I promise I won't.'

'You can't have sex with me.'

He found her frankness disarming. '*What?*'

'You can't have sex with me.'

Proctor attempted a little levity. 'That's a relief. You're not my type. Now get in.'

But Stephanie looked as serious as before. 'I mean it.'

'I don't believe this. Look, you asked me. Remember? I was the one who was working at home, who pulled on his shoes and drove up here to collect you.'

She clutched her coat at the throat. 'I won't let you –'

'I don't want to have sex with you. You look like death warmed up. Now are you getting in the bloody car or not? Because I'm not hanging around here all night waiting for the police to arrest me for kerb-crawling.'

Once again, Proctor saw a look that could have been sorrow, hatred or fear. Or all three. After a final suspicious pause, Stephanie got into the car.

Proctor kept both hands on the wheel and looked straight ahead. 'I'm sorry. I shouldn't have said that.'

'Forget about it. You've no idea how refreshing the truth can be.'

It takes me time to remember where I am. This sofa is not in Brewer Street. It is in Bell Street, which is between the Edgware Road and Lisson Grove. I am in the living room of Proctor's flat.

My life is precarious enough without climbing into strangers' cars. Last night, I needed to get off the street, and to rest, so I was grateful for his intervention. But now that it is morning, I've got to think ahead and make plans. I have to keep moving – moving prey is harder to catch – until I can find somewhere secure to lie low. And for that, I'll need money. The three hundred and fifty-five pounds that I lifted from the businessmen in King's Cross will fuel me for a while but it does not represent a passport to a new life.

As I rise from the sofa, I become aware of how ill I feel. This doesn't seem like a regular hangover; I ache all over and I feel sick. I am simultaneously hot and cold. Maybe this is my body protesting yet again at the way I have treated it.

I assume that Proctor is still asleep. I move quietly. When we returned here last night, we didn't talk much. He showed me where the bathroom was and I changed into the jeans and sweat-shirt that I was carrying in my rucksack. Then he sat me on this sofa and poured me one whisky after another. I don't remember how many it took to eradicate my in-built sense of caution. Exhaustion was to blame, but by the time I was ready to talk, I was ready to sleep. Proctor realized this and fetched me a pillow and some blankets. I suppose he thought we'd talk this morning. He's going to be disappointed.

He was wearing a worn leather jacket when he picked me up. I cannot see it in this room so I put on my shoes, gather my things, fasten the rucksack and pull on my overcoat. Then I open the door as quietly as I can and I tiptoe past Proctor's bedroom, which is on the left, and make my way down the hall.

My temples throb. I feel nauseous.

Before I reach the front door, there is a final room on the left. Somebody could have used it as a second bedroom. Proctor uses it as an office. There are two tables in it; on one, there are box-files and correspondence, on the other, a computer. On the back of the chair between the two hangs his leather jacket. I creep into the office and run my hands through the pockets until I find his wallet. I open it up and ignore the cards. I am only interested in cash. He has eighty pounds; three twenties, two tens. I fold them in half.

Which is when I hear him behind me.

'Are you looking for something of yours?'

Stephanie spun round. Proctor was filling the doorway, blocking her exit.

'Or just something of mine?'

The wallet was in her hand.

Proctor was wearing track-suit bottoms and the same black shirt he had worn the night before. There had not been time to fasten the buttons. On one side of his head the hair was flat to the skull, on the other it stood out like bristles on a brush.

He looked dejected, not angry. But Stephanie had long since learned to distrust appearances. He said, 'All you had to do was ask. I would have given you money.'

'Yeah, right . . .'

'It's true.'

44

She squinted at him. 'And why would you do that?'

'Because I know about you.'

His hand was outstretched, waiting for the return of his wallet. Stephanie stepped forward to give it to him. And then she charged, ramming his chest with her shoulder, knocking him off-balance. Clutching the wallet as tightly as she could, she sped across the hall and reached for the front door. But Proctor's hand grabbed her shoulder, spinning her round. In an instinctive continuation of the movement, she raised a fist and punched him on the jaw. Proctor recoiled, amazed by her speed and strength.

She tugged at the front door catch repeatedly but couldn't open it. The knowledge came to her gradually, sapping her strength. She let go of the catch, her hand falling limply to her side. When she looked round, she saw the keys dangling from the key-ring that was hanging on the tip of his forefinger.

His other hand was massaging his jaw. 'Double-locked, just in case,' he said.

The front door was at the end of the corridor. Proctor had her penned in; there were no rooms to run to, no surprises left to spring. Stephanie's reactions were automatic, a by-product of experience. She retreated into the corner and slid to the floor. Mentally, she began to go blank, closing everything down, numbing herself. When Proctor took a step towards her, she wrapped her arms around her head and pulled herself into the smallest human ball possible.

'What are you doing?'

She braced herself for the first blow.

'I'm not going to hit you, Stephanie. I don't want to hurt you.'

Those very words had been the preface to a savage beating more than once. She knew that Dean West always tried a little kindness before administering his punishments. She stayed still, knowing better than to lift her head.

'I'll tell you what, I'm going to move back. All right?

45

I'm going to move back to my office doorway and then I'm going to sit down on the floor, like you. And when I have, you can look up. Then we can talk. Is that okay?'

There was no reply.

'That's all I want to do. Just talk.'

She sensed his retreat before allowing herself to peep through crossed arms.

'See? I can't hurt you from here.'

Stephanie felt dizzy. She swallowed.

'Where were you going to go?'

No answer.

'*Is* there anywhere? Anyone?'

She was trembling.

'What about last night?' he asked. 'Do you want to tell me what that was all about?'

She kept her head protected.

'Look, I know you don't trust me – there's no reason you should – but I really have no interest in you, apart from what you can tell me. I have things to tell you too but if you don't want to hear them –'

'I don't want to hear anything,' she whispered.

Proctor shook his head. 'This is your family we're talking about.'

Stephanie shrugged.

'How about if I asked you some general questions? Would you answer them?'

'No.'

'Why not?'

'There's nothing you need to know about me or about my family.'

'I see. Well maybe you could just sit and listen. I'll tell you what I'm working on, what I've found out, how I'm –'

'Don't you get it yet? I don't care.'

'No. I don't get it. I don't get it at all. If it was my family on that 747, I'd want to know why it went down and who was responsible. I'd want justice. For them and for everyone else on board. And for all their relatives and friends who've had to deal with the aftermath. That's what this is about, you know. That's what this investigation was when I started. A human interest story. What happens to the families and friends of the dead a couple of years down the line when it's no longer news? How do they cope in the long term? You may not talk to me but there are others who have. I've seen their grief. I've felt it. Two years plus hasn't diminished it. They've learned to live with it – some of them, anyway – but the wounds haven't healed. And they probably never will. Every single one of them has suffered and –'

'Do you think that I haven't?' she snapped. 'That I still don't?'

'Of course not. It's just that –'

'Just what? Odd that I don't like to talk about it to journalists? I bet you think my situation is a consequence of the crash, don't you? That would be a good story for you if it was true, wouldn't it?'

He wanted to say yes, but said, 'I don't know enough about you yet. I can't tell.'

'You see? You're lying like everyone else. I can see your outline from here: a family in ruins, four dead, two survivors, one who copes and one who can't. Like you said, a human interest story.'

'My story is changing.'

'What makes you think I want to see my life in print?'

'You wouldn't necessarily feature.'

'Not unless I improved the story. Then you'd include me. Right?'

For a moment, Proctor considered the temptation to lie. 'It's my job. It's what I do.'

'Yeah. Fucking people for profit. It's what we both do.'

She looked in worse shape than she had the night before, outside the Underground station, when her skin had been a riot of goose-bumps tinted by the harsh light falling from street lamps. Now, wherever he looked, she was bones. Her cheekbones were too prominent to be attractive, her wrists looked swollen because her arms were so fleshless, and when her knees showed through the tears in her jeans they looked sharp enough to cut through her blotchy skin.

Proctor said, 'I'm not writing the same story any more. This isn't human interest. It's gone way beyond that. Every day, I learn something new and the angle alters.'

'Well, you're a real one-man Woodward and Bernstein, aren't you?' He was surprised and it must have showed because Stephanie smiled humourlessly. 'Yes, I know who they are and what they did. You think just because I sell my body I have the intellect of a footballer?'

'No. I know that's not true.'

Stephanie ran her hands through her tangled blonde hair. 'So, all these other people you've been talking to – all the other ones like me – what do they think?'

'About what?'

'Your bomb theory.'

Proctor looked at the floor. 'They don't know.'

'What?'

'I haven't told them yet.'

Stephanie felt herself tensing again. 'Why not?'

'I spoke to most of them before I found out. And when I did find out, I wasn't sure it was true.'

'But you are now?'

'As sure as I can be, yes.'

'When did you discover this?'

'Three days before I came to see you for the first time. I never meant to say a word about it but when you refused to talk to me, I just blurted it out without thinking. It was frustration. It was unprofessional. And now it's too late to take it back.'

Stephanie shivered and then felt hot. 'Who else knows?'

'No one. It's just you and me.'

She made no attempt to conceal her incredulity. 'You don't expect me to believe that, do you?'

'It's true.'

'Why haven't you told anyone else?'

Proctor bit his lower lip for a moment. 'Because I'm scared.'

The building in which Proctor lived was a small Victorian mansion block. It was not smart but his apartment had some style, although most of it seemed to have been lifted from a magazine. There was a Bose sound system, a widescreen Sony TV, and Danish furniture – armchairs, lamps, bookcases – all of it minimalist and clean. A beautifully-made wooden table dominated the centre of the sitting room. There were Turkish kilims on the floor, African batiks on the walls.

Stephanie lit a cigarette and noted his reaction, a grimace. When she asked him for an ashtray, he produced a saucer.

She said, 'What do you know about him?'

'I know that he's young, probably no more than thirty, and that he's a Muslim. I know that he's living somewhere in this city. And I know that this is known at MI5, SIS and the CIA. And I'd guess we could include the FBI in that group, although I don't know that for sure.'

'Does he have a name?'

'He probably has several but I don't know any of them.'

'Nationality?'

'Same answer.'

'What about a photo?'

'I haven't seen one.'

'You've hardly narrowed the field much, have you?'

'I can tell you that outside of those groups I've already mentioned, you and I are the only two people who know about this. And that we're not supposed to.'

Stephanie's cigarette was making her feel worse. She stubbed it out, half of it unsmoked. 'That's another thing. How come *you* know all this?'

'I was contacted by a man at MI5.'

'Who?'

'I don't know.'

She pinched the top of her nose, squeezing her eyes shut, trying to will the pain into recession. 'Why did he get in touch with you?'

'Apparently, he discovered what was going on and couldn't live with it.'

'But when it comes to leaking classified information, he has no problem living with that?'

'I don't know what his deeper motive is. I think it's possible that he had a relative or a friend on the flight. The point is, when it became apparent that the bomber was in London, MI5 were detailed to do the surveillance on him.'

'Why wasn't he arrested?'

'I still don't know that.'

'Your whisperer at MI5 didn't say?'

'No. I think if he had and then it had come out straight away, it would have been too easy to trace back. He wants me to work it out myself so that it can look like it's all my own effort. He needs to protect himself.'

'And you believe that?'

'Increasingly. At first, I was sceptical. But not now.'

'How come he picked you?'

'Because he discovered I was preparing this series of articles. There aren't many journalists who are still working this story. For most people, it's yesterday's news.'

'But if this is true, there's no journalist in the world who wouldn't take the bait. This story will make a legend out of the one who breaks it. He could have given it to anyone.'

'He wanted someone who had a genuine interest, not an opportunist.'

'Is that what he told you?'

'No. It's what I think, but . . .'

Stephanie suddenly felt faint. Her vision shimmered. She closed her eyes and hoped the moment would pass. It didn't.

'Are you okay?' asked Proctor.

She swallowed and found her throat hot and dry. 'I think I'm going to throw up . . .'

She rose to her feet and was dizzy. She stuck out a hand for balance. Proctor took her by the arm, guiding her swiftly to the bathroom. He left her there and returned to the living room, trying to ignore the sound of her retching. When she reappeared, her skin was grey and damp with perspiration.

He said, 'I hope you don't feel as ill as you look.'

The muscles in her stomach were trembling. 'I thought it was some kind of hangover . . .'

'Sit down. I'll get you some water.'

'I'll be fine in a minute.'

'I'm not so sure about that.' When Proctor returned with a glass in hand, Stephanie had put on her coat and was fetching her rucksack. 'What are you doing?'

'I've got to go.'

'Why?'

'That's none of your bloody business.'

'Look, you don't have anywhere to go to.'

She looked insulted, then defiant. 'I can't stay here.'

'Why not?'

Her eyes said it first. 'Because I don't trust you.'

'Well, I don't trust you, either. But I'm willing to take that risk.'

'Then you're an idiot. If you knew what I know, you wouldn't say that so easily.'

'I'm sure you're right but if I was going to harm you, I'd have probably done it by now. You can leave if you want to. I won't stand in your way. But if you want to stay here, you can.'

It was a savage strain of influenza that laid Stephanie low. Proctor offered her his bed but she refused, preferring the sofa. He made her soup, brought her tea, fed her aspirin. She was sullen and silent. For four days, she did little more than sleep. Her temperature fluctuated wildly and during the first forty-eight hours, she vomited repeatedly. The aches never ceased. It was like narcotic withdrawal, the destructive drug being Stephanie herself, her body rejecting every aspect of her poisonous life. At one point, Proctor considered consulting a doctor but Stephanie was adamant that he shouldn't. When she awoke on the fifth morning, she knew she was getting better.

Proctor was making coffee. Not instant coffee, but real coffee. Stephanie enjoyed watching the little rituals of preparation, from the grinding of the beans to the cup. She noticed that Proctor was a man who enjoyed practical precision. She saw it in the way he kept everything so clean, in the order that ruled his flat and his appearance. There was no chaos around him and, she suspected, none inside him, either.

They returned to the living room. On the cherry table there were two bulging files, a folder, which was open, and an enlarged colour photograph of a Boeing 747. The fuselage and the engines were deep blue. Running forward of the wing's leading edge were three enormous, crimson letters: NEA. North Eastern Airlines. The letters reached from the belly to the upper deck, and almost as far forward as the flight deck. On the tail, there was a white circle with two arrows pointing out from the centre, one heading north, the other heading east.

Proctor saw Stephanie looking at the photograph and said, 'Flying in a pressurized aircraft at altitude is like flying in an aerosol can. Now if you imagine –'

'I don't want to imagine anything. Just tell me what happened.'

Proctor flicked through one of the files and unclipped a sheet of paper from it, which he then spread across the table-top. It was a diagram of a 747, seen from the front, from both sides and from above, this view including the lay-out of the seating. The North Eastern logo was in the bottom right-hand corner.

'There were two explosions. The first one – the smaller of the two – occurred at an altitude of thirty-seven thousand feet. It blew a hole in the fuselage just in front of the wings, here –' He pointed at one of the side views. ' – and, less destructively, at the same point on the other side. Critically, the force of the blast was not powerful enough to tear the aircraft in two. As soon as it happened, the 747 fell into a steep descent while the flight crew tried to regain control. They were experienced enough – they had over forty-five thousand hours of accumulated flying time between them – but in this situation, there wasn't much they could do.

'At this point, it's probable that most of the casualties were behind the blast. Those in the nose and on the upper deck – first and business class, mainly – would have been less likely to suffer the worst of the deceleration injuries, although they'd still have been damaged by them. In the end, of course, it made no difference. At twelve thousand feet, there was a second explosion and this was what tore the aircraft in two. Or rather, into pieces.'

Proctor poured some coffee into a pale lilac cup which was sitting on a saucer. Stephanie lit her first cigarette in almost a week, then took the cup and saucer and returned her attention to the diagram between them. 'So what was all that stuff about electric wiring?'

'The official verdict was inconclusive. The eventual findings dealt only in probability and theory, one of which suggested that a section of electrical wiring may have been faulty. There are lawsuits pending against both Boeing and North Eastern Airlines but while the cause remains only "probable" they are unlikely to be found culpable. If there was more conclusive proof that the cause was something mechanical or negligent, you can be sure that both Boeing and NEA would be investigating the matter more thoroughly, looking for ways out. With this verdict, they're as happy as they can be in an unhappy situation. It's no coincidence that pilot error is so frequently the cause of a crash; when the accused is dead, he can't provide awkward answers to tricky questions. Pilot error is a lot cheaper than structural, mechanical or procedural failure.'

'But there must be investigators who know the truth. What about the ones who discovered the evidence?'

'Normally, when there's a tragedy of this nature, there are investigators all over it. FBI, FAA, members of the NTSB – the American National Transportation Safety Board – to name but a few. They swarm all over the debris and all over the dead. In this case, however, the crash site was in the middle of the Atlantic. That severely reduced the number of agents who could physically get there. What's more, the FBI reduced the number yet further by vetting those allowed to make the trip.'

'I wasn't aware the mid-Atlantic was part of their jurisdiction.'

'It isn't. But ultimately the ships and planes involved were, since the FBI was heading the investigation. Which is how they came to have the final say. They were very careful – and influential – about which FAA agents and, more specifically, which representatives from the NTSB were allowed out to the crash site. The same security applied to the testing conducted on recovered debris and human remains when they were returned to the United States.'

'What are you saying?'

'According to my source at MI5, the FBI received two warnings that a terrorist attack was on the cards. The first was about six months before, the second was just three weeks before. In their wisdom, they decided not to pass the warnings on to the airlines.'

'Why not?'

'I don't know. They'd probably say that they get a lot of dud information – and a lot of hoaxes, too – and that they have to make a tough call each time. Perhaps they weren't convinced of the sincerity or legitimacy of the warnings.'

In one of the two files that were on the table, Proctor had stored all the relevant articles he could find. They ranged from newspaper and magazine reports published in the immediate aftermath of the crash to coverage of the investigations executed by the FAA, the FBI and the NTSB. The initial assumption had been that flight NE027 had been brought down by a terrorist bomb. In the first forty-eight hours, all the usual suspects were accused; Arab terrorist organizations, Colombian drug cartels, home-grown fanatics from the mid-western militias. But during the months that followed, each potential villain was removed from the equation. Cocooned by her decline, Stephanie had still retained enough awareness of the outer world to recall the glacial progress towards a verdict that favoured structural or mechanical failure, 'favoured' being as close as it ever got.

There were photographs with the articles. Some were familiar; the section of pockmarked fuselage floating on the Atlantic's surface, the huddle of women clutching one another for support at Heathrow. Other photographs were new, like the small collection of recovered items laid out on the deck of one of the salvage ships; several shoes – none of which matched, two soggy passports, a portable CD-player, a denim jacket, a necklace with a gold heart, a teddy bear with one of its legs missing. There was another set of photographs from inside the vast hangar where the retrieved wreckage was gathered and sorted. A series of struts running back from the 747's nose to its hump were twisted like spaghetti. There was a seat that had been toasted to the frame, which was all that remained of it. Sections of fuselage had been burned black. In one shot, an investigator stood over some fragments of engine cowling. Behind him, fading from focus as the lines of perspective came together, was the rest of the hangar, its entire floor carpeted by debris. Disbelief was etched into the investigator's face.

Stephanie said, 'There must be some kind of evidence somewhere.'

'There is. And wherever it is now, it's conclusive. High explosives leave clues. A fuselage puncture is distinctive to look at. It's petal-shaped and the petals themselves are bent in the direction of flight. The metal is super-heated by the roasting gases created by the explosion – we're talking about a temperature as high as 5000°C – and is then instantly cooled by the freezing, speeding air outside. The heated forces generated by high explosives stretch, fracture and blister the aluminium skin of an aircraft in a way that leaves no doubt as to the cause. Similarly, those super-hot gases leave their mark on those who inhale them, in the form of severe burns to the mouth and lungs.

'According to my source, the evidence shows that there was a bomb on board and that it was probably a shaped charge; that is, it was placed against the fuselage and designed to blow outwards, creating a hole in the aircraft's skin. The smaller hole on the other side is really incidental.'

'Why this flight?'

'Who can say . . . ?'

'There wasn't anyone important on board?'

'Not really. Some prominent businessmen, a Congressman from Alabama, a French diplomat, a Swiss heart surgeon. But no one who ranks for something like this.'

The dismissive tone in his voice stung because it rang

true; her family didn't merit consideration. They were simply there to make up the numbers. 'What about the second explosion?'

'That was almost certainly a consequence of the damage sustained by the initial blast and by the descent that followed it.'

'So how come Boeing and North Eastern bought the faulty electrics theory?'

'They haven't bought anything yet. But that theory is technically possible. The 747 is a very safe aircraft. A lot of trouble is taken to avoid the possibility of any kind of spark or electrical charge being released inside any of the fuel tanks. No electrical wires run through the central fuel tank in the belly of the aircraft. The pumps are housed on the outside. However, on some of the older 747s, there are wires running through the fuel tanks on the wings. But as a precaution, these are coated with aluminium, as well as two protective layers of Teflon.'

'Was the North Eastern 747 one of that generation?'

'Yes. It was the oldest aircraft in their fleet. It was still in operation after twenty-six years of service. Not that there's anything unusual about that, you understand.'

'So what was their theory?'

'Their theory is that compromised wiring in one of the wing tanks caused flames to ignite. These travelled rapidly to the tip of the wing and then blew back into the centre tank along a venting tube that is supposed to let fuel vapours escape. Like I said, since this is only a possibility, it's hard to blame anybody. For Boeing and for NEA, it could be a lot worse. Also, since this only affects ageing 747s, the cost of the alterations won't be nearly so high for the industry. In fact, the proposed changes aren't even mandatory. All that's mandatory is close inspection, to see if wiring changes are necessary.'

'And since there's officially no terrorist involvement, no intelligence agency comes under scrutiny for ignoring the warnings?'

'Correct. As a compromise, this works for all the parties involved. Everyone gets to breathe a sigh of relief.'

The following morning, Stephanie ventured outside for the first time since Proctor had brought her back to the flat. It was a crisp day and the chill cut through to the bone. When she'd seen her reflection in the bathroom mirror, she'd been shocked to see how thin she had become. Her ribs and collar-bones had never been so prominent. The hollows beneath her cheeks were as deep and dark as those in which her eyes hid. As a teenager, her full breasts had made her popular with the boys in her school despite her acid tongue. Now, she was almost flat-chested and only her mouth retained elements of voluptuousness. At least, it did when her lips weren't cracked or blistered.

She walked past the old book shops, the Willow Gallery, the bike shop and the antiques shop. Bell Street felt stranded in time. At one end, it opened on to the Edgware Road so that, in a matter of a few short steps, one could stride out of the Fifties and into the present.

She drank a cup of tea in Bell's Café, which had a green façade and a net curtain in the window that looked on to the street. Stephanie sat at a small table and toyed with the spare keys to the flat that Proctor had given her at breakfast. His sense of trust was easier to win than hers.

Part of her wanted to leave immediately but a growing part of her was content to stay. She was increasingly convinced that he would do her no physical harm; so far, he'd had her at his mercy for six days and he hadn't tried anything. Furthermore, Stephanie had seen no sign of it within him. Besides, she had nowhere to go and no one to see. There was no genuine reason to leave. Except that sooner or later, there would be some sort of price to pay for Proctor's apparent kindness. Experience had taught her that much.

*　　*　　*

They were in the kitchen. It was early evening and Stephanie was sitting on a wooden stool watching Proctor cut chicken breasts into thin strips. When he'd finished, he started to slice broccoli and courgettes with a clean knife on a clean board. Out of the corner of his eye, he noticed her staring.

'Are you laughing at me?'

'I'm smiling, not laughing.'

'What about?'

'Watching you chop food reminds me of my father. Not that you're similar in any way. It's just that he liked to cook and he was good at it. He taught me how to cook.'

'Do you enjoy it?'

Stephanie shrugged. 'I don't remember.'

'What about your mother? Didn't she cook?'

'Very well. But she didn't enjoy it the way he did. I preferred to learn from my father. I liked to watch him work with knives. He always cut things really quickly. He had these huge hands but he was so precise with a blade. There'd be a blur of steel and suddenly everything was beautifully sliced.'

'I guess that comes from being a doctor.'

'He was a general practitioner, not a surgeon.'

Proctor nodded and then wiped his hands on a tea-towel. 'What were they like, your parents?'

Stephanie's smile vanished. 'They weren't *like* anything. They were my parents.'

It was five-thirty in the morning. Stephanie was unable to sleep. She rose from the sofa and dressed quickly; it had been a bitter night and the central heating didn't come on until six. She made herself coffee the way Proctor made it. Then she took the mug back to the living room and lit herself a cigarette. Down in the street, a man was scraping ice from the windscreen of his Vauxhall. Frozen breath shrouded his head.

On the cherry table were the reports that Proctor had

been going through the night before. Stephanie sat down and began to leaf through the photo-copies. On the front cover of one plastic folder, a date had been scrawled in fluorescent green ink. It was only three months old.

There was some analysis on the causes of death for those bodies that had been recovered. Twenty-eight passengers remained unaccounted for. Given the crash site, Stephanie felt that number was remarkably low. The divers had made almost four and a half thousand dives to retrieve the debris and the dead. Their task had been made harder by the vast area over which material had been scattered and by the violent storms which settled over the region twenty-four hours after the crash. Approximately two dozen of the recovered bodies were more or less intact. The condition of the rest of the corpses ranged from 'partially' to 'totally disintegrated'. Of all the photographs of the dead that were taken, only eight were deemed suitable for circulation for the purposes of identification, according to a psychologist assigned to handle the liaison between the authorities and the relatives of those on board. In the end, none of the eight was used.

There was another section from one of the FAA's reports that described the impact of explosive deceleration on the passengers. Many of them had been killed instantly. The force with which their bodies had been thrown forwards was so powerful that some of them had been decapitated, while others perished due to the violent separation of the brain stem. Those who survived this were then subjected to numerous alternative forces. The pressurized air leaked from the puncture points in the fuselage with a power ferocious enough to strip a body of its clothes, to rip contact lenses from eyes. During the free-fall, some passengers were burned to death while others were cut apart by structural debris.

In another file, Stephanie came across a passenger manifest. Proctor had made several copies of it and scrawled notes over most of them. His comments were mostly concerned with structural damage from the first explosion. Stephanie looked down the list until she saw their names.

Seat 49A: Patrick, Sarah
Seat 49B: Patrick, David
Seat 49C: Douglas, Martin
aisle
Seat 49D: Patrick, Monica
Seat 49E: Patrick, Andrew

In that part of the 747, towards the rear of the economy section, the seats had been in a three-four-three configuration, split by two aisles. Seeing their names in print, seeing where they had been positioned within the aircraft, Stephanie felt numb. She could deal with the emotions that she saw in others; the instant despair, the long-term despair, the bewilderment and the rage. What she found harder to cope with was the brutal, clinical truth. Printed statistics, cause of death on a signed certificate, names on a passenger manifest.

She knew Proctor was looking at her before she saw him. He was in the doorway.

'Are you okay?' he asked.

'I couldn't sleep. Did I wake you?'

'I heard you in the kitchen.'

'The man in seat 49C, Martin Douglas,' she said, staring at the name between her brother and her mother. 'Do you know who he was?'

'He was an architect from a place called Uniondale. He lived and worked in Manhattan.'

'An American?'

'Yes.'

She nodded to herself slowly. 'So, an American architect condemned by an act of petulance from an English teenager he never knew existed.'

'I'm not with you.'

61

'I should have been in that seat. It was booked in my name.'

'How come you weren't?'

'It was a family holiday but I didn't go. I said I couldn't be back late for the start of my university term. Not even forty-eight hours, which is all it was. But that wasn't the reason and they knew it.'

'What was?'

Stephanie smiled sadly. 'I don't even remember. Something petty and hurtful, I expect.'

'Why?'

'Because that's how I was back then. Spiteful and rebellious.' She looked up at Proctor. 'Now, I'm just spiteful.'

'Martin Douglas would have got another seat, Stephanie.'

'Maybe . . .'

'The flight was almost full but not every place was taken. If you'd been on board, he'd have sat somewhere else and the death toll would have been greater by one.'

'How old was he?'

'If my memory serves me correctly, he was thirty-three.'

'Married?'

'No.'

'Good.'

Stephanie wondered whether those in row 49 had survived the first blast. Or even the second blast. And then she hoped that they hadn't when she thought about the speed at which the flaming remains of flight NE027 had fallen towards the sea. At an impact speed of around five hundred miles an hour, the gentle waves below might as well have been made of granite.

2

STEPHANIE'S WORLD

6

This is my last *cigarette. I draw the flame to the tip and inhale deeply. Proctor looks cross, as he always does when I smoke, but then he doesn't know that I'm giving up. It's a secret that will gradually betray itself, hour by hour and day by day.*

It is almost exactly a month since Proctor collected me from Warren Street Underground station. I have lived with him since that night and I have started to change. Giving up cigarettes is a part of that process. A symptom.

I can't pretend that I am any easier than I ever was but Proctor has earned some trust from me. He has allowed me to stay with him. He has not asked me to contribute to my keep. He has not made a move on me. He has not got angry at my continued reluctance to trace the bomber of flight NE027; he cannot understand my unwillingness, but he accepts that it is a fact. In truth, I cannot fully understand it myself.

I have not seen much of Proctor in the last month and his investigation into the crash has not advanced at all. Being a freelance journalist, he has no organization behind him to help finance his research. Instead, he writes travel articles for newspapers and magazines. At the moment, this is his only source of income. He tends to cram several trips together, if he can, thereby allowing himself uncluttered months in-between. Since I came to stay here, he has been to Israel for a week and to Indonesia for a fortnight. And today, he returns from a long weekend in Miami. He hates the work but he needs the money.

Within this flat – and the immediate area surrounding it – I have learned to feel safe. That is something new. When I stray beyond the confines of the Edgware Road or Lisson Grove, however, I begin to feel anxious. I think of Dean West, of Barry

Green. I think of how I was when Proctor walked into my room on Brewer Street and how I regarded him as just another punter prepared to rent me for sex.

Then I think about how I regard him now and I am confused. He has resurrected my family but he has resolved nothing. Perhaps the reasons for my reluctance to seek answers are not so unusual. Perhaps I feel safer with the uncertainty than with the truth. What if the truth is worse than ignorance? I can cope without answers. It is more important to me not to be undermined. I do not want to relapse.

I have taken no drugs since I have been here. I am drinking less, too. I finished Proctor's spirits within three days and he did not replace them. I could have bought replacements myself but felt too ashamed to. Ashamed. Given all that I have done in the last two years it seems strange to me that I should feel like that. But I did and, consequently, I adapted. Proctor himself rarely drinks and my habits have fallen into line with his. If he has a glass of wine and offers me one, I'll accept. If he chooses not to, I won't drink either.

Since I got here, there has been only one serious lapse.

Stephanie dialled the code and another three numbers before replacing the receiver, replicating the same action for the fourth time in five minutes. Her hand hovered over the phone. She knew she would see it through eventually because, until she did, the matter would continue to haunt her. Half an hour later, she dialled 1–4–1, followed by the entire number, and then pressed the phone to her ear. When it began to ring, she hoped there would be no reply. But there was.

'Hello?'

Her vocal cords were paralysed.

'Hello?'

This time, she managed a response. 'Chris?'

'Speaking.'

He was waiting for her to introduce herself. His voice had been instantly recognizable to her. If he'd cold-called her, she would have known straight away that it was him. But he had no idea who she was and the significance of that was not lost on her.

'It's Steph.'

The pause was as predictable as it was lengthy. 'Steph?'

'Yes.'

His voice dropped from a deep boom to a whisper. 'I don't believe it. Is it really you?'

'Yes.'

'My God. How long's it been? How are you? *Where* are you? What are you doing?'

Stephanie closed her eyes and saw him clearly. Six foot two, dark hair that was thinning, unlike his waistline, which was expanding. That was how she remembered him. A sense of dress that followed the seasons without imagination. Today, since it was the weekend and he was home, he would be wearing blue jeans, a check shirt, a thick jersey – probably navy – and a pair of sturdy shoes. She felt the wind clawing at their farmhouse, which overlooked the small Northumbrian village of West Woodburn, not far from where they had all been raised. It was a bleak and beautiful place, sparsely populated. On the lower ground there were farms, while the higher ground was fit for nothing but grazing sheep.

'Are you okay, Steph?'

'I'm fine. How about you?'

'I'm well.'

'And Jane, how's she?'

'She's well, too.'

'What about Polly and James?'

Polly was her three-year-old niece. James, her nephew, was fourteen months old. Christopher said, 'They're both great. Polly's been a bit feisty over the last six months, just like Mum always said you were at that age.'

Stephanie was aware of the pounding in her heart. 'I just wanted to hear how you were, you know?'

'It's been a hell of a long time . . .'

67

'I know.'

'We lost track of you after you left that place in Holborn. What was her name? Smith?'

'Karen Smith.'

'That's it. She said you walked out one day and didn't leave a number.'

And you didn't make the effort to look harder. It was a vicious circle. She'd never kept in touch with them so they'd made less and less effort to keep in touch with her. How long had it been since their last acrimonious conversation? Nine months? Ten?

Christopher had been instrumental in helping Proctor to trace Stephanie. Proctor had contacted him late the previous summer and had asked for an interview which had been granted. He'd travelled north to West Woodburn in the autumn and it was during the course of his interview with Christopher that he sensed there might be a story in Stephanie. The two remaining fragments of the family had not clung together for support in the aftermath of the tragedy. Instead, one had tried to cope with it and continue with as normal a life as possible, while the other had disappeared into the ether. Christopher had an old phone number – Karen Smith's – but had insisted that she'd be unlikely to know where Stephanie was and that even if he found her, she wouldn't speak to him. When Proctor had asked what Stephanie did, Christopher had been evasive and then dismissive.

'I have no idea,' he'd replied. 'Probably nothing. In fact, probably less than nothing.'

But Proctor was persistent, spurred on by an instinct for a story. He'd contacted Karen Smith who, as predicted, had no idea where Stephanie was. But she knew some names and pointed him in the right direction. Moving from one shady acquaintance to the next, a picture gradually emerged of a girl with a future sliding into nowhere. From promising student to chemically-infested prostitute, she was perfect. Of all those who were connected to the dead of flight NE027, Stephanie's tragic decline was the worst. And, therefore, the best.

'What have you been doing?' Christopher asked her.

'Bits and pieces. You know . . .'

'Like what?'

'Odd jobs. Anything to help pay the rent.'

'Where are you living?'

Stephanie felt the onset of panic. The conversation was already drifting the way of so many of its predecessors. She could hear it in Christopher's tone, which was cooling. It was always the same. Off the top of her head, she said, 'Wandsworth.'

'Let me take your number.'

It was slipping from her grasp. All the things she wanted to say were still unsaid and, instead, she was being sucked towards the familiar vortex.

'Chris, there's something I have to tell you. About the crash . . .'

'Hang on, I can't find a pen.'

'You don't need a pen.'

He wasn't listening to her. He never did. 'Okay, what is it? You might as well give me the address, too.'

'Chris, please!'

'What?'

Stephanie shook her head. It could not be done over the phone. The moment was gone and the dark storm clouds were gathering at the horizon. 'Nothing.'

'*What?*'

'It doesn't matter.'

'Are you in trouble?'

'No.'

'Are you sure? Do you need money?'

For some reason, that was the question that had always hurt the most. 'No.'

After a pause, Christopher said, in a fashion that was equally critical and concerned, 'Steph, you're not doing anything . . . *stupid*, are you?'

'Not any more.'

'What do you mean by that?'

'Nothing. Forget it.'

'Okay, so give me your number and address.'

Stephanie fell silent.

'Steph?'

The power of speech had abandoned her.

'Steph?'

I got drunk that evening. I had plenty of vodka at the Brazen Head, which is at the far end of Bell Street, and then I returned home with two bottles of bad red wine. They slipped down as quickly as they came back up, which was shortly before I passed out. As an attempt to rinse the conversation from my memory, it worked, albeit temporarily. For two days, I felt I had the flu again.

Proctor is a fitness fanatic. He eats healthily and takes exercise, running three or four times a week. He performs a variety of stretches every morning before breakfast. He says stretching is more important than running or weights or any other form of exercise. I have caught him during his routine several times and we have both been embarrassed by it. It is not that I dislike what I see, or that he dislikes being seen. What makes us awkward are the things we think but which we do not articulate. On each occasion, I have noticed what good shape he is in. He is lean. Nearly all the bodies I have seen in the last two years have been flabby.

Although I have no feelings of affection for Proctor, I have wondered what it would be like to have sex with him. I cannot remember what sex was like with real people. For me, Proctor now has a personality – not to mention a genuine name – whereas all my clients were anonymous. They lied about their identities and the sex we had was purely physical. I faked the gasps of pleasure where required. I never felt anything, apart from occasional pain. In the last month, however, as I have gradually learned more about Proctor, I have speculated on how we would be together. Would the fact that I know him affect the way

70

the sex would feel, or have I been permanently numbed to its pleasure?

How would I react?

I know that he has been thinking about it too. I see it in the glances he steals when he thinks that I cannot see him. And perhaps it is this more than anything else that has fostered the new self-consciousness that I feel for my body. As a prostitute, I will strip for anybody if the price is right. Nudity is nothing for me, nor is the exploitation of it by a stranger, as long as I am profiting from it. But Proctor's gaze – even when I am fully clothed – can make me uncomfortable.

Over the last fortnight, I have started to perform some stretches myself. I have been amazed at how creaky and stiff I am. In general, the last month has been a great boost to my health; I have started to eat healthy food at regular intervals and I am sleeping properly. I have put on some weight and my skin looks less blotchy and grey. The smudges around my eyes are fading. But I am not supple in the way that I was when I was a teenager. I am upset by my physical condition and I am determined to improve it.

Christmas has been and gone. Proctor was in Israel, then. I was here, alone. It was the best Christmas I've had since the crash. New Year's Day has gone, too. For that, he was in Indonesia. Now, we are in January. For everyone else, it is just another year. For me, it is another life. The changes that I have initiated have a momentum of their own and I cannot stop them.

Proctor was still frowning. Stephanie rolled an inch of ash on to a saucer. It had been less than an hour since he walked through the door, suitcase in hand, fatigue on his face. Now, after a shower and a change of clothes, he looked revitalized.

Stephanie said, 'How was it?'

'Terrible. If anybody ever takes you on a holiday to Miami, you can assume they hate you.'

'So what are you going to say in your article?'

'That it's a winter weekend paradise.' They were in the

living room. Proctor was on the sofa, Massive Attack was on the sound-system. Noticing for the first time, he said, 'New haircut?'

Stephanie ran her hand through it and nodded. 'Do you like it?'

It was shorter than before, not quite touching the shoulders. The dark roots had been dyed.

'Sure. It looks good, although I thought you were going to let the blonde grow out.'

She shook her head. 'I couldn't do it.'

'Why not?'

'I always wanted to be blonde. When I was younger, you know . . .'

'And now?'

'It makes it easier to believe I'm someone else.'

'I thought you were getting past that.'

Stephanie stubbed out her final cigarette. 'I'm never going to get past that.'

Later, Stephanie came across Proctor in the bathroom. He was lying on the floor, beneath the sink, unfastening the panel at the end of the bath.

'Is there a leak?' she asked him.

He grinned. 'I certainly hope not. Not after this kind of precaution.'

She saw that there were three computer floppy-disks on the floor beside him. 'What are you doing?'

'A bit of home security. This is where I keep the important stuff. The floppy-disks and my lap-top. There's nothing on my desk-top of any significance – I back up information down a phone-line and then erase it – and I don't keep any good material on paper. The juicy bits are here.'

'Isn't that rather primitive?'

'Primitive is sometimes best.'

'Why don't you just get an alarm or something?'

'In a place like this? Are you kidding? That'd be an invitation to a burglar.'

72

He put the three disks in an airtight plastic pouch already containing four. Then he re-sealed the pouch and replaced it, taping it to the underside of the bath. The lap-top, which was in a protective cover, was inserted between two filthy floorboards. Finally, he re-secured the panel with a screwdriver.

It was a soulless place, catering for the rush-hour trade in Victoria. There were fruit-machines along one wall, Sky Sport on a vast TV suspended over the bar and a sound system that played at a deafening volume. Proctor bought himself half a pint of Guinness and ordered a Coke for Stephanie. They sat at a small circular table with a good view of the bar.

Proctor wriggled out of a leather coat which he folded and placed on the bench beside Stephanie. He wore a denim shirt. The ironing creases were still sharp on the sleeves. Stephanie wore what she wore almost every day; faded jeans and a sweatshirt over a varying number of short- and long-sleeved T-shirts. Her blonde hair was scraped back and gathered by a clasp, which was a new look for her. Before, her face had been too gaunt to justify it. She wore no make-up, which was also a departure for her and one with which she felt increasingly comfortable.

Proctor said, 'You see the guy on the stool, the one with the half-moon glasses and the charcoal jacket?'

'Yes.'

'That's who he's coming to see. I don't think Bradfield usually comes here but the man on the stool likes it because it's crowded and noisy, good for anonymity.'

'Who is Bradfield?'

Proctor took a sip from his glass and then wiped the thin line of cream from his upper lip with the back of his hand. 'I told you. He's a document-forger.'

'I know. But why's he important?'

'It's possible he forged a passport for our man. There's

73

this guy in Whitechapel – Ismail Qadiq – he's an Egyptian T-shirt importer. His brothers run the manufacturing end of the business in Cairo and Qadiq brings the product over here and sells wholesale. But that's not the only thing he's importing. He brings in stolen documents for reprocessing, or brand-new documents, ready for use.'

'Brand-new?'

Proctor nodded. 'Genuine passports or driving licences from Syria, Iran, Iraq, Egypt, Algeria. Anywhere. They get stolen over there – or bought on the sly – and then they're distributed all over Europe. There are dozens of ways into this country. Qadiq is just one. The point is, he may have actually seen our man, but he's not sure. At least, that's what he says but then he's a compulsive liar. An intermediary brought a stranger to his Whitechapel warehouse – the place where he stores all his merchandise – and asked Qadiq to help process some documents as quickly as possible, including one Israeli passport and another in the name of Mustafa Sela. Money was no object. Qadiq says he never saw the stranger fully, that he was lurking in the background, but he told me that he organized it for the two men to meet Cyril Bradfield.'

'So why do we need the man on the stool?'

'Because Cyril Bradfield's number isn't in the phonebook. Because no one seems to be sure what he looks like or where he lives. Because Cyril Bradfield's name probably isn't even Cyril Bradfield.'

Stephanie sipped some Coke. 'And he's some kind of sympathizer, is he?'

'Bradfield? No. He's non-political. He's not even in it for the money. Apparently, he's in it for the love of it. For him, it's art. And a question of quality. So naturally, he draws attention from the worst kind of people.'

'How does the man at the bar fit into this?'

'He's a go-between for some low-life in Birmingham who reprocesses passports for the criminal fraternity and who prefers to have the artwork done down here. The

74

go-between ensures Bradfield and his client never have to meet, which is better for all concerned.'

'How did you discover this?'

Proctor smiled. 'Slowly.' He drained his half-pint glass and rose to his feet. 'I'll be back in a minute.'

Stephanie thought about Barry Green and his sideline in altering the PIN codes on stolen credit cards. It felt as though she had borrowed the memory from someone else.

'Straying a little, ain't you?'

She looked up. The man before her had emerged from the sea of boozing suits, from the waves of accountants, local government officials and cut-price travel-agents. She checked Bradfield's contact; he was still perched on his bar-stool, nursing a pale gold pint and a slim cigar.

She said, 'I'm sorry. What did you say?'

'You're straying a little.'

He wore a suit as badly-fitting as any other she could see; tight trousers eating into a medicine-ball gut, a jacket with spare room at the shoulders, sleeves that ended inches short of the wrist. His face was pink and his neck was coated in shaving rash.

'I don't know what you're talking about. I think you've mistaken me for someone else.'

'Nah. At first, I thought I might've – you look different with your kit on – but not now. I couldn't place your face and then it clicked. You work up west, not down here. Brewer Street, top floor, near the Raymond Revuebar. Right?'

Stephanie was reintroduced to one of her least favourite sensations as her stomach turned to lead and seemed to seep through her bowels, through the floorboards and deep into the earth below. Mentally, she reached for the mask; the hardness in the eyes, the firmness of the mouth, the determination to betray no sign of weakness. But there was nothing there and it showed.

'It's Lisa, ain't it?' The man was leering, enjoying her shock. 'Remember me now, do you?'

Truly, she didn't. He could have been one in a thousand. He might have been *every* one in a thousand. The pub seemed to shrink, the crowd grew taller, the lights dimmed, until they were the only two people in the room.

'You've put some meat on. Don't look bad on you, neither. You was well thin the last time I had you. But now you got more to sink into, know what I mean?'

There was no stinging comeback, there was no response at all.

He lowered his voice. 'You on the meter?'

'What?'

'You working or what?'

'You've made a mistake –'

His bravado was in his piggy eyes, which dropped to her thighs, as much as it was in his voice. 'I got eighty quid in my pocket says you've got something for me down there.'

'I told you –'

'And I'll go to a ton for a bit of A-level.'

Suddenly, Proctor was back, standing beside the man, looking at Stephanie, reading her alarm and saying, 'Are you okay? What's going on?'

Once again, the words stalled in her throat.

Bristling with aggression, the stranger turned to Proctor. 'Who are you?'

Proctor stared him down in silence. Stephanie watched the arrogance subside and the confusion surface. The man turned to her and said, unpleasantly, 'Should've told me you was busy.'

'I don't have to tell you anything.'

Then he turned to Proctor, in a futile attempt to salvage some gutter-born self-respect. 'I'm telling you, she'll cheat you, that one. Bleed your wallet dry and won't give hardly nothing back. So do yourself a favour and make sure she gives you full value, know what I mean?'

Before Proctor could protest, he was gone, back into the sea of suits. Proctor looked at Stephanie, grabbed his

76

leather coat from the bench and took her hand. 'Come on, we're getting out of here.'

'What about Bradfield?'

'He can wait.'

The wind was brisk along Victoria Street. They stood on the pavement, waiting for a taxi. Stephanie was trembling, a fact that was more disconcerting to her than the cause of it.

Proctor said, 'Are you okay now?'

'I guess I'm cold.' She looked down at her hands. 'I'm shaking.'

He took hold of one of them. It was icy. She lifted her gaze to meet his. He traced absent-minded lines across her palm. Then his fingers threaded themselves through hers.

She said, 'We shouldn't throw this chance away.'

He moved closer. 'No.'

'I'm talking about Bradfield.'

His cloudy vision cleared. 'What do you mean?'

Stephanie smiled at his mild embarrassment. 'I can get home all right. You should stay. If there's a chance you'll find him, you'd be crazy not to take it.'

Proctor knew she was right. 'Are you sure you're okay?'

'I'm fine. He was just some wanker trying it on. It's happened a million times. I don't know why it got to me this time. But it's over now.'

They were still holding hands.

7

'**What are you doing?**'

'What does it look like? I'm cooking. Or at least, I'm going to.'

Proctor appeared in the kitchen doorway. 'What is it?'

'Stir-fried vegetables with noodles.'

'You've been waiting all this time? It's midnight.'

Stephanie sliced the leeks that were on the chopping board. Then she placed a pan of water on to the blue circle of flame.

'How did it go?' she asked.

'Bradfield showed up a couple of hours after you left. He was only there for about ten minutes. I followed him and he went to a place called Gallagher's in Longmoore Street, not far from where we were, maybe a ten-minute walk. He stayed there until closing time and then went home. It turns out the pub's his local; his house is right down the same street.'

'What happens now?'

'I'll go and see him.'

'And what will you say?'

'I don't know yet but I'll think of something. Do you want a glass of wine?'

'Are you having one?'

'There's a bottle open in the fridge.'

'Okay.'

The glasses were balloons on tall, thin stems. He handed her one and half-filled it.

'Can I ask you something personal, Stephanie?'

'You can ask.'

'I know you told me once that you didn't want to talk

about your family, but would you tell me about them now? I'd like to know. Not for an article – in fact, I promise anything you tell me will be in confidence – but for me.'

'You think a personal appeal cuts more ice with me than a professional one?'

Proctor smiled and shook his head, the two things coming to a sum total of weariness. 'I don't understand you. Every time I think we're making a little progress, you say something and we're back to square one.'

'In that case, I'll try not to raise your expectations again. That way, you won't ever be disappointed. As for my family history, it's very boring.'

'I doubt that. There's always something.'

My father, Andrew Patrick, was a doctor for Falstone and the surrounding area. Falstone is in north Northumberland, not far from West Woodburn, where my brother, Christopher, now lives with his family. The area my father covered was large, even for a rural practice. It is a wild, rugged place and it is perhaps the one thing that I have not poisoned in myself. I cannot rinse my love for it out of me. In the summer, it can be idyllic; warm days and nights where the light never fades – I have read books outside at one in the morning. In the winter, it can be hard and cold. During those months, it doesn't get light until nine and it's dark by four. But I have no favourite season when I am there; I love them equally, just as I love everything else about the land.

Both my parents possessed strong puritanical streaks and so the life we led was hard without ever being uncomfortable. It was an outdoor existence, mostly. They were keen on walking and were both expert climbers, a legacy of my mother's nationality – Swiss – and my father's fondness for Alpine holidays. They passed this love on to all of us. We lived for the land and off it, growing many of our vegetables and summer fruits, as well as rearing chickens and a small number of sheep. There were always dogs at home and they were always Boxers; we never had less than two, we frequently had four. All in all, we lived a life that might seem perfect to many.

But Proctor is right. There's always something. And in our family, it was probably me.

My parents' puritanism was matched only by their stubbornness. Consequently, our house was a fiery place to be. They argued with each other, they argued with us and we argued among ourselves. Except for David, who was the youngest of us, and who was crippled by shyness. When confronted, he always withdrew deeper into himself. My parents were strict with all of us and often expressed their disappointment at our behaviour or lack of achievement. But by far the largest share of their exasperation was reserved for me, their brightest child and their greatest frustration, a fact that was not lost on me, even at an early age. I under-achieved deliberately and I took a perverse delight in it. I was the archetypal 'difficult second child'.

I never cried. I was sullen and cold. When provoked or angered, my resentment was usually silent and ran deep. I rarely forgave, I never forgot. I preferred my company to that of anyone else. The social aspects of family life held no attractions for me. Independence was what I craved. I longed for a future free of the family.

It wasn't that they were unpleasant. It was that I was unpleasant.

My teenage years must have been a particular form of Hell for my parents. I rarely missed an opportunity to anger or disappoint them. I found academic work much easier than anyone else of my age but I frequently failed exams as an absurd act of rebellion. When my parents lectured me on the perils of alcohol, I went through a phase of getting drunk at every available opportunity and, if possible, in public. Even losing my virginity was an act of spite. It was genuinely nothing more. I treated the boy who took it as contemptuously as I treated my parents, whom I told the following morning. They were disgusted, then distraught. I was delighted.

I think about these things now – the pointlessness of it all, the needless irritation and sadness for which I was responsible – and I try to console myself with the fact that at least there was a reason for it, an explanation. But there isn't. And now it's too

late to apologize. They're gone. Dead. And if I hadn't been such
a spoilt bitch and refused to go with them, I'd be dead too.

There really is no justice in this world.

'How did you find out what had happened?'

Stephanie cupped her glass of wine between both her hands. 'It was when I was at Durham University –'

'So you didn't totally under-achieve, then.'

'I was smart enough to know when it mattered and then I'd always do enough to get by. And I wasn't going to miss out on a place at university. It was a chance to move away.'

'What were you reading?'

She smiled. 'German – I was already fluent. My mother was Swiss-German. We were all brought up trilingual. My father was fluent in French.'

'Why didn't you choose something more challenging?'

'Because I wasn't really interested. If I had been, I'd have made sure I went to Oxford or Cambridge. But for me, university wasn't about degrees leading to professions. It was just a phase to be endured.'

Stephanie poured a small amount of walnut oil into the wok and then moved it over a flame. The vegetables were on the wooden board beside the chopping knife. Proctor was behind her and in this moment, she preferred it like that.

'The night before I found out, I was with this second-year student. He was living in a rented cottage in Sherburn, an old pit village a few miles outside Durham. There was a party, we all got drunk, I stayed over. I didn't get back to Hild and Bede – my college – until eleven the next morning. I was in my room, changing, when there was a knock on the door. It was another first year, like me. She was ashen-faced, she looked sick. I hadn't heard the news or seen a paper, but she had. She said the Principal was looking for me so I went across to his office and he told me. I remember how hard it was for him, how he struggled to find the right words.'

Stephanie turned around. Proctor said, 'How did you react?'

'Predictably. No gasps, no tears. It didn't seem real until I saw it on TV. Even at the funerals, I couldn't absorb it. I kept expecting it to end, for someone to say that it had just been a macabre practical joke.'

'And when that wore off, what then?'

'Then I had to get away. From Durham, from Christopher and his family. From myself. And so I came down here. The rest . . . well, you know most of that already.'

'You stayed with friends at first?'

'They weren't really friends, just people I knew. I moved from one place to the next – a couple of nights here, a couple of nights there. To ease the pain, I drank and took drugs. I'd done a bit of both at Durham, but when I got to London, I started to do more. Before long, and without really being aware of it, I gravitated towards similar people. Instead of wine and beer, I started drinking cheap cider and stolen spirits. Instead of a sharing a couple of social joints, I started scoring Valium, speed, coke, heroin. Anything to take me up or bring me down, I didn't really care which. You know how it is. The habit gets worse, the crowd becomes seedier, the circle becomes more vicious. It didn't take long for me to run out of money – six weeks, maybe two months, I don't remember – so that was when I started trading sex for cash.'

'That must've been hard.'

'Not as hard as you might think. I was wrecked most of the time and I'd already been screwing a heroin dealer in return for a steady supply of tranquillizers. That was like a stepping-stone to the real thing. I got away from everyone else by moving to London and then I got away from myself by getting out of my head. Selling myself was the price I had to pay for that.'

Proctor shook his head. 'I can't even begin to imagine what that's like.'

'Oh, I'm sure you've tried.'

'What do you mean?'

'I mean the reality's not as titillating as you'd like it to be.'

He looked indignant. 'I've never thought there was anything titillating about prostitution.'

'No?'

'No.'

He saw that she didn't believe him. She said, 'Whatever you say. The truth is, it's dirty, monotonous and depressing. Occasionally, it's dangerous. But most of the time, it's as routine as any nine-to-five. Except we tend to work p.m. to a.m.'

'How many days a week did you work?'

'I'd say four to five, averaging five clients a day, at thirty to eighty pounds a go. Some days you get no one, other days you lose count.'

'What kind of people?'

'A mixture of regulars and one-offs.'

'Can I ask you the most obvious question?'

She guessed what that was. 'How do I do it with someone I find repellent?'

'Yes.'

'The same way a lawyer does his business with a criminal he's sure is guilty. Dispassionately and professionally.'

'But this is your *body* we're talking about.'

'Exactly. It's not my soul – my spirit – so it's not the real me.'

This time it was Stephanie who saw that her answer was doubted.

'What do they tend to be like?'

'They're mostly middle-aged, mostly married. There are one or two who are nice enough – they tend to be the regulars – but the rest are wankers. Especially the ones who try to bargain. I mean, it's bad enough without having to explain to some tosser that I'll open my legs for eighty but I won't for forty. Then you get the guys who can't get it up or who can't come. They're the ones who are most likely to get abusive. They're also the ones most likely to cry. But the ones I like the least are the macho ones who insist on the full half-hour – not a minute less – and are determined to try to break some kind of ejaculation record. It's like some kind of virility test they have to pass. They're pathetic.'

'Do you have to see so many of them?'

'Why? Do you think I enjoy it?'

'No. But five clients a day at eighty quid a session, that's four hundred pounds. Five days a week makes two grand.'

'Let me explain something to you. Firstly, not all punters want, or can afford, the full service, so it's not eighty quid a time. Then there's rent. I paid a full rent to Dean West, my landlord. I also paid protection to him. If I'd gone outside him, I'd have had to pay a full commercial rent but I'd also have had to pay someone to take the flat in their name, since no agency is going to lease a place to someone who doesn't even have a bank account.'

'What?'

'That's right. No bank account, no National Insurance, nothing. And whoever rented the flat on my behalf would probably have skimmed some more off the top. Then I had to pay the maid – she cost fifty quid a day plus ten percent of what I made. On top of that, I had the cards to pay for. That's twenty pounds for a thousand and ten pounds to the carder for every one hundred he stuck in a phone-box. And now that British Telecom is clearing some phone-boxes up to four times a day, that's a hell of a lot of cards we're talking about.'

'I never really thought about the details,' Proctor admitted.

'No one ever does. The truth is, it's bloody hard work.'

Proctor nodded. 'It sounds rough.'

'It is.' When it looked as though he might be about to say something sympathetic, she cut him dead by adding: 'But not as rough as the ride on North Eastern Airlines.'

He reached inside the fridge for the bottle and replenished

their glasses. She shovelled some of the vegetables into the wok. The oil spat.

She said, 'Did you know that they never found David? All the others were eventually identified – God knows how – but David was one of the twenty-eight they never recovered.'

'No. I didn't know that. I'm sorry.'

Stephanie shrugged and seemed surprised at herself. 'I don't even know why I mentioned it. I mean, what difference does it make?'

Half an hour later, they had eaten. The topic of conversation had changed and so had the mood.

Stephanie said, 'It's my turn to ask you something personal.'

'Go ahead.'

'Are you gay?'

'*What?*'

She wasn't sure whether he was merely surprised by the question, or angered by it.

'Are you gay?'

'What makes you think I might be?'

'I haven't seen you with anyone.'

'In case you hadn't noticed, I've been away a lot.'

'I know. While I've been here. And no one called. At least, no one personal and female.'

He smiled at her analysis. 'In answer to your question, no. I'm not gay. I'm just busy.'

Stephanie gathered their plates and took them through to the kitchen. Proctor followed. She placed the plates in the sink and turned on the cold tap. Proctor was behind her, but closer than before. She knew he would touch her before he did. He placed a hand on her hip and kissed her on the ear. It was a little peck followed by: 'Thank you. That was delicious.'

The cold water was running over her hands. 'It was nothing.'

'It was thoughtful.'

He hadn't moved away. He'd waited for a response, some form of rejection. There hadn't been one and he took this as a sign of encouragement. He placed a hand on Stephanie's shoulder and slowly turned her around. She let him. This was a moment that had been coming for a while.

Stephanie's curiosity was marginally stronger than her trepidation. Proctor kissed her. He was tentative and closed his eyes. She kept hers open and never blinked. His hands moved around her, from the shoulders to the small of her back. Her lips felt numb against his.

She broke the kiss.

'Are you all right?' he murmured.

She recognized the sensation; the tension of a guitar string on the verge of snapping. Her pulse quickened, her fingers flexed.

He lowered his face towards hers once more, reading her silence as acceptance. But she turned her face away, grabbed his arms and pushed him back. If he was surprised by the vigour of her rejection, he was utterly amazed by the look on her face. Her eyes were aflame. The bitterness in them superseded anything he had seen in her before.

'What's wrong?'

'Keep away from me,' she hissed.

He was dumbfounded. 'Stephanie, what the hell's going on?'

'What did you think was going to happen?' Even her voice had changed. Instead of rising to a hysterical shriek it had dropped to a growl. 'That I'd find relief by letting you fuck me all night?' She spat every word. 'Is that what you thought? Me with tears on my face, you with a grin on yours?'

'What are you talking about? It was just a kiss. I didn't mean to . . .'

He took a step forward, she took a step back, until she found herself pressed against the sink. Her elbow knocked a wine glass to the floor. It shattered but her eyes never left Proctor. She felt the cold water splattering off the plates on to her arms. And then she felt the knife on the chopping board. She grabbed the handle and thrust the blade at Proctor who froze.

'Come one step closer to me and I'll kill you. I swear to God, I will.'

He raised his hands. 'Take it easy, Stephanie. Just calm down –'

'I mean it.'

'Look, I'm sorry if I upset you.'

'*Sorry?*'

'If I misread the signals, I apologize. I didn't want –'

'Signals?'

'I thought there was something . . . *happening*. Between us.'

'Like what?' Her fury was still building. 'Do you see some neon sign over my head? *You can fuck me if you want.* What bloody signals?'

Proctor was bewildered beyond reason. 'Stephanie, please . . .'

She was shaking. Her face had reddened at first but now the colour had drained from it entirely. He had never seen eyes so black or so brilliant. Her voice quietened to a brittle whisper: 'If you ever touch me again . . .'

Proctor slowly extended his right hand towards her and said, softly, 'Give me the knife.'

The swipe was so quick that neither of them saw the blade properly.

Stunned, Proctor looked at his palm, at the slice that extended from the base of the index finger to the edge of the wrist. For a second, it was a perfect scarlet line. Then the cut started to flow, streaming over his hand and fingers, curling around his wrist, coiling itself around his forearm, slicking the sleeve of his shirt, splattering on the tiles of the kitchen floor.

It was the sound of the front door closing that prompted

him to gather his senses. Stephanie was gone and he needed medical attention.

At two in the morning, the busiest places in London are the night-clubs, the police stations and the Accident and Emergency departments of the city's hospitals. Proctor descended from the first floor of St Mary's Paddington and stepped out on to South Wharf Road. His palm had been stitched and bandaged. It was a freezing night. He glanced both ways, wondering which direction would most likely lead him to a taxi, even though Bell Street was not far away. To his right, he recognized the vast curved roof that covered the platforms of Paddington Station. Only a handful of lights were burning in the high-rise beyond. It stood out against the night, lit by the glare from the streets below.

Proctor turned left. He never saw Stephanie standing still in the shadows of the hospital. And she never saw him alive again.

8

I open the door to Proctor's flat with my key – with his key – and my breathing stops.

I have spent the night on the streets. This is nothing new for me. I am familiar with the city as a bed. Like so many others in London, I've slept in shop doorways and close to the warm air exhaled by Underground ventilation units. I've sneaked into hotel service areas and stolen a few warm hours. Sometimes, a train station – or a bus station – has been the best place to rest. But tonight I wasn't looking for sleep. I was looking for answers.

So I walked through the streets, mindless of my direction and only vaguely aware of my surroundings, which is unusual for me. I have learned to be cautious. Working at night in the seamier areas of the city, one quickly develops a sixth sense for danger. I can see behind me. I can feel a threat, smell its scent on the polluted air. Unless the drugs or the Special Brew have kicked in. Then I'm useless and vulnerable, which was how I was last night. All my defences were down.

I cannot believe what I have done. Until dawn, I don't honestly think I even accepted what I had done. It seemed like a dream. But morning tends to bring clarity, in all its painful guises.

I don't understand why I reacted the way I did. I knew Proctor was going to touch me, to kiss me. I wanted him to. The moment had been telegraphed; I had plenty of time to kill it before it even happened but I chose not to. I knew he would be tender and understanding. When he put his hand on my hip and his lips on my lips, it was much as I hoped it would be. No, it was better than I hoped it would be. And then . . . I snapped. Just as I did with my last client, even though the two situations could hardly have been more different.

Around seven this morning, I stopped at a café for a cup of

coffee. I only just resisted my craving for a cigarette. For an hour,
I agonized about what I should do before stumbling to a decision.
It was a cowardly choice; to sneak back to Bell Street, collect my
things and flee. I prayed Proctor would be out to make it easier
for me. Then I could leave my keys with a hastily-scribbled note
of apology. A month ago, his absence would have been an invi-
tation to scour for valuables. But not now. I owe Proctor. He is
the only man who has shown me any kindness in the last two
years. And how have I repaid him for that kindness? By cutting
him with a knife.

I cannot believe myself. What kind of cold-blooded creature
have I become?

There were papers strewn across the floor in the hall of
Proctor's pristine flat. They were the first thing that Stephanie saw. The self-pity and the shame evaporated. Her
skin prickled, her throat dried. She paused for a moment,
pushing the door completely open and listening for the
sound of movement. Nothing. Then she stepped inside and
quietly closed the door behind her.

The paper trail led to the office on the right. From the
short hall, she could see empty desk-drawers on the floor,
the swivel chair on its side, the activated computer screen.
She turned left. In the kitchen, every cupboard and drawer
had been investigated. The fridge was empty. Its door was
open, all its contents spread across the tiles. Clean cutlery
cluttered the steel sink. Proctor's bedroom looked no more
dishevelled than that of the average student but, normally,
it was clinically clean and tidy. The mattress had been
removed from the bed and sliced apart. The sheets were
screwed into a bundle in the corner. The cupboards had
been checked, all the slatted doors were open. In the bathroom, the bath itself contained all that had been inside the
medicine cabinet and the cupboard beneath the sink.

Proctor was in the living room, an island in a scarlet
ocean.

Stephanie stood over him and found she was unable to

cry out for help, to gasp in horror, to shed a tear. This wasn't Proctor. It was only his body. Just as she wasn't Stephanie when a stranger was using her. The spirit was gone but the sight still stopped her heart.

Proctor had been shot in the forehead and through the left hand. Also, there were dark glossy stains on his shirt and on his trousers, one on the left thigh and one around each knee. The bandage that had been wrapped around his right hand during the night lay in a crumpled heap on the sofa. The stitches had been plucked free of the injury that Stephanie had inflicted upon him and the gash had been deepened and extended. There were four cross-cuts on the same palm and she could see that the little finger, the index finger and the thumb had all been broken. His eyes were frozen open. A fat drop of blood sat on the left pupil.

She could not imagine the agony he had endured before his death and wondered how his torturer had prevented Proctor from screaming; howls of pain would surely have alerted the other residents of the mansion block. Ransacking suggested the killer had been looking for something specific. Torture suggested the killer hadn't found it. Stephanie wondered whether the prize was what lay behind the panel in the bathroom. She had noticed that it was intact. Or maybe the killer was after something else – something that was actually retrieved. A piece of hard information, perhaps? A secret locked in Proctor's mind? Would he have surrendered it? He must have known that he was going to die so did he try to take it to the grave? How resistant had he been to the pain? How resistant would she have been?

Stephanie picked up the phone. She pressed nine once, then twice. *Think about it.* Then she stopped, before replacing the receiver. There was nothing she could do for Proctor now. She was all that was left. She wondered whether she was in danger herself. Had the intruder expected to find both of them in the flat or was Proctor the only target?

And who had the intruder been? Bradfield? An associate of his? Or someone else, someone invisible to her?

She needed time to think and somewhere safe to do it.

Auto-pilot engaged and emotions temporarily suspended, she drifted through the flat. Her little rucksack was in the corner of the living room, its contents scattered across the cherry table. The money she had stolen from her King's Cross clients was gone, everything else – the worthless stuff – had been left. The panic rose within her but she beat it back. She returned her belongings to the bag and searched for Proctor's overcoat. That was what he had been wearing when she had seen him leaving St Mary's Paddington. She found it in the bedroom among a heap of clothes on the floor. The wallet lay beside it. The cash was gone. Only the cards remained; Barclays Connect and Visa. She rummaged through her own pockets and found six pounds seventy.

She put his wallet into her rucksack and went into Proctor's office. She examined the computer screen. It was a letter to a features editor of a magazine she did not recognize. She scrolled down the page. The content was innocuous. Then she remembered that he had told her that he kept nothing of value on his desk-top. The necessity for torture became more apparent.

It seemed Proctor had kept his filing cabinet locked and had not been forthcoming over the whereabouts of the key since it had been prised open with a hammer and a screwdriver, which had both been left lying on top of it. The files had been examined and discarded. Stephanie got down on her hands and knees and began to sift through the papers.

It took thirty-five minutes to find the slip of paper with the PIN code for the Visa card on it. She found no number for the Connect card but made a note of Proctor's birth date, his phone numbers, his fax number, his National Insurance number, his passport number. A three-month-old bank statement revealed a nine hundred and eighty pound credit in Proctor's current account. She hoped his Visa card was as healthy.

She took the screwdriver from the top of the filing cabinet and went to the bathroom, where she unfastened the panel and retrieved Proctor's lap-top and the plastic pouch containing the seven floppy-disks. There was too much to squeeze into her rucksack so she found another small shoulder bag on the bedroom floor. She helped herself to a tatty Aran jersey, a relic from a bygone era in Proctor's personal fashion history. She also took some thick socks, three T-shirts and a navy blue silk scarf, which she wrapped around her throat. On the cherry table, by her rucksack, she noticed Proctor's portable phone, which was recharging. She took it.

Her scavenging concluded, Stephanie wanted to do something about Proctor, to cover him, or to arrange him in some way that looked less awkward – less pained – and then to alert someone. But she did none of these things.

Instead, she gathered her bags and left the flat, taking care to double-lock the front door as Proctor had always insisted she should.

It had started to rain when she stepped on to Bell Street. She looked left and right, half-expecting an approach from a stranger, or a dark-windowed car to screech to a halt beside her. Or the cold dart of pain as the tempered steel slipped between her ribs, courtesy of an invisible hand. But there was no one and nothing. She turned right and headed for the Edgware Road. Cash was her first consideration.

She tried the Connect card at the first two ATMs she came to, using variations of the month and year of Proctor's birth and the last four digits of his phone number for the PIN code. All were rejected. At the Halifax ATM, on the junction of Edgware Road and Old Marylebone Road, Stephanie played safe and inserted the Visa card for which she had a valid PIN number. She withdrew two hundred pounds and turned her attention to the next priority: getting off the street.

Sussex Gardens offered plenty of cheap, anonymous accommodation, the dingy terraced hotels set back from the road behind railings and hedges. She could have picked any one of two dozen places but settled for the Sherburn House Hotel for the flimsiest of reasons: its name. Sherburn was the village outside Durham where she had stayed on the night that flight NE027 had plunged into the Atlantic.

She paid cash and registered under a false name that she forgot almost instantly. Her room was on the second floor. The single bed had an orange bedspread, the curtains were maroon. There was a single-bar electric heater mounted on a wall. The wallpaper had been buttercup yellow once – the original colour was preserved in a rectangle where a picture had hung for years – but now it was dirty cream, with patches of brown where the damp was worst. In the corner, there was a sink with a small green bucket beneath it, to catch the drips leaking from the U-bend in the pipe.

Alone, Stephanie dumped her bags on the floor and sat on the bed. The springs squeaked as she sank into the quicksand mattress. She put her head in her hands.

What now?

A cigarette. I'd give anything for a cigarette right now. And maybe a drink. Maybe two. A shot of vodka would help, especially if it was a double. The first of several, perhaps. And then maybe something a little stronger, just to be sure.

I am standing at the crossroads. Again.

I have been here before. Of the choices that are available to me, I know one well and I can feel it drawing me towards it. It is the path that offers to numb the pain. It is the path which promises the bliss of ignorance as a solution. It is the path I chose last time.

Proctor's lap-top was operating Windows 98. The last time

Stephanie had used a computer she had been a student and Windows 95 had been the freshest thing on the menu. She never cared much for computers, or for the sad souls who were so infatuated by them, but she had learned the basics. At the time, she had been surprised by how easy she found it. Now, two corrosive years later, she felt less complacent. Working cautiously, it took her two hours to refresh her memory to a standard that allowed her through the system.

There was a list of the material stored on Proctor's desk-top. Most of the files from the original investigation were on that; the interviews with the families and friends of those who had perished aboard NE027. She supposed that included Christopher and wished she could have seen what he'd said to Proctor. How had *he* coped over the last two years? Stephanie had done all she could to bleach her own memory but her brother wasn't like that. Since his emotions rarely rose to the surface, what lurked beneath remained a mystery.

There was a form of diary on the second of the seven disks that she inserted into the computer, a chronological report for Proctor's investigation. It showed the order in which he had contacted the bereaved and each of their responses to his request for an interview. Where granted, there was a file reference for the interviews themselves, all of which were stored on the desk-top. Most people had only been interviewed once, either by phone or in person, but some had been interviewed twice or even three times. The chronology also showed Proctor's travel schedule and the actual dates for all the interviews he had conducted. Stephanie saw that Christopher had only been questioned once.

The computer record also told Stephanie something about Proctor's MI5 contact. At first, she thought Smith was part of Proctor's initial enquiry, someone close to one of the three hundred and eighty-eight dead. But the name cropped up more frequently than any other and Stephanie

was then forced to reconsider her original opinion when
she reached the following entries.

Dec 10   Tried Smith. Phone disconnected.
Dec 15   Smith called. Use outside phones from now on.
Jan 06   Smith called. Watching and watched.

Watching and watched? Stephanie travelled through
time, scrolling up and down the pages of the diary. She
traced Smith's first entry into the journal.

Jul 22   Spoke to Beth Marriot, widow of NE027 captain
          – turned down request for an interview. Contacted
          by 'friend' who wants to help. Will deliver infor-
          mation.
Jul 25   Contact of 22nd left package this morning. Incred-
          ible – clearly a crank! Signed Smith. Question –
          how did he find me? How did he know?

Stephanie proceeded slowly, assembling the bare bones
of Proctor's information. From the abbreviated notes in
the diary, she saw how his initial opinion of Smith was
gradually undermined. Each entry seemed to nudge him
a little further along Smith's path. The other contacts – the
relatives and friends of the dead – made fewer and fewer
appearances in the log until, on November 30, they ceased
altogether, apart from Proctor's first contact with Stephanie in mid-December. In passing, she saw two familiar
names – Bradfield and Qadiq – which brought her back to
the central questions: who killed Proctor? Why? And what
about her? If Proctor's flat had been under surveillance,
the killer would have known that she was living there.
Perhaps his murder had been more impulsive than that.
   One of the disks had 'Smith' scrawled across the label
in green felt-tip. Stephanie placed it into the computer.
There were only three files on the disk. One of them
detailed Smith's version of the story, as told to Proctor.

Smith had become aware of Caesar – the name he, or maybe someone else, had ascribed to the alleged bomber of NE027 – when he had access to knowledge of an MI5 surveillance operation. It wasn't clear whether Smith was actually part of the surveillance team detailed to watch Caesar, or whether he was running the operation, or whether he had no part in it but had, one way or the other, learned of its existence. Stephanie supposed the obfuscation was deliberate. It was clear that Smith had questioned the suitability of such an operation, only to be rebuffed by a higher authority. He claimed that SIS were aware of Caesar's presence in London, as were factions within Scotland Yard. He also claimed that Caesar was currently masquerading as a student at Imperial College at the University of London, and he had even noted the course he was taking: a Postgraduate Study in Chemical Engineering and Chemical Technology.

Smith's outrage, Proctor noted, had felt genuine. And justified. Here was a man who had placed a bomb on an aircraft full of innocents – who had murdered them all – and who was now walking around London, as a free man, in the full knowledge of those agencies whose job it was to hunt such people and bring them to justice. Worse still, he was passing himself off as a student, living off government-funded grants paid for by the British taxpayer. Proctor, it seemed, had been persuaded of Smith's integrity simply by the tone of his voice, since the two men never actually met.

During another conversation, Smith had warned Proctor to be careful about those with whom he spoke. Questions to the police, for instance, would inevitably be referred upwards and, sooner or later, someone on the inside would see his name. A direct approach to MI5 or SIS would obviously be swatted aside, in the first instance, and who could say what the longer-term consequences of such an action might be? The inference was clear. *Tread cautiously, stay in the shadows, whisper it softly.*

* * *

I am lying in bed, fully-clothed beneath the sheets, blankets and orange bedspread. The wall-mounted heater is on and radiating a pathetic amount of warmth. I am shivering but it has nothing to do with the fact that I am cold.

It is ten-to-midnight. There is a prostitute in the room to my left. She's been intermittently busy since half-past-eight this evening. The headboard of her bed smacks the wall between us when she's earning. I'm surprised she doesn't break it since the partition is so thin I can hear nearly everything that is said between her and her clients. Those sad exchanges; the insincere teases and the lies. The whispers and moans of encouragement, the grunts and groans of faked release, I know her vocabulary in all its depressing entirety. I am her.

As for my shaking frame, who can say? It's shock, certainly, and it was only a matter of time before I succumbed to it. Frankly, I'm surprised I lasted this long. But is there also something else?

Every time I close my eyes, I see Proctor, twisted and torn, drained, quite literally, of life. Or I see him as a kind man, someone who didn't deserve to die, someone quite unlike me. All day, I was ruled by reason and protected from emotion. But now I am too tired to resist. An overwhelming sadness rises up within me and threatens to drown me. I think of his injuries and the sickening process that created them. And the fact that but for a cruel coincidence of timing – a coincidence born of my brutal behaviour – I would have been there when Proctor's killer called. And either the two of us, as a team, would have survived, which is a jewel to add to my treasure-chest of guilt, or I would have gone the same way as him.

So, what of me now? Proctor's kindness gave me a chance. Six weeks ago, my fate was sealed, as it had been for the last two years. A gradual slide towards an inevitable end, perhaps as a consequence of an overdose, perhaps at the hands of a psychopathic client, perhaps as a suicide. But he changed that and offered me an alternative. The way he treated me acted as a buffer between who I used to be and who I'd become. He showed me there was a choice. He was dependable and honest, and it seems that I'd come to rely upon him more than I ever realized because now that he's dead, I already feel as though I'm losing control again.

It is only now that it's really starting to sink in. He's never coming back. The rock is gone. I'm by myself. Shock aside, I'm petrified, that's why I'm shaking. I'm terrified of myself because I know what I can do to myself and there's no longer anyone around to stop me. I am my own enemy.

Despite the fear, however, there is something else I feel. It is lurking in a small, dark corner deep within my soul. It is festering, feeding on itself, waiting.

It is anger.

9

A new morning, a new mood. Stephanie wasn't sure what time it was when she finally fell asleep but it was after four. In the end, sheer exhaustion conquered shock. Now, three hours later, she was awake again. The fear was still with her, just beneath the surface, but for the first time since Proctor's catastrophic kiss, Stephanie felt she was in control of herself again.

She spent three hours checking the remains of the contents of the floppy-disks. Then she packed her two bags, left the Sherburn House Hotel and ate slices of toast and drank coffee in a nearby café. Afterwards, she found the nearest ATM and drew another two hundred pounds against Proctor's Visa card. She bought a pack of floppy-disks so that she could make copies of the originals for her own protection. She needed somewhere safe to hide Proctor's information and that was a problem since anywhere that required her to provide proof of her identity was out of the question. There was one place that came to mind, but there were other, more serious risks associated with it. In the end, however, she saw little alternative. So she bought a small torch.

She checked into another hotel, close to Waterloo Station. It was no smarter than the Sherburn House Hotel and was equally anonymous. For most of the rest of the day she went through Proctor's disks again, selecting the files she wanted to copy, filling two new disks in the process. Late in the afternoon, she was ready to conceal the lap-top and the original seven disks.

She thought a hot bath might have a calming effect. For half an hour, she let the water work its way into her body, turning her skin pink. When the temperature cooled, she added more hot water. Steam rose from the surface, shrouding her head, drawing beads of sweat to her face. When she climbed out of the bath, she wiped the condensation from the mirror and examined herself. Although hardly voluptuous, there was more flesh on her than at any time in the past two years. Her breasts had grown, her thighs had assumed some muscle, her ribs were less prominent. As for her face, much of the gauntness had gone. So had the dark smudges beneath the eyes and her skin looked incomparably healthier. By any standard, the changes of the past six weeks were extraordinary. But they were not enough. She was still Stephanie. Or rather, she was still Lisa.

The prospect of returning to Brewer Street made her extremely nervous.

Waiting for darkness had been a good idea; there was less chance of her being recognized. To make it yet harder, she had bought a black baseball cap with Newcastle United written across the front in silver letters from a pavement trader on New Coventry Street. She'd pulled it low, creating a greater shadow across her face. Wearing Proctor's Aran jersey, not her customary sweatshirt, as well as his blue silk scarf, she'd also tried to alter her gait a little. With her heart hammering, she had walked through the familiar streets, homing in on the one place she had sworn to avoid for the rest of her life.

Now, however, the darkness was a handicap. She was on the fire-escape at the rear of the building next to the one in which she used to work. She thought it safer not to use the torch she had bought that morning; she didn't relish drawing any attention to herself. The only source of light came from cracks in curtains and the gaps left by badly-fitted blinds.

The fire-escape was steep and narrow. It felt unsafe and seemed to sway under her weight, threatening to tear free from the crumbling bricks. She didn't remember it being so frail. She reached the top, a small square landing leading to a door with a padlocked bolt. Except that the bolt had nowhere to slide to; the frame was rotten. It took three heaves with the shoulder to force it open, the bottom scraping against naked floorboards.

Only when she was inside and had closed the door behind her did she dare use the torch. The attic was identical in basic design to the attic in the next building. Originally, the buildings had been one. When they were sold separately, the new owners of the building next door had converted their attic into a small apartment, whereas the owners of the attic in which she now stood had left it empty. There was a door set in the wall between the two. She shone her torch at the door. The fact that no one in the other building knew about it was not a surprise. It was stuck behind a wardrobe that hadn't been moved in years. Besides, men like Dean West were not renowned for their interest in the structural developments of the buildings they owned; they were only concerned with the money-making enterprises that occurred within them. Stephanie had discovered the door by accident when trying to recover a lost earring that had rolled beneath the wardrobe. Later, from Brewer Street, she had seen that the next-door building's attic windows were boarded up. When she investigated the building from the alley behind, she'd climbed the fire-escape and learned that the door at the top of it was not secured, as it appeared, but open to anyone prepared to give it a good push.

Inside, it was lightless, musty and mostly empty. Just like it always had been. Stephanie suspected that she was the only person to have been in the place for at least a decade. There was an old water-tank that was no longer in use, some discarded packing cases and several tightly-bound piles of newspapers and magazines dating back to the Seventies. Stephanie had learned that on the floor below there was a private pornographic screening-room and that when the room was being sound-proofed the builders had sealed and concealed the access to the attic.

Having originally discovered the attic, she'd begun to treat it as an occasional bolt-hole, always taking care to make sure she was not seen entering or leaving. Quite frequently, it had served as her bedroom for the night, which was a less than pleasant experience. It was draughty and cold, and a home to rats. But when nowhere else could be found, it was better than sleeping in rain. Now, having served as a part-time hideaway, the attic was to serve as a safe deposit box.

She placed the computer inside the empty, rusted water-tank. Then she removed one of the many loose floorboards and taped the plastic pouch containing the seven disks to the underside of one of its secure neighbours. Finally, she replaced the floorboard and then counted the wooden planks back to the door that opened on to the fire-escape, noting how far left she had moved.

I remember the Christmas when my father broke his ankle. He slipped on ice and fell awkwardly. I remember the crutches he used and the cheap lights on our Christmas tree. I remember the snow that fell that year and that our Swiss grandparents came to stay with us in Falstone. These things are my first memories. At least, I think they are. But maybe this is a cosy invention of the imagination; I would not be the first person to rewrite history.

Now, at a moment when I am at my most lonely, the memory is unleashed. These are the things that rise up and overwhelm me: chewing-gum stuck beneath my school desk; me picking on David and then feeling guilty, and that guilt eventually fermenting into an anger which was directed at him since he was the source of it; the winter night that Jimmy Craig – a local farmer who sold us lamb and beef – drowned in the North Tyne; our first family holiday abroad in Switzerland; Sarah biting me because I'd been teasing her about her acne; 'Transformer' by Lou Reed – the first album I bought; 'Perfect Day' – the first song to send a shiver through me; my parents arguing in the

kitchen over whether Christopher, aged sixteen, should be allowed
to spend a weekend in London with a friend of his; my first
suspension from school for drinking alcohol; the death of Matilda,
our first brindled Boxer – I cried myself to sleep for a week;
chicken pox – we all had it; me sipping red wine for the first
time and finding it filthy; Christopher's first girlfriend – Laura,
a chubby blonde with metal girders restraining her buck teeth;
being car-sick on a hot afternoon on the way back from Seahouses;
shopping at Fenwick's in Newcastle – my mother's temper was
never shorter than when she was in a crowded store; my first
cigarette, a Benson & Hedges, given to me by Michael Carter, a
thirteen-year-old classmate, in exchange for a kiss – his was the
first tongue to touch mine; the smell of Sunday lunch wafting
from the kitchen to every part of our house; standing outside on
Midsummer's Eve beneath a sapphire night sky; my first driving
lesson in a Ford Fiesta with an instructor whose eyes spent more
time on my breasts than on the road; Polly's christening – I
found it hard to believe that Christopher had become a father
and that I had become an aunt; the blow-job that was my first
paid act of sex – I got twenty pounds for it.

It is four in the morning, the hour at which we are at our
most vulnerable, the hour at which we most want to rewrite our
history and secure our future.

In the morning, Stephanie changed hotels again. She took
the Underground to Queensway. She drew another two
hundred pounds from a Barclays ATM on the junction of
Queensway and Moscow Road, before finding a hotel
in Inverness Terrace. A long, black TV aerial cable hung
from the roof of the King's Court Hotel. It fell to within
fifteen feet of the ground and swayed in the stiff wind.
The first-floor French windows opened on to crumbling
balconies. Weeds sprouted miraculously from flaking
plaster. There was a handwritten sign taped to the pat-
terned glass of the front door's window. It said: 'No Jobs,
No Dogs'.

Later, Stephanie took the Central Line to Tottenham

Court Road, and then walked down to Shaftesbury Avenue, near its junction with Wardour Street, where Barry Green's ticketing agency was located. The agency was on the first floor, its ground-floor entrance sandwiched between a newsagent and a restaurant.

The previous evening, Stephanie had been scared to return to this part of the West End. Now, with determination outweighing anxiety, she was cold to the risk.

The agency was familiar territory. This was where Green sold drugs to customers he knew well, although he never kept any product on the premises; the agency was too useful a cover to place in such obvious jeopardy. Stephanie knew the routine only too well. One entered the office and placed an order with Green, who then made a phone call to establish where and when it could be picked up. But the cash had to be in Green's hand before one left the room. There were no exceptions to this rule. Those who preferred a direct exchange were invited to conduct their business elsewhere.

Stephanie climbed the stairs to the first floor, aware of the tightness in her stomach. She entered the office, its windows sporting gold painted letters in reverse so that from Shaftesbury Avenue one saw: BARRY GREEN – London's Premier Ticket Agency. On the walls, there were promotional posters for *Chicago* and every other West End hit. There was a board on an aluminium easel that listed a string of pop and rock acts, beside their dates, venues and prices. A sign by the tan leather sofa claimed to guarantee seats for any home fixture for Arsenal, Spurs or Chelsea.

Behind a pair of matt-black desks sat a pair of bottle-bleached blondes. They wore too much make-up, powdered peach cheeks clashing violently with rose-red lips. Stephanie suddenly felt acutely uncomfortable rushing to such a quick and damning judgement.

Sitting in the far corner, apparently minding his own business – he was reading a copy of *The Sun* – was a man who might have been a customer waiting for tickets. He wore a pale grey suit, a khaki shirt and a thin, purple tie. Stephanie recognized him as a man paid to prevent undesirables from reaching Green's private office, or to eject those who had already sneaked in. She couldn't remember his name. His head snapped up from his tabloid when Stephanie marched past the receptionists and headed for the door behind them. Normally, he would have intercepted her before her fingers touched the handle but recognition, followed by astonishment, dulled his reaction.

Green was standing by a window overlooking Shaftesbury Avenue. He was on his mobile, laughing coarsely, sharing a joke. 'Nice one!' he chortled several times.

He was short and stout with a fat face, a collection of chins and thinning black hair. What remained was combed tightly back over the ears. He had bushy black eyebrows, a broad nose, thick lips and a swollen tongue. He was wearing black slacks, fake Gucci slip-ons and a Nike sweatshirt with JVC across the back. Five of his fat fingers sported rings, three on the left, two on the right. A thick gold identity bracelet circled his left wrist and clinked against an Omega watch designed for deep-sea divers.

When he turned round and saw her, his conversation dried up. So did his good humour. He lowered the mobile and stared. Stephanie was aware of the protection moving into the room behind her.

'Sorry, boss, but . . .'

Green silenced and then dismissed him with a flick of the hand. The door behind Stephanie closed. Green switched off his mobile and moved back behind his desk, apparently happier to have something solid between them. He flipped the lid on an onyx cigarette box and took out an Embassy Regal. Stephanie smiled; that had always amused her, even in the darkest moments. He lit it with the gold Cartier lighter that Dean West had given him as a small gesture of appreciation in the aftermath of the Gary

106

Crowther incident; Green had organized the dumping of the body in Docklands.

Eventually, he recovered himself. 'You've got a fucking nerve, ain't you? Walking in here like that. Where you been the last couple of months?'

'A long way from here but not far enough.'

'What the fuck happened to you?'

'Plenty.'

Green was used to seeing her in a state of desperation. Usually, when she came to the agency, she came to score drugs, accepting any insult or indignity, just so long as Green sold her relief through release.

'Why've you come back?'

'To see you, Barry.'

Now she saw he was unnerved. Surrounded by the comfort of familiarity, Green was a barrel-chested bully. Confronted by anything unexpected, he shrank. It was the tone of her voice and the way that she looked at him that were causing the damage.

He made a clumsy attempt at small-talk. 'You look good, Steph. You've put on some weight.'

'So have you.'

He ignored the jibe. 'Suits you.'

'You're too kind,' she replied, as flatly as she could, holding his gaze.

'Looks like you've moved up in the world.'

'Any move was going to be up from where I was.'

'Been fucking the towel-heads on Park Lane, have you?'

She let the question go.

Green sat down and began to sound less anxious. 'After you vanished, West went berserk. That wanker you poleaxed with that bottle of champers ended up in hospital. Plod was all over West like flies on shit, and he was all over the rest of us twice as bad. So if you're here looking for favours, you can forget it. You owe us. You owe *me*. You owe me big time.'

'I don't owe you anything.'

'Maybe you'd like to tell that to Deano?'

'And maybe you'd like to be fingered as an accomplice in Gary Crowther's unfortunate death? Or should I say murder?'

'Give over, Steph. Why don't you play a different record for a change?'

'Because I don't have anything to lose. Unlike you.'

Green frowned, his large black eyebrows meeting over his nose. He sucked on his cigarette. When his mobile rang, he ignored it.

'So what do you want? Cash? I hope not. I'm fucking skint.'

'I doubt that. But don't wet your Calvin Kleins. I don't want your money.'

Green's smile was unconvincing. 'Oh, I get it. You want medicine, right?' She continued to stare at him. 'What's it gonna be?'

'A gun.'

He assumed he'd misheard. 'What?'

'I want a gun.'

His jaw slackened. 'What the fuck do you want a gun for?'

'That's none of your business.'

'Bollocks it ain't. I'm making it my bloody business.'

'I've got money – your favourite kind: cash – so what do you care?'

'What do you reckon? Suppose I sell you a gun and you take a pop at my good friend Deano? Understandable under the circumstances, I know, but what if the word gets out that I was the tosser who sold you the weapon? See what I'm getting at? I'd be as popular as a bacon sarnie at a bar mitzvah. Even if you whacked West – which I reckon's no more than a fifty-fifty chance – I'd be next in line for the slab.'

'It's not West.'

'And I have your word on that, do I?'

'Yes.'

108

Green overplayed his exasperation. 'The word of a washed-out whore? Excuse me, love, but you can kiss my fucking ring-piece.'

Stephanie's inscrutability remained intact. 'I'll get a gun, one way or another. If not from you, then from someone else.'

'Fine. Then piss off. I don't care who you get it from as long as –'

'But I'll be sure to let it slip that you were the one who sold it to me. You can count on that.'

Green looked incredulous. 'Are you threatening me?'

'I'm suggesting a trade.'

'I could have my lad out there make you disappear –' He clicked his fingers in front of his face. ' – like *that*!'

'Grow up, Barry. You don't honestly think I'd walk in here after six weeks – after everything that happened in Brewer Street – without some kind of protection, do you?'

'What protection?'

'That's for me to know.'

'Bollocks. You're bluffing.'

'Then make me disappear.'

An hour later, as arranged, Stephanie was standing outside the Hippodrome when Green's Shogun pulled into the kerb. The minder was driving. Green was sitting in the back and beckoned Stephanie. She climbed in beside him and the four-by-four pulled away.

'Just drive around in circles and make sure you don't get hauled up by Plod.'

Lying between them, on the back seat, was a plastic John Lewis bag. Green reached inside and pulled out a bundle of cloth which turned out to be an old sweatshirt. He unfolded it, revealing a gun.

'Browning 9mm, army issue,' he told Stephanie. 'Do you know how to use it?'

She raised an eyebrow. 'Point it and pull the trigger?'

'Don't be a fucking comedian, Steph. I'm not in the

mood.' Green handled the gun, keeping it low, beneath the height of the windows. He showed her the clip and then slapped it home and pointed at the safety-catch. 'You ease it off like this and then she's ready to pop. I'm giving you one up the pipe, five in the clip, six in total. You need any more than that and you can get them yourself.'

'I'll only need one. Maybe two.'

'Then that's all you need to know. But I'll give you a tip. Get as tight as you can to your target. These things are bollocks at any distance. If you're wondering whether you're close enough, you're not. You've got to get in so it's harder to miss than to hit.'

Green rubbed the gun with the sweatshirt before re-wrapping it in the material and returning it to the John Lewis bag. Then he cleaned the palms of his hands on his trousers and lit a fresh cigarette. He was nervous, Stephanie saw. That was why he was taking care of it personally.

She produced a roll of cash from her pocket. 'How much?'

Green looked at the notes greedily and almost gave her a figure, but then reined himself in. 'It's on the house.' Stephanie couldn't believe what she was hearing and it must have showed because he added: 'Use the cash to buy a one-way ticket to New Zealand when you're done. After this, we're through, you and me.'

'With pleasure.'

'And I want your word that you ain't gonna take a pop at West.'

'I didn't think my word was good enough.'

'Stop fucking around, Steph!'

She was almost able to take pleasure from his discomfort. 'Okay. I promise. But when you next see him, you can tell him to stop wasting his time looking for me. I'm going to be out of touch. Permanently.'

'Oh yeah? Gonna do us all a fucking favour and top yourself, are you?'

110

Stephanie shook her head sadly. 'Didn't anybody ever teach you that it isn't grown up to swear?'

Stephanie was in her room at the King's Court Hotel when she saw the news on TV. A journalist had been found dead in his flat in Marylebone. Police described Keith Proctor's injuries as 'appalling' and confirmed rumours that he had been shot several times. They urgently wanted to speak to a young woman who had been seen with the journalist in recent weeks. The physical description of her was unremarkable; white, medium height, medium build, blonde hair, mid-twenties. They also wanted to speak to a man who had been seen leaving Proctor's block of flats several nights before. He was described as short and stocky, of Middle-Eastern extraction, with a beard.

A Middle-Eastern man. Not Bradfield then. The bomber, perhaps? But how could he have known about Proctor? Or was it another man and, if so, who?

All afternoon, Stephanie had considered how to handle this moment. In the end, she opted for the direct approach, simply because she could not think of any clever alternative.

She had found Gallagher & Sons without any difficulty, on the corner of Wilton Road and Longmoore Street. Inside, it was warm. There were small tables on a green carpet, wooden panelling to waist height and then mustard yellow paint to the ceiling. In appearance and position, Cyril Bradfield was just as Proctor had described him to her; he was sitting at the back, a mirror on the wall behind him, directly above his head, he was drinking Guinness. There were three pensioners arguing at a table, none of them listening, all talking. One of them was either half-witted or very drunk. Stephanie couldn't decide which. Having glimpsed Bradfield, she left, confident that he had not noticed her.

His address, further along Longmoore Street, had been

on one of Proctor's priceless disks. She walked past the house, with its grimy façade of blackened brick and rotten window-frames, before turning right into Guildhouse Street, passing the rear of an office block to her left, housing, among others, the Civil Service Appeal Board and the Pensions Ombudsman. She paid attention to the security cameras covering the service area. She completed a circuit and re-entered Guildhouse Street from Warwick Way and then stopped at the junction with Longmoore Street. She kept moving to keep warm and to avoid suspicion, not that there was anybody around.

Forty-five minutes later, Bradfield appeared and the moment arrived.

She felt the weight of the Browning in her pocket. As Bradfield neared his front door, Stephanie emerged from Guildhouse Street. It was dark. Bradfield heard steps and turned his head. *It's just a young woman.* He put his key in the door. As it creaked open, he heard: 'Excuse me.' He turned round. The young woman was standing at the foot of the three steps that rose from the pavement.

'I'm lost. I'm trying to get to Victoria Station.'

'Oh, it's not far from here . . .'

Smiling sweetly, she climbed one step, then two. Her hand emerged from her coat pocket. She waited until he'd seen the gun, which she held close to her body, and then said, 'We're going inside.'

For a moment, Bradfield was too stunned to move at all and Stephanie didn't know what to do. But then he nodded and led the way in. Stephanie kicked the door shut with her heel.

'What do you want?'

They were in a narrow hall lit by a single bulb inside a dusty globe of frosted glass. Cyril Bradfield looked to be in his fifties. He was an inch shorter than Stephanie and shuffled when he moved. His silver hair was wiry and disobedient. Stephanie was drawn to the watery blue eyes beneath the furrowed brow.

'Is it money? I'm afraid I don't have much on me . . .'

He's going to see through me. He's going to realize that I'm a fraud, that I don't have a clue.

The gun felt clumsy in Stephanie's hand, as alien as the controls of a train or a conductor's baton. Bradfield was unfastening the buttons of his overcoat.

'It's not money,' she told him, aware of the tremble in her voice. 'It's work. *Your* work.'

This seemed to unsettle him more than the prospect of being robbed. He squinted at Stephanie and whispered, 'Who are you?'

'I need information about someone you did work for.'

Bradfield winced. 'Confidentiality is crucial in my line of work. I can't talk about those things.'

Stephanie waved the gun just enough to draw his attention to it. 'I think you'll find you can.'

He sighed, his brief flirtation with resistance over. He began to climb the stairs. Stephanie followed. The doors on the first-floor landing were closed. They rose to the attic in darkness until Bradfield found the switch on the wall. The entire space had been converted into a studio. There were two work-benches, a desk and stool in the farthest corner, and three machines that Stephanie couldn't identify. Running the length of one side of the attic there was shelving, containing jars of ink, tins of solvent, paints – some prepared, some not – adhesives, knives, a multitude of different papers, photographic equipment, developing fluid, a vast array of pens, a franking machine, batches of plastic strips and thirty or forty labelled box-files.

'This is my office.'

Absent-mindedly, Stephanie murmured, 'I used to work in an attic, too.'

'Doing what?'

'I'll be the one asking the questions.' She looked for signs of security but saw none. 'You made a document for somebody I'm looking for. A passport, possibly. It might have been Israeli.'

113

'It wouldn't have been the first.'

'The man was referred to you by a third party. He probably came with a minder, maybe two.'

'Who referred him?'

'Ismail Qadiq.'

'Never heard of him.'

'Try again. An Egyptian. An importer of T-shirts, among other things.'

'He might well have referred the man to me but I wouldn't necessarily have met him. I have someone who acts as a go-between for me.'

'Yes. I know. He smokes panatellas.'

Suddenly, Bradfield looked a little shaken. 'Why do you want this man?'

Stephanie ignored the question and remembered another name from Proctor's file. 'There might have been other documents. An Algerian passport, perhaps, and a driving licence in the name of Mustafa Sela.'

Proctor had suspected that Sela might have been the name – or the alias – of the bomber of NE027. Stephanie thought she saw a flicker of recognition. Or a change of some sort.

'How long ago?' Bradfield asked.

'More than six months, less than a year.'

Bradfield walked over to the box-files and selected one. He placed it upon one of the work-benches, opened it and started to go through the hundreds of items within: documents, receipts, photographs, scribbled notes.

Stephanie looked around the attic and said, 'I'm surprised you work at home. I would've thought it might've been safer to keep your studio somewhere else.'

Bradfield shrugged. 'Why bother? If anyone wants to find me – like you, for instance – how hard is it going to be to find my studio? Or if I'm in my studio, how hard is it going to be to discover where I live?'

'That's a very fatalistic attitude.'

'That's the way I choose to live.'

'Is that why you don't seem concerned by the fact that there's an armed intruder in your house?'

His hands paused and he looked up. 'No. That's something different.'

'What?'

Their eyes locked. 'Let me give you a piece of advice,' Bradfield said. 'Don't carry a gun unless you're prepared to use it.'

He dropped his gaze and continued sorting, leaving Stephanie stranded. She felt humiliated. Had it really been so glaringly obvious? She stopped pointing the Browning at Bradfield, letting her arm fall to her side. But she still felt ridiculous holding the gun, so she slipped it back inside her coat pocket.

'Anyway,' Bradfield said, continuing their original conversation, as though the embarrassing exchange had never occurred, 'I'm a poor sleeper. I do a lot of my work in the small hours so it's convenient to work from home.'

Stephanie was still trying to cope with her sense of deflation. 'You knew straight away?'

He nodded. 'On the steps, outside.'

He was still sifting through the remaining contents of the box-file.

She walked over to him. 'Then why are you doing this?'

He shrugged again. 'Because I might be wrong about you. Because you know where I live. Or maybe because most of the people in my line of business are unattractive men, not attractive women.'

Three answers, none of them honest, of that she was sure. He smiled and Stephanie didn't know whether to smile back or shoot him dead; she was, in equal measure, relieved and outraged. She wondered what the real reason was.

Bradfield said, 'I remember that the man involved – the subject – did not recover the documents himself. Someone else did.'

'Who?'

'I don't know. It was the only time I saw him. But I know that they were destined for the man who organized everything. What did you say his name was?'

'Ismail Qadiq.'

'Who knows, maybe he was the one who collected them? It's possible, don't you think?'

Bradfield's fingers stopped and then he plucked a photographic contact sheet from the box-file. He walked over to a light and held it close to the bulb.

'Ah, yes,' he purred. 'Here he is.'

Bradfield emerged from his dark-room, which was little more than a light-sealed cupboard at one end of the attic. He handed the photograph to Stephanie. The head and shoulders shot was in black and white. It showed a man in his late twenties to mid-thirties with smooth, dark skin, black hair cropped short and a full but well-trimmed beard. His hooded eyes stared straight into the camera, straight into Stephanie, straight into the past. She felt a coldness in her chest.

'This is Mustafa Sela?' she whispered, not looking up.

'No. That is the man who pretends to be Mustafa Sela. Who can say what his real name is?'

Now, Stephanie felt inclined to hoist her gaze. Cyril Bradfield was rolling a cigarette for himself. He had thick, gnarled fingers, grooved by years of accumulated cuts and scratches, hardened by solvents and adhesives, made crooked by age. But the dexterity was still in them. He rolled the cigarette in a moment, without ever looking at it, and it was perfect. No creases, no unfortunate tapering.

'And who do *you* think can say?' Stephanie asked him.

He offered her yet another Gallic shrug. 'Your friend Qadiq, maybe?'

'Why?'

'It was a rushed job. Good money but very urgent. Whoever organized it must have known what they were doing.

116

So it seems likely – but no more than likely – that they knew who they were doing it for.'

Stephanie watched Bradfield light the roll-up. Then they were looking at one another and she felt their eyes were engaged in some form of conversation but that her brain was failing in the translation.

'Your memory suddenly seems to be working rather well.'

'Some experiences are more memorable than others.'

'And this was one of them?'

'In its own way, yes.'

'What way, exactly?'

She saw that Bradfield was eager to talk, but that some part of him – fear, perhaps, or some lingering respect for the remains of his confidentiality – was making it difficult for him. But she knew from experience that if she waited long enough, he would unburden himself. They always did. The dithering helped soothe the guilt, making disclosure seem a more honourable choice. Stephanie had always been amazed by what her clients told her. And by the fact that of all the people to tell, she was the one they chose. This was no different.

Eventually, when the silence could no longer be endured, Bradfield said, 'They refused to use my go-between. For me, it's an important form of protection. In fact, it's my only protection, as you've seen for yourself. And generally, I'd say it was a precaution that is mutually beneficial. But they insisted on side-stepping it.'

'Insisted?'

Bradfield nodded. 'In the way that only such people can.'

And the underlying message was clear: *I shall not be unhappy if harm comes to them.*

10

I remember all too *vividly what Cyril Bradfield said to me
last night.* Don't carry a gun unless you're prepared to use
it. *I know that I'm not going to kill Ismail Qadiq but he doesn't
know that. In fact, he thinks he might be about to die. Two
things are helping me to create this illusion. Firstly, there is Qadiq
himself. Unlike Bradfield, he is an aggressive man – a rampant
misogynist, I suspect – and I am finding it easy to dislike him.
Secondly, I have already fired the gun at him. It was an accident.
I was thrusting the Browning at him menacingly and, in an
effort to reinforce my sincerity, I released the safety-catch. The
trigger was much lighter than I had imagined. When the weapon
discharged, I was as shocked as Qadiq. Fortunately, he was too
concerned with the bullet embedding itself in his office wall to
recognize the expression on my face. The truth is, I missed him
by a yard but that margin was still narrow enough to persuade
him that I am a serious threat.*

Qadiq turned round. He was a short man whose girth
strained the beige silk of the shirt beneath his quilted
climber's jacket. He wore tinted glasses with lenses that
magnified his eyes enormously. There was a minuscule
mobile phone clipped to his trouser-belt. He was shaking,
his podgy hands half-raised, as if in surrender. Stephanie
gathered herself quickly, fixing him with as hostile a stare
as she could muster. She hoped he wouldn't see that she,
too, was trembling.

Had anyone outside the warehouse heard the shot?
Would the police be called?

She tried to think of something sinister to say. 'The next
one's going to hurt.'

It had still been dark when she arrived in Whitechapel, an hour earlier. There had only been one other passenger on the Underground for most of her journey; an old man with silver stubble and bags beneath his bloodshot eyes. His head had lolled to one side as he snoozed, whereas she had been uncomfortably alert, the adrenaline making her jittery. Whitechapel had been mostly quiet, a few early traders opening up, a dog investigating rubbish on the pavement, the aroma of Balti cooking on the icy air. Ismail Qadiq's warehouse was in a small side-street. Down one side, there were the blackened backs of small commercial buildings whose façades lined the parallel street. On the other side, there was a row of small ware-houses, each garage door with a large white number painted on it.

Stephanie had found Qadiq's premises and had then looked for a vantage point from which to watch and wait. That was how she came to pass an hour crouched behind a skip full of snapped wood and splintered glass. Her hands froze in minutes, her fingers becoming lifeless around the grip of the gun in her coat pocket. She clenched her teeth to stop them chattering. The buildings on either side of the street only allowed her a small slice of sky to glimpse. She watched the gradual change from sapphire to aqua-marine. It was going to be a brilliant, bitter day.

When Qadiq arrived, she waited until he'd unfastened the padlock and heaved open the garage door. Then she slipped out from behind the skip. Qadiq had pulled the door down again but had left an eighteen-inch gap at the bottom which was quite sufficient for Stephanie. She rolled over the concrete threshold. It was damp and cold inside. There was a baby fork-lift truck by the entrance. She saw unopened crates, recently arrived from Cairo. On the left, there were cardboard boxes filled with T-shirts of all colours. There were others that had had designs or logos printed on them; they were individually wrapped in plas-tic. Stephanie passed half a dozen hanging rails sagging under the weight of leather jackets. Their scent was powerful.

She tailed Qadiq through the gloom until he entered a small office at the rear of the warehouse. That was when she coughed and he spun round, a hand held to his chest.

'Who are you?' he barked at her.

Stephanie hoped coldness would give her authority. She held out the photograph that Bradfield had developed for her the previous night and said, 'Take a look. Where can I find him?'

Qadiq's shock subsided and was replaced by hostility. 'Get out! Leave!'

'Not until you answer the question.'

He glanced at a desk overrun by paperwork. There was a telephone on it. 'I'm going to call the police.'

Stephanie took the gun out of her pocket. 'No you're not.'

His eyes widened behind his magnifying lenses, each pupil a dark golf ball. 'Who are you?'

'Just answer the question and then you can forget I was ever here.'

Beneath the superficial composure, Stephanie was a collection of electrocuted nerves. Qadiq took a peep at the photo and shook his head.

'I've never seen him. Now please go!'

'He came here. You helped him.'

'I told you, I've never seen this man before.'

'He needed forged documents. You organized it.'

Increasingly angry, Qadiq raised his voice. 'I'm an importer of T-shirts!'

'Among other things?'

'I don't know what you are talking about.'

Despite her determination to suppress it, doubt was entering her mind. 'I'm talking about passports. Stolen or fake.'

'Okay, where are they?' Qadiq swept a hand over the warehouse. 'Show me where you think they are.'

Stephanie was stumped. She saw the contempt in his eyes. 'I thought not. So why don't you put your stupid little gun away and leave?'

The look on his face suggested that it was inconceivable that she – a mere woman – could pose a threat to him. For her part, Stephanie found herself flummoxed for the second time in twenty-four hours. She was the one with the gun but Qadiq, like Bradfield before him, was the one in charge.

'Go on! Get out of here!'

That was the moment she released the safety-catch, which was all she had intended by way of menace. Perhaps it was frustration, perhaps it was nerves, but whatever it was, her jittery right forefinger squeezed the trigger.

The accidental shot changed everything. Having convinced himself that he had read the situation correctly, Qadiq was now confused, his fear compromised by lingering disdain. He gawked at the hole in the collection of receipts that were pinned to the wall, while Stephanie looked at the gun with alarm, as though it had mutated into a living creature with a mind of its own. However, by the time Qadiq turned back to face her, she had found a familiar mask; in a moment, she was clinical dispassion.

Qadiq was blinking in disbelief, a reaction inspired by the change in her as much as by the shot itself. Stephanie showed him the photograph again. 'Why don't you take another look? And then tell me where I can find him.'

Qadiq shook his head. 'I don't know.' Stephanie raised the gun again. 'Please,' he wailed, 'I don't know where he is. I was never told.'

'Then give me a name.'

Qadiq paused for a moment before saying, 'I don't know his name.'

That pause betrayed him. They both knew it.

'You're lying to me.'

'No. I swear . . .'

'This one's going to hit you between the legs, Ismail.'

She adjusted her aim and Qadiq gasped. *'Mohammed!'*

'Mohammed?'

He nodded vigorously. 'Yes. That's his name. Mohammed.'

'Well, that narrows it down to a few hundred million, I suppose. Mohammed who?'

She watched Qadiq agonize. Eventually, he whispered, 'Reza Mohammed.'

'Is that his real name or just the name he's using here?'

'I don't know.'

'If you were a cat, you'd be eight lives down. Now, where can I find him?'

'I swear, I don't know that, either.'

According to Proctor's information, Mohammed was a student at Imperial College. 'What's he doing here in London?'

'I don't know.'

'He must have a job of some sort.'

'Probably, yes . . .'

'I'm losing my patience with you, Ismail. What does he do?'

'Please! I was never told such things.'

Stephanie let him stew, wondering whether an uncomfortable silence would loosen his tongue. When it appeared that it wouldn't, she said, 'I'm leaving now but I want you to listen to me first. I'll find Reza Mohammed. You can count on that. But if he gets a sniff of trouble and disappears, I'm going to know where it came from. Then I'm going to come back here and shoot you in both knees. And then I'm going to tell the authorities what you've been doing, so that when they've finally rebuilt your legs and let you out of hospital, they'll throw you in jail for twenty years. Do you understand?'

Qadiq nodded feebly.

Stephanie raised the gun and pointed it at the small spot between his ludicrously magnified eyes. 'I want to hear you say it.'

*   *   *

122

Back at the King's Court Hotel in Bayswater, three telephone calls established two things. Firstly, Reza Mohammed *was* currently a student at Imperial College. Secondly, Mustafa Sela *had* been a student at Imperial College, until eighteen months ago. Stephanie worked it out. That was before Reza Mohammed procured the Mustafa Sela documents from Bradfield. But that didn't necessarily mean that the early Sela and the late Sela were not one and the same man, neither of them Mustafa Sela himself. Perhaps Mohammed had lost the originals, or had them stolen. Or maybe there were two Mustafa Selas, one legitimate, the other an impostor. For that matter, maybe there were more than two. Why not?

On her way from Bayswater to South Kensington, Stephanie tried to withdraw another two hundred pounds on Proctor's Visa card but the ATM denied her and retained the card. She succumbed to a stab of panic but allowed logic to tackle it. It was to be expected. She was fortunate to have collected as much cash as she had.

The buildings of the Imperial College of Science, Technology and Medicine at the University of London are situated between Exhibition Road and Queen's Gate. Stephanie found the administration centre in the Sherfield Building, an unattractive block at the centre of the complex. Mustafa Sela's UCAS course code number – H402 – had been on one of Proctor's disks. Using it, Stephanie was able to obtain a prospectus for the undergraduate course itself: Aeronautical Engineering with a Year in Europe. She also picked up a prospectus for Reza Mohammed's course: a Postgraduate Study in Chemical Engineering and Chemical Technology.

Reza Mohammed appeared at half past three in the afternoon.

He was in a group leaving a lecture, several of whom were of Middle-Eastern or Arabic appearance, but Stephanie picked him out straight away. Compared to his photograph, the hair was a little longer and the beard had been thinned to little more than heavy stubble, but the aquiline nose and the hooded eyes were unmistakable. Although he was in the middle of the group, he was alone. Others chatted in pairs or clusters, but not Mohammed.

At a discreet distance, Stephanie followed him on to Queen's Gate, where he turned left. At the Cromwell Road, he turned right and she guessed he was heading for Gloucester Road Underground station. She closed the gap between them so as not to lose sight of him once they reached the station. As it turned out, he bypassed it, only turning off the Cromwell Road when he reached Knaresborough Place, which leads into Courtfield Gardens. He entered a building on the corner with Barkston Gardens.

Stephanie held back for a minute, before making the first of several passes. From the pavement, stone steps rose beneath a first-floor balcony to an entrance which, through the glass door, looked like some sort of reception area; there was a young man slouched behind a desk, smoking a cigarette. He looked bored. Most of the surrounding buildings were private and residential – once substantial homes converted to flats – or cheap hotels. This one seemed to be neither. Sticking close to the railings, she was able to peer into the basement; two large rooms divided by a corridor. In one room, there was a soft-drinks vending machine, plastic chairs on a linoleum floor, an old TV in the corner. In the other room, she saw a rowing machine, a set of weights on a rubber mat and a stair-climber. On the wall, in the corridor, she noticed there was a pay-phone. It was just inside the fire-exit door, at the foot of the steps which descended from the gate set in the railings at pavement level.

There was no sign on the front entrance, but there was a small side entrance and next to this, on a grubby brass plate she saw: al-Sharif Students Hostel. In the corner of one window, there was a sticker, white on a green background, a crescent and a star.

During the third pass that she made, she saw Reza

Mohammed downstairs, apparently watching TV, his back to the window. There was another young man sitting close to him but they were not speaking.

She dialled Directory Enquiries and got the number of the al-Sharif Students Hostel, which she then called. A male voice answered. She asked for Reza Mohammed and was told to wait for a moment. Another phone began to ring. From the pavement, she watched a young man emerge from the gym into the corridor. He picked up the pay-phone's receiver. She saw and heard him utter a word that she did not understand before she switched off Proctor's mobile.

I am consumed by a rage that cannot be expressed by words. Over the last couple of days, I would have appeared to the casual observer to have been quite calm and composed. Nothing could be further from the truth.

Over the last two years, my life has been conspicuously free of bitterness. I was too stoned, too drunk or too tired to find the energy for anger. I couldn't hate Dean West, or Barry Green, or any of the others who exploited me. I didn't feel rage towards those who bought me by the hour. And I'm not sure that if I'd known then that the cause of the tragedy was terrorism it would have made any difference. My behaviour was determined by me, not by events around me.

But now, things are different. Now, I do feel the fury. And I feel it in a way that suggests it was there all along, locked away in some secret deposit account, earning astronomical interest. I feel angry towards Christopher for cheating death, I feel angry towards the rest of my family for succumbing to it. I feel hatred for West, Green and all the other users. Even Proctor does not escape my wrath: how could he leave me just as I had come to depend on him? And then, of course, there is Reza Mohammed, the man with the bomb. Mostly, however, I am angry with myself. I despise my decline and I am now bitter about everything that has happened to me in the last two years. I am angry about the way I behaved during all the years before that. What makes it worse is knowing that I can't change any of it, that I can only act retrospectively.

So that is what I will do. Tomorrow.

I consider Mustafa Sela's undergraduate course. Aeronautical Engineering with a Year in Europe. Did the knowledge gleaned from Imperial College help blow NE027 out of the sky? Sela would have been in the third year of his four-year course at the time. I look through the prospectus. Areas already covered include topics such as Aircraft Structures, Materials, Mechanics of Flight and Airframe Design. If Sela and Mohammed are one and the same person, which seems quite likely to me, then that course has a particular, personal sting to it. Either way, Reza Mohammed's current course looks potentially alarming: a Postgraduate Study in Chemical Engineering and Chemical Technology. Armed with such knowledge, the nightmares that he can surely transform into reality are too horrifying to consider.

I open a can of Coke and study Reza Mohammed's photograph. I look at him looking at me. Are his parents still alive? Do they know where he is and what he does? Does he have brothers or sisters? Maybe they are like him. Will he be mourned or missed?

As for my own future, I do not care beyond what happens tomorrow. I shall not succumb to alcohol and narcotics again, but my future may be no brighter for that. Then again, I'm used to living in the darkness. The question I am asking myself has nothing to do with what follows tomorrow but is this: when the moment comes and I look into Reza Mohammed's eyes – the eyes of a fellow human being – will I be able to pull the trigger? I have done it accidentally – and missed – but can I do it deliberately and hit? Despite the rage, it runs against every natural instinct within me.

Can I really kill in cold blood?

There had been no sleep during the night. She watched TV instead, hoping it would distract her. It didn't. Nor did the arguing couple in the next room, or the sirens in the distance, or the occasional squeal of car brakes.

Stephanie wanted a cigarette, then a whole packet.

She wanted vodka, then heroin, then anything so long as it stopped her thinking. She wanted to be a child again; safe, at home, in a warm kitchen with her mother moving around her, spinning the protective web of parental love. She wanted Reza Mohammed to disappear. She wanted to go to sleep and never to wake up. She wanted to be someone else, someone who wasn't scared and exhausted.

Dawn brought drizzle to the city. Perfect. She tried breakfast and was sick almost instantly. The day moved like a glacier. She kept expecting the adrenaline to run out and the nervous collapse to begin but it never did. Now, at eight-thirty in the evening, with her body running on empty, and with her thinking as fractured as it was ever likely to be, Stephanie was a wreck.

Reza Mohammed was in full view, a sight that forced her heart into her throat. There were half a dozen students watching the TV. Mohammed sat behind them, his chair turned in the opposite direction. He was talking to an older man, the two of them facing one another, sitting forward, elbows on knees. Mohammed held a paper cup between his hands. Stephanie guessed their voices were lowered; there was a conspiratorial look to their body-language.

In her mind, the plan was thoroughly rehearsed. She would get Reza Mohammed to the pay-phone. Next, she would open the gate in the railing – she had already established that it was not locked – and would then go down the steps and shoot him through the window in the fire-exit door. She had estimated the distance from barrel to bone at less than ten feet. This way, there was a chance of escape. Shooting him through the fire-exit window meant she didn't have to enter the building, which lessened her chances of being caught, or even seen. And since she imagined that gun-shots would cause confusion, she hoped that this and the night would offer her some form of cover as she tried to get away. With five rounds left in the gun, there was no reason for her to fail unless the failure was her own; she was the only weak link in the chain.

It felt as though her entire life had been crystallized, reduced to a single, defining moment. And this was it. All that had gone before had led to it, and all that was to happen after would be as a consequence of it.

She dialled the number and pressed Proctor's mobile phone to her ear. It rang three times before it was answered.

'Good evening.'

It was the voice of the receptionist.

'Could I speak to Reza Mohammed, please?'

'Who is speaking?'

She plucked names from nowhere. 'Mary Stuart. I'm Professor Pearson's secretary at Imperial College.'

A pause. Then: 'Please hold the line.'

She was standing on the pavement by the railings. The gate was fractionally ajar. Her left hand held the phone, her right hand held the gun in her pocket. Icy rain was dripping down the back of her neck. As before, another phone started ringing in her ear, the one she could see through the fire-exit window. A stranger answered and she asked for Reza Mohammed again. She saw the man disappear along the corridor, only to reappear, moments later, in the room next door. She watched the silent movie; Reza Mohammed's head turning, his mouth moving – a quick word to his companion – his body rising from the plastic seat. He wore khaki trousers, old trainers and a navy fleece over a white T-shirt. She imagined the bloodstains to come.

Stephanie nudged the gate open and moved on to the broad, top step. Reza Mohammed arrived at the phone and reached for the dangling receiver. Stephanie withdrew the gun from her pocket.

Don't carry a gun unless you're prepared to use it.

His voice was deep. 'Hello?'

'Is this Reza Mohammed?'

'Yes. Who is this?'

The phone was gone, the gun was gone.

There was a hand over her mouth stifling a word, then a scream. Now there were hands all over her, fingers digging into her flesh through her clothes. She was going backwards, upwards, being dragged, her heels scraping against stone steps. Strong arms bound her. She heard terse exchanges she could not absorb. There was rain in her eyes. And then there wasn't.

Suddenly, she was in a vehicle of some sort – a van, perhaps – being pushed on to an uncovered floor. It was dark inside. She heard: 'Go, go, *go*!'

She managed to twist her face slightly and this allowed her to bite the hand that had covered her mouth. A man let go and cried out in pain. Stephanie struggled as violently as she could and, finding a leg free, lashed out, connecting with something that recoiled and grunted. The vehicle swung round a corner. Everyone shifted.

Someone else muttered, 'For God's sake, get her fixed!'

There was no time to think, less time to act. Stephanie went emotionally blank, not even finding time for fear. She kicked and flailed as wildly as she could, finding unexpected reserves of strength, until a fist the size of a boot crashed into her eye. Twice. Once would have been enough. After the second punch, her power evaporated completely. Rough material was wrapped around her head and shoulders – a coarse blanket or a sack, something damp that reeked like a dustbin – while her body was subdued by invisible arms and legs. Fingers of steel were clawing at the sleeve of her right arm, tearing the material away. Then the arm itself was pinned to the cold metal floor by two powerful hands.

A voice murmured, 'We're ready.'

11

When she opened her eyes the darkness was as absolute
as it had been when they were closed. Stephanie drifted
back towards consciousness slowly. She felt dizzy and the
darkness didn't help, not allowing her a visual anchor. She
had never seen – or rather, not seen – or even imagined
what total absence of light might be like. Her cheap plastic
watch had been removed, so that even the feeble back
light behind the digits was denied to her. This, surely, was
the utter darkness of the dead.

She was lying on a hard surface. A floor, presumably,
but how could she know? Maybe she was on a ledge one
hundred feet from the ground. She ran her palms over the
surface. It was cool and smooth.

She knew she had to discover the dimensions of her
confinement. There had to be limits and definition. Darkness and infinity were too terrifying. Already, she was
aware of her brain sowing seeds of panic in her stomach.
She got to her hands and knees with some difficulty; her
balance was impaired. The darkness was bad enough but
whatever was oozing through the blood in her veins was
making it worse. She retched violently, her spine drawn
out like a stretching dog's.

Apart from her watch, her coat, shoes and belt had also
been removed. Her pockets had been emptied. On her right
arm, the puncture point left by the needle was tender to
the touch. She was cold. She crawled slowly, sliding one
palm forward, then the other, increasingly nervous about
what her fingers might find. With her navigational senses
damaged, she hoped she was moving in one direction.
Otherwise, she could be crawling in circles inside a small

room while believing she was travelling as straight as an arrow through a vast hall.

Her fingers stubbed themselves against something hard. She flinched, retracted her hand and caught her breath. Then she reached forward again. Smooth, hard, cold, vertical. A wall. She pressed both palms to the surface and used it for support as she rose unsteadily to her feet. She chose to go left. A corner followed, then another wall and another corner. The third wall provided the first break: the finest of lines running vertically to the floor and then along it and then up again. An outline, a door. But a door with no handle. She hammered it and called out but her hands told her that no one would hear her. There was no give in the door; it was as solid as the wall in which it was set. It had clearly been built to be airtight, which meant one of two things: either her air was being provided through a vent that was out of her reach – she wondered how high the ceiling was – or there wasn't a vent and her air supply was limited. Stephanie tried to dismiss this idea. The last thing she needed was another reason to panic. But the possibility, once thought, lingered.

She travelled the fourth wall and the length of the first wall again, to complete an entire circuit. She estimated each wall to be roughly twenty-five feet in length. What kind of room was it? A cell? A storage room? And wasn't that exactly what a cell was? A human storage room.

Stephanie retreated to the first corner and sat down in it, hugging her legs close to her body. At least she now had some frame of reference, even if it was invisible; there was no longer any emptiness behind her. Along with the darkness, it was all in front of her.

I urinate in the third corner. I waited as long as I could but I have no idea how long that was. Half an hour? An hour? Several hours? The isolation of darkness is affecting my judgement. With no watch to glance at, no sky to monitor, I am suspended in time.

I make my way back to the first corner, physically relieved, but ashamed. I am being reduced.

Where am I? Who brought me here?

These are the two questions that won't go away. The answer to the first seems obvious. I am nowhere. As for the second question, the possibilities are less clear. I never saw any of my abductors. They grabbed me from behind and dragged me backwards. By the time I had the chance to catch a glimpse of one of them, I was in the gloom of the vehicle, being pinned to the floor. This is not the work of the police, I am sure. But is there another agency involved? Proctor's informant at MI5 – alias Smith – warned of potentially sinister consequences if the authorities ever learned of Proctor's investigation. Is this the work of MI5, or SIS, or of some service of which I have never heard? I find this prospect alarming but I also find it strangely comforting because the alternatives are worse. Suppose my captors are linked to Reza Mohammed, or Ismail Qadiq? My runaway imagination reminds me of the way Keith Proctor looked when I last saw him.

I am truly frightened. All the frosty aggression that kept me focused has gone. Nothing I've experienced in the last two years has felt like this. Even in the worst situations, I always felt that I would have a chance, that there was something I could do to help myself. But not now. I am alone and there is nothing.

Total darkness getting darker, emptiness getting closer. To me, this is what claustrophobia is. It's my first experience of it and it's petrifying. Logic abstains. I can't see anything – I hold my hand close enough to my face to feel my breath on the palm without even a suggestion of an outline for the eye – but I know the walls are closing in on me. The darkness is shrinking. I can feel it. The air is crushing my lungs. I am sweating. My breathing grows yet shallower. Is this anxiety or is this the last of the oxygen running out?

A fear of being trapped, of small spaces. The emptiness and the darkness are simultaneously infinitely vast and terrifyingly close. They are amorphous yet they form a second skin that is choking me. My mind is buckling beneath the pressure. I am disintegrating.

Forget fractured aircraft. This is what explosive decompression feels like.

The light was painful. Stephanie cowered in the corner, shielding herself from the brightness until she could adjust to it. When she finally raised her head, she saw the silhouette of a man standing in the doorway.

He said, 'Follow me.'

She didn't think to ask where she was or where they were going. Anywhere was preferable to the darkness. She rose to her feet and, still blinking, stepped barefoot into a passage with rusting pipes running along the low ceiling. There were lights on the wall, behind protective wire covers.

The man led her to the end of the passage and up a staircase of concrete steps. The walls had been painted grey and green many years before; now, they were peeling. The hard surfaces gave an echo to the tap of his shoes. They passed the ground and first floors. Stephanie looked through filthy stairwell windows and saw nothing familiar, just an industrial estate in the distance and a building site masquerading as a car park. It was nondescript urban. She supposed she was still in London but couldn't be sure. On the second floor, the man pushed through a set of swing doors and led her down a corridor that bisected an abandoned office. He showed her into a room, told her to wait and then locked her in. She tried the handle, just to be sure.

A wooden desk dominated the room. On its top, there was an old Bakelite telephone. She picked up the receiver but the line was dead. There was a Rolodex, which she flicked through. The cards were yellow with age; the London phone numbers were still prefixed by 01. On a side-table, there was an old typewriter, a relic from the pre-electric era. There was no hint of a computer or a fax machine. Stephanie felt as though she was in a social museum: a middle-manager's office from the Fifties. The dust added to the impression. The air was stale.

She rubbed the crook of her arm, then looked down and saw the dark bruise around the needle's puncture point.

By the time she heard the key scraping in the lock, she had grown weary of inspection and was sitting on a swivel chair, her bare feet on the desk.

One man entered the room – not the one who had escorted her into the office – and she saw two more in the corridor. He closed the door. There was a fat file under his arm. Stephanie guessed he was in his fifties, although his hair was almost completely white. He was no taller than she was and had a slim build and fine features; a long, narrow nose, almost Slavic cheekbones and a severe mouth bordered by thin, pale lips. His skin was ruddy, as though wind-blown. But it was his eyes that were most striking; they were pure aquamarine. He wore an old overcoat over a thick, check shirt and a pair of worn corduroy trousers. His tan brogues were scuffed.

He dumped the file on the desk by her feet. The impact blew a cloud of dust into the air.

'Miss Stephanie Patrick. Age? Twenty-two. Profession? Prostitute. Home? Anywhere and nowhere.' He withdrew a pack of Rothmans from his pocket and pointed at the file on the desk. 'Your life is collected in there, Miss Patrick. At least, the life you led before you dropped out of society and slithered beneath it. But what of you now? *Who* are you now? You don't have any bank records, doctor's records or tax records. You have a driving licence, apparently, but the address is out of date. Your passport has expired and has not been renewed. You are not registered to vote, you don't pay Council Tax. You don't have a National Insurance number. Actually, you do, but they don't know if you are dead or alive. And they're not the only ones.'

His accent was Scottish. It wasn't strong but it was unmistakable. The voice itself was, somehow, deeper than suited a man of his physique.

'Where am I?'

'It seems you have always attracted trouble. Expelled from two schools, once for persistent smoking and drinking offences, and once for sexual misconduct. At Durham University, it only took a month before you received a warning –'

'A lecturer made a pass at me.'

'That's not what it says in the file.'

Stephanie removed her feet from the desk. 'Who are you?'

'It says exactly the opposite. And that when he rejected your advances you lied to his wife to punish him.'

'Believe me, my punishments are more imaginative than that.'

He smiled but it was an expression entirely without humour. He withdrew a cigarette from the pack and lit it. 'What it doesn't say in the file is how you came to be in Earls Court with a loaded gun, apparently prepared to fire it into the back of an unarmed man's head. But let me take an extravagantly wild guess. You are the young woman who was recently seen in the company of Keith Proctor, the murdered journalist.'

'And you are?'

'My name is Alexander.'

'Alexander who?'

'*Mister* Alexander.'

'What are you? Police?'

'No.'

Stephanie considered the other options. 'MI5, or something?'

'Something. Something else.'

Something you never knew existed.

Alexander said, 'The file makes interesting reading. Apparently, you are a very intelligent young woman with a particular gift for languages. Frankly, I find that hard to believe. What I find less hard to believe is that you have an extraordinary capacity for self-destruction. Personally, it is of no interest to me that you feel you can kill someone

135

in cold blood. I'm sure you'd be very good at it. You seem to have a genuine taste and talent for those practices that the rest of us take trouble to avoid. All that concerns me is that Reza Mohammed is not harmed.'

Stephanie rediscovered a little of her anger. 'Where's the justice in that?'

'You're prepared to shoot an unarmed man in the back of the head yet think you can lecture me on justice?' Alexander watched her through a veil of blue cigarette smoke. 'Mohammed is more useful alive than justly dead.'

'He'd still be alive if he was doing twenty-five years in a maximum-security prison.'

'Alive but useless. He has to be free and . . . *uninhibited*.'

'Why?'

'That is not your concern.'

'He killed my parents, my sister and a brother, and you're protecting him. How much more of my concern could it possibly be?'

'You have a point, I agree. But that's all you have.'

'That isn't good enough.'

'I'm afraid it's going to have to be.'

'Then tell me why I'm here. Wherever here is.'

'You are here to be assessed. By me.'

'For what?'

'Risk. You have to convince me that you pose no further physical threat to Reza Mohammed and that your silence is assured. I need to feel you can make those promises and keep them.'

'Or what?' she retorted.

Alexander shrugged casually, as if it was of no importance. But Stephanie saw what was in his eyes and, then, what was in her mind: charred aluminium wreckage in the Atlantic, Keith Proctor's shattered knees, Reza Mohammed in a lecture theatre.

'I can't do that.'

Alexander raised an eyebrow. 'You'll find I'm not a humorous man, Miss Patrick. So you can assume I'm not

136

joking.' He looked at his watch. 'I have to go now. Perhaps you'd like some time to think about it, although it seems simple enough to me.'

'You think I'm going to let it go just because you're threatening me?'

'I don't think you appreciate what a serious situation you're in.'

Stephanie tried to forget the claustrophobia. 'Don't you get it? I don't care. Besides, I find myself in a curiously strong bargaining position.'

'You're not in any position to bargain.'

'On the contrary. All the information that Proctor collected is on disk.'

He smiled again, as lifelessly as before. 'Yes. I know. They were recovered with your personal belongings from the King's Court Hotel.'

Stephanie tried to maintain her momentum. 'And have you checked the contents yet? Of course you have. Let me guess. Heart-breaking stories of human interest on two disks. Tragic accounts of how the families and friends of the dead are coping with their grief two years down the line. In fact, nothing remotely threatening to you, whoever you are.'

Alexander smoked in silence. The contents of Proctor's desk-top had also been stored on his set of seven. Stephanie had transferred them on to two new disks. Alexander's expression gave nothing away but Stephanie instinctively knew that she needed more.

'There are seven disks. Or rather, there *were*. In fact, there are now twenty-one, three complete sets. And there are four printed copies, too. I can't pretend that I've been through all the material, or that I even understand most of it. But I've seen enough to know its value. Flight NE027 was brought down by a shaped Semtex charge. The evidence was all over the wreckage and the dead but this has been suppressed. I don't know why. What I do know is that Reza Mohammed – currently a postgraduate student

137

at Imperial College – was the man responsible. The disks prove that he is alive and in London, and that the relevant authorities know this and have sanctioned it. Maybe there *is* a perfectly good reason for this but I just can't believe it's going to look that way when it's splashed across the front page of a newspaper, can you?'

She watched his pupils dilate. 'You don't honestly think a newspaper's going to be allowed to print such ludicrous, unsubstantiated allegations, do you?'

'They are substantiated but I take your point. Which is why I sent most of them abroad. I've got one set of disks with a firm of lawyers; they have their instructions if anything happens to me. The signals have been established. As for the rest? Well, they could be anywhere.'

Alexander's smile was now patronizing. 'Very good.'

'Germany, Argentina, South Africa, Canada – who knows? It could be a large TV network or a small independent publisher. Money doesn't come into this equation. It could just be an individual who likes to float stuff on the Internet.'

'And who would you know in Argentina?' he asked. 'You're lying to me, Miss Patrick.'

'As I understand it, you're offering me the chance to walk away unharmed just as long as I keep my mouth shut. Why would I reject that? It wouldn't make sense. Not unless I had some serious protection.'

Alexander was quiet for almost a minute but it seemed longer. Perhaps he had expected her to say something when the stillness became uncomfortable, but Stephanie was good at icy silences.

Eventually, he checked his watch again and said, 'You've bought yourself some time, that's all.' He took a final drag from his cigarette and then dropped the butt on to the floor, grinding it beneath his heel. 'But not much.'

Two men came for her in the evening. One remained outside, the other entered the room to return her belongings.

Stephanie strapped her watch to her wrist and saw that it was ten to eight.

'How long have I been here?'

'Since yesterday.'

'Where are we going?'

'You'll see.'

It was cold outside. There was a blue Mercedes waiting, its engine idling, its exhaust breathing heavily. Stephanie noticed an estate agent's 'For Sale' placard outside the building. It looked as though it had been there a long time.

One of the men opened the back door and waved her in with his hand. She looked around but there was nowhere to run to. Reluctantly, she obeyed. The man joined her in the back, while his companion rode in the front next to the driver. The doors locked centrally and the car pulled away.

They slid silently through the cones of orange light cast by street lamps, past semi-detached houses set back from the pavement, past small industrial estates, past furniture superstores whose names sparkled against the night in huge letters of bright neon. Stephanie saw a sign for Wembley. It was only a mile away. They were in north London. And as the architecture changed, it became clear they were heading back towards the city centre.

Half an hour later, the Mercedes followed the tight descending curve of Lower Robert Street as it twisted round and then, apparently, through the building above, which was on the corner of Robert Street and Adelphi Terrace. The car did not carry on into Savoy Terrace. Instead, it halted outside a door set in the wall. One of the men opened it by tapping a code into a metal key-pad. Stephanie followed him into the building and found herself in a small reception area; there was an unmanned desk with a monitor on it. Ahead, there was a lift, which her escort summoned. They stepped inside and he pressed 'three'. Stephanie looked at the lights on the panel; they were starting on a level designated 'minus four'.

The doors parted to reveal a carpeted hall with cream wallpaper. On the walls, there were prints of engravings depicting idyllic rural scenes. The man showed her into a room. There was a single bed by one wall, a TV, a desk, two armchairs, a full bookcase and a door leading through to a small bathroom. On the desk, there was a tray with a glass and a plate of sandwiches.

'Get some rest. Someone will come for you in the morning.'

He closed and locked the door.

Stephanie checked the windows. They were sealed. Over the tops of the trees in Victoria Embankment Gardens, she could see the Thames and, on the south bank of the river, the Royal Festival Hall. She left the curtains open.

She took a long, hot shower and then wrapped herself in a thick white towel before sitting on the bed to eat the sandwiches. Ham and cheese. She turned on the TV and flicked through the channels but found herself unable to concentrate. She examined the books in the bookcase; mostly paperback fiction, mostly well thumbed. Neither the room nor its contents said anything to her.

Despite her exhaustion, she could not relax. It was after two when she fell asleep and just before nine when she awoke. She had another shower. Stepping on to the bath mat, she glanced at her reflection in the mirror and ran a hand through her bright blonde hair. Her roots were beginning to show, as dark as her pubic hair. In the early days, before she asserted herself and came to an uneasy understanding with him, Dean West had forced her to shave her pubic hair because it was, he'd told her, better for business. She found the implication behind this explanation disgusting but had been too scared to protest. West had insisted on watching her perform the ritual and this memory always left a knot of nausea in her stomach, which inevitably matured into seething resentment.

She wrapped a towel around her dripping body and returned to the bedroom to find a small, round-shouldered woman carrying a tray towards the table. Coffee, toast, butter, jam. Stephanie's head spun towards the open door. A man with a complexion like uncooked steak was blocking her putative escape. A second, fatter man lurked in the corridor. Stephanie feigned indifference as the woman collected the tray from the previous evening and left. Not a word was spoken.

An hour later, the door opened again. This time, it was Alexander. He was smarter than before, wearing an immaculately tailored double-breasted, navy pin-stripe suit. His shirt was white, his tie was maroon silk, his oval cufflinks were gold. Her own clothes, which were now filthy, lay in a heap on the carpet. She was wearing a white-towelling dressing-gown that she had discovered on the back of the bathroom door. It was for a man; the sleeves concealed her hands.

'Have you slept well?'

'What am I doing here?'

He offered her a Rothmans, which she refused, before lighting one for himself.

'I'm going to ask you one simple question. Will you let Reza Mohammed go?'

Yes. That was the instinctive response. Stephanie hoped it didn't show because she now knew that the matter was no longer one of choice. Somewhere between anger and obligation, the answer was almost as clear as her desire to deny it.

Alexander looked pained by her silence. 'I understand your position entirely. The problem is, you don't understand mine. You *can't*.'

'What is this place?'

'Are you listening to me?'

She disliked the way he now looked. Like an investment banker, or a lawyer. 'So what am I supposed to do? Try to forget about it? Pretend he doesn't exist, that none of this ever happened?'

'The honest answer is, I don't know.'

'The honest answer!' she scoffed. 'The reality is, there's nothing left for me.'

'You're twenty-two. You could have any future you like.'

'My future's history.'

'It doesn't have to be. You can change.'

'Why don't you fucking change?' she snapped.

Whatever Alexander had expected from her, this was not it. 'Is that your answer?' When Stephanie declined to reply, he sighed sadly. 'Then we have a serious problem. Serious for you, that is. Because I can solve my problem, if I have to.'

'Not without public exposure, you can't.'

Alexander shrugged. 'Only if you're telling the truth. Personally, I think you're lying but I don't want to be proved needlessly wrong. On the other hand, if push comes to shove, I'll take my chances. You might want to think about that. You're as expendable as anyone else.'

'As long as that anyone isn't Reza Mohammed. Right?'

Alexander held her gaze. 'You can't save your family, or anyone else who was on that flight. You can't save Keith Proctor, either. But you can save yourself, Miss Patrick. There's still time. But I'm warning you, it's running out.'

Stephanie supposed it was a tactic, to suggest time was expiring and then to keep her waiting. She was confined to her room. Lunch and supper came and went on trays, borne by the same, silent woman. She even avoided eye contact whenever possible. Stephanie was not unnerved by her isolation. She dipped in and out of the paperbacks, surfed the TV channels and slept. Alexander did not return that evening or at any point during the following day. On the third morning, however, he accompanied the breakfast; there were two cups on the tray the woman brought into the room. Once she'd left, Alexander closed the door and poured coffee for both of them.

'You've been here for more than forty-eight hours. It's more than seventy-two since you disappeared.' He checked his watch. 'More than eighty-two, in fact. Can you guess what I'm wondering?'

Stephanie knew precisely but said nothing. Alexander handed her a cup and saucer.

'How long do we have to wait before your insurance kicks in?'

She was sitting cross-legged on the bed. Alexander turned one of the armchairs to face her and then sat down. He took a sip of coffee. 'On the surface of it, it looks as though you and I are locked in stalemate. But there may be a way forward. I've been looking into it, looking into *you*. But I want you to understand that this is my compromise and it's as far as it goes. It's a take-it-or-leave-it offer and it will require you to compromise too.'

Stephanie felt her skin creep. So this was it, the subtext revealed.

'You could come to work for us.'

What work? Stephanie only just resisted the temptation to blurt out the question. Hauling people off the streets, drugging them, imprisoning them. How did one describe such work? What job title might she be given?

'We would train you. Then we would operate you.'

Operate? She was to be a machine again?

'And in return, you would get Reza Mohammed.' Almost as an afterthought, Alexander added: 'But only if you were successful.'

'At what?'

'At whatever we required of you.' When it seemed she might protest, he qualified his answer. 'I can't imagine there is too much that you would consider off-limits. Not after what you've been doing for the last two years. Not after what you were about to do in Earls Court, the other night.'

'That was different. Those were special circumstances.'

'Meaning?'

'Meaning that what I'd be prepared to do would always depend on the circumstances.'

'The circumstances would be – would *always* be – that we ordered it.'

'And that's my compromise, is it?'

Alexander shook his head. 'No. That's just one of the conditions. The compromise is this: you'll have to wait for Mohammed. I don't know how long it would take to train you. I don't even know if it's possible – you might not make the grade. But if you did, and you were successful, thereby rendering Mohammed irrelevant, we would not be talking about a matter of weeks, or even months. We'd be talking about a year, maybe two, maybe more.'

Stephanie felt lead in her chest.

'Can you be that patient?' Alexander wondered. 'Maybe your anger will burn itself out –'

'You'd like to think that, wouldn't you?'

'Personally, I couldn't care less. I only mention it because if you accept my offer, you're in and, once you're in, you can't just walk out.'

'What if I don't make the grade?'

'Then you won't be of any use to us. Which means we'll still need Reza Mohammed.'

'Why?'

'At the moment, you are not entitled to an answer to that, no matter what you might think.'

'But if I do make the grade, then he's mine?'

'If you're successful, yes. You have my word on it.'

Stephanie wondered how good a bond that was. 'And if I don't make the grade, what then?'

The question seemed to catch Alexander by surprise. He had no prepared answer and so thought about it for a while. 'This is what I'll do: if you quit the training course – or you fail it – I'll allow you to walk away in return for a vow of silence. In other words, a deal just like the one I've already offered you. No more, no less, the same rules apply.' He stood up and placed his cup and saucer on

144

the tray. 'We'll speak again this afternoon. Think about it between now and then.'

'How did you find me?'

'Does it matter now?'

'Yes.'

'Easily. That's how we found you.'

Recognizing a dead-end when she saw one, Stephanie let it pass. 'How long would I have to work for you for?'

'For as long as we decide. You will belong to us. That is the price you have to pay for Reza Mohammed.'

How biblical. A life for a life. When I was planning to kill Reza Mohammed, I only saw my life in terms of the hours and minutes leading up to the pulling of the trigger. The future didn't exist. So why should this be different? Five minutes, a year, five years, does justice really have a time limit? Does it exist only in the here and now?

I have no statute of limitations.

For two years, I had no reason to live. I was dying slowly. But Keith Proctor changed that. If I accept Alexander's original offer – his conditional discharge – I know that I will relapse. The dead must be avenged. This, I know, is a thought that would never leave me. It would live inside me, festering, gnawing at my self-respect until, finally, I'd find the pain had become intolerable and I'd surrender to the craving to take something – anything – to make it go away. And that would be it. One moment of weakness and the damage would be done. In no time at all, I'd be Lisa again with no Proctor to save me. That kind of intervention only happens once in your life, if you're lucky.

As for working for Alexander for as long as he decides . . . well, we'll see. I don't belong to anybody and the world is a big place.

The decision isn't hard to make.

'I – that is, we – belong to no organization. We exist in the ether, which is the only safe place to be.'

They were standing on Adelphi Terrace, overlooking the Thames. Alexander had suggested that Stephanie might welcome some fresh air and a chance to stretch her legs. It was a slate-grey afternoon, a stiff wind stirring the river. Behind them, on the corner with Robert Street and dwarfed by the huge Adelphi building to their left, was the building in which Stephanie had spent the previous three nights. It was really an amalgamation of two separate buildings; an old one of black brick and cream columns married to a smaller, squatter one in front.

An age-worn brass plate by the front door announced: L. L. Herring & Sons Ltd, Numismatists, Since 1789. Their office was in the front building, a musty collection of rooms staffed by musty men and women, all comfortably coco-oned in their time-warp. Just inside the front door, there was a board that listed the other companies with offices inside the Siamese buildings: two small investment houses, one English, the other Spanish; three companies registered to Galbraith Shipping (UK), all of which were based in a single, cramped room at the rear of the larger building; Truro Pacific, an Anglo-Australian mining company; a property firm named Porterhouse Services; Adelphi Travel, a travel agency with no obvious customers.

'We used to operate out of a building on the Edgware Road called Magenta House,' Alexander explained. 'It was a terrible place. Post-war rubbish where nothing ever worked. Most of the companies were in tele-sales, flogging advertising space for DIY magazines and the like. Established one week, bust the next. You never knew who was who. That was an advantage. In the end, though, the building had to be demolished. Talk about built-in obsolescence; it lasted less than forty years. That was when we moved down here. I only mention this because sometimes we refer to ourselves as Magenta House; you'll never hear that name from an outsider.'

'You don't have a real name?'

He shook his head. 'Just as we have no employees and

no records. This is not a department of some greater organization. We do not exist. So we are travel agents, mining consultants, landlords, collectors of coins.'

'I don't get it.'

Alexander leaned against the wall, resting his arms on the cold stone, his hands clasped together. He gazed at a flat-bottomed barge struggling against the tide. Screeching seagulls hovered over the rubbish it was transporting.

'We live in an era of increased global terrorism. And of increasingly sophisticated and dangerous terrorism. But we also live in an era of accountability. The end of the Cold War created an illusion of safety. Politicians argued successfully for cuts in expenditure and more openness. Consequently, secret services became more answerable to politicians than they ever had been, just at a time when they needed to be more furtive. I suppose I could say that we are an ironic by-product of this new culture. The era of wholesome accountability and transparency gave birth to us. Every nation needs intelligence services and those services need to be secret, not something for politicians to play with. Much of what we do is distasteful but somebody has to work in the sewers, somebody has to defend the paedophiles in court.'

Alexander turned to look at Stephanie. 'This is not a question of nationhood, of flags and monarchs. It's a question of order, a question of protecting those conditions that allow the majority to live peacefully. It's a numbers game. We know it, our enemies know it. The problem is, how do we confront and defeat these people? What if the solutions aren't politically acceptable?'

'What solutions?'

Alexander considered this for a moment.

'Let me put it this way: you catch the terrorist, you put him on trial, you find him guilty and sentence him to life. Suddenly, he's not only a hero, he's a martyr. His imprisonment inspires the easily misguided into action. His punishment invites reprisals. All of a sudden that initial moment of triumph – the capture and incarceration – is gone, blown away by the bullets and bombs of those who follow.'

Stephanie concluded the argument for Alexander. 'So you kill them, instead?'

He nodded. 'Efficiently and anonymously.' His dispassion was predictable. What other way could there be for a man in such a business? 'Where possible, we try to make it appear accidental. Or, if we can, we lay the blame at someone else's door. Anything to avoid being credited. It may not be morally defensible – not to mention being completely illegal – but it is increasingly the only realistic solution to some terrorist problems.'

'And this is what you people do?'

She knew the answer before she asked the question. In her bones, she had known – or at least suspected – it from the start. She didn't find it shocking, or even particularly surprising. Her opinion of all forms of authority and establishment had always been low.

'Yes.'

'And is it *all* you do?'

'Yes.'

'No wonder you like to keep a low profile.'

Alexander smiled genuinely for the first time. 'A low profile is best for people in low places.'

'And this is what you expect me to do?'

'Not quite. You'll be different. A one-off, something customized, you might say.'

The following morning. A blue Mercedes cruised down the damp Cromwell Road. In the back, Stephanie sat beside Alexander. He was on the phone, she was staring out of the window, through the drizzle, at the billboards, the hotels and the turning for Knaresborough Place. She thought of how she had tailed Mohammed to the al-Sharif Students Hostel from Imperial College.

Alexander finished his call and seemed to read her mind.

'Reza Mohammed placed the device on board flight NE027 but we're still not sure how he did it. What we do know is that it wasn't his idea. He was simply a delivery-boy working for someone else.'

'Why did he do it? I mean, why that flight?'

'We don't know.'

'I don't suppose it makes a difference now,' Stephanie muttered. 'He's still going to be the one that pays.'

'Eventually, yes. But not until you find Khalil.'

'Khalil?'

'The man behind Mohammed. The brains.'

'Khalil who?'

Alexander raised his eyebrows. 'What a question. Throughout the Arab world, it sometimes seems that every other man is a Khalil. What his real name is, God only knows. He's used so many aliases, I wouldn't be surprised if he's forgotten who he is. And if he has, I wouldn't be surprised if that were deliberate. No one knows his true nationality, or what he looks like; there are no verified photographs of him. He's probably in his late thirties, possibly in his early forties. I can tell you that apart from master-minding the destruction of the North Eastern flight, he has been responsible for three bombings in Beirut, the assassination of a French diplomat in Chad, the murder of an Israeli businessman in Antwerp, and the transport of Sarin nerve gas from Japan's Aum Shinri Kyo sect to Kurd separatists in northern Iraq. He organized the kidnap, torture and murder of two Mossad agents in Athens in 1995. He is also suspected of being the force behind a foiled attempt to plant a bomb at the 1994 World Cup Final in Pasadena. Those are just some of the edited highlights.

'As far as we can tell, Khalil is not part of any group, which makes it harder to track him. He forms temporary alliances through intermediaries who, themselves, tend to be temporary. We don't know whether he is ideologically motivated or whether he's in it for the money; there are strong arguments for both. What we do know is that Reza

Mohammed is one of the very few who has direct, lasting links to Khalil, although how well established those links are is a mystery. That's what makes him valuable.'

The A4 became the M4, three lanes of slow-moving traffic shrouded in a spray stained scarlet by brake lights. The driver took the Heathrow spur, the Mercedes ducking into the tunnel beneath the runway.

'Where are we going?' Stephanie asked.

'*We* are not going anywhere. But you are.' Alexander reached inside his jacket pocket and produced an air-ticket. 'You'll be met at the other end.'

'What about my things?'

'I imagine you're referring to the stuff we collected from your hotel.'

'Yes.'

'We've disposed of what there was.'

'What?'

'You're leaving everything behind.' Alexander let the vague statement float for a second before cruelly adding: 'Besides, there didn't appear to be much worth keeping.'

Stephanie checked her anger, determined not to let him have the satisfaction of seeing it. The car pulled up outside Terminal One.

Alexander said, 'This is the last time I'm going to say this: it's not too late to quit.'

Still annoyed, she replied, tartly, 'Don't bother.'

'I know what this is about. It's a question of revenge, pure and simple –'

'You worked that out all by yourself, did you?'

'– but I also know this: when you get your retribution – *if* you get it – there will be no relief and no answers. The pain will still be there. The dead will still be dead. And the search will have taken years off your life. Years you could more profitably spend pursuing a productive and happy future. I am asking you not to make this choice.'

'And I've already told you, it's not a choice.'

'Revenge is empty. It's as hollow as a prostitute's promise.'

Stephanie took the ticket from his hand. 'You don't need to tell me that, Mr Alexander. As a prostitute, I broke more promises than you'll ever keep.'

12

Stephanie stepped into the terminal building at Inverness Airport, glad to be out of the wind that had made the landing so uncomfortable. She scanned unfamiliar faces, hoping that one of them would come forward. None did. Then, from behind her, she heard, 'Miss Patrick?'

Startled, she turned around. He was tall – about six two, she supposed – and she could see that he was thin, despite the bulky fleece that he wore. His coarse, blonde hair was cut short, almost to stubble down the back of his neck. He had a broad, flat-featured face and huge hands with fingers almost as thick as her wrists.

She was momentarily confused. 'You were on the plane?'

He nodded. 'I was at Heathrow, watching you. To make sure you caught the flight and didn't try to vanish into thin air.'

His accent was more pronounced than Alexander's.

'And if I had?'

'Let's just say it's a good thing you didn't. I'm Iain Boyd. The vehicle's outside.'

The vehicle was a thirty-year-old Land-Rover. Stephanie sat in the cab with Boyd who mashed the gears and wrestled with the wheel as they headed north on the A9 over the Moray Firth and across the Black Isle. It took more than an hour and a half to reach Lairg, where Boyd filled the Land-Rover with petrol. He wasn't the talkative type. Stephanie sat on the passenger seat, hugging her legs to her body, watching the landscape grow bleaker and, to her mind, more beautiful. Her parents would have loved it. She wanted a cigarette.

From Lairg, they took the A838, a narrow road with regular passing places, which meandered along the shores of Loch Shin, Loch Merkland and Loch More. The further north they travelled, the steeper the snow-capped hills seemed to be, a collection of jagged slopes and sheer rock faces. The weather was capricious; one moment a sun dazzled, the next, low, swollen clouds rolled through the ravines, smothering the peaks. The wind stirred the water into choppy ripples on one loch while on another, the surface was a perfect, dark mirror. As the brightness and gloom took their turns, so the colours changed. From gold, sapphire, amber and rust, suddenly everything was the colour of bruises and lead. Stephanie watched a patch of sunlight rolling across a hill and a loch, brilliantly illuminating all beneath it, surrounded by an area of light so flat that it reduced three dimensions to two.

At the Laxford Bridge, they turned right on to the road to Durness, a small settlement on the north coast. A few miles after the turning, they left the road, veering right on to a rough track. Twisting and turning through boggy grass, craggy outcrops of rock and pools of icy black water, it took quarter of an hour to reach the last bend, which revealed a small loch. On the far side, a steep slope rose from the water for several hundred yards before rising vertically for three hundred feet. On the near side, there was a cluster of buildings close to the water's edge and, fifty yards further back, a stone house.

Boyd parked the Land-Rover in a large garage next to two vehicles of similar vintage. Attached to one of them was a small trailer carrying an Argo-Cat. At the back of the garage there were a dozen kayaks racked against the wall.

The buildings by the shore were fairly modern; long, single-storey cabins made from wood with roofs of tar-paper or corrugated iron. Boyd led Stephanie into the nearest one. It reeked of damp. Two-thirds of the building was a dormitory, iron-frame beds set against each wall at regular intervals. There were no mattresses. The other third was partitioned and divided into six small, single rooms. Boyd showed her into one of them.

'This is where you sleep.'

The bed was the same as the others she'd seen, except there was a thin, lumpy mattress on top of it and a pillow that was turning brown with age. On the end of the bed were some sheets, a pillowcase that was so worn it was almost see-through and two heavy blankets made from a material that scratched like sandpaper. There was a cupboard, a set of drawers, a tiny circular mirror and a sink. A small window overlooked the loch.

He led her outside again and told her to wait for him by the garage. She watched him stride towards the stone house. Once he was inside it, she peeped through the windows of the other buildings. There was a canteen that was clearly closed, a small block with two baths, four lavatories and a set of showers, a hut containing a diesel generator, a large workshop, and another building that was empty.

Five minutes later, Boyd reappeared, wearing track-suit bottoms, running shoes and a rugby shirt over two T-shirts. He was carrying a bag from which he took two sweatshirts, a pair of track-suit bottoms sawn off at the knee and a pair of walking boots. He tossed them on the ground at Stephanie's feet.

Her fingers were already starting to go numb.

'Put that lot on. Then put the clothes you're wearing in the bag and stick it in the garage.'

She picked up the garments and started to head for the garage.

'Where are you going?'

'To change.'

'You change out here, for Christ's sake!'

It started to rain.

Stephanie slipped and tumbled into a peat hag. The black mud cushioned her fall and doubled the weight of her clothes. It was like quicksand. Boyd looked down on her from the slick grassy ledge above. Despite the cold, Stephanie was on fire. Her lungs felt as though they were bleeding, her cheeks were pink and hot, and across her brow sweat mingled with the rain that slithered into her eyes. She felt humiliated by her lack of fitness and tried to close her mind to what was to come.

Boyd shook his head in disgust. 'What the hell are you doing out here? You should be back in the city. Filing your nails, gossiping with your little friends on your mobile. I'll tell you one thing for nothing: you'll quit. If you get to the end of the week it'll be a bloody miracle. I give you seventy-two hours.'

Stephanie found some air from somewhere. 'I won't quit.'

'Look at you. We've not even been gone half an hour and you're thrashing around in the mud, not a clue what's going on. Right now, you'd be out of your depth in a car park puddle.'

Stephanie clawed at the black banks of the hag, her feet squelching beneath her. She scrambled on to a nearby rock and then hauled herself up to where Boyd was standing. He was not out of breath.

They continued with Boyd trotting behind her, as sure-footed as the deer that lived among the peaks and saddles, while Stephanie lurched from one stumble to the next. Boyd drove her on, muttering obscenities and threats every time she slowed. And when she ceased to care, he nudged her forwards with his hands. She collapsed, threw up, and was hauled to her feet while still retching.

'Fucking drama queen!' Boyd hissed in her ear.

By the time they returned to the loch, Stephanie could barely stand. She had executed most of their descent on all fours, much to Boyd's mounting displeasure.

Now, they were outside the garage. He handed her the plastic bag containing her clothes and pointed at one of the huts. 'There's a shower in there. Get yourself cleaned up and then come up to the house.'

The shower was painfully powerful and hot but Stephanie welcomed that as she staggered beneath the jet. She tripped and fell against the tiles, jarring her shoulder, before sliding to the floor. She made no attempt to stand and, instead, curled herself into a ball, letting the water and steam do their best for her.

The door swung open, crashing against the partition wall, which shuddered. On came the light, a feeble, solitary bulb hanging from the ceiling but the brightness of which was now as penetrating as an anti-aircraft searchlight.

'Get up!'

Boyd's voice was yet another element in her bad dream. *'Now!'*

The bed was moving. Stephanie opened her eyes. Boyd had yanked the bed away from the wall and was now tipping it on to its side. She tumbled to the floor, still swathed in blankets and sheets, still, by any practical definition, asleep.

'Outside and ready to run in two minutes. If you're late, it'll be worse.'

With that, he was gone.

Every muscle hurt. Some seemed to have locked solid and were hard to the touch, there was no flexibility left in them. She thought her joints had become prematurely arthritic overnight. Stephanie had known countless grim mornings but she wasn't sure she had ever felt quite so miserable.

It was freezing in her room so she struggled into her clothes as quickly as her body would allow. Despite being hung to dry, they were still damp from the day before and stank heavily of peat. Outside, it was dark. Frost crackled beneath her feet.

'Jesus!' she exclaimed, clouds of frozen breath erupting from her mouth and nostrils. 'What time is it?'

Evidently, this pleased Boyd. She made a mental note not to do it again.

They ran in the dark, along the rough track that led, eventually, to the main road. To Stephanie, it seemed like a tease. A reminder that this was the way out – that there *was* a way out – and all she had to do was take it.

The run was a revelation. She had never experienced such pain before, not even at the hands of a violent client.

Later, Boyd made breakfast for her in his kitchen at the stone house. This was a sanctuary; it was dry and warm, the heat coming from a coke-fuelled Rayburn. She sat at the wooden table while he moved around her in silence. Prepared previously, the porridge had been left to cook slowly in a warm oven. He placed the bowl in front of her.

'How very Scottish,' she muttered.

Boyd made her sweet tea and replied, 'It's good for you. Eat it.'

'I don't want it.'

'I'm sure you don't. But you're going to need it.'

A routine was quickly established: a wake-up call at an ungodly hour; exercise before breakfast; breakfast at the house; an hour afterwards, more exercise; lunch at the house; an hour being lectured on some element of outdoor survival; more exercise as the brief afternoons faded into night; a shower or bath depending on which Boyd prescribed; supper at the house; more pearls of wisdom dispensed by Boyd, usually in the warmth of the kitchen; finally, bed, at an hour that was absurdly early but which still did not allow her enough time to recuperate before the morning.

I don't have the energy to remove my clothes. It's all I can do to crawl beneath the blankets on my bed rather than collapse on top of them. If I wasn't so exhausted, I know that I'd be terrified. I have made an awful mistake. Alexander was right. So was Boyd. I can't do this. Physically and emotionally, I am shattered. I thought I was immune to pain but Boyd has shown me that I was wrong.

My bones are cracking, my skin is cracking, my brain is cracking.

On the sixth evening, Boyd told her that between Easter and late September, he ran outward-bound courses for pale office workers whose bosses sent them north to get fitter and to bond. Mostly, it was beneficial, Boyd claimed, although there was always a certain percentage for whom the entire exercise was not only an appalling experience but also a negative one. During the long winter, the place was closed, although he continued to live in the stone house that he and his wife had renovated. She had died two years previously from cancer – a fact that might usually have elicited some sympathy from Stephanie. But not at that moment, not when she was in so much pain and he was the cause of it.

He alluded to a military background, told her that during the closed winter months small army units were sent to him for 'discreet' training. There were also certain climbers for whom he was always available, regardless of season. They came to him for tailor-made preparatory regimes.

The short days seemed endless, the nights seemed as brief as a blink. Along with every other muscle in her body, her brain alternated between bouts of extreme discomfort and total numbness. Most of the time, she existed on some form of excruciating auto-pilot, responding mindlessly and mutely to Boyd's barked orders.

On the seventh day, Stephanie got her period. The usual warnings were masked by the pulverizing cramps that ran right through her and by an exhaustion so complete she could easily believe she was already dead.

She found Boyd hauling coke from a storage hut to the kitchen. 'I need tampons.'

He frowned at her. 'What?'

'I need tampons. I've got my period.'

'That's none of my business.'

'It will be when your lovely mattress gets stained.'

158

Boyd scowled at her. 'You bleed on that and I'll make you eat it.'

'What am I supposed to do?'

'What do you think? Sleep on the floor until it's finished.'

He was glaring at her but she was glaring back. 'Fine.'

During a run the following morning, they reached the edge of a small loch. Boyd stopped and began to strip. Stephanie guessed she was hallucinating and supposed it was inevitable. She was so crushed she had no idea why her body was still functioning. No amount of Valium had ever dispersed the contents of her mind quite so successfully.

Boyd turned round, as he dropped his trousers. 'Get your clothes off.'

There was steam rising from his shoulders.

Stephanie shook her head as he stepped out of his shorts and was naked. 'Why?'

'Why? Because I say so, that's why. Now get them off!'

Stephanie stripped clumsily. She was hot, there was perspiration all over her, but as soon as her skin came into contact with the air, she was cold.

They stood naked on the rough grass. There was a strange, glazed expression on Boyd's face. It was one with which she was depressingly familiar. It made her alert. Boyd seemed to be encouraging an awkward silence, perhaps to allow the worst elements of her imagination to get to work. She looked him in the eye and said, 'So, are you going to fuck me or what?'

Boyd bristled at what he perceived to be a challenge. 'You think I wouldn't?'

They stared at each other, each as dead as the other. It wasn't just Stephanie's body that was going numb. 'I've had nastier than you. Uglier, too. It won't be the worst thing you can do to me.'

She looked down and saw the blood on the inside of

159

her thighs and the stains on her clothes. Then she looked up and saw that Boyd had noticed them too. It was impossible not to; the deep crimson – almost purple – against her white skin.

Boyd suddenly dropped to a crouch, stretched out his trousers on the ground and then began to roll his shoes and the rest of his clothes in them. Without making eye contact, he said, 'Put everything into a bundle like this, so you can hold it above your head when you swim.'

Stephanie glanced at the water in the small loch. It looked black. She was glad she was already freezing. She tried to stop herself from wondering about the temperature.

'That's right,' said Boyd, heartened by her silence. 'We're taking a short cut.'

'That's okay,' she replied flatly, hoping to mask her anxiety. 'I could do with a clean.'

Wind buffeted the side of the house. The windows shuddered. It was night. Stephanie sat at the kitchen table and watched Boyd dump the plates into the sink. For all the brutal drill outside his home, he never allowed Stephanie to lift a finger inside it. His aggression stopped at the door. When they were inside, she sat at the table and listened to him while he cooked and served them food, before clearing it away. She wondered if this was how it had been while his wife was alive.

He disappeared for a moment and returned with a wooden board, a wooden box and a thick book. 'Do you play chess?'

'I know *how* to play. The basics . . .'

He set the chequered board on the table between them and opened the box, revealing thirty-two cream and black pieces. Stephanie wondered whether this was the first sign of a thaw in his attitude towards her.

He said, 'The mind is a muscle. Yours has withered. Like every muscle it needs to be exercised to stay healthy. You need to learn how to absorb vast quantities of information at short notice and to retain it. You need to learn how to keep that information flexible, so that you can adapt it to any situation you find yourself in. You need to learn how to think tactically. Chess can help prepare your mind for those techniques.'

Boyd pushed the book towards her. Stephanie picked it up. Modern Chess Openings, more than one thousand five hundred pages of annotated moves in tiny print.

'Looks like a riveting read.'

'You're going to learn the defences I select for you. You'll memorize all the variations I want to a depth of coverage that I specify. And once you've got those nailed, I'll expect you to apply a little mental elasticity to a solid foundation during the middle game.'

'Okay.'

'Okay?' Boyd smiled coldly. 'Every error you make will be punished. So will every lapse in memory. And whatever the punishments are, you can be sure that they'll be unpleasant enough to be worth avoiding.'

Stephanie bit her tongue for a second. Then: 'And when am I supposed to learn all this stuff?'

'At night. You don't need to sleep half the hours I'm allowing you.'

I am awake. I slide out from beneath the blankets and place my feet on the wooden floor. I know the floor is cold although I can no longer feel it through my soles. Instead, what I feel are the blisters and the bruises. The first bleeding blisters have healed, leaving hard scabs in place of skin. The second set are still raw but they too are hardening and mending.

This is what is happening to all of me. Every laceration and every twisted joint serves not to cripple me, but to fortify me. The incident on the shore of the loch has proved pivotal. It took me back to another time; Dean West forcing himself on me with ever-increasing vigour and ever-decreasing success. Each attempted act of brutality backfired, empowering me and

161

unmanning him. Boyd and I are experiencing something similar, although I don't think he realizes it.

I won't ever quit. Not now. I would sooner die.

The cramps are lessening. I am remembering something that Proctor told me. He said stretching was the best exercise one could take. When Boyd and I return from a run and I am banished to the showers, I stretch in secret. It can be agony at the time but the reward is rich; my muscles are starting to stay flexible, to become more flexible.

I pull on my clothes and start to go through a small stretching routine that I have devised for myself. I feel stiff but, as the stretches progress, I am aware of the flow of blood warming me. I become supple. I feel energetic and strong. For this, I thank Proctor, remembering him with fondness each time I perform an exercise of his. And, in turn, each of these exercises acts as a spur, reminding me of why I am here and what I must do.

This is the first morning since I've been here that I've been awake before Boyd's rowdy entrance. It's an important milestone for me. I keep stretching until I hear him outside.

When he throws open my bedroom door, he finds me standing beneath the bulb, fully dressed, ready to run. He makes an attempt to conceal his surprise but it is too late; I have already seen it. Just as I see the anger that follows it. Our eyes lock, a battle of will ensues.

Eventually, he whispers, 'You'll still quit. Believe me.'

And I shrug rather casually and say, 'Whatever . . .'

During the fourth week, there was a blizzard that lasted five days. Driven by a howling wind, the snow blew horizontally through the passes. The days seemed to go straight from dawn to dusk and once the temperature plunged, it failed to make zero for almost a week.

Confined mainly to the lodge and outbuildings, Boyd managed to maintain the routine. On the first day, they ran in circles around the loch, keeping close to the water's edge. By the second morning, the snow was knee-deep and so Boyd led Stephanie to the empty cabin beside the canteen. It was hardly any warmer than outside; there was a thick glaze of ice on all the windows. The cabin itself was a general purpose assembly room. At one end, beneath dust-sheets, there were stacked chairs. The floor was made from varnished wooden boards and it was on these that Stephanie exercised for four days. During the dark afternoons and evenings, they played chess. Boyd continued to win but Stephanie began to make it harder for him, using a selection of the Najdorf variations she had learned, as well as a selection of Sicilian defences that she had memorized without his knowledge.

Towards the end of the fifth week, Boyd told her that a small group of soldiers was arriving for some specialist training and that she was to have no contact with them. That afternoon, when she returned to her cabin from their run, there were mattresses on a dozen of the beds in the dormitory.

They came at night. It was raining hard. Stephanie was listening to the drops hammering the roof when she heard the grumble of engines. Momentarily, fragments of light played across her ceiling. She heard movement and muffled talk in the dormitory for half an hour, then nothing, except the rain.

By the time Boyd came for her in the morning, the men were gone, although she had seen them running around the far side of the loch. As she and Boyd stepped outside, she noticed there were two men working in the canteen. Boyd told her that she would still be eating with him in his house.

Over the next twelve days, Stephanie hardly saw them. It might as well have been just her and Boyd. Occasionally, she heard them leaving in the morning or returning at night, or caught a glimpse of them in the canteen. Sometimes, they left in the truck and returned by foot, sometimes it was the other way round. At one point, they were absent for three days. At least, Stephanie thought they were; it was not possible to be sure.

163

On the thirteenth morning, Stephanie was detailed to run with the soldiers. Boyd had told her the previous evening and had said, 'They were pretty underwhelmed when they learned you'd be joining them.'

When she was introduced to them just after dawn, it appeared the feeling had not run its course. They were a stony dozen. There was nothing faked about the menace they radiated. Stephanie had known plenty of men who thought they were hard, mostly petty criminals who surfed on their inflated reputations. Even the genuinely tough ones would have been no match for any of the twelve in front of her. Only Dean West had the same brutal charisma and that wasn't because he was hard, it was because he was psychopathic.

One of the twelve wasn't running. The other eleven were split into pairs with Stephanie being assigned to the man left over. His shoulders sagged a little at the prospect; the others were visibly relieved. Each pair was handed a different route.

Stephanie ran as normal in lightweight walking boots, thick track-suit bottoms, two loose-fitting T-shirts beneath a heavy sweatshirt and a Gore-Tex vest. The men ran in combat dress with heavy boots and loaded packs on their backs. Stephanie's partner might as well have been naked for all the difference the weight made; he sprinted over the treacherous ground. Stephanie tried her best to keep up and assumed it was military male pride that was driving him on, and that soon enough he would tire and she would catch up. But that never happened.

Instead, she was saved by the weather. The mist came down in a matter of seconds.

They were running along a high ridge between two peaks. There had been clouds in the pass below them but that was not unusual. Although it had been murky since first light, there had been no serious problem with visibility. Then, seemingly from nowhere, the mist descended, as thick as smoke. One moment, the soldier was ahead of her, the next she was alone in a world of grey cotton wool.

Her universe shrank to ten feet by ten.

He called out to her and told her to stand still and then to call out for him. She did and he tracked back to find her. A rough wind was blowing rain with the mist.

The soldier said, 'We'll have to wait until this passes.'

She agreed; Boyd had repeatedly stressed the importance of not moving in the mist. Disorientation was almost instant and automatic for the uninitiated. Even with the aid of a compass for direction, there was no way to judge distance effectively.

The soldier led her off the ridge to escape the worst of the wind. They moved cautiously until they found partial shelter behind a collection of jagged stones at the edge of a peat hag. They crouched low and pressed their backs against the side of the hag, which was wet, but which was a preferable discomfort to the full force of the wind and rain.

'Fancy a tab?' he asked.

She shook her head. He produced a small metal tin and took a cigarette from it. He used a match to light the cigarette. Then he extinguished the match between his thumb and forefinger and put it into a thigh-pocket on his trousers.

'What's your name?' Stephanie asked.

He shook his head. 'No names.'

'Make one up.'

'Geordie.' It fitted his accent.

'I'm from the north, too.'

'Don't sound like it.'

'I've been away.'

'Down with them soft, southern shites, I'll bet.'

'That's right.'

He grinned. 'That's a fucking tragedy, that is.'

He was shorter than she was by a couple of inches, but he was amazingly broad and she was sure it was all muscle. She supposed he wasn't much older than she was but his face was creased by a permanent scowl that remained in place even when he smiled. His soaked buzz-cropped blond hair allowed her a view of his scarred scalp. He kept the glowing tip of his cigarette inside his fist.

'What you doing here?' he asked her.

'I don't know. You?'

'This and that.'

'What part of the army are you?'

He shrugged. 'Who can say?'

'You *are* army, aren't you?'

'Could be.'

The rain was getting fiercer. Icy water was dribbling on to them from the lip of the ledge above. The mist rolled by. The wetness and the cold were starting to work their way into her; Stephanie tried to close her mind to them. She thought about herself on the top step of the al-Sharif Students Hostel, Reza Mohammed on the other side of the glass. Would she – *could* she – have done it?

'Have you ever killed anyone? Not in self-defence.'

Geordie glanced at her suspiciously. 'What you asking that for?'

'Because I'm curious.'

'You canna know what it feels like by being told.'

'I don't want to know what it feels like. I just want to know how you actually make that leap from planning to do it to actually pulling the trigger.'

'I wouldn't know about that, like.'

Geordie smoked and appeared almost content sitting in the dismal weather. When he'd finished the cigarette he extinguished it on the wet sole of his boot and then placed the butt in the same thigh-pocket as the used matchstick.

Neither of them had spoken for a couple of minutes when he said, 'It's a question of self-control. Everything's a question of self-control.'

Stephanie looked at him and he was peering into the mist.

166

'When you're in a tight situation, you canna be panicking. You gotta keep hold of yourself.'

'How do you do that?'

'By looking after your rhythm section.'

'What?'

'When you panic, you gotta get your breathing sorted. Once you do that, you're in control of yourself again. But if you can't, you've had it, you're dead meat on a hook.'

'I don't understand.'

'It's like in music. Drums and bass are the rhythm section, right? Your heart is the drums, your breathing is the bass. You get those two sorted, then *you're* sorted. You can't panic when your breathing's under control and you've got your pulse in check. It's not physically possible. That's what you gotta remember. Keep the rhythm section tight and the rest of the song plays itself.'

When Stephanie got up the next morning, she and Boyd were alone again.

They ran for forty minutes before reaching the face. Stephanie's leg muscles worked in harmony with her ankles, knees and hips, rolling with the ground over which she passed. Her movement was no longer a series of spasmodic lurches; stumbles followed by clumsy over-compensation. Now there was a fluidity which allowed her confidence. She enjoyed the improvement in her own condition as much as the feeling that she was somehow forming a bond with the environment that had been so cruel to her when she first arrived.

Stephanie looked up at the wall of rock. She had wondered whether Boyd would bring her here. They had run past the face before, and above it, having ascended the hill by the gentler slope on the far side. Climbing was a new element in the routine and one that she had taken to instinctively, surprising Boyd and stirring within herself a conflict of emotions. For the first time in her life, she felt

167

a strong spiritual connection to her mother. And as ever, warm feelings confused her.

Monica Patrick – or Monica Schneider, as she had been then – had been one of the most respected young climbers of her generation in Switzerland. Both her parents had been famous climbers and by the time Monica met Andrew Patrick she had been to the top of Everest (at the second attempt), K2, and many of Europe's most famous mountains. Love, however, led to marriage and then family, which brought her serious climbing career to a halt, although she and Stephanie's father had always enjoyed a cliff face, or a sheer slice of rock. Stephanie remembered that her mother had regarded the Eiger as her only true defeat. Twice she had tried to climb it, twice she had failed. And on both occasions, she'd been lucky to walk away with her life.

'I'll go first,' Stephanie said.

Boyd shook his head. 'No. You go second.'

She smiled on the inside as Boyd scrambled up a channel carved by a stream. By taking the lead, he was denying her the opportunity to leave him behind. During the first climb they had made, Boyd had gone second, presumably as back-up, if it were needed. It had quickly become clear that it wasn't. Stephanie seemed to see the fissures and crevices quicker than Boyd. She found she could read a rock face, a route presenting itself to her as surely as if it were painted on to the surface.

The climb ahead was not a matter for ropes and crampons. It was not vertical, although there were several short vertical sections. Generally, it was a combination of rock, of heather ledges, and of occasional, unlikely trees which seemed to sprout out of the steeper, stonier areas. They were ugly and stunted but, given their location, the fact that they existed at all made them impressive.

She looked up and saw the three ledges which she had already identified as natural breaks. Boyd was heading for the first. She followed. There was no proper climbing

168

before the first ledge and she reached it a moment after Boyd had, noting that he seemed slightly shorter of breath than she was. Between the first and second ledges, there was a tricky screen of rock that was only thirty feet in height but which was almost completely smooth. The second ledge was fifty feet to their left.

Boyd said, 'You can go first to the next ledge and I'll take the lead to the last.'

Stephanie saw no direct route and so moved cautiously across the rock face, staying low on it, where there were more holding opportunities. Moving off the ledge left her with a forty-foot drop on to grass-covered stone. Her hands and feet moved quickly and surely, fingers finding cracks to slip into, nodules of rock to clutch. She tested every grip before committing to it. At the far side of the face, there were deeper grooves, providing an uneven ladder to the second ledge, which she reached quickly. She turned round to watch Boyd following her path. It took him longer. He looked less agile. She wondered whether that was really the case or whether it was more a question of confidence.

Boyd didn't pause when he joined her. Or speak. Instead, he immediately embarked upon the next stage, a longer section with two short vertical climbs of thirty to forty feet each, about sixty feet apart. Stephanie looked up. From the third ledge to the top was only twenty feet and it wasn't a climb, just a steep, rocky slope. From afar, she had seen stags and hinds clambering over it, totally sure-footed. When Boyd reached the third ledge, Stephanie started, using the same route. Having completed the first climb, she followed the cut in the face, which dragged her high to the left and through a baby waterfall. The water was icy. She raised her face into the stream and drank, before tackling the second climb that rose to the third ledge.

Now Stephanie knew what it was that had pumped through her mother's veins as an integral part of her blood.

Although Monica Patrick had graduated to the prestige peaks of the world, the elemental thrill was to be found here. What was important was not the height you achieved, or the magnitude of the fall below you, but the way you adhered to and moved over the surfaces. The feeling of supple limbs in motion, of balance and power in partnership, of physical economy. The sense of a challenge accepted and successfully completed.

These were the thoughts running through her mind when the rocks hit her.

Above her, and unseen by her, Boyd had become impatient and had decided to complete the ascent before she joined him on the third ledge. He moved off the flat ground and slipped, dislodging several rocks before scrambling to safety.

The dirt hit her first. She looked up, saw what was following and tried to flatten herself against the rock face. To no avail. The largest stone clipped her right shoulder, wrenching her right hand from the fissure. Her body swayed, her right foot slipped. She tried to scramble for a new hold. A stone glanced off the left side of her face.

And then she was free.

For half a second, she was in the air. Then all four limbs were scrambling for purchase before gravity's acceleration proved terminal. She was lucky. Her right hand fastened on to a tiny, jagged outcrop. It wasn't enough to stop the fall, but it slowed her and she jammed her left hand into a V-shaped crack before the right hand was torn free, leaving the skin of her palm on the stone. The rest of her body swung like a pendulum. She felt popping in her fingers.

Her right boot found a small inlet and stopped the swing, allowing her to take some of the weight off her arm. There was blood seeping into her left eye, blurring her vision. She ran the fingers of her right hand over as much rock as she could, until she found a stony peg to cling to. Then she located a ridge for her left boot.

She was temporarily secure.

'Stephanie?'

She closed her eyes and pressed her cheek to the cold, hard rock. The adrenaline was pumping furiously, making her shake.

'Stephanie?'

She couldn't recall Boyd using her first name before.

He was lying on his belly on the ledge, leaning over the lip, looking down at her.

'Are you hurt?'

Her eyes opened. Out of the right, she saw what was below her. Rock, trees, more rock. And a gap of two hundred feet.

'You've got to get back down to the second ledge.'

He was right. Despite her damaged left hand, retreat was possible. Even the smooth sheet of rock between the first and second ledges was bridgeable. She tried to release her left hand but it was stuck. She needed to be higher to pull it out. There were pins-and-needles spreading through the fingers.

Slowly, Stephanie found new footholds for herself and nudged her body upwards.

'What are you doing?' Boyd shouted at her. 'You've got to go down. *Down!*'

She yanked her left hand free of the V-shaped crack and the pain made her cry out. She saw that the forefinger and the middle finger were broken.

'For God's sake, go back to the second ledge!'

Her left shoulder was sore but didn't appear to have lost any mobility.

Inch by inch and hour by hour – for that is how it seemed to her – she continued to climb upwards, closer to Boyd, who continued to scream retreat at her. After ten excruciating minutes, she found herself within six feet of the ledge.

Boyd's expression revealed a truth; he was astounded she hadn't fallen.

He was reaching down to her, saying, 'Not far now. Reach up. Take my hand.'

Between staccato breaths, Stephanie muttered, 'I don't need your hand.'

'For Christ's sake, don't be an idiot. Give me your hand!'

'I made it this far without you. I'll make it the rest of the way, too.'

Boyd's temper had been under strain, pressured by the twin forces of shock and guilt. Now, it snapped. 'Believe me, sweetie, you'll get plenty of opportunities to get yourself killed, so at least have the good grace to make it count. Not like falling off a rock in the middle of nowhere when it doesn't mean a fucking thing!'

Stephanie ignored his hand, which was now just four feet from her. 'I'm not quitting.'

'Fine. Now give me your hand.'

'I said I'm not quitting.'

'I heard you the first time.'

She turned her face upwards, so that he could see the cut above her left eye and the blood that was flowing from it. And so that he could feel what was burning behind both eyes. 'Ever.'

It took a moment. Then Boyd averted his gaze and replied, quietly, 'I know.' Stephanie recognized an act of submission when she saw it. He said, 'Now please give me your hand.'

13

The clouds parted, revealing rough fields over hilly land, a few woods, occasional farm buildings and a web of small winding roads. Gusts of wind rocked the helicopter as it made an almost vertical descent towards a field of coarse grass with a dilapidated barn in one corner. By the barn, on the narrow track that bordered one side of the field, there was a parked car.

The day had started routinely with a short run before breakfast. Afterwards, Boyd had driven Stephanie to Durness, where they had run along the beach and through the dunes. It had been a beautiful morning, cold and bright, a sparkling sun turning the Atlantic into liquid jewels. Stephanie had enjoyed the cold sand between her toes and the salt on her lips. She had enjoyed the young Golden Retriever that had run wildly at her side for half the length of the beach. She had enjoyed seeing Boyd struggle to keep up with her.

When they returned to the loch, there was a helicopter on the grass by the water's edge. Boyd did not seem surprised to see it. He left Stephanie in the Land-Rover and went across to talk to the pilot. When he returned, he said, 'You've got ten minutes to have a shower and get dressed.'

Stephanie had never been in a helicopter before. As the machine soared into the sky and wheeled away to the south, she found the climb exhilarating. She kept her face pressed to the window, absorbing all that passed below until they ran into thick cloud over the Grampian mountains. They rose to a higher altitude to clear the worst of the weather and only encountered it again during their descent. When Stephanie asked where they were going, the pilot said he'd been instructed not to tell her.

Now, the helicopter was on the ground. The pilot turned round and waved Stephanie out. She was immediately assaulted by the power of air beating down on her. The downforce had flattened the grass beneath her feet. She slammed the door shut and scuttled forward, half-crouched. The whine intensified and, before she had cleared the blade circumference, the helicopter was air-borne again. She watched it surge up towards the clouds.

When she turned round, she saw Alexander standing by the gate next to the barn, patting his white hair back into place. He was wearing grey flannel trousers, a navy cashmere polo-neck and a charcoal overcoat. There was no verbal greeting. Instead, Stephanie followed him out of the field and into the black Rover that was waiting for them. They both sat in the back.

Alexander said to the driver, 'Are we going to make it?'

'Should do. We're a bit behind schedule. But not too much.'

It only took Stephanie two minutes to realize where she was. That was when they turned on to the A6088, south of Hawick. She caught Alexander looking at her black eye and then at her hair. More than ten weeks of dark roots beneath the bleached blonde had made it look particularly striking. She wore it drawn back into a pony-tail.

'How are your fingers?' he asked.

They were still bound together, having been re-set in Lairg. The doctor had also stitched the cut above her left eyebrow and had disinfected and dressed her skinned right palm.

'I won't be doing any tapestry for a while, but apart from that, they're fine.'

'Iain says you're making satisfactory progress.'

She allowed herself a small mocking smile. 'He says that, does he?'

'He says your fitness levels have come on well.'

'I can imagine. He certainly tried his best to break me. On your instruction, I have no doubt. I still can't decide whether he underestimated me or overestimated himself.'

'You've genuinely surprised him.'

'And genuinely disappointed you?'

For a moment, it looked as though Alexander might deny it. But then his expression changed from insincere protest to resignation. 'It's not the first time and I'm sure it won't be the last.'

They took the turning to Saughtree, passing through Deadwater and Kielder before driving down the west bank of Kielder Water. The closer they got and the more familiar the surroundings became, the more uneasy Stephanie felt.

They came round a bend and the driver braked. Ahead, there was another car – a mud-splattered Cherokee Jeep – parked on the left-hand side of the road. The Rover pulled in behind it, close to a sign informing them that Jedburgh was thirty-three miles to the north.

To the left, rough grass fell away from the road. There were horses grazing on it. On the right, the land rose sharply. There were sheep to the edge of the softwood plantation. Half a mile ahead, there was a turning to the left which went past Falstone Cemetery and led into Falstone itself, the village where Stephanie had been born and raised. All of this was visible from the vantage point by the road.

There were three men in the Jeep, one of whom got out as Alexander and Stephanie approached. Alexander said, 'Are we too late?'

'No, sir. You're bang on time.'

Spits of rain fell as tiny darts. Above, every shade of grey was reflected by the clouds that rumbled eastwards. The wind made Stephanie's eyes water but through her streaky vision she noticed, for the first time, black cars parked along the wall of the cemetery. One or two people were emerging, shuffling through the gates into the small patch of gravel that passed for a car park. From this distance, and in this light, the figures, being predominantly dressed in black, were mostly lost against the dark background.

Alexander peered through a pair of binoculars that the driver of the Cherokee had handed him. He passed them to Stephanie who raised them to her eyes with a sense of dread. Pale faces, hair tousled by wind, dark clothing. More people were leaving the cemetery, but none that Stephanie recognized. Until she saw Jane, her sister-in-law, who was only three years older than she was. On her hip, she was carrying James, Stephanie's nephew, while guiding Polly, Stephanie's niece, towards one of the black cars. Her hand was on the girl's shoulder. Stephanie saw a flash of white handkerchief dabbing an eye.

She searched the mourners for her brother but could not find him.

'Oh God, no . . . *Christopher!*'

As she scanned the gathering, other faces began to stand out. Karl and Claudia Schneider, her mother's parents. Karl's white hair was brilliant against his Alpine tan, knocking twenty years off his eighty. Stephanie remembered the hot chocolate Karl made for her when, as a young child, she had stayed with them in Switzerland. They drank it at breakfast out of bright blue glazed clay bowls. Karl always added cinnamon to it. Stephanie could smell the aroma across fifteen years. Claudia, who was now seventy-five, was hiding behind a pair of dark glasses and a black scarf. Isabelle Fouchard, Stephanie's aunt, had made the journey from Paris. Her copper hair shone against the drabness. Stephanie's father's parents were there too; at seventy-seven, Richard Patrick was still standing ram rod straight at six foot six, with Angela beside him, now walking with the aid of a stick.

Stephanie lowered the binoculars and turned to Alexander. 'What happened to him?'

'Who?'

'My brother. Christopher.'

'Nothing. He's there somewhere.' Alexander was trying

to light a Rothmans in the wind, both hands cupped around the tip as he fired his lighter repeatedly. Out of the corner of his mouth, he said, 'This isn't his funeral. It's yours.'

She felt sick.

'What?'

Finally successful, Alexander puffed on his cigarette and nodded. 'It had to be done.'

'Why?'

'You know why.'

She raised the binoculars to her eyes again and eventually caught sight of Christopher. She kept her sense of relief private.

'How did you do it?'

'A car crash. A *nasty* car crash. Head-on. One of the cars – a stolen car, as it happens – caught fire. The driver and the passenger were burned beyond recognition.'

'Who were they?'

'Does it matter?'

'To someone.'

Alexander seemed disappointed. 'The stolen car was being driven by a fifteen-year-old joy-rider. There was no one else with him. You were added later, as it were.'

'Do my family know?'

'The circumstances? That you were with a fifteen-year-old car thief who was drunk when he veered across the road into an oncoming vehicle? Yes, they know.'

'*Why?*'

'To be consistent. It was considered better to have you die as you'd been living. Identification was made through your dental records. The funeral took place earlier, at St Peter's, your local parish church over there in Falstone. And the cemetery's where you're now buried.'

Stephanie was momentarily speechless.

Alexander said, 'This is what you chose. Remember?'

'I never chose this for Christopher.'

'Indirectly, you did.'

'And is this what you brought me here for? To show me this?'

'No. You're here for something else. But I thought you might want a last chance to see your family. Even if it's only from afar.' Stephanie could not tell whether Alexander was being genuine or merely cruel. He looked sincere enough. Then he rubbed salt into her wounds, as casually as he could, when he said, 'By the way, your sister-in-law is pregnant again.'

Her reply was pure reflex. 'How do you know?'

It was a question that Alexander was not going to answer and, on reflection, one that Stephanie didn't want answered. She peered through the binoculars again.

'When's it due?'

'In six months.'

Christopher was crying. Stephanie could see him wiping his eyes. Jane was looking after the bewildered children. It broke Stephanie's heart.

It was too painful to see his tears and to recall how terribly they had fought, how impossible it had been for the two of them to find comfort in each other after the others had died. This was a moment where she might have cried, but Alexander's presence guaranteed her stoicism. Looking at Christopher, she tried to persuade herself that she was following this path for both of them but she knew that was a lie. Whatever the differences between them, she saw now that her presence in the world had, after all, mattered dreadfully to him. To see his grief – to be the cause of it – was too painful to witness. Had he not suffered enough without this?

Momentarily, she thought she could repair the damage, that she could run down the hill and tell them all that she was alive and that everything was all right. Then reality infected the illusion and she realized that she could not. Not today, not ever. To do that would be to place them all at risk. Alexander didn't even need to say it.

She turned away and handed the binoculars back to the

Cherokee driver as four large files were transferred from the back of the Jeep to the Rover. Alexander and Stephanie got back inside the car. The driver pulled off the windswept verge and executed a U-turn.

For a while, they drove in silence. Then Alexander patted the four bulging files between them and said, 'This is all for you.'

'What is it?'

'Information. Every detail must be memorized. Absorbed.'

'What kind of information?'

'It concerns a German terrorist, who started out as an anarchist but who has renounced her ideals in favour of commercial considerations. She is, you could say, a *professional* terrorist. Her name is Reuter. Petra Reuter.'

Stephanie picked up the file nearest her and began to flick through it, scanning fragments of information. Petra Reuter was born in Hamburg in 1968. During the Second World War, her father, Karl Reuter, had been a teenager in the 371st Infantry Division under Lieutenant-General Stempel at Stalingrad, part of Paulus' doomed Sixth Army. After the war, he'd become a policeman, moving to Stuttgart in 1959. In 1965, at the age of forty-two, he'd married Rosa Holl, twenty years his junior. Petra was their only child. Rosa had died in a car crash in 1985. At the time, she'd been an archivist at the *Bibliothek für Zeitgeschichte* in Stuttgart. A life-long smoker, Karl Reuter had succumbed to lung cancer in 1987.

Stephanie skipped the bulk of the file and flicked through a section near the back, which contained education details, a photo-copied set of fingerprints, details of Reuter's sexual history, photographs of a dark-haired woman whose features were blurred to the point of anonymity. With each photograph there was a tag containing a date and a place.

'I've never heard of her,' Stephanie said, setting the file back on the seat between them.

'You wouldn't have. But over the past two years and, in particular, over the last year there are plenty of people who have.'

'Does she have links with Khalil? Or Reza Mohammed?'

'No.'

'Then what's she got to do with me?'

'Everything. Stephanie Patrick is dead. You are Petra Reuter.'

3

PETRA'S
WORLD

14

The air-conditioning unit was broken so it was baking inside the hotel room on the fifth floor. The window was wide open but it made no difference. It was another sweltering, airless day. At the centre of the floor, a naked woman was stretching, her skin slick with sweat, her mind focused on her breathing. By a glass of water on the bedside table, there was a watch. She glanced at it.

She completed the routine and closed her eyes for a minute, more aware of the heat within her than of that which surrounded her. Her short, thick hair, which was so dark it was almost black, was soaked with perspiration. Through the open window, she heard the ceaseless riot of the traffic – sirens, engines and horns in competition – and could smell the choking exhaust fumes that contributed to the permanent mustard haze that hung over the city. She rose from the floor and caught her reflection in the mirror. She saw her muscles and sinews – the human cables – moving beneath the skin, she saw her lack of body-fat. She saw her animal power.

At nine-thirty in the morning the temperature passed 35°C, on its way towards the previous day's high of 40°C, the humidity as close to one hundred percent as made any difference. In Brazil – in Rio de Janeiro – winter had arrived as a heat-wave.

The blue-and-yellow taxi was weaving across the road, cutting in and out of all the other cars; it seemed every male driver fancied himself as Ayrton Senna while driving like a drunk. Sitting on the slashed back seat, Petra Reuter stared out of the window at Guanabara Bay and tried to ignore the motorized mayhem around her. They passed Santos Dumont, the city's mid-town airport. Yesterday, when she had been on top of the Sugar Loaf, she had watched the planes taking off from the airport. She had watched the sun set behind the mountains, seen the beach lights flicker to life in the dusk, seen Christ silhouetted against a sky of blood on top of the Corcovado. Yesterday, she had been an American tourist.

At the end of Flamengo Beach, the taxi headed for Centro, Rio's financial and commercial district. She got the driver to stop on Avenida Presidente Antonio Carlos. From there, it was only a short walk to Rua Araujo de Porto Alegre. The pavements were as congested as the roads: sweating businessmen in lightweight suits; food-vendors working at stands on street corners; shoe-shine boys touting for business; perspiring policemen with guts over their belts and guns on their hips; young girls selling individual cigarettes or sticks of chewing gum. The roasting air smelt of diesel.

The office block was home to fifteen different companies. Petra took a slow lift to the sixth floor. The reception area for the suite of offices belonging to Boa Vista Internacional was freezing; machismo in machines – only in Brazil, perhaps, could an air-conditioning system feel the need to prove its virility. Petra asked for Eduardo Monteiro and was shown into a large office with tinted glass forming the rear wall. She could see into the ageing office blocks on the other side of the street. The man who entered the room a minute later was small and desiccated; his skin looked like brown wrapping paper. His nose was hooked like an eagle's beak, the bridge forming a perfect perch for small, wire-framed glasses. His beige suit was as creased as his forehead. Petra asked if he was Senhor Monteiro.

He smiled and shook his head. 'No. Senhor Monteiro is not available. He asked me to speak to you on his behalf.'

'What about Marin?'

'He's not in the city. He's at his house in Búzios with his family and friends.'

'I came here on the understanding we would meet.'

'If everything is satisfactory, you will. He has a helicopter that can bring him into the city. But only if it is necessary. That is why he and Senhor Monteiro want me to speak to you.'

'And who are you?'

'My name is Ferreira.' He sat behind the desk and in front of the window. 'Would you like a *cafézinho*?' Petra shook her head. 'Coke? Mineral water?'

'Nothing.'

She sat down opposite Ferreira, who said, 'I'm sure you appreciate Senhor Marin's caution. He was unaware that he was in business with you. And he has no desire to end up like Lehmans.'

'Lionel Lehmans died from a cardiac arrest.'

'We heard that, too. But in this world, you can never be sure.'

'You should check with his doctor. For a man with a weak heart, he took very poor care of himself. Too much rich food, too many young boys – sooner or later, one or the other was bound to get him. In the end, it was a fifteen-year-old Greek – and not the *foie gras* – that killed him.'

Ferreira shrugged. 'Why have you insisted on coming here? You could have waited until Senhor Marin returned to Europe.'

'I'm on a schedule. I thought Lehmans explained this to you.'

'No. It was never mentioned.'

Petra knew that was a lie. 'So I'm mentioning it now.'

'He talked about delivery in two to three months. That's not a rush job. Not for us.'

'But I need guarantees. And I need them now. So that if there's a problem I still have time to look elsewhere.'

'And for this, you come out into the light?'

185

Petra's expression darkened. 'It would be better for you if you didn't try to second-guess me.'

Ferreira smiled feebly. 'Of course.'

'I understood that I would be able to inspect everything in the order. Just as Lehmans would have, if he'd been here.'

'That is true.'

'Good. So let's do it.'

'Today?'

'Now.'

'Right now?'

The unique opportunity that Alexander could not overlook was created by two separate occurrences, one deliberately planned, the other a stroke of luck. What actually produced the chance was timing; the second incident took place within sixty hours of the first.

In 1967, at the age of just twenty-one, Lionel Lehmans deserted the Belgian army and became a mercenary, seeking the Siamese twins of money and conflict in Zaire, Angola, Ethiopia, Somalia and Chad. By 1987, however, he'd grown weary of spilling blood and of having his own blood spilled. His list of injuries was lengthening, his stamina was waning and his appetite for warfare was rapidly being usurped by an appetite for indulgence. No longer content to limit himself to the whores and bars of the lost communities of Africa, Lehmans decided to relinquish the sharp end of the business for the softer, financial end. Trading on the surviving contacts made over two decades, he went into the arms business. Unlike Gustavo Marin, the Brazilian whom he met in 1994, Lehmans had no direct contact with manufacturers. His sources were all buyers. Marin, on the other hand, knew everybody and, for the right price, would play any role; supplier, recipient for and deliverer to the end-user, middle-man, guarantor. Even manufacturer, it was rumoured.

Lehmans returned to Brussels, his home town, and

began to engineer deals, casting himself as a middle-man and taking a cut of everything that passed through his hands. As his reputation spread, his work took him further afield but it was in Brussels that he first encountered Grigory Ismailov. Ismailov was a Georgian who had served in the Red Army for the duration of the doomed Afghanistan campaign. After the retreat from Kabul, Ismailov was discharged from the army and took to crime, killing being the only profession for which his Afghan experience had fully trained him. He worked for criminal organizations in Sverdlovsk and Perm, in the Urals, before moving back to his native Georgia in 1994. In Tbilisi, he made a name for himself as a man for whom no job was too distasteful providing the pay was right. In 1996, he began sporadic work for Chechen gangs operating in Moscow who wished to take anonymous retribution for Russian atrocities inflicted upon Grozny. With no family to bind him, with no conscience to undermine him, Ismailov was the perfect choice. Most of these jobs simply involved killing – policemen, politicians, journalists, the usual targets – but somewhere along the line, Ismailov was entrusted with a greater programme of terror. That was what brought him to Brussels and, ultimately, to the attention of Alexander in London.

Lehmans was under Magenta House observation on account of his business links with Gustavo Marin. Marin was under observation because he was known to have links with Marc Serra, a Frenchman suspected of conducting business on behalf of Khalil. When Grigory Ismailov came to Lionel Lehmans with a list of 'special requests', Lehmans approached Marin because he was known to cater for customized weaponry. The line of communication thus established, Alexander had the order traced back to its source. At that time, Ismailov was planning a domestic – 'domestic' meaning purely Russian – bombing campaign against Aeroflot offices. Besides, as the local joke ran, with a safety record as poor as theirs, what would be the point of bombing their aircraft?

What concerned Alexander was not the proposed assault on Aeroflot but the new assassination programme that Ismailov was also planning. Three of the names on the hit-list drawn up by the Chechens were based in London, including the Russian ambassador himself. It was this consideration which prompted Alexander to sanction Ismailov's execution, which was carried out by a Magenta House operative who travelled to Grozny, coinciding with a visit by Ismailov to the Chechen capital for a meeting with his employers. The operative used a car-bomb activated by a mercury tilt-switch. The device killed Ismailov and his Chechen driver instantly. As anticipated and desired, the blame for the killings was placed upon a rival Chechen gang and bloody retribution followed almost instantly, the resulting confusion covering any lingering trace of the real perpetrator.

This was the first occurrence. The second was the heart-attack that killed Lionel Lehmans.

Lehmans learned of Ismailov's death within six hours of it occurring. Keen to stop the deal that Ismailov had initiated, Lehmans tried to reach Marin but failed because the Brazilian was on his yacht and had deliberately severed all communication with the outside world. Unfailingly sentimental when it came to family matters, Marin would tolerate no interference when he was with them. Frustrated, Lehmans consoled himself with the fact that the deal could still be halted and that the weekend would not be without its Greek pleasures. On Sunday evening, however, Lehmans was dead on his bedroom floor, his heart's failure being the only true indication that he had ever had one.

Suddenly, Alexander saw a remarkable opportunity. He knew that as far as Marin was concerned, the transaction was between him and Lehmans; where the order ended up was a matter for the Belgian, along with the size of his commission. Alexander also knew that Lehmans operated alone; the chance of anyone else knowing about his deal with Ismailov was negligible. When Marin learned of Lehmans' death, he was going to be looking for someone to inherit the deal. Either that, or he was going to abandon it and take the loss.

By instinct, Alexander was a cautious man. The operation he ran was small and he had never harboured desires to expand it. He pressed his operatives into action as a last resort and disliked having to do so. As for Petra, she had been a matter of permanent reluctance for him. He had not wanted her in the first place. Having been forced to accept her, he had been unwilling to train her as an assassin and so had been compelled to treat her as a one-off, choosing to have her trained as an undercover operative instead. This fell outside the organization's mandate which was another source of pain for him. Now, however, he was faced with his greatest dilemma yet. With the deaths of Ismailov and Lehmans, a space had been created that could be filled by Petra but the window of opportunity was bound to be limited. Marin would not wait long. If he could not find someone to carry the deal forward, he would walk away from it. On the other hand, Petra was not yet fully trained.

Under any normal set of circumstances, Alexander would have let the moment pass. Had he had his way, Petra would have spent another year – perhaps longer – moving from city to city, following the routines he devised, offering stage-managed glimpses of herself for hand-picked viewers. But here was a chance to penetrate Gustavo Marin's inner circle and, potentially, to forge a direct line to Marc Serra. The two men trusted one another, just as Marin had trusted Lehmans. This was an opportunity to buy into that by proxy, something that could not be achieved from the outside. And it was this consideration, in the end, that outweighed the serious concerns over Petra's readiness.

From London, via Brussels, Alexander orchestrated contact with Marin, masquerading as Petra, allowing her identity to be revealed – something that was guaranteed to grab the Brazilian's attention – and informing him that she was on the other end of his deal with Lehmans. Petra, Marin would discover, was keen to finalize their business quickly and, on account of her own circumstances, would be prepared to meet him face to face in Brazil. Alexander reckoned this would be enough of an incentive – the name of Petra Reuter was known, the face was not – and was proved right. Marin agreed to see her and to conclude the half-negotiated deal in Rio de Janeiro.

Petra's function was clear: fly to Brazil and negotiate a price with Marin. Then fly home and let Alexander take care of the rest. The important thing was to strike up a relationship with the Brazilian. From that, a creditable approach to Marc Serra could be engineered.

Physically, she was in superb condition, her strength and fitness complemented by a range of self-defence techniques taught to her by Iain Boyd. Mentally, she seemed tougher than ever – certainly Alexander had seen no sign of weakness in her. But what was lacking was background; the legend she had assumed was still thin, her knowledge was still patchy. And what of her real nerve, the kind of nerve that was only tested in extremity? These were the things that had preoccupied Alexander as he'd prepared to allow the paper terrorist to become real.

They parked on the pier and stepped into a crucifying sun that was now directly overhead, apparently hot enough to burn their shadows from the ground. Petra peered into the water lapping the pier; it was filthy, pools of dark froth floating on the oil-slick that encircled the rusting hulls of docked ships. She glanced at the home ports painted across their sterns: Osaka, Vancouver, Rotterdam, Magadan. The cranes on the dock were idle. To her left, she watched a vast tanker pass beneath the raised section of the Niterói Bridge. On the far side of Guanabara Bay, Niterói itself was blurred by haze.

Ferreira led her into a cavernous warehouse with Boa Vista Internacional painted above the entrance in peeling yellow and green. The air inside was stifling. There were old rail-tracks set into the ground and creaking gantries overhead. Some men were stacking crates on the left, others were slouched around packing cases, smoking cigarettes, killing time. Petra felt their gazes and recognized the intent in each one.

In an office at the rear of the building, two men were waiting for them. They were clad in ill-fitting suits, perspiration stains beneath the armpits, stubble on their jaws, sunglasses masking their eyes. On the desk, there was a piece of tarpaulin. On it were different pieces of off-white plastic and a small, black metal box. One of the men handed Ferreira a thick file as he closed the office door.

He said, 'You understand that we have not yet assembled or manufactured the products that Senhor Lehmans requested.'

'Of course.'

'But we can show you something similar. And in here,' he said, tapping the file with his fingertips, 'we can show you alternatives with specifications.'

What Gustavo Marin offered was a cornucopia of destruction. Explosives and weapons of all sorts and in any quantity imaginable, delivery guaranteed. Ferreira said there was nowhere beyond their reach. And if a client had more specific needs – the sort of dark needs not specified in the catalogue – then those, too, could be met. Just recently, for example, one of Marin's laboratories had doctored two packets of Camel cigarettes for an Iraqi client, coating the filters with anthrax spores, a practice developed by and bought from South Africa's biological warfare programme. Even nuclear material was available, Ferreira claimed.

'But first,' he said, handing Petra a sheet of paper, 'here is the list that Lehmans sent us.'

Petra took her time running through the contents which

were printed in English: twenty-five Memopark safety-arming switches, one hundred kilos of Ammonal – a Russian manufactured explosive – one hundred kilos of Czech-manufactured Semtex, fifteen Iraco detonators, twenty Heckler & Koch carbines, ten infra-red sensors. All in all, enough to cause plenty of mayhem in Moscow and elsewhere. At the bottom of the list, and separate from the rest of it, were two entries she did not recognize: six Series-410/5s and three CBTs.

Choosing her words cautiously, she said, 'The two at the bottom – I'm not familiar with the names.'

Ferreira smiled and turned his attention to the pieces spread across the tarpaulin. 'Series-410 is a range of customized weapons that we manufacture as a by-product of a larger industrial process at one of our plants in São Paulo. Made from plastic resins and ceramics, they are designed to be carried through automatic security checks.'

Such as might exist in the homes or offices of Ismailov's targets, Petra thought.

'They are easy to assemble,' continued Ferreira, 'so that they can be carried unassembled if a physical check is a possibility. The pieces can be disguised as everyday objects; a glasses case, a mobile phone or pager, a Walkman, a pen, a lighter, a key-ring.' He waved a hand over the pieces on the tarpaulin. 'As you can see, these components are plain at the moment, but you can get an idea of how they work.' He began to assemble the weapon. 'This is the Series-410 prototype, a basic one-round unit. An experimental model, really. The 410/5 that you have ordered is an automatic, taking up to fifteen 9mm rounds.'

The fully assembled gun looked more like a plastic camera grip with an unsightly stubby cylinder attached, but the principle was neat enough. Petra nodded in appreciation and then pointed at the black metal box on the tarpaulin. 'And in there?'

'A CBT. A customized barometric trigger. A real work of art.'

Ferreira opened the box. Set in a grey foam cushion was a single, slim glass capsule, almost oval in shape, about an inch and a half in length. He picked it out and held it between his thumb and forefinger before passing it to her. The surface was perfectly smooth except for one minuscule dot halfway down the capsule. Ferreira saw her squinting at it and said, 'A pressure valve.'

'How does it work?'

He turned round and took a box off the top of a filing cabinet, from which he produced a small, spring-loaded switch in a glass frame. With his fingers, he withdrew the spring creating a gap in the housing. 'The capsule goes in here and then the trigger is attached to the device. When the correct pressure is attained, the capsule disintegrates, the spring is released and the device is detonated. Or maybe the trigger is attached to a timer, in which case the timer is initiated.'

'I still don't see how it works.'

Ferreira smiled. 'That's because you *can't* see how it works. The truth is there are two capsules, not one. There's a second capsule inside the first. There's a pressure differential between the two and when the outside pressure changes, the built-in fracture lines crack and the capsule shatters, releasing the spring. The trigger is then activated.'

'Ingenious.'

'And beautiful. All of these are individually made for us in Minas Gerais. Each one is precisely calibrated to be triggered at a pre-selected pressure. Lehmans mentioned that all three of yours were to be used on helicopters. Is that right?'

I have no idea. She looked up at him and smiled coldly. 'That's right, yes.'

'Will they be operating from sea-level?'

Any answer was better than a pause. 'Yes.'

'Are they pressurized?'

'No.'

Petra ran her fingers over the smooth glass. The connection was unavoidable. A timer ran risks. Commercial flights were so frequently delayed. Also, if one was anxious that an aircraft should be brought down over a specific location – the middle of the Atlantic, for instance, where corpse and debris recovery would prove hardest – then a barometric trigger allied to a timer was ideal; the timer would only be activated once the aircraft was airborne and once the cabin pressure had passed through a designated level. Additionally, a glass barometric trigger was close to perfect, the evidence being totally destroyed by the blast it provoked, so that if the remains were scattered across land, even the craftiest investigator would be defeated.

Petra wasn't sure whether she wanted to crush the capsule or keep it close to her heart for ever. She looked up at Ferreira. 'This looks like it would be the perfect trigger for a device on a commercial aircraft.'

He said, 'It already has been.'

15

The traffic was slow along Avenida Niemeyer, which snaked around the foot of the Morro Dois Irmãos, the double-humped mountain dividing Leblon from São Conrado. Rising steeply from the right of the road was Vidigal, one of Rio's notorious *favelas*. To the left, with typical Brazilian insensitivity, stood the Sheraton Hotel. Vidigal was a stew of narrow concrete steps and corridors, of hastily cemented breeze-blocks and corrugated-iron roofs, of stray dogs and stray children. The car swung left towards the hotel entrance, past the permanently manned police-booth on the island at the centre of the road.

The heat and humidity remained oppressive so the hotel's lobby was a refreshing relief, instantly cooling her. She strolled past a group of American tourists who were being corralled by a flustered tour representative. At the desk, she asked for Eduardo Monteiro. They told her she was expected and that he was in room 1625, on the sixteenth floor.

In the lobby, in full view of the reception desk, sat a man in a tan linen suit and an open-necked light blue shirt. He was folding a copy of the *Jornal do Brasil*. She never noticed him – there was no reason that she should – but he was watching her.

There were six lifts in the lobby and she had one to herself. She checked her reflection in the coppery metal that surrounded her. A simple cotton dress – navy with a few, small white polka-dots on it – and white Superga gym shoes. She carried a black canvas bag over her shoulder containing a beach towel, a paperback swollen by dampness and two bottles of sun-cream. Plain enough, then, a tourist dressed for her holiday. She kept her sunglasses on.

She turned right out of the lift. 1625 was at the end of the corridor. She knocked on the door and it was opened by a tall man with suede for hair and badly pock-marked skin. There were two other men inside. Neither of them was Eduardo Monteiro. One was Ferreira, the other was Gustavo Marin. She recognized him from the photograph Alexander had shown her in London. She scanned the room, making a check-list. There were two single beds on her right, a table and a cabinet against the left wall, a TV on top of the cabinet. At the far end of the room, sliding glass doors opened on to a narrow balcony overlooking the Atlantic.

Marin dismissed Ferreira. Petra heard the door close behind her and then, a moment later, heard the gentle thud of the door to the neighbouring room. Marin was fat with thinning, curly, grey hair that was heavily-oiled and combed back over a scalp peppered with liver-spots. He wore a large Fila tennis shirt and black Adidas track-suit bottoms.

'Petra Reuter, the woman without a face.' He took a deep breath and exhaled slowly. 'You don't mind if we speak in English, do you? Living in Switzerland has not helped my French or German as much as it should.'

'I don't suppose you spend much time there.'

Marin chuckled. 'No. You are right.' He nodded to the man at Petra's side and then said to her, 'You'll forgive me, but I need to know that you are not armed.'

She handed the protection her bag. He went through it carefully, even removing the towel and unfolding it. He put it back and shook his head at Marin, who said, 'You don't mind if he frisks you, do you?'

'That's why I chose the dress. So that you could see I was unarmed.'

'I've heard so many stories about you. About your ingenuity. Luiso will be quick.'

Luiso lingered. Particularly once his hands were up her dress and crawling over her thighs.

Marin enjoyed the show and said, 'I like my men to be thorough.'

Petra held his gaze and was expressionless. 'Me too.'

When Luiso had finished, Marin offered her a drink, which she declined. He hauled himself out of his armchair and shuffled to the mini-bar which was housed in the cabinet to Petra's left, where he mixed himself vodka and orange juice.

'I come home to Brazil for a month each year. To see my family, to see my friends. When I'm here, I don't do much business. When I'm at my house in Búzios, I never do *any* business. So this meeting is unusual. But apparently, you are a woman in a hurry.'

'That's right.'

'Please show me the scar.'

The request was not unexpected. Petra unfastened the zip on her dress a little and shrugged her left shoulder clear of the material, exposing the sealed wound. Then she turned round to show him the exit wound before covering herself again and fastening the zip.

'How did you get it?'

'Belgian police.'

'Where?'

'Mechelen.'

Wherever he was, Marin liked to conduct business in hotel rooms selected at random and at the last minute; he never met customers on private property. The hotel rooms in which his meetings occurred were never booked in his own name. Instead, he had one of his people register at the hotel in their own name. Typically, the room would be booked just an hour or two before the scheduled meeting, and whoever booked it would stay in it until Marin and his entourage arrived. In this instance, the room had been booked by Eduardo Monteiro, the man Petra had failed to meet in Centro earlier in the day. Monteiro was a forty-four-year-old Harvard-trained lawyer and a very well paid full-time employee of Marin's. She wondered where he was. Next door, perhaps, with Ferreira?

After her inventory check in the warehouse on the pier, Ferreira had driven Petra to Flamengo, where he'd dropped her. She'd declared herself happy with the list and he'd promised to contact Marin to set up a meeting so that a price could be agreed. He'd given her two phone numbers. She'd called the first one at three and had been told that the meeting would occur between six and seven in the evening. At five, as instructed, she'd called the second number and had been told that the location was the Sheraton and that she should ask for Eduardo Monteiro. Which was how she came to be in room 1625.

'Look at this,' said Marin, who was standing by the glass doors leading on to the balcony. 'It's beautiful, no?'

Petra stepped forward to admire the view. The sliding glass doors were parted, a hot sea breeze blowing into the room. The curtains billowed, waves of material as a sixteenth-floor extension for the ocean outside. Dusk was descending over the Atlantic. Curving to the left was the Leblon-Ipanema beach-front, the street lamps curving too, countless pinpoints of incandescent white. The hotels and apartment blocks seemed to glow against the early evening light.

'In Rio, we say God created the world and everything in it in six days and then on the seventh day, he created Rio de Janeiro. It could be true, don't you think?'

'From this distance, maybe. But not close up.'

Marin turned round and looked irritated. 'Tell me about Mechelen.'

'I thought we had business to discuss.'

'We do. But I'm curious. The two who were with you – who got killed – who were they? It said in the papers they were drug dealers.'

'Then that is who they were.'

Marin took the wrapper off a pack of Hollywood

cigarettes. 'Did you know the guns were destined for Irish terrorists?'

'I know they would never have made it. They were under surveillance.'

'But you didn't know that at the time.'

'What's your point?'

Marin shrugged. 'How do you find the Irish?'

'They're out of my sphere. I don't have any contact with them. Republicans or Loyalists, they're all the same to me. They're not terrorists, they're not political, they're criminal.'

Marin considered this for a moment and said, 'I agree. In the past, I've sold to both and that's the impression I have. It's all about money.'

'Precisely.'

'In this case, *my* money.'

Marin was pointing a gun at Petra's stomach and, as surely as she could see the darkness down the barrel, she knew Luiso was holding a gun behind her. For several seconds, she was a slave to confusion. Marin was supposed to be setting a price for her. They were meant to seal the deal. That was why she had come to Brazil. The contract with Lehmans had been real. What was happening?

Her mind went to automatic.

The sunglasses she was still wearing were circular. The lenses were completely flat, allowing her to see fragments of reflected movement behind her, at the outer edges of the dark disks. A change in light suggested movement and triggered movement of her own. Luiso wouldn't shoot for fear of hitting his master, but Petra knew that Marin would have no reciprocal qualms. So she lunged forwards, feinting to the left and then ducking to the right. Marin fired his gun but missed her. The bullet hit the door.

Luiso stood still for a second, stunned by what he was seeing and unsure of how he should react to it. Petra reached Marin and grabbed the wrist of the hand holding the gun. In a series of movements that were concluded in a moment, she altered her grip and broke his wrist. He buckled at the knees and squealed. The gun went off again. She tore the weapon free of his fingers and then spun round to confront Luiso. But he wasn't where she had pictured him. He was tilting, his left hand still clutching his gun but also resting against the cabinet for support. His right hand was clamped to the right side of his torso. Mouth agape, his eyes were wide in astonishment. Blood began to seep from between his fingers.

Somewhere deep inside Petra, a computer was at work, assessing priorities, directing function. It was calculating the seconds since the first shot, pinpointing the rumble of feet from the room next door. Petra trained Marin's Colt on Luiso and then back on Marin himself, who whimpered.

Spinning on her left foot, she lashed out with her right, catching Luiso on his wound. He gasped as he collapsed. She yanked the Beretta from him and tossed it on to the carpet between the two beds. Then she grabbed him by the back of the collar of his shirt, twisting it tightly, choking him, sapping his strength yet further. She pressed her body behind his and forced him to his feet. Having proved to be useless protection for Marin, he was now to serve as more practical protection for Petra. With one quick monitoring glance at Marin – he was retreating towards the balcony, desperate to get as far away from her as possible – she pointed the Colt at the bedroom door.

It burst open, the lock splintering. It was Ferreira. As predicted, his eye-line was distracted by the sight of Marin cowering in front of the window, clutching his fractured wrist. Petra fired shots in quick succession. He went down, dead before he hit the carpet, but not before he managed to squeeze off three shots. One hit Luiso in the shoulder. He screamed like a child, high-pitched and frantic. The blow punched hard, knocking Petra off-balance. A second shot pierced a sliding glass door. The third winged Petra. There was a searing pain down her right side. She and Luiso tumbled to the floor, his weight winding her.

She scrambled out from beneath his body. Marin was mewing by the window, unable to prevent himself from urinating into his track-suit bottoms. Luiso was going into shock, his mouth flapping uselessly; he looked like a fish out of water. His legs twitched violently. Ferreira's glasses were shattered. His left eye-socket was a crimson tear. Petra pressed her palm to her right side, feeling the heat of her blood coming through the cotton. The percussive crack of the shots rang in her ears, their scent was strong in her nostrils.

She dropped Marin's Colt into her shoulder bag and picked up Luiso's Beretta from the carpet. She checked the clip – eight left – and slapped it back into place. Then she pointed the gun at Marin. 'Why?'

'Please, don't shoot!' he wailed.

'Why?'

His mind was too scrambled for coherence. *'Please!* No! I have money. We can –'

She thought of the glass barometric trigger. And of smoking bodies falling towards a black sea.

He was crying when she shot him.

The lift took an eternity to arrive. She checked the corridor again. Nothing. The doors parted, revealing five people inside, three men, two women. She saw sunburned shoulders, beach towels, a Dallas Cowboys cap, five jaws dropping. She raised the Beretta.

'Get out!'

They hesitated and she read their minds: *maybe the doors will close and save us.* She aimed at the woman nearest her, a skinny creature with beetroot burns beneath gold jewellery.

'Do it now!'

They moved like sheep; one of the men tentatively taking the lead, scraping past her before breaking into a scamper, the others following blindly. Petra stepped into the lift. The doors closed. She dropped the Beretta into her shoulder bag, where the Colt was. Then she examined her copper reflection. There was nothing to be done about the stain on her dress and she was thankful that the cotton was mostly navy. She took the dark green towel from the bag and wiped Luiso's blood from her thighs and left shoulder. She watched the floors counting down to the lobby. The lift slowed.

When the doors parted, there were people waiting. She stepped out and walked past them, not looking back. *Move confidently, don't draw attention to yourself.* The lobby seemed larger. The American tourists were still there, pink-faced and slack-bellied, bewildering their guide. Outside, the heat was a slap in the face. A man in uniform asked if she wanted a taxi. She brushed past him, turning right. A few yards on, there was a door leading to the underground car park. The lift was out of service so she took the stairs.

She reached Level Four. The heat was worse than outside, incredible, hotter than anything she had experienced so far. The smell of evaporated fuel and exhaust fumes was overpowering. She heard voices and withdrew the Beretta from the shoulder bag.

How long would it take for the panic to spread? How many people had heard the shooting? By now, those she had ejected from the lift were doubtless on the phone. From there to hotel security to the police, how long would it be before the hotel was sealed?

She moved out from the passage connecting the stairs to the level. The ceiling was low, and was made lower by a chaotic grid of pipes which were hanging from it, many of which seemed to be leaking. She tiptoed through stagnant puddles of oily water. Voices echoed but their owners were invisible to her.

The black Omega was parked by a pillar. She knelt on the ground and examined the underside but saw nothing out of place, so she climbed inside, fastened her seat-belt and turned the ignition. She drove slowly towards the barrier, her ticket on the passenger seat. She kept the passenger window a third open. As the attendant raised his hand to halt her, she heard the squeal of tyres on smooth, painted concrete. She looked round but saw nothing. The attendant waved her through. She turned right and headed up the ramp, fumbling with the dashboard, trying to find her headlights. Instead, she activated the windscreen wipers. When she reached ground level, she powered the engine, accelerating past three parked coaches outside the hotel's entrance. She reached Avenida Niemeyer and began to turn right, wanting to return to Leblon as quickly as possible.

Normally, Avenida Niemeyer is a two-way road but not during rush-hour. Rio de Janeiro's legendary traffic had prompted the authorities to take drastic action to alleviate the worst of the congestion. One of their solutions had been to turn Avenida Niemeyer into a one-way road heading into town during the morning rush-hour, and a one-way road heading out of town during the evening rush-hour. Ignorant of this, Petra had planned to barge into the nearest lane for Leblon. As she began to turn, she saw two lanes of traffic coming straight at her. She pounded the brake and yanked the wheel. The car skidded. A white Volkswagen swerved to avoid her and mounted the kerb. A rusting blue Ford drove into the back of the Omega.

Tyres screeched, horns blared, fists shook. The driver of the Ford opened his door. There was no time for civility. Any moment now, the alarm would be raised in the hotel. Perhaps it already had been. Running the steering-wheel through her hands, she reversed into the side of a purple Fiat, went forward to the rock face at the road's edge and then reversed into the Fiat again. The startled policeman in the booth on the central island was now striding towards her, his hand heading for the holster on his hip. Her brutal three-point turn accomplished, Petra engaged first gear, spun the wheel and crushed the accelerator to the floor.

Moving up through the gears, she glanced in the rear-view mirror. The policeman had his gun out but his attention was distracted by the fury of the drivers she had left behind. Petra knew that somebody would have made a note of the number plate. She needed to dump the vehicle as quickly as possible. The dented boot and bonnet would only make it easier to identify. The twisting road began to descend. Petra saw São Conrado beach ahead, curving for a mile. The road broadened as she sped past the Inter-Continental and the empty, cylindrical, glass tower of the Nacional. She got stuck behind a local bus. Hopelessly overcrowded and with its suspension shot to pieces, it leaned to one side, limping more than motoring. The road started to curve to the left when Petra caught a glimpse of a Retorno sign on the right. She braked as fiercely as possible and swung right, clipping the kerb and narrowly avoiding a blur of pedestrians. She just made the Retorno slip-road, which rose to join the dual carriageway heading into the tunnel back to Leblon.

Only now did she become aware of how violently she was shaking. Every muscle seemed to quiver. She checked her mirrors constantly, half-expecting the chilling siren of a pursuing police car. She cursed herself for taking the wrong turning out of the hotel. Had she driven a little slower, she would have had time to see the change in traffic direction. But under the circumstances, driving slower would have seemed like an invitation for trouble. Another check in the rear-view mirror and there were still no police behind her. She spied dirty light at the end of the tunnel and began to feel calmer. Once she was through it, she had an entire city to lose herself in.

Petra watched the pink water circle the plug-hole before slipping down it. Then she clutched her right side with her right hand, letting the water rinse her skin before she turned off the shower. By the basin, the contents of her medical kit were laid out on a paper towel. She disinfected the cut, which stung, and then, squeezing the two walls of the wound together, applied the butterfly sutures as well as she could. She knew she had been lucky. The bullet had grazed her close to the bottom rib. She didn't know whether the rib itself was damaged – the whole area was painful – but a few inches the wrong way and the bullet could have proved fatal.

She wrapped a towel around her body and walked into the bedroom. The air-conditioning kept the temperature cool and the sealed windows kept the noise of the street muted. Although by no means a smart establishment, the Hotel Plaza on Rua Joana Angélica, between Rua Visconde de Pirajá and Rua Prudente de Morais, was far more comfortable than the hotel in Copacabana where she had spent the three previous nights. But then Marina Gaudenzi had a more comfortable lifestyle than Susan Branch.

Susan Branch was a mature student at New York University, who was on a four-day visit to Rio for the wedding of an old friend of hers. Marina Gaudenzi was Swiss, a native of Geneva, and she was in Rio on business for one night only. That night had been last night.

As Susan Branch, Petra had flown into Rio on a United flight – the cheapest available – from New York. Apart from the absence of a wedding to attend, she had existed in the city as Susan Branch until her meeting with Ferreira. Marina Gaudenzi had been established by someone else – a courier she had never met – and she had arrived in Rio late the previous evening from Buenos Aires. She had gone straight to bed and then left the hotel early in the morning after a breakfast delivered by Room Service. Petra wondered where she was now.

The courier had left some money – reis and dollars – and all Marina Gaudenzi's documents in an inner pocket of the suitcase, which was secured by a numbered padlock. Petra knew the number. On the desk, the courier had also left some of her faked business correspondence. Her air-ticket showed the itinerary: Geneva-Buenos Aires-Rio de Janeiro-London-Geneva. A week from start to finish, although the final section would never be used.

Having driven through the tunnel back into Leblon, Petra had needed to dump the damaged car quickly. She had been glad it was dark, the evening offering cover despite the street lights. She'd parked in Rua General Venáncio Flores, placed the shoulder bag containing the guns in the boot, and then walked the short distance to the Hotel Plaza. As she'd entered the hotel, she'd draped the dark green – and slightly stained – beach towel over her right shoulder to cover the wet wound on her side.

Now, she examined the clothes on the bed. A white silk blouse, a navy jacket, pressed Armani trousers. There was a pair of oval Calvin Klein glasses to complete the effect. Susan Branch had been a jeans and T-shirt girl, whereas Marina Gaudenzi was a serious European professional.

Petra sat in the back of the car, peering out of the window as they cruised along Avenida Brasil. The driver had given up trying to make small-talk to her with his limited English.

The *zona norte* was mostly industrial. By the side of the multi-laned highway there were pockets of habitation between large crumbling factories. Ramshackle housing had grown up around the manufacturing plants as randomly as the weeds. Dead cars rusted to dust beside make-believe kerbs. Children slept beneath the billboards promoting Chevrolets and Brahma beer.

They crossed the bridge to Ilha do Governador and Galeão, Rio's international airport. It was cool inside the departures terminal, but crowded; the great majority of flights to Europe and North America left during a four-hour period at night. Also, Brazilians tended to come in numbers to bid farewell to their travelling relatives or friends. Petra felt the congestion would work to her advantage.

She walked slowly through the terminal for a second time to confirm what she had suspected the first time; there were more officials around the United desks than anywhere else. Police and airport security hung back from the desks themselves, waiting for some signal from airline staff, who had presumably been briefed. Susan Branch was due to return to New York that night. Marin was dead but his operation was not; somebody had told the police who to look out for because they could not have made the connection themselves. Arriving at the Sheraton reception desk, she had been careful not to use her name. Or rather, the name of Susan Branch.

As Marina Gaudenzi, Petra checked in at the Varig Executive Class desk and then got in line for Immigration. The official in the booth took his time, poring over her Swiss passport and the Immigration counterfoil the courier had retained the previous evening on arrival from Buenos Aires. Once through, Petra ignored the private lounge that was available to her, preferring to keep moving until her flight was called. Through the terminal windows, she saw her Varig MD-11 parked outside, the gantry attached to the aircraft like a vast umbilical cord. She drifted through the duty-free shops and past the stalls selling easy-to-carry packs of Brazilian coffee and three-bottle boxes of *cachaça*.

The United flight to New York was delayed for an hour. Petra was not surprised. Then more delays were announced, including her Varig flight to London, also by one hour. Most of the other flights, however, were getting away on time and, as the night's quota of departures neared completion, the number of passengers cruising the concourse began to diminish.

At quarter-to-midnight, her flight was finally called. A stewardess took her boarding pass and showed her to seat 9L. As the other passengers boarded, she read a copy of the *Frankfurter Allgemeine*. Out of her window, she could see the New York-bound United 747 at the next-door gate. Even when her own flight rolled back from the stand, she

207

remained tense, a part of her still expecting the aircraft to be recalled. It was a sensation that persisted as they taxied to the runway and which was only lifted as the wheels of the MD-11 lost touch with the ground.

Her face pressed to the window, she watched the sparkling lights of Rio de Janeiro vanish beneath her.

No longer the robot, Petra panicked. She opened her eyes. The wound in her side hurt but the pain in her head was worse. There was darkness and noise; it took her a moment to remember where she was. Both hands were clamped tight to the arm-rests, her entire body tensed to rigidity. She forced herself to deepen each breath, to slow the rate. As her eyes grew accustomed to the half-light, she looked around. The cabin was virtually empty; she was the only passenger in row 9.

Aware of creeping wetness around her ribs, Petra found the small medical kit that she had put in her hand-luggage and went to the washroom. She unbuttoned her white silk blouse. There were bloodstains on the garment. She peeled off the covering plaster and saw the sutures had not fastened the wound properly. She wiped away the blood, dried the area and covered it with fresh plasters.

Looking in the mirror, she saw herself as she really was, not as she was programmed to be; a scared and confused fraud. For a few seconds, she was not Petra Reuter. She was Stephanie again. And when she closed her eyes she saw Marin crying, she saw Ferreira falling, she felt the weight of a gun in her hand. When she opened her eyes again, she didn't recognize the pupils which stared back at her from the mirror.

In the galley, she found a stewardess and asked for coffee. Curled into a ball in her seat, she raised the blind a little and daylight spilled into her lap. She marvelled at the sky, at the curvature of the horizon where sapphire turned to purple then black, and at the first fiery tongues of sun.

When it came, the coffee was strong and sweet.

16

At Heathrow, Petra cleared Customs and made her call from a pay-phone. A familiar and comforting voice answered. 'Yes?'

'It's . . .' Who was she to him? It took a moment to remember. 'It's Stephanie.'

'Ah, yes. And how are you?'

'That's what I want you to tell me. Can I come now?'

'Where are you?'

'Heathrow.'

'Yes, all right. I'll expect you in an hour, then.'

She took the Underground and sat with her head against the dirty window, watching the suburbs of west London slip by. The doubt persisted. What had gone wrong? Why had Marin suddenly turned the gun on her? On account of Mechelen? Unlikely. After all, Alexander – masquerading as Petra – had contacted Marin, not the other way around. Perhaps she had made some mistake that had betrayed her. She tried to remember her conversation with Marin but found she could only recall inconsequential fragments.

Marin had been a monster, it was true, a man responsible for more deaths than could reasonably be calculated. But he had been a husband, too. Thrice over, in fact. He'd also been a father of five. And what of Ferreira? Was he also a husband and father? If not, he had still been a son and, maybe, a brother. Grief was a chain reaction and through Marin and Ferreira, Petra had touched the lives of many.

She felt suspended between two different states; the woman she had once been and the woman she was supposed to be now. In Rio, she had been Petra. Now, if only temporarily, she felt she was Stephanie again; confused, isolated, vulnerable – not things one would have associated with Petra. What alarmed her the most was how easily she had been the other woman, how natural it had felt. Her reactions had been automatic, correct and clinical, just as Boyd had taught her, just as Alexander demanded of her. It was only now, in the aftermath, that she felt the effect of her actions. The narrowness of the margin of her escape chilled the part of her that was Stephanie just as surely as it thrilled the part of her that was Petra.

At Green Park, she changed from the Piccadilly Line to the Jubilee Line, which took her to Bond Street. From there, she walked to George Street. Dr Brian Rutherford welcomed her warmly, as usual. A lean man, with salt and pepper hair and a sallow complexion, he was wearing a heavy tweed suit, the sort of ill-fitting garment so beloved of British films from the Fifties. He led her through to his surgery where she stripped from the waist up.

Her sutures prompted raised eyebrows. 'Who did these?'

'I did.'

'I'm glad to hear it. I'd hate to think a fellow professional was responsible, no matter what part of the world they came from.'

'That bad, are they?'

'For a novice, they could be worse. Especially considering the awkward angle. But they'll have to come out.'

'I thought as much.'

Rutherford straightened himself. 'I need to know where you've been.'

'Brazil.'

'The Amazon?'

'No. Rio.'

He reopened the cut, disinfected it thoroughly with antiseptic and then re-sealed it neatly with new sutures. Then he checked the bruising around her ribs.

'You'll be fine. You've got nothing broken. The bruising will start to go down in a day or two. I'm going to give you some antibiotics for the wound. Make sure you finish them. Do you need pain-killers?'

Stephanie fastened her bra. 'Nothing too strong.'

Rutherford nodded and then glanced at the scar on her left shoulder. 'That's come out nicely, I must say. Very realistic.'

Mechelen. What a sad catalogue of errors that had been: a consignment of firearms destined for Belfast; a surveillance operation that had been corrupted; tarnished information sold at a price; an armed gang who thought they were intercepting cocaine, who thought they were on the verge of the easiest score of their criminal lives. The plan had been simple enough: when the lorry reached the warehouse in Mechelen, they would deal with the single, unsuspecting driver – the gang believed he was unaware of the illegal cargo hidden among the TVs and VCRs – and then drive the lorry to a rendezvous outside the town where all the merchandise would be transferred to a vehicle of their own. The French police officer who had sold them the information had assured them that the cocaine was stored inside the VCRs themselves, in the slots that held the tapes.

The gang had executed six successful armed robberies in Belgium over four years. Originally a quartet, they were now a trio and of the three, Anna Gerets was the only one who survived Mechelen. As it turned out, the driver of the lorry, far from being naïve about his cargo, was armed and had an accomplice, who shot Guy, Anna's boyfriend. So she shot the accomplice. That was when the Belgian police, who had assumed control of the surveillance from the French police, intervened. During the shoot-out that followed, Jean, the third member of the gang, and the driver were shot dead, along with one police officer, while another four were injured. Anna escaped through the back of the warehouse, but not before she had been shot through the left shoulder.

A fortnight later, the French policeman who had sold the information was dead. An apparent suicide, it seemed he knew the investigators were closing in on him and couldn't face the consequences. A week after that, Anna Gerets drowned. It was not witnessed. Her body sank in the Channel, unnoticed and unmourned. As far as the police were concerned, however, she was still at large.

After three months, a new rumour began to circulate: the gang had not been ignorant at all; they had known there was no cocaine in the lorry. They'd known about the guns. The guns were what they were after but as for what purpose, who could say? The whisper was that although the two dead men had belonged to the original gang, the woman had not been Anna Gerets. Quickly, another rumour spread: Anna Gerets was alive and well and living in Thailand. Or was it Indonesia? No one could say for sure but, yes, she was definitely in that part of the world. It was said that she had split from Guy a year before and was now living off her cut from their previous heists. She was drifting, contemplating a new life in a new country under a new identity. And who knew this for sure? Well, it was hard to say. *I didn't meet her myself, you understand, but I met this Dane in a bar in Manila and he'd heard it from someone else. Someone who actually met her. Apparently.* And so it went. A culture of rumour was created which, in time, gained sufficient critical mass to pass into some form of fact.

A question that had seemed answered slowly became unanswered: who was the woman whom the Belgian police had shot through the left shoulder? The woman who had, miraculously, escaped.

A season changed and a gruesome possibility surfaced. The name was whispered quietly. Petra Reuter, the human plague. The physical descriptions were not dissimilar – although with Reuter you never knew; she was such a mistress of disguise – and the ability to avoid capture was entirely consistent. In fact, Reuter hijacking weapons seemed an altogether more plausible explanation than

Anna Gerets and her two accomplices mistakenly attempting a cocaine heist.

This was how fiction ram-raided truth.

Just as she had never questioned the need to have surgery for the cosmetic scars, Petra had never asked Alexander whether the French police officer had really committed suicide. Or how they had traced Anna Gerets, or who had killed her and dumped her body into the sea. She preferred not to know how the rumours were planted and nurtured. She just accepted it for what it was: another slice of real life to be added to the fake life created for her. She was a collage of impersonation and deceit, mostly assembled while she had still been Stephanie, or a prostitute named Lisa.

Originally, the Petra Reuter legend had been created as an open-ended option, one of a set of four artificial identities, two male and two female. Stephanie became Petra because she was the closest physical match of the two female legends. Of the four legends, Petra was the only one that had been activated. It was strange to think that while Stephanie had been destroying herself, her next life was gradually and painstakingly being manufactured by Magenta House. The Mechelen incident had occurred six months before Keith Proctor had walked into her room on Brewer Street.

This was what she was thinking about as she turned off John Adam Street, into Robert Street. She paused for a moment by the sign: L. L. Herring & Sons Ltd, Numismatists, Since 1789. Collectors of coins. It wasn't the only thing they were collecting inside the building; lives, also, were being amassed, sorted and stored. Deaths, too.

Alexander's secretary, Margaret, was a large woman with a generous nature, as if to compensate for the frugality of her master's. Once upon a time, she had been married. Now, she was professionally wedded to Alexander and the extraordinary hours he kept. Petra wondered whether she had any social life at all.

'Nice to see you again, Stephanie.' Margaret was one of the few who continued to use the name. 'He's waiting for you. You can go in.'

Alexander's office was on the top floor of the smaller of the two buildings, the one closer to the river. It was old-fashioned, two computers on a mahogany desk being the only genuine concessions to modernity. In many ways, it resembled a library; full shelves from floor to ceiling, reading lamps on Alexander's desk and on a small table by the door. It had an air of antiquity and a sense of tranquillity. Within the rest of the twinned buildings, there was enough technology for the present and for the future, so this seemed like a small sanctuary, a place to let the mind work uncluttered by microchips.

Alexander was at one of the computers behind his desk by the bay window. Petra crossed the carpet and sat down. Still gazing at the screen, he asked, 'Were you hurt?'

'Not seriously. I was lucky.'

He considered this for a while. 'In time, you'll find it's as important to be lucky as it is to be good.'

'I was nearly killed.'

'Nearly but not quite. If you had been, it would merely have proved that we were wrong about you, and that you weren't good enough. You may or may not be interested to know that Marin's bodyguard – I think his name is Luiso – survived.'

Petra shrugged.

Alexander said, 'Apparently, you used him as a human shield.'

'It's what Boyd taught me.'

He nodded to himself and then abandoned the computer. On his desk, there was a coffee pot sitting on a tray with two cups and saucers, a silver sugar bowl and a small jug of milk. Alexander began to pour.

Petra said, 'Marin was involved with Mechelen. He was the gun-seller.'

214

Alexander stiffened for a second. 'Was he now?'

She wondered whether his reaction was provoked by the information itself, or by the fact that she was in possession of it. She waited for something more from him but that was all he offered her, so she said, 'I'd like to know how you missed that.'

He handed her a cup and saucer. 'We can't know everything. Even the largest organizations can't know everything.'

'You absorbed the Mechelen situation for me but didn't know about Marin's involvement? I find that hard to believe.'

'We first knew of Marin through another source.'

'Even if you didn't know much about Marin, you presumably knew all there was to know about Mechelen. Otherwise how would you have known it was safe to claim the role for me?'

'He must have used an intermediary.'

'Like Lehmans?'

'Possibly. All we can say for sure is that Marin's name didn't come up.'

'Who was the original source?'

'Marc Serra.'

That made some sense. 'You sent me out to Rio to agree a price with Marin. You told me it was going to be routine.'

'It should have been.'

'Marin's people were surprised that I made the trip just to conclude the deal. And now that I think about it, so am I. A price could've been agreed over the phone.'

'What's your point?'

'Something's not right.'

'Marin was completely untrustworthy. For all I know, perhaps he decided to kill you just so that he could boast that he was the one who got rid of the infamous Petra Reuter. That's the kind of man he was.'

Petra knew more about lying than most people. Next to her, Alexander was an amateur and it showed. The least palatable explanation for what had occurred in Rio was starting to look like the most plausible.

She said, 'So what happens now?'

'You wait. Serra is the same lead as Marin. He's just further along the line.'

Petra halted, tripped by an instinct. She knew she was missing something but couldn't see it.

Alexander said, 'My advice to you is that you should relax for a couple of days. Recuperate. Your sites are up and running, aren't they?'

'Yes.'

'Then all you have to do is check them from time to time. Let's see what happens.'

'Do you really think he'll come looking for me?'

'Who can say? One thing is for sure, though. You're not in the shadows any more, no longer just a legend. You're identifiable now, a myth made flesh and blood.'

Petra returned to her flat, a one-bedroom place in a block that filled a gap between Half Moon Street and Clarges Street; her apartment looked on to the former, the building's entrance was on the latter. It was just six days since she had left for New York to become Susan Branch. It was only a fortnight since she had moved in.

She had turned down the heating before leaving so it was now cold. She altered the thermostat and the boiler fired. Compared to most of the flats she had stayed in over recent months, this one was not bad. It was small but comfortable, if a little soulless; typical, in other words, of the corporate flats that formed the majority within the building. Hers belonged to Brillex-Martins, the Belgian pharmaceutical and chemical company for whom Marina Gaudenzi worked.

She remembered the other places without fondness. There had been a freezing two-room apartment above a café in Ostend. That had been March. The days had crawled by. She'd spent hours waiting for the phone to ring, staring vacantly at the harbour and the gunmetal smudge of sea and sky. Three months later, the ageing owner of the café – the one who had rented her the place – would confirm her description to the police, but only in the broadest terms. After all, what could he say? He had only seen her on three or four occasions. He would tell them what he knew of her, but how much was that? She didn't appear to have gone out much. She had paid the rent in cash, in advance, and had been no trouble. Had she said why she was in Ostend? Not that he could recall.

After Ostend, she had travelled to Berlin for a miserable month in a decaying tenement block populated almost exclusively by Turkish immigrants. From Berlin, she'd moved to Zurich for a fortnight, slumming down with heroin addicts and petty thieves.

Barcelona, Sarajevo, Marseille, Bucharest. So the list went, the cities already blurring in her memory, linked only by her desire to leave them. It was not that they were unappealing places. Rather, it was the life she was forced to lead in them that was unappealing. She had to be glimpsed but not seen, a presence, not a person. In isolation, she waited for instructions. *Go out to the airport. You're meeting a passenger off the Lufthansa flight from Frankfurt. They will not be on it so call the following number from the nearest pay-phone in the terminal. When it's answered, don't speak. Put the receiver down. Then return to your apartment.* She never questioned the purpose of such routines. If there was method in the madness, she did not want to discover it. Sometimes, her instructions would send her further afield. A weekend in Oslo, perhaps, or a three-day trip to Milan. But the destinations were always an irrelevance because the reality was always the same; a hotel room, a phone, a long wait watching TV in a language she did not understand.

Often, exercise was her saviour, toning both the body and mind. She increased her strength and suppleness, devising new routines to occupy the empty hours and save

217

her from negativity. In this, she was only partially successful. She had become a nomadic loner and no matter how
hard she tried to combat it, there were times when the
isolation and the tedium were depressing. Especially when
she considered the future. Alexander had told her this was
how she would live her life for at least a year, maybe more.
It was necessary, he said, in order to build up Petra into
a convincing three-dimensional reality. It was not good
enough for Stephanie to masquerade as Petra; she had to
become Petra and that took time. In the end, however,
the process lasted just six months. The deaths of Grigory
Ismailov and Lionel Lehmans changed everything.

'Are you all right?'

The enquiry came as a shock. It took her a moment to
adjust to the real world. His face was familiar. So were the
surroundings. She was in the over-priced Europa supermarket on the corner of Curzon Street and Clarges Street.
She remembered now. There had been no food in the flat.

The man said, 'It's Miss Gaudenzi, isn't it?'

'Yes.'

He was holding a bag of apples. 'You dropped these.'

She looked at them. 'I did?'

'Are you sure you're okay? You look a little . . . *lost.*'

'I'm fine.'

'You're shaking.'

It was true but Petra snapped at him anyway. 'I said I'm
fine.'

That was a lie. One moment, she had been shopping for
groceries, the next, she had been shooting people in a
hotel room. The thought of it had overwhelmed her. The
memory had played like a dream – it felt unreal – but it
was still a memory, a record of something that she had
done.

The man wore jeans and a heavy, black jersey over a
white T-shirt. Petra guessed he was six foot two. His hair
was as dark as hers – almost black – and just as thick. He

218

had a large Roman nose and sharp blue eyes, as clear as the blue she had seen from her aircraft window earlier in the day. His name had temporarily deserted her.

Flustered, she said, 'I'm sorry, I've forgotten –'

He handed her the apples. 'I'm Frank.'

Frank White. That was it. They lived in the same building. They had passed one another in the entrance hall a couple of times during the week before New York. They had exchanged the odd phrase; a greeting, a farewell, a comment about the weather.

Petra said, 'I didn't mean to be rude.'

'It was nothing. Forget it.'

'I'm just tired. Jet-lagged, I guess.'

'You've been abroad, then?'

'Yes.'

'Where?'

The questions were too quick, too direct. 'On a business trip. A couple of places.'

He seemed to sense the resistance in her. They paid for their goods and stepped on to Curzon Street. He examined the change in his hand and said, 'That place is like the Bermuda Triangle. Money just disappears in it.'

In front of them, on the other side of the street, was the façade of the Third Church of Christ, Scientist. Carved into the stone portal above the entrance were three phrases: HEAL THE SICK; CLEANSE THE LEPER; RAISE THE DEAD. Again, Petra pictured Marin standing by the sliding glass doors, crying like a child, the first bullet hitting him in the throat. A father of five. She closed her eyes for a moment and tried to banish the image.

Frank White was still making small-talk. They entered their building and waited for a lift to descend. On the hall table there was a large padded envelope addressed to her. She looked at the reverse side and recognized the smudged inky stamp. It was from Adelphi Travel. Or rather, Magenta House. Yet more information to be processed and stored, she supposed.

She glanced at her watch. In Brazil, afternoon would be making way for early evening. She wondered what Marin's villa at Búzios was like. That was where the children had been while she was shooting their father. Her head ached. She put a hand to her temple.

'Are you sure you're all right?'

'Yes. Thank you.'

'Perhaps I could offer you a cup of coffee?'

Petra tensed. 'Coffee?'

'Or tea, if you'd prefer it.'

Somewhere deep within her, inexplicably, she felt anger towards Frank White. The trigger was a mystery but the feeling was familiar. 'I don't think so, Mr White. I don't think I want anything from you.'

There was frost outside. Petra saw it on the windscreens of the cars parked beneath the street lamps. It was still dark at ten-to-seven in the morning. She sipped from a mug of green tea and then sat down at the Compaq lap-top that was on the smoked glass table-top. The modem squealed as its electronic tentacles spread out, hunting for other tentacles to cling to. She reached Magenta House at Adelphi Travel. The computer in Adelphi Travel then looked for a host and came up with a short-list to choose from: Bank of America, RTZ, Nike, Finnair, Renault, DuPont, Crédit Suisse, Marriott. Out of dislike, she chose Nike. Each day, the short-list varied, between five and ten firms picked at random. From then on, the selected firm was, effectively, making the link. That was where the line of communication would be traced back to.

She visited the first of her web-sites, Heavens Above, which was dedicated to stargazers, comet-prophets and all things pertaining to alien abductions and UFO sightings. Ken and Bryon, the two men – or boys, perhaps? – who ran the site and edited the on-line newsletter, were based in Urbana, Illinois. There was a discussion forum for visitors, each message being displayed in chronological order, next to the name of the sender and the time at which it was received. When the list grew too long, it was edited by Ken and Bryon, which was what had happened while Petra had been abroad. She prepared a new message of no significance; what mattered was the name she used.

Can anybody tell me whether they saw a strange light over Hamburg on December 3?
It occurred at about 2.45 a.m.
It was a white disk about twice the length of a commercial aircraft.
V. Libensky.

She ran two e-mail addresses, one through AOL as Rosario Alcon, the other through MSN as Andrew Smith. She checked those. There was nothing on either. Nor was there anything at any of the other three sites she used.

She switched off the screen.

I am not meant to be a human being any more. That's the whole point. Yesterday, I was a perfect machine. Designed by experts, built to specification and flawlessly programmed, I functioned just as I was supposed to. I followed instructions so deeply ingrained that they have become instinctive. I was automatic and lethal, an entity without conscience.

I take another sip of green tea and hope that the hangover will pass quickly. Last night, alone in this depressing flat, I drank vodka. Not to ease the anguish, it should be understood, but to ease the lack of it. I have been shocked by what I did, but I have experienced no regret. I have examined the consequences of what I did and concluded that every action I took was correct. And I have thought about the friends and relatives of the two that I killed and I know that they will be grief-stricken, although I can feel no grief for them. I can analyse anything but, emotionally, I am numb. If those who created me could see me now, they would be so pleased.

I have the heart of a computer.

17

There were several photographs of him, some in colour, some in black and white. He had thick, brown hair that was turning silver at the temples. The skin on his face was dark and creased, a combination that suggested too much sun. Against this background, his blue eyes looked paler than they probably were in reality. Petra checked his age. Forty-four. For a financier – for that was what he called himself – he looked in reasonable shape.

His father, Paul Serra, had been a dentist in Marseille while Claudette, his mother, had been raised on a small farm in Provence. Marc was the eldest of their three children; Luc, his brother – the middle child – had died of leukaemia, aged thirteen. Françoise, his sister, was married to a doctor in Lyon. Academically bright, Marc Serra had been a difficult child and had been expelled from two schools in Marseille, a fact that struck a chord of solidarity with Petra. Despite this, he achieved excellent grades and later attended INPG – the *Institut National Polytechnique de Grenoble* – before deciding to travel the world. He was supposed to have been away from France for a year but there was nothing further in the file until, aged twenty-nine, he landed a job at Crédit Lyonnais, where he stayed until he was thirty-three. That was when he moved to Banque Henri Lauder, a small, private firm with a single office in Zurich. Hardly a distinguished career move, it seemed, unless one's chosen career was not really in banking anyway.

He was still an employee of Banque Henri Lauder – a director, in fact – but this appeared to be more of a technicality than a working reality. In the last five years, he had taken two 'sabbaticals', each lasting a year. The file also claimed that he travelled extensively and spent less than a month a year in Switzerland. That in itself was unremarkable; there were plenty of businessmen who spent more nights in aircraft than with their wives. But the firm he was working for was not a multi-national with massive foreign interests.

Petra spread the contents of the file that had been inside the padded envelope across the living-room floor. As was so often the case with such dossiers, the gaps were more interesting than the solid information in-between. What had Serra done between INPG and Crédit Lyonnais? Where had he gone to for his two year-long sabbaticals? The file didn't say. It didn't even float theories.

Serra lived in Paris now. He had a small circle of friends, two of whom were members of the Communist Party, as he had been during his time in Grenoble. He was unmarried and, as far as could be ascertained, heterosexual; there was a list of old lovers in the file. Petra flinched. If their names were included it was because someone had imagined they might be valuable at some point in the future. More than most, she knew how painful sexual indiscretion could be.

Reza Mohammed's postgraduate course in Chemical Engineering and Chemical Technology had been paid for by the French-Arab Scholarship Society, which had also funded his living expenses, making small monthly contributions to the al-Sharif Students Hostel and to a current account at a branch of NatWest in Earls Court. The course money due to Imperial College arrived at the Society direct from Banque Henri Lauder. But the money for Mohammed's living expenses was paid into NatWest by the London branch of the Islamic Industrial Bank. This had been the same arrangement that Mustafa Sela had enjoyed during his time at Imperial.

The French-Arab Scholarship Society was based in Paris and had been established by Marc Serra in 1991. Its aim was 'to promote greater understanding between the French and Arab peoples, a hope best achieved through the mutual exchange of promising students'. The file said the exchange was lop-sided; ninety percent of the students were Arabs travelling to Europe, with only ten percent travelling in the opposite direction. Although the Society was French, the Arab students were dispersed throughout Europe, not just in France. It was not known how wealthy the Society was but, currently, they were sponsoring one hundred and thirty-five students across the EU.

Petra sifted through the remains of the file. There were pictures of Serra with directors of Telegenex, a French firm who designed missile guidance systems. There was a fuzzy shot of him on the back of a sun-drenched boat, a bleeding barracuda on the deck, sunburned men on either side of him, laughing. They were executives of Murray-Gardyne, a Canadian arms manufacturer with a completely illegal sideline in land-mine production, which occurred at a plant belonging to a wholly-owned subsidiary in Guadalajara, Mexico. In another photo, taken at a fund-raiser in Dallas, Serra was shaking hands with Jim Buchanan, a senior figure with the National Rifle Association.

Petra began to develop an instinctive feel for Serra. A bright and cultured man, he found it easy to move among others, to make contacts without ever having to step out of the shadows. Even in the photographs, he was, somehow, never the focus of attention. The list of his known associates was impressive but Petra was more interested in the way he adapted to any situation in which he found himself. Serra lied to everyone. Just like she did. Which was how she knew it was impossible to know Serra just by reading a file.

I lie on the sofa and watch TV, flicking through the channels. I see a game-show where contestants are trying to win a bright blue hatchback. I see a football match where teenage millionaires with bad haircuts roll around on the grass kissing each other. I see tomorrow's weather. I see EastEnders. *I see an arts pro-gramme where a young female author is talking aggressively about women taking control of their lives. She has an acerbic wit and uses it to denigrate men. She talks a lot about self-respect and empowerment and I am left to wonder what she's talking about.*

Women of my age go out to work; they do the nine-to-five for a pittance. They tolerate the Underground or the bus twice a day. They go out to cinemas and clubs with their friends. They bitch about each other, they stagger from one hopeless man to the next. They buy groceries when they're tired and cold and when it's the last thing they want to do on the way back home. They fumble for clean clothes in the morning just like the person they wake up next to. They're mothers and daughters. They're pro-viders and home-makers, they're professionals, they're terminally unemployed. They keep fit, they smoke thirty a day. They dream about two weeks in the sun and winning the National Lottery. They're not looking for Brad Pitt – they're looking for a man who's kind and honest and can make them laugh. Or they're not looking at all because life's too short to waste sorting out the good ones from the bad. They're fragile and mean, they're resili-ent and generous, they're anything you can imagine. They're normal.

Not like me. And that makes me sad because at this very moment, that's all I want to be.

The pavements of Piccadilly were congested but from the sea of faces, one emerged. Petra saw him before he saw her and prayed he wouldn't look her way, knowing that he would. Of all the directions available, his gaze chose hers.

Frank White.

The opening exchanges were a clumsy dance. *Hi, how are you? Nice to see you. What are you doing? Just picking up a few things. What about this weather? I know, but they say it'll get warmer by the weekend.* The words sounded shallower than usual, made more pointless by the words that were not being spoken.

Eventually, Petra brought it to a halt. She averted her gaze and said, 'Look, Mr White –'

'Frank.'

'Frank. Look, Frank, about yesterday, I'm –'

'What about it.?'

'I'm sorry for cutting you dead like that. I just –'

'It doesn't matter.'

Petra rubbed her eyes. 'Actually, it does. It matters to me.'

'Well, it was only a cup of coffee.'

'No, it wasn't,' Petra insisted. She saw a Pret A Manger thirty yards behind him. 'But why don't you let me buy *you* a cup of coffee? By way of an apology.'

'What, now?'

'Why not?'

It was crowded inside Pret A Manger but they managed to secure a couple of stools by the window overlooking the street. He ordered *latte*, she drank *mocha*. He'd been to Hatchards. He placed the peppermint bag beside his cup.

'What are you reading?' she asked.

'A history of Namibia.'

'Namibia?'

'I may be going there next month. I always like to try to read up on the places I visit.'

'What takes you there?'

'Work. I'm a geologist.'

'Really?'

'I work for a small firm of mining consultants. When a client wants to know what's underneath his feet, they send me to check it out.'

'So you travel a lot?'

'Yes.'

'Do you like that?'

'Actually, I do. A lot of people complain about it, but not me. I get restless if I'm in one place for too long. What about you?'

Petra had forgotten what it was like to have a real home.

'I move around more than I'd like, but that's the job.'

'Who do you work for?'

'Brillex-Martins.' He shook his head and she said, 'It's a Belgian chemical and pharmaceutical company.'

'What do you do for them?'

A pause. 'Trouble-shooting.'

'And that keeps you fully occupied?'

'Oh yes.'

'How long have you been in London?'

'About a fortnight. The first time we bumped into each other in the hall – I think that was my first day in the flat. And I've been away for the last week.'

He took a long sip from his paper cup of *latte*. 'I met your predecessor.'

Petra felt her pulse surge. 'My predecessor?'

'The man who lived in the flat before you. What was his name?'

Petra hoped she didn't look too flustered. *Take a deep breath in, let it out slowly. Look lost in thought. And then say*: 'To be honest, I'm not sure. I don't know who was here before me.'

Frank White shrugged and looked sympathetic. 'That's the way it is with these kinds of places, I guess. People come, people go, the furniture remains the same.'

The expression on his face was warm. Genuinely friendly. And just as she had felt fury towards him the last time they'd spoken, Petra now felt something equally inexplicable and fundamental. Sadness. She smiled and was sincere. 'You're right. Everywhere I go, I'm in exactly the same place as I was before.'

Six days after her return from Rio, at four in the morning, Petra found she couldn't sleep. First she was hot, then she was cold. Eventually, she got up and paced back and forth for a while, hoping boredom would tire her. When it failed to, she checked her computer. There was a hit on the Heavens Above site.

227

To V. Libensky.
My sister noticed the light on December 3 from my home,
in Zeven.
The newspaper said it was due to atmospheric conditions
but I don't believe that.
What do you think?
R. Julius.

Julius was one of three names that Petra had chosen for
a call sign. The sight of it sent a shiver through her. The
first letters of the first three words denoted the server – in
this case MSN – and the letters between the comma and
the full-stop of the first sentence provided the name:
inzeven; clearly an e-mail address that had been established for one conversation only. Whoever Julius was, he
or she could now be contacted at inzeven@MSN.com.

Using her Andrew Smith address, which was also at
MSN, Petra replied.

To R. Julius.
Got your message. Awaiting return enquiry.
V. Libensky.

She knew she was unlikely to receive a reply at that
hour but the petty thrill kept her alert in front of the
screen's blue glare for a while. There was no prospect of
a return to sleep now. She hit the hot-water switch,
stretched for an hour and then had a long bath. Afterwards,
she made breakfast. At twenty-past-eight, she got a message on Andrew Smith's e-mail.

To V. Libensky/Andrew Smith.
I understand we have a mutual interest in South America.
It would be good to meet you to discuss it. And to discuss
the future.
Is this possible?
R. Julius.

And so a dialogue began that lasted all morning. Oblique messages were received and sent, their contents construed carefully before a reaction was shaped. Proposal and counter-proposal and, eventually, an agreement. A rendezvous was scheduled for two days later, in Paris at the heart of the *huitième arrondissement*, on the junction of Boulevard Haussmann and Avenue Matignon. Petra tapped an affirmative response on to her screen and stared at the reply for a minute. The machine asked whether she wanted to send the message or not. Yes.

Then she called Alexander. Two hours later, they met at the Round Pound in Kensington Gardens. They headed for the fountains by Marlborough Gate on Bayswater Road. It was a cold morning, a low grey sky allied to a blustery wind that sent shivers through the branches of the trees. They passed a few hardy joggers, their heads in clouds of frozen breath, their cheeks the colour of red cabbage. One or two dog-owners were walking their pets. Apart from that, the gardens were almost empty.

Petra said, 'I've been through the material you gave me and I'm wondering what Serra's status is with other agencies.'

'Not high. Certainly, the French don't rate him. The closest shave he's had there has been two investigations for tax evasion, both of which came to nothing. In Germany, the BKA suspected him of associated involvement with a group of Ukrainian smugglers who were trying to sell nuclear material to Pakistani Muslim militants. But Serra was no part of it.'

'So nobody else knows what's in the file?'

'Most of that material could be gathered from public records of one sort or another. As for the rest, well maybe one agency knows a little piece, and another knows another piece. Or maybe they know most of it and they don't think it adds up to anything. Who can say? Besides, we can hardly share our information, can we? We don't even exist. And even if we did, I'm not sure we'd choose to spread it around.'

'I don't see why not.'

'Because you never know where such information will end up. In the past, any Irish information that MI5 or SIS shared with the CIA or FBI found its way to the IRA within forty-eight hours. Unlike the Americans, we don't feel that psychopaths who blow children to pieces in shopping centres are heroes in need of support – or Hollywood beatification, for that matter – so we keep our Irish information to ourselves. The same goes for anything related to Khalil, a category that includes Marc Serra. The last thing we need is for him to get spooked and disappear like Reza Mohammed.'

Petra stopped walking. *'What?'*

The wind ruffled Alexander's hair. 'Don't look so shocked. You must have known it was a possibility.'

Her initial instinct was to be angry, to be true to herself. But she quickly suppressed that. She had no doubt that Alexander's casual attitude was deliberate. He left nothing to chance. She assumed he wanted to provoke a reaction and so she chose to deny him.

'Where did he disappear?'

'Where so many disappear. In Athens.'

'What was he doing there?'

'We don't know. We supposed he was acting as a courier.'

'He'd left Imperial?'

'No. We contacted the college the following week and they said he was ill. Someone from the hostel had phoned to say that he had flu.'

'And that was it?'

Alexander nodded. 'We had him tailed to Heathrow where he boarded a flight for Athens. I arranged to have him placed under surveillance at the other end but they lost him.'

'When did this happen?'

Alexander lit a Rothmans. 'A little while ago.'

'When?'

'Six weeks ago.'

'Why didn't you tell me?'

Alexander shrugged. 'There didn't seem much point. Khalil is the one who matters to all of us. Without him, there is no Mohammed. At least, not for you. Besides, Mohammed will surface again. Men like him always do. You'll still get your chance, if you earn it.'

I don't really believe in female intuition. I think some people are intuitive and some people are not, and that the difference has nothing to do with gender. As I watch Alexander disappear through Marlborough Gate, the danger signals are going off in my brain like a fireworks display.

I know that the only thing keeping me alive is that Alexander has invested his organization's time and resources into me and that he is in no hurry to write that off. My fictitious insurance is now largely discredited. During my training, there were periods when my communication with the outside world was severed and there were no damaging consequences; no German tabloids claiming a 'world exclusive', no Malaysian TV network breaking sensational news, no related conspiracy theories drifting across the Internet. On the other hand, I suspect Alexander still believes I have something that is potentially damaging to him and, in that assumption, of course, he is correct. But an unspoken agreement has been reached between us: I tricked him into this and he hasn't forgotten or forgiven me, so I'd better not let him down.

Now, however, I suspect there is another agenda. A sub-agenda of which I have no knowledge. I know that I am expendable – that is a risk that comes with this life – but I am not prepared to be a sacrifice. I have no evidence to support such a suspicion but I don't need any. This is instinct and I need protection.

'Mr Bradfield?'

He turned round. They were outside the Victoria Arcade, pedestrians passing by them on either side.

'Who are you?' he demanded, his voice a rasp.

'You don't recognize me?'

A challenge offered, he squinted at her. She thought she saw some flicker of recognition but then he shook his head. 'No . . . not really, no. I don't think so.'

Petra found that interesting. His profession was invested in faces. Real ones, forged ones, those he was happy to remember and those he could not forget. She watched his eyes going over her, trying to recall the where and when.

'I had blonde hair the last time you saw me. I was thinner, too.' Somewhere deep inside the memory something was stirring, but it wasn't enough. 'I had a gun. You told me I shouldn't carry one unless I was prepared to use it.'

Cyril Bradfield's bushy white eyebrows arched. '*You?*'

'Yes. Me.'

'Were you the one who sent me the note?'

Petra nodded. The previous afternoon she had slipped an envelope through the letter-box in the front door of Bradfield's house in Longmoore Street. Inside, there had been a single sheet of paper. The message had been short and simple: *I'd like to talk to you. Tomorrow, the Victoria Arcade, at eleven in the morning. Yours, a friend.* At ten-to-eleven, he'd left his house in Longmoore Street and walked up Wilton Road. Petra had followed at a discreet distance. Once Bradfield was in the arcade, she'd kept one eye on him and one eye on anybody else who might be looking out for him. She didn't spot anyone. At quarter-past-eleven, he decided he'd had enough and stepped out of the arcade, which was when Petra called his name.

Bradfield was wearing an old jacket with leather patches on the elbows. To keep the chilly air at bay, his coat was buttoned to the throat, the collar upturned. His hands were thrust deep into age-worn bottle-green corduroy trousers.

'What do you want?'

'I want you to do some work for me.'

At first he seemed surprised, then relieved, then suspicious. 'What kind of work?'

232

Petra looked around, anxious not to be overheard. 'The kind that you do best. How about a cup of coffee? It's freezing out here.'

They settled at a table in a warm café, where condensation streamed down the window and where the petals on the plastic flowers were losing their colour after too many years in sunlight. Cyril Bradfield stirred two spoons of sugar into grey milky tea.

'What would you want?' he asked.

'Driving licences. Identity cards, too, where necessary.'

Bradfield opened his rusty tin of tobacco and peeled a paper from a packet of Rizlas. 'What nationality?'

Their voices were low, murmurs that were inaudible to anyone else over the radio that was on the Formica counter by the cash-register.

'I want three complete identities, not British. They can be English-speaking, though, or French-speaking, or German-speaking.'

'And all three require passports? Or just national documents?'

'Each one must have a passport. That's the most important thing.'

'What about your appearance? As you are now, or something different?'

'Basically, something close to how I am now.'

He peered over the top of his half-moons at her. 'In other words, something that can be used in a hurry?'

Petra held his gaze. This was not, she quickly realized, a devious moment. It was more an issue of trust. 'Yes. If I want something radically different, I'll ask for it later.'

Bradfield nodded, appreciating her candour and the fact that she had understood him. He licked the paper and sealed the cigarette. 'Do you want completely fresh identities or can they be stolen?'

'What are the pros and cons?'

'Well, with identity theft you assume a real person's identity. For one thing, it makes it possible for you to use their credit-rating to get bank accounts, loans and credit cards, which means you have money at your disposal. You can apply for a legitimate driving licence rather than buying a forged one.' Bradfield lit the cigarette and then examined the glowing tip. 'These days, identity theft is a growth industry in this country.'

If Petra ever needed to use one of the identities, there wouldn't be time to arrange bank loans. She would be using cash. 'I think fresh identities would be better.'

'Are you going to provide the blank documents or do you want me to do that?'

'I want you to do it.'

'Do you want stamps in the passports?'

'A few might be good.'

'Then you'll have to provide me with a list of the places I can include and the ones I can't.'

'Okay.'

Petra sipped some coffee. It was disgusting. Bradfield seemed happy with his tea. He said, 'I remember you now. Bit by bit, it's coming back. You've changed.'

If only you knew. She said, 'A little, maybe.'

Bradfield shook his head. 'A lot. I look at you now – the way you move, the way your eyes move – and I see some-one new.'

'I'm the same person on the inside.'

'I doubt it. From where I'm sitting, you look empty.'

She stood on Boulevard Haussmann, a rapier wind cutting through her woollen coat and all the clothes beneath. She had goose-bumps on her skin. In Rio, early winter had burned. In Paris, it froze.

She checked her watch. The car appeared from Avenue Matignon, a black Volkswagen Golf with a battered passenger door. Petra had expected something smarter. She had also expected Serra to be travelling with protection but he was alone. He leaned across and opened the passenger door.

'*Fräulein* Libensky?'

His tone was gently mocking. Hers was harsher. '*Herr* Julius?'

She got in and Serra pulled out into the stream of traffic without checking his mirrors. A car horn blared behind them.

'Lights in the sky over Hamburg?' he said.

'It was the first thing that came to mind.'

'I thought we could talk over lunch. Would that be okay?'

'I've already eaten but I'll watch you.'

'Well, we'll just get coffee, then. Are you staying in Paris?'

'No. I'll be leaving today.'

Petra had taken the Eurostar from Waterloo. The credit cards she was carrying had been issued in London to the name of Susan Branch. Her passport was in the same name but it was not the American one that had admitted her to Brazil. This one was Canadian.

They drove to Montmartre. Serra forced the Golf off the partially cobbled street and on to a crumbling pavement, ignoring the protests of a spindly, steel-haired woman who was loitering in a nearby doorway. She spat on the ground and cursed them. Serra led Petra down some steps to a café on the corner of a narrow street. It was gloomy inside; the walls were painted dark green, the floorboards were naked and worn smooth, the ceiling was stained by years of nicotine. Serra chose a table near the back, sat down and lit a cigarette.

'Are you sure you don't want anything to eat?'

'I'm sure.'

'Would you like a drink? Some wine, maybe? Or coffee?'

'I'll have a can of Coke.' She looked up at the waiter who had shuffled over to their table. 'And I'll have it unopened.'

Serra smiled. 'No cigarettes, no food? Only drinking from unopened cans? You don't have to be so cautious, you know.'

Petra had already identified three potential escape routes from the café. As for weapons, there were knives and forks, cheap tumblers, an ashtray and the book of matches that was in it, a two-pronged candlestick, salt and pepper pots, toothpicks in a glass dispenser, the pencil wedged behind the waiter's ear and the corkscrew hanging on a cord from his belt. She looked around. The staff looked diffident in a typically Parisian fashion, as though they would sooner boil their customers than serve them.

Petra was keen to start and finish. 'So, what is this meeting for?'

'It's partly curiosity. I wanted to meet you. To be face to face with the woman without a face.'

'Just so you know, I'm allergic to small-talk and flattery.'

'And it's partly business. I wanted to meet the woman who's cost me so much money. Marin and I did a lot of mutually lucrative business together. When he died, that died.'

'I'm sorry about that.'

'Not as sorry as me.'

Petra shrugged in an off-hand way. 'This arrangement you had with Marin was purely business?'

'Yes.'

'Well so was mine. From one to another, I'm sure you can understand that. It was nothing personal.'

The waiter returned with coffee and Coke. There was an uneasy silence until he had retreated. Then Serra said, 'You should know that I'm talking to you on behalf of a client.'

'Who?'

'I can't say. You know how it is.'

'Go on.'

'He wishes to retain your services.'

'What services?'

'He's heard about you, about what you did to Marin – not from me, I might add – and he's also heard that you are – how shall I say it? – *available*?'

Available? Petra had a history of availability. Especially for clients who wished to remain anonymous.

'There is a man in New York,' Serra continued. 'A prominent man who has become a problem for my client.'

Petra opened the Coke can. 'I don't think so.'

Serra looked surprised, which she found strange. What had he realistically expected? 'You won't even hear the offer?'

'It's not a question of money. Besides, I never negotiate. I fix a price and that's it.'

'Okay, so what is your price?'

'I don't work for anonymous clients.'

'He'd be generous.'

'I told you, it's not a question of money. I'm sure you'll find someone else to take care of it. Now if you don't have anything else to say, we're finished.'

Anxious to keep her, Serra said, 'Why don't I speak to my client and see if I can get him to change his mind?'

Petra shrugged. 'If you want. Who's the target?'

'I think that should wait, don't you?'

'If I have an objection to the target there will be no deal anyway. In which case, going back to your client will be a waste of everyone's time.'

Serra ground out his cigarette while he considered this. Then he nodded in agreement. 'Okay. The man's name is Giler. Leon Giler.'

18

Margaret, Alexander's secretary, was wrapping a small
box in pink paper. In silence, Petra watched her fasten the
box with green ribbon. When Margaret looked up, she
blushed, her cheeks turning the same colour as her blouse.

'It's for my niece,' she explained. 'A birthday present.
It's her first watch.'

Through a pair of binoculars was how Petra had last
seen her own niece. Standing on the verge of the road
overlooking Falstone, she had watched her family mourn
her. She remembered now that Alexander had said that
Jane was pregnant again. The sudden lurch in the pit of
her stomach was surely guilt; she had forgotten about the
pregnancy. Now she wondered whether she was, at
twenty-three, an aunt again. And if so, to what? A boy or
a girl? Or twins, perhaps?

Margaret was leaning across her desk. She seemed to
sense the turmoil and took hold of Petra's hand and
squeezed it. 'You take care of yourself, Stephanie.'

The look in her eyes said more than that. Petra thanked
her and entered Alexander's office.

It was three days since her trip to Paris and it had been a
relaxing time. She had exercised her body and eased her
mind. With no phone calls to wait for, the days had been
hers. She'd read two books for pleasure, which was a long-
lost pastime, and, on a morning of persistent drizzle, she'd
walked through Regent's Park before visiting the British
Museum and the Tate Gallery, neither of which was familiar
to her. She was a tourist in her home town and she liked it.

When Alexander finally managed to look at her, he
winced. Petra supposed it was the clothes she was wearing.

Beneath her tatty, corduroy jacket, which was far too large for her, she wore a black sweatshirt with a day-glo green slogan across the chest:

WOMEN WHO SEEK EQUALITY WITH MEN LACK AMBITION.

Or perhaps it was the black boots he didn't like. Or the khaki combat trousers. It was hard to tell. Alexander himself looked dapper enough in a Paul Smith suit and a chocolate polo-neck.

'We have a problem,' he said. 'Do you want to sit down?'

'Am I going to need to?'

Alexander sat down himself. 'Two weeks ago, a Mossad team lifted a young Muslim – an Iranian – off the streets in Rome. Within forty-eight hours, they had him back in Israel ready for interrogation.'

'That sounds nasty. Who is he?'

'Abbas Karim Kassir. He's part of Hizb'allah's military wing, operating just beneath the military command council. For the last two years, he's been stationed in Rome as a representative of the Islamic Cultural Association at the Islamic Republic's embassy. Last month, though, he flew to Zurich and guess who he met there?'

Petra shrugged. 'You tell me.'

'Gustavo Marin. Just before Marin went back to Brazil for his winter break. Needless to say, the Israelis were keen to find out what they had discussed and, in this at least, they were successful. Kassir had placed an order with Marin for a delivery of SAM-7 anti-aircraft missiles. Their problem was that they were unable to discover where and when the order was to be delivered, or how large it was. So they decided to snatch Kassir and ask him in person. He'd been a thorn in their sides for years, so they figured they'd be doing themselves and the rest of the world a favour. And once their specialists got to work on him, he turned out to be quite productive.'

239

'You've started talking about Kassir in the past tense.'

Alexander opened his hands to her. 'Well, it's no secret that Israeli methods of interrogation can sometimes be a little . . . *vigorous*.'

'I like a bit of understatement.'

'Mossad is pleased that Marin has also been removed from the equation but they have not been especially forthcoming with the results of their interrogation of Kassir. Nevertheless, we have learned that he had connections with Khalil. He never met him personally, but Kassir was under the command of Sheikh Ismail Mahmud Hussayn who also controlled Khalil, until Khalil decided that he didn't want to be controlled at all. Despite that, lines of communication continued to exist between Khalil and Hussayn, as they did between Hussayn and Kassir. Shortly before his death, Kassir revealed that Khalil is currently planning a spectacular terrorist assault on the West but he didn't know what it involved or when it was going to happen.'

'That could've been a bluff.'

'The Israelis don't think so. Apart from employing some rather crude and destructive chemical processes on Kassir, they've also had elements of his claim confirmed by independent sources, including something that Kassir revealed right at the last. There is a phrase that is associated with Khalil's plan. We don't know whether it refers to the operatives who will be used, or whether it is the name of the plan itself. But the phrase is: Sons of Sabah.'

'Sons of Sabah?'

Alexander rose from his desk and led Petra out of his office. They passed Margaret, who smiled at them, and then walked down the narrow corridor to the landing. Alexander pressed the brass button on the panel and the ancient cage-lift coughed into life.

'The Sons of Sabah,' he said, 'are named after Hassan Sabah, who is considered by many to have been the man who developed political murder as a crucial element in the acquisition and maintenance of political power.'

'I don't think I've heard of him.'

'Unless you're a student of Islamic history, that's not entirely surprising. He lived in the eleventh century.'

The lift arrived. Alexander opened the door and drew the brass cables to one side. They both stepped in. He pressed the button marked 'five' – there wasn't a fifth floor – and, rather than rising, the lift began to descend.

'Hassan Sabah has a special place in our hearts,' Alexander said, 'since he gave us the word "assassin".'

'How?'

'Assassin comes from the word *hashasheen*, which means, literally, smokers of hashish. Sabah's followers – the *Fedayeen* – used to smoke hashish. Not understanding the chemical properties involved, they mistook their hallucinations for glimpses of Paradise, which made it a lot easier to kill in the name of Allah.'

The lift halted at a subterranean level. Alexander led Petra along another narrow corridor but this one retained none of the creaking character of the one above. The floor was stone, the walls were painted matt cream. They went through a door at the end into a small conference room with an oval table at its centre. There was a screen at one end of the room and a bank of nine television monitors on the left. An Indian woman whom Petra knew only as Rosie was waiting for them. She wore black pleated trousers, a purple shirt and a silk wrap. Her glasses were the same Calvin Klein design that Petra had worn as Marina on the night she left Rio.

Rosie dimmed the lights and, on the large screen at the end of the room, an image of a man appeared. It was a head-and-shoulders shot. He was heavy-featured and hirsute. Despite thinning on the crown and despite the rest of his scalp being neatly clipped, thick, black hair was exploding out of the top of his shirt. He looked like a man who needed to shave hourly.

Petra peered at Alexander through the partial darkness. 'Abbas Karim Kassir?'

241

'No. Leon Giler.'

'I don't get it.'

Alexander was lighting a Rothmans. 'Kassir had links with Marc Serra but Mossad don't know that. They're looking for a Dane named Preben Olsen. Kassir revealed that he'd learned about Sons of Sabah from Sheikh Ismail Mahmud Hussayn. Mossad tried to find out who else knew about it. Kassir could only come up with one name. Preben Olsen. Kassir knew that Olsen had visited Hussayn twice in Tehran and that he was something to do with Sons of Sabah.'

'How?'

'I don't know. Maybe Hussayn told him. Or maybe Olsen actually met Kassir and told him himself. Who can say? The point is, we know that Preben Olsen is, in fact, Marc Serra. It's one of the identities that he uses. Mossad do not know this. No one does apart from us.'

Petra looked back at the picture on the screen. 'I still don't get it.'

'You're going to have to take the contract for Leon Giler.'

She stared at him and a stalemate of silence ensued until she eventually broke it. 'You're not serious.'

He said, 'You should know me better by now.'

'I was supposed to get close to Serra to see if it was going to lead somewhere. I was supposed to agree to consider taking a job from him – which is what I did – and then to reject it on the grounds of prior commitment. Or something equally vague.'

'The circumstances have changed.'

'Maybe that's true but I didn't join your organization to start killing third parties who have nothing to do with Khalil or Reza Mohammed.'

'You joined this organization to do exactly what it tells you to do. Those were the conditions. And frankly, after what you did to Marin and Ferreira in Rio, I find your reluctance unconvincing.'

'That was self-defence.'

242

'Really? According to the statement that Luiso, Marin's useless bodyguard, gave to the local police, you shot Marin in cold blood.'

'It was in the heat of the moment.'

Alexander's irritation began to show through. 'We're straying from the point, which is this: you've made contact with Serra and now that his links to Khalil have been confirmed, we need to ensure that you keep close to him.'

'By killing an innocent?'

'Leon Giler is hardly an innocent.'

'Let me guess. Unpaid parking fines?'

Alexander drew deeply on his cigarette, letting the smoke linger in his lungs, letting words linger in his throat. Rosie avoided looking at either of them, and busied herself with the file on her lap.

'You'll take this contract. I want you to close it as soon as you possibly can. I want you to impress Serra. Or rather, his client.'

'You don't know that the client's Khalil.'

'Not for sure. But I've a strong suspicion it is. Khalil has a personal history with Leon Giler. And it makes perfect sense for him to put this job out to tender. For one thing, Giler spends most of his time in the States and Khalil wouldn't want to take the risk of travelling there for this kind of work.'

Petra glanced at the face on the screen again. She knew there would be no denying Alexander – not here, not now – so she nodded her compliance. Alexander said, 'Rosie has gathered some information for you, which she'll now take you through. You'll get a more detailed briefing on Giler when you've confirmed the contract with Serra.' He rose to his feet. 'There's one more thing. I don't know how efficient Serra's network is but he may place you under surveillance so you're not to come here any more. Not unless you have clearance. The less contact there is between us, the better. Use the usual channels and wait for instructions.'

*   *   *

I am in the darkness looking at the screen. It is a larger room, a larger screen and a darker darkness; I am in a cinema. Frank White is sitting next to me. When I returned from Magenta House I found a note that had been slipped beneath my door. Marina, I was wondering whether you would like to come to the cinema with me later today. Call me when you get back. Yours, Frank. *The message seemed shy and awkward. I liked that. Besides, in the age of mobile phones and pagers, it's rather nice to get a piece of paper slipped beneath the door.*

I have seen Frank once since our cup of coffee on Piccadilly. It was yesterday. We met in the entrance hall. I was going out, he was coming in. We should have had a conversation that was typical of two people on their way to do something else; a few pleasant exchanges and then a 'well, I must be getting on'-type comment. Instead, we talked for quarter of an hour, stranded, half in the building, half out. I can't remember a single thing we said. But I do remember that when we realized how long we had been there, we were both embarrassed and that we both tried to laugh it off. Unsuccessfully.

The cinema we are in is the Curzon Mayfair on Curzon Street. The film we are watching is part of a Kieslowski retrospective. It's Three Colours Red. *Sitting here in the darkness makes me feel like a schoolgirl truant once again. I am reminded of boys in the back row, of hungry tongues and clumsy fingers, of stolen cigarettes. When I was Lisa, I used to go to the West End cinemas in the afternoons. It was cheaper and the theatres were emptier and that was where I found solitude when I needed it. Sometimes, I went to the cinema to hide, to nurse my bruises in the darkness, to stare into nowhere in a place where no one would notice.*

Afterwards, Frank suggests dinner and we go to a small bistro in Shepherd Market where I eat sea bass baked in salt, and where Frank eats seared tuna. We drink lusty, Sicilian red wine. I am quite cold towards him and he doesn't seem to mind this; it really appears he has no expectations. Part of me is offended but the greater part is relieved. I don't feel any pressure and I don't believe that he does, either. We talk easily in the knowledge that this isn't going anywhere. On our way back home, he asks

if he can cook for me one night. I say I don't know – can he
cook for me? He doesn't get it at first, so I'm embarrassed. And
when he does, he recognizes how poor the joke is and he's embar-
rassed. So I cut my losses – our losses – and say yes, that would
be nice.

They met at the Jardins du Luxembourg on a freezing
afternoon when the grey air was so damp it felt like the
roadside slush that snow becomes in any city. Marc Serra
was wearing a long, fawn, cashmere overcoat that Petra
instinctively disliked. She was wearing a North Face snow-
jacket and faded jeans tucked into thick grey socks that
were themselves tucked into sturdy walking boots. They
walked among the chestnut groves and the formal terraces.
The coldness gave them a degree of privacy.

'Can I ask you something personal?' asked Serra.

'You can ask.'

'How old are you?'

'How old do you think I am?'

'I'm not sure. That is to say, my sources aren't sure.
Around thirty-two, maybe? Some say thirty, others say
thirty-five . . .'

'But you say thirty-two?'

'Like I said, I'm not sure. You look kind of young for
thirty-two.'

'And you look kind of old for forty-four but I'm not
going to hold it against you.'

Petra was pleased to see that the remark stung and she
could tell that Serra was surprised that she had bothered
to discover his age. She had suspected him of vanity from
the first moment she had seen him. She wondered what
he would have guessed as her true age. Twenty-seven,
twenty-eight? These days, when she looked in the mirror,
she didn't feel that her face reflected twenty-three. Too
much had happened in the four years since nineteen for
her to still look twenty-three.

They stood at the edge of the Grand Bassin, the octagonal

pond at the centre of the terraces. Petra watched clouds of grey pigeons explode from the tops of the trees to her right. They circled her twice and then wheeled away towards the Palais du Luxembourg which seemed to be floating on a bed of mist.

'Has your client changed his mind?' she asked.

Serra lit a cigarette. 'I regret that he hasn't, no. Have you changed yours?'

'Yes.'

Serra seemed genuinely puzzled. 'Yes?'

Petra nodded. 'But I need to know about timing. Is there a schedule?'

'As quickly as possible.'

'Does it matter where it happens?'

'No. Our information says he will be in New York for the next fortnight. If it could be done by then, that would be perfect.'

'We'll see.'

'How will you do it?'

'I'm not sure yet.'

Serra exhaled smoke slowly. 'My client will be very pleased to hear this news.'

'I doubt it. His decision to remain anonymous is going to prove expensive.'

'How expensive?'

'One million dollars American. Half now, half on completion.'

'A million dollars? For Giler?'

'Correct.'

'That's ridiculous! It's ... it's ... *extortionate*!'

'So take me to court.'

Serra began to gesticulate with his hands. 'But you could walk up to him on the street. You could get him anywhere. His bodyguard is almost as out of shape as he is.'

'I'm aware of all this.'

'He's a businessman, not the President of Israel. Be reasonable.'

'This isn't a reasonable business.'

'I could get some climbing-the-walls junkie to do this for a hundred bucks. It's not an assassination, it's an errand.'

'Then get an errand-boy. My price is a million dollars. And that's final.'

Serra looked disconsolate and shook his head. He muttered something beneath his breath that Petra didn't hear. They turned away from the pond and headed for the nearest exit, which was close to the station. When Serra finally gave his answer, Petra was silent for a moment. She had fully expected – and hoped – to be rejected. Serra's capitulation could only mean one thing: he had to hire her. She could have asked for two million and he would have agreed.

'How can you justify a million?' he wanted to know.

'Easily. This is a job I don't need or want. Think of me as a lawyer who hires himself out to wealthy clients but who also does a lot of *pro bono* work. The fat fees I charge my wealthy clients subsidize the *pro bono* work. Now think of yourself as a wealthy client. It shouldn't be too hard. You look like one.'

Serra glared at her for a moment and then smiled. Perhaps he thought she was teasing him – she wasn't – or perhaps he liked women who talked back.

'And where would you want the money deposited?'

Blankness fell over her. She had never even considered this. 'What?'

'The bank? The account number? For the first five hundred thousand dollars?'

I am buying clothes in Joseph and I am not enjoying it because I am buying for Marina. She wears garments that are well cut, she wears black a lot, she wears suits, she wears designer labels. These are not the things that Stephanie and Petra choose to wear. Their preference for scruffy clothes is, perhaps, the one thing they have in common. Apart from the body they share.

A skeletal assistant runs a Gold Amex in the name of Marina

247

Gaudenzi through the machine. The total comes to one thousand four hundred and eighteen pounds. Absurd, definitely. Rather like charging a million dollars to kill a businessman. Or eighty pounds to let someone fuck you.

When I'm Marina, I am a single Swiss Catholic, aged thirty-one, although the way I behave might give the impression that I am forty. I have two sisters – one older, one younger. I have a degree in chemistry and a love for classical music, particularly Sibelius. I like sailing and was taught by my father, who had a boat on Lake Geneva. When I speak English, I speak it with the same accent as Petra. Unlike Petra, I like to wear scent – always Chanel.

The sales assistant is placing my clothes in two bags. I can tell that she doesn't like me. It's mutual. She's a snob, she doesn't believe I belong in this shop despite the money I've just spent. I don't mind because she's right. This is strictly Marina's territory. I find it difficult being her and have started to ignore some parts of her. She never touches alcohol but I drink it occasionally. My temper sometimes betrays her self-control. And as for Sibelius, I'm happy to listen to his music from time to time, but not as often as I choose to listen to Radiohead or Manic Street Preachers, and that's something that Marina Gaudenzi would never do.

I leave the shop with a bag in each hand. I'm not quite sure who I am as I walk along the pavement but what I do know is that the clothes I am carrying belong to someone else.

According to the Fortune 500, Leon Giler was worth $3.5 billion. Petra sat cross-legged on her living-room carpet and spread the documents before her. Newspapers had provided Giler's initial wealth; in 1977, he'd acquired his first daily in Baltimore. Others soon followed in Washington, Pittsburgh, Philadelphia and New York. In the Eighties, Giler had moved into radio and television and, in 1989, he'd fulfilled a childhood dream when he'd purchased an ailing Hollywood studio. Although his was essentially a sentimental investment, his business methods were notoriously ruthless and, for a while, his name passed into common usage. Those who were unceremoniously fired from their jobs talked of 'getting Gilered'. Now, he was carving a new fortune for himself in satellite communication.

Apart from a mansion on Long Island and two Manhattan apartments, he also owned an apartment in Paris, a small Greek island, a permanent suite at the Dorchester in London and a ranch in New Mexico that he had never visited. Giler was ostentatious yet hated publicity. A hugely generous contributor to charitable causes, he was a famous penny-pincher when it came to accounting of any sort, from corporate level down to a child's allowance. He liked to portray himself as the respectable family man, the loving husband and ideal father, yet he couldn't resist gorging himself on hookers. To Petra, Giler seemed like a man who was at war with himself.

This inner struggle seemed to extend particularly to the question of his Jewishness. He was not an observer of the *halacha*, the corpus of Jewish law, and this appeared to have left him with a guilt he could not assuage, no matter how hard he tried. He was a contributor to New York's Yeshiva University and paid for large amounts of housing in apartment blocks in Borough Park, Brooklyn, a predominately Jewish section of the city. He was an active sponsor of the Lubavitcher Hasidim in New York and was also a patron of the Jewish Museum.

Giler had also provided financial support for the Israeli government's programme of building Jewish settlements in the Occupied Territories. Those who had compiled the file suggested that this might be the reason that Khalil wanted Giler killed. Petra paused. Was that enough? It was certainly a contentious issue but she found it hard to believe that someone like Khalil – whoever he was – would order the execution of someone like Giler over such an issue. In the end, it made no difference. Serra had hired Petra to do a job. His reasons were a private matter and nothing to do with her. She was simply a contractor.

Later, she came across a photograph of Giler's wife and their five children, four boys and a girl. She turned them over and laid them face-down on the carpet.

The whore's golden tongue had been replaced by no tongue at all. Or so it seemed. Petra was standing in Frank White's living room as he poured her a glass of chilled Saint-Véran. White wasn't saying anything either but he seemed easier with it, which was strange because Petra considered herself an expert at awkward silences.

She glanced at her watch. It was four days since she had met with Serra in Paris. This time tomorrow, she would be in Manhattan. The thought of it made the hairs stand up on her arms.

On a coffee table at the centre of the living room there were several ornamental rock samples. She picked one up. It was turquoise in colour and shot through with veins of rust. The sample was surprisingly light and was jagged, its shape not entirely dissimilar to a chunk of quartz.

'Beryl,' said Frank, as he handed Petra her glass.

'What?'

'That's beryl. One of the beryllium minerals, which are used in alloys of copper, nickel and aluminium. They're used in X-ray tubes and nuclear reactors. Emerald and aquamarine are the gemstone varieties, but beryl is the commercial source of beryllium, although if it's clear and transparent it can also be gemstone. I got that piece in Mozambique.'

'Ah yes. The geologist. The man who checks what's under people's feet.'

'A long way under, usually.'

She put the beryl down and picked up another sample, which was vaguely cylindrical in shape and dirty yellow in colour. 'What's this?'

'Apatite.'

'I'm sure you could make a bad joke out of it with a name like that.'

'You'd find it more useful if you were to make fertilizers, pesticides or cleansing products out of it. Or even smoke-bombs. It comes from the Kola Peninsula in northern Russia, near the border with Finland.'

'You've been there too?'

He nodded. 'I've collected all these pieces personally.'

Petra put the sample back on the table. 'So it's sort of like a photograph album, then? Except with these, you can feel them. It must be nice to be able to feel the places that you've been to.'

Frank was wearing black jeans and black shoes. His shirt was bottle-green. Even though Marina would not have done so, Petra wore jeans too because she had not wanted to dress up. No effort equalled no encouragement which, in the end, equalled no nasty surprises. So there was no little skirt, no skimpy top, no jewellery, not even make-up. Just her jeans, a navy jersey and a coarse-bristled brush rushed once through her hair; she was Petra pretending to be Marina dressed as Petra.

Frank put on music that she didn't recognize but liked. She looked at the CD cover. John Martyn, 'Solid Air', released in 1973, before she was even born. But not before Marina was born. It was at moments like this that Petra had to remind herself that for Frank, Marina was who she had to be.

In the kitchen, she saw something that was painful to her; Frank preparing food. The knife was a blur, the thud of the blade on the board a drum-roll. In seconds, the vegetables were sliced and cut. She could have been watching her father. She could have been watching Keith Proctor. She held her wine glass tight to her breasts. Frank caught her staring at him. 'Is everything all right?'

She nodded. 'I was somewhere else.' And someone else.

Frank's flat was a little larger than hers and he had breathed some life into it. Apart from the rock samples, there were pieces of real furniture, like the oak table at which they sat to eat. There were also enlarged photographs

251

that he had taken around the world; astonishing skies over desolate stretches of Patagonia, tidal waves of golden sand in the Sahara, the sun haemorrhaging over Siberia. She noticed that there were no people in any of the shots. She thought of her own flat, and of all the other places, and found the comparison depressing. But this was not an evening for decline.

The hours melted slowly.

Frank brought food to the table and, when they were finished, removed the plates. When Petra tried to help he told her it was unnecessary, so she remained seated and watched him work. They finished the Saint-Véran and he opened a bottle of Nuits-St-Georges. Later, he placed a board of cheese between them, next to a bowl of fruit. They were virtually silent while they ate and, even when they talked, silences peppered their conversation. And as the night grew older, these silences became longer and easier.

Frank had been a father once. As a young man, he had fallen in love with a drama student named Karen Cornwell. They were different people entirely; she was impulsive and hot-tempered, he was serious and balanced. But they were in love so it didn't seem to matter. Six months later, Karen was pregnant. She was thrilled, he was shocked. But once he was over the shock, he was happy. Not because he wanted to be a father especially – he didn't – but because he had brought joy to Karen. He proposed to her and she stalled him. Not until after the baby was born, she said. She wanted to be sure he was marrying her for *her*, not just because she was pregnant. He agreed to be patient. Three months after the birth of Rosa, he proposed again. It was too early, Karen said. They needed to wait a while, to get over the sleepless nights, to settle down into a routine. Once again, he agreed. Six months later, she landed her first major acting part in a soap opera. A month after that, she moved in with one of the show's writers.

Frank finished this story by saying, 'And ever since then,

I haven't been able to watch any kind of soap opera on TV.'

Petra frowned. 'Is that true?'

Frank grinned; it was the first time she had seen him do that. 'No, of course not. I don't watch them because they're crap.'

Petra grinned too. She took an orange from the bowl and began to peel it. 'Do you still see her?'

'Karen?'

'Yes.'

'No. She lives in Paris now. She's married to a French film producer. I'm glad to say it didn't work out with the writer.'

'What about Rosa?' Petra asked, suddenly remembering that Rosa was the name of one of her mothers. Rosa Holl, later to become Rosa Reuter. Petra wondered whether the woman had ever actually existed or whether, as with so much else, she was simply another illusion, another Magenta House lie.

Frank said, 'Rosa died three years ago.'

Not a flinch. His answer was as flat as the kick in Petra's stomach was pronounced.

'Oh no, I'm sorry . . .'

He shrugged. 'It was a motor accident in Paris. She was on a bus. A school trip. The driver lost control and there was a pile-up. None of the children were wearing seat-belts. You know how it is on buses.' Frank refilled his glass. 'That was five years ago this October.'

'Five?'

'She was in a coma for two years. At first, the French doctors thought there might be a chance that she would make some kind of recovery. But in the end, there was nothing. Persistent vegetative state is what they call it here, I think. Karen and I had to take the decision to let her die.'

'God . . .'

Again, Frank shrugged. 'That sort of decision gets made over time, not in the moment.'

Petra reached across the table and placed her hand upon his. 'I didn't mean to pry.'

'You didn't pry. You asked a question, that's all. I don't mind talking about it if people don't mind hearing about it.'

Frank had a larger build than Keith Proctor. His face told of the places he had seen as surely as the rocks he had brought back from them. Lashed by wind, burned by sun, stung by salt and cracked by ice, his travels were etched into him. In motion, he looked powerful but clumsy, but Petra saw that this impression was incorrect because he was as nimble with precision movements as Proctor had been. Despite the differences between them, there were startling similarities. When she watched him making coffee it was *déjà vu*; Frank took the same care that Proctor had during the ritual of preparation.

When she glanced at her watch for the second time since entering his flat, it was ten-past-two in the morning. She looked up and saw Frank watching her.

'I have to go,' she told him. 'I haven't even packed yet.'

He nodded. She rose to her feet, still clutching her glass. The wine had stoked a small fire within her. She was pleasurably numb, not drunk; the feeling was infinitely better than drunkenness and she could not remember alcohol being so kind to her.

At Frank's front door, she thanked him for a lovely night and handed the glass back to him.

That was when he said, 'Marina, can I kiss you?'

Who?

'I need some information.'

'Type and level?'

'Person. A Grade Two profile.'

'Name?'

'White. First initial, F for Frank. I don't know about any other names.'

The male voice on the other end of the phone wanted

254

to know what else she knew about him. Apart from the fact that he was a geologist – or at least said he was – and that they lived in the same building, nothing. When the call was over, she replaced the receiver on the cradle and sat in the darkness. It was half-past-three.

She picked up a framed photograph from the table. Who were these people? Actors? She held it close to the window, allowing their faces to be illuminated by moonlight. A man with his arm around a woman's waist. They smiled for the camera. The background was out of focus; a house surrounded by pine trees. These were her parents. Marina's made-to-order Gaudenzi parents. They had been waiting for her when she moved into the flat. She'd already known their names – Alberto and Francine – but it had been a surprise to discover their faces.

Petra spun round and hurled the frame across the room. It hit the wall and shattered. Then she prowled through the flat in darkness, collecting the other 'family' photographs that had been left for her. She tore them into pieces and threw them into the bin.

Marina, can I kiss you?

She'd wanted Frank to say, 'Petra, can I kiss you?' Or, even better, 'Stephanie, can I kiss you?' And, of course, she'd wanted to say that he could. But she'd been too scared to do that. In his eyes, she saw the kiss, the knife, the blood seeping from the cut across the palm. In Frank's eyes, she'd seen Proctor walking away from the hospital into the night.

So she'd reverted to type. She could actually feel her heart chilling, her stare turning to stone. It was easier to be this way, to shut everything down until it was impossible to feel anything. Now, alone in her cold flat, she saw how she'd treated Frank the same way she'd treated Proctor. And now, as then, she shuddered at the memory of it, hardly able to believe she'd let the words escape from her throat.

'It was nice wine, Frank. But not that nice,' she'd replied.

And when he'd opened his mouth to speak – to protest, perhaps, or maybe just to say something nice – she'd cut him off. 'What did you think? That you'd get me drunk and fuck me? Is that what you thought?'

She couldn't cry; the coldness in her would have frozen tears to ice.

At quarter-to-four, she rang Magenta House and cancelled her request for the profile.

19

Petra answered the phone. It was a woman's voice on the other end. 'Miss Shepherd?'

'Yes?'

'This is reception. Mr Brewster is here to see you.'

'Thank you. Please send him up to my room.'

Petra moved from the bedroom to the sitting room and peered out of the window on to East 63rd Street. A garbage truck was blocking the road and the drivers of the cars that were forming a queue behind it were leaning on their horns. There was a knock on the door.

Andrew Wilson was wearing a grey anorak over a shabby grey suit. He wore a brown polyester shirt, a scarlet paisley tie and a pale blue V-neck jersey. An Englishman in New York, he couldn't have looked more out of place.

He was immensely tall, six-foot-five and skinny, with a build incapable of grace. He had thick, wild, wavy hair that was maturing from light brown to silver. Petra wondered whether he'd run a comb through it since arriving in New York. Tortoiseshell glasses with thick lenses distorted bloodshot eyes. Wilson's skin was as grey as his suit and his teeth were the essence of an American nightmare.

'You should see the place I'm in,' he muttered, his jealous gaze absorbing the furniture, the antiques, the Persian carpet, the two vases of roses, the sheer size of the room. 'Who are you?'

'Elizabeth Shepherd. A management consultant.'

'Management consultant, eh?'

'Yes. Feeding off juicy expense accounts and corporate fat. What about you?'

'Simon Brewster, a secondary school teacher from Brent on a short winter break.'

'Well, that's why I'm staying at the Lowell and you're staying in a cesspit. Coffee?'

'Tea, please.'

Of course. One only had to look at him to see that. Petra rang Room Service.

Wilson said, 'Giler's got an enormous mansion out on Long Island, near Centerport, overlooking Long Island Sound. That's where his family spend most of their time and it's very heavily protected. He's also got two places here in New York. There's a family apartment on Park Avenue – I say apartment but it's actually the top two floors of the block – and he has another place on Fifth Avenue. That's where you'll do it.'

'Why?'

'Because that's where he fools around. His wife doesn't even know the place exists.'

'He has a mistress?'

'No. He uses call-girls. Which is how we'll get you in.'

Petra's stomach turned. She wondered if Wilson knew anything of her past. 'How?'

'Easy. Giler always uses the same escort agency, Premier International. We'll get the phone in his Fifth Avenue apartment fixed so that when he calls Premier International's number it gets diverted.'

'Supposing he calls from somewhere else?'

'He won't. His routine's pretty stable. He goes to the apartment in the early afternoon. As soon as he arrives, he calls the agency. Then he has a shower and a drink so that he's nice and relaxed. An hour after phoning Premier International, the call-girl arrives.'

'How will you get the phone fixed?'

'There's someone who can get us inside at NYNEX.'

'What about in the apartment? What kind of protection can I expect to find?'

'That's the beauty of this option. Giler trades security

258

for privacy when he's there. He doesn't like to be watched or heard. His bodyguard stays downstairs and checks the call-girl in the lobby before she gets into the lift. Then he chats to the porter or goes and waits for Giler in the limo.'

Petra thought about it for a second. 'Does Giler have a type of girl that he prefers?'

'Blonde and busty.'

What a surprise, thought Petra. Having seen a few photographs of him, she would have guessed as much. Stereotyping didn't become stereotyping without being rooted in fact.

'I'm not going to dye my hair so I'll need a wig. Can you arrange that?'

'Yes.'

'As for being busty, well, these'll have to do.' Wilson blushed violently. Petra said, 'Besides, he won't get close enough to know they're not big enough. What kind of security has the block got?'

Petra awoke with a jolt. She scrambled for the light and it took her several seconds to remember where she was, who she was and what she was doing. Then she thought about Frank and the way she had treated him. Her skin crept. She rolled over in the large double bed. It was half-past-four in the morning. Her body-clock had not yet adjusted to New York.

At six, she went through a stretching routine and then relaxed in a hot bath for twenty minutes. Afterwards, she lost herself in a large dressing-gown and ordered breakfast. While she was waiting for it to be brought to her room, she sat cross-legged on the bed with the phone in front of her. It was nearly seven in New York and just shy of mid-day in London. The call ran completely contrary to procedure – at the very least, she should have used a public pay-phone – but Petra didn't care. She dialled the number anyway. It began to ring but then she stopped it. She realized she wasn't ready yet. She had to think about what she was going to say. Yes, it had to be an apology but it also had to be more than that. It needed to be an explanation too, otherwise how would she ever repair the damage? *Could* she ever repair the damage? And what explanation was there?

Breakfast arrived. As she ate fruit, yoghurt and freshly-baked rolls, she tried to invent a plausible excuse but found she couldn't. After breakfast, she called again and, this time, let the phone ring. No answer. She wondered what Frank was doing. Perhaps he was with another woman. The possibility made her queasy.

Until Giler's phone could be fixed, there was no need for her to be on call. For a day, she was a tourist. She went to the top of the Empire State Building, she walked through the Village and SoHo, she visited the Museum of Modern Art and the Guggenheim. In the evening, she stayed in her room and allowed American TV to numb her senses. After a sleepless night, she rose early the following morning and called Wilson at his hotel. They agreed to meet at eleven. He gave her the address and she decided to walk there.

She crossed over to Seventh Avenue and headed south towards Times Square. The saying seemed to be true for her: one is never more alone than in a crowd of strangers. She walked through the city – Manhattan in Christmas mood – but was untouched by it. Except, perhaps, when it came to the matter of coldness. She and the temperature were as one, they froze everything with which they came into contact.

Wilson's hotel was near the Port Authority Bus Terminal. His room was not much larger than her bathroom at the Lowell. It unsettled her because it reminded her of hotel rooms from her past: the single, tacky picture on the wall, the Seventies TV set, the wardrobe with an orange curtain instead of a set of doors. When Wilson suggested they go out, Petra agreed in a hurry.

They found a diner a couple of blocks away. Petra ordered coffee, Wilson ordered a full breakfast. The waitress brought two huge glasses of iced water.

'The NYNEX thing is done,' he told her.

She nodded. 'So now we just have to wait.'

'Not for long. Giler's busy today, but he's blocked off two hours tomorrow afternoon. Chances are, that'll be what it's for.'

'It'll be good to get it over and done with.'

'Yes. Then we can get out of here.'

'You don't like it?'

Wilson held open his hands. 'I'm not really a city person.'

'And New York's more of a city than most cities . . .'

'Exactly.'

'Don't you like living in London?'

'I don't live in London. We moved out ten years ago.'

'We?'

'My wife and I, and our three children. We bought a place down in Surrey.' Wilson looked out of the window at the human tide. His mind seemed to drift with his gaze. 'Of course, our eldest has moved out now. He's got a place of his own in Ealing.'

Petra tried to guess Wilson's age. Mid-fifties, perhaps. And then she tried to marry this image of middle-class suburbia to working for Alexander at Magenta House.

'How do you do it?' she asked him.

Wilson returned to reality. 'Do what?'

'Work for Alexander. I mean, with a wife, a *family*, I just don't get it.'

'It's a job. That's all.'

Petra shook her head. 'No it isn't. It's a . . . it's a . . .' She couldn't think of an appropriate description. 'I mean, what do you say to her? When you get home in the evening and she asks how your day went, what do you say? Oh, it was so-so, dear. We rubbed out a group of Russian Mafiosi.'

'My wife doesn't know. She thinks I'm an accountant. Which in many ways, I am.'

'Doesn't that hurt? To have to lie continuously to someone you love?'

'Of course. But it's what I have to do. There is no other way.'

'You could quit. Get a normal job.'

Wilson looked genuinely puzzled. 'Quit? What do you mean?'

His breakfast arrived, loaded on to a plate the size of a tray. Eggs and bacon for four in an order for one. To Petra, it looked like a heart attack waiting to be eaten. With a side order of waffles, just to make sure. As Lisa, she'd eaten less than that in a week.

A black canopy led off Fifth Avenue to the entrance. A doorman in an ankle-length green overcoat and black leather gloves smiled and held open the door for her. The entrance hall was vast. A Persian carpet lay on a veined marble floor. There were three chandeliers between the door and the lifts. Behind the desk, both men wore dark grey uniforms with brass buttons and scarlet epaulettes.

'I'm here to see Mr Giler.'

The fatter one nodded and pressed a button. A door opened on the other side of the hall and a man beckoned her. Petra recognized him from the photograph that Wilson had shown her. Ken Randall, former offensive lineman for the Cleveland Browns, now Leon Giler's bodyguard. Wilson had told her that a serious injury to his right knee had forced Randall to retire from the sport; it was always useful to know people's points of vulnerability. He ushered her into a small room with a table, two chairs and a camera mounted high in one corner.

'I ain't seen you before.'

'Madeleine's sick. I'm her replacement.'

'I gotta check you out.'

'Be my guest.'

He frisked her thoroughly, not gratuitously, as Luiso had. Then he examined the contents of her bag; wallet, keys, lipstick, eye-liner, tampons, a pair of lacy black knickers. As he picked them up, their eyes met and Petra smiled. 'You never know when you'll need a spare pair.'

Randall came across a small canister and struggled with the name on the label. 'What is this? Sal . . . Salbamol . . . Salbumol . . . no, wait . . . Salbu –'

'Salbutamol.'

'What's that?'

'I'm asthmatic.' Petra reached inside the bag and pulled out the plastic device. 'You stick the canister in the inhaler and then breathe through this mouthpiece.'

Randall began to return her things to the bag. 'Asthmatic, huh?'

'Yes.'

He broke into a large, sloppy grin. 'Must be all that heavy breathing you do, right?'

Petra took the lift to the fourth floor, where the doors parted to reveal a small crescent-shaped atrium. Ahead, the double doors were slightly ajar. The atrium led into a large oval hall ringed by fluted columns. The floor was a chess-board of black and white stone. At the centre of it, there was a small pool with a bronze dolphin rising vertically from its heart, water spouting from the mouth.

A voice called out to her. 'Close the door, then turn left and come down to the end.'

The drawing-room windows offered a stunning view of Central Park, which was the only stylish thing she could see. Parquet flooring, white leather sofas, Picassos on the wall and gold everywhere; the room was reverential, a monument to tastelessness.

Leon Giler was wearing a plain white shirt. He'd removed his tie and rolled up his sleeves, revealing powerful forearms carpeted with thick black hair. He held a tumbler in his left hand, ice cubes clinking in amber liquid, his Cartier watch clinking against a chunky gold bracelet.

'I'm Eva,' Petra said.

'Where the fuck's Madeleine?'

'She's got the flu.'

'The woman at Premier never said anything about that.'

'She didn't know until she called Madeleine. Then Madeleine called me.'

'You a friend of hers?'

'We help each other out from time to time.'

'What kind of fucking accent is that?'

Good question, thought Petra. 'Swedish.'

He raised both eyebrows and Petra knew that she was right, that she could list the tedious preconceptions in his mind. 'So you're Swedish, huh?'

She nodded. Giler's eyes scraped over her and then he sniffed dismissively.

'Is there a problem?' Petra asked.

'Yeah, there's a fucking problem.'

'What?'

'Forty fucking inches. That's what. You're not forty inches. No fucking way. You're what? Thirty-six max, right?'

Petra was unfazed. 'At least they're natural.'

Giler seemed neither amused nor impressed. 'I told her – the woman at Premier – that I wanted forty inches minimum. Forty inches, blonde and good with her mouth.'

Feeling dead inside, Petra tried to look flirtatious. 'Well, two out of three ain't bad. But maybe you don't want me. Perhaps I should leave.'

Giler took a long sip from his glass while he thought about it. 'I don't know. Do you do all the same stuff that Madeleine does?'

'We don't compare lists. Like what?'

'I get to fuck her any way I want. And she lets me slap her around some.'

Not an unusual request, in Stephanie's experience, Petra recalled. Especially among businessmen who spent all day surrounded by suits in sterile offices. It wasn't enough to order people around via memoranda. To feel truly powerful, they had to be abusive to someone and what better way was there than by humiliating them physically? Yet it amazed Petra that these people never understood that they were the ones who were humiliated. They never behaved in the same way with the people who really mattered in their lives. They didn't treat their porcelain wives like that, only anonymous professionals who were paid to squeal when slapped but who felt nothing.

'You got a problem with that?' Giler asked.

Say what you like, you'll be dead in five minutes. She smiled. 'No, I don't have a problem with that.'

'Then let me see what you got.'

'Here?'

'Yeah, of course here. What, there ain't enough fucking room for you?'

The rough talk was predictable. Too much time spent in the company of CEOs and on the boards of charitable foundations had left Giler with a surplus of frustration in need of release. This was his way. Petra was familiar with it. The coarse language and general aggression were a precursor to the pinches and slaps that were themselves a precursor to the clenched fist.

'I need to go to the bathroom first.'

'You can go later.'

Petra tensed. 'I need to go now.'

Giler scowled at her and then grumbled, 'Down the hall, turn left, go through the octagonal room and it's the second door on the right.'

His minor capitulation proved what she already knew. She was in charge. Men like Giler never saw that, which was just as well for women like her.

She locked herself into the bathroom and shrugged off the black ankle-length overcoat. She emptied the contents of the handbag on to the inevitable slab of marble into which the basins were sunk. Her fingers found the tag at the bottom and lifted the black panel to reveal a small hidden compartment. It wasn't large enough to conceal a gun but it was large enough for a double-edged blade and a stainless steel handle. She fastened the two pieces of metal together and checked they were secure. Then she replaced the panel and all the contents of the bag except for the canister, which she inserted into the inhaler. It was an ingenious piece of invention by Magenta House. The canister could be loaded with any gas or spray, turning the life-saving device into a weapon that could be taken through any conventional security check.

Petra then stripped naked before stepping back into her high heels and pulling on the overcoat. She slipped the knife into the right pocket. The blade sliced through the lining but the metal guard kept the handle in the pocket itself. The inhaler went into her left pocket.

It was going to be easy, she told herself. A man like Giler would probably enjoy the sight of her entering the room in nothing but high heels and an open overcoat. He'd like the glimpses of flesh beneath the material as she moved. And this would distract him until she was close enough to ensure she could fire the CS gas out of the inhaler and into his face. Blinded and gasping, he'd be vulnerable to the blows that would send him helpless to the floor. At that point, Petra would take out the knife, kick off her shoes and shed the coat. When the work was bloody, it was an advantage to be naked; she'd need the coat when she left the building so she didn't want it stained. The first cut would be to the throat, taken from behind Giler, her left arm securing the head while her right went to work with the blade. She'd remember to cut deeply, as Boyd had shown her, drawing her arm away, being sure to sever the wind-pipe and the vocal cords. The second cut, which would merely quicken his death, would start in the upper thigh and go up through the groin and into the hip flexor, severing the femoral artery. Once he was dead, Petra would find a shower and clean the blood from her skin, before getting dressed and walking out.

*   *   *

I walk down the corridor and I am aware of the air on my naked skin. My hands are in my coat pockets. The left one feels the inhaler, the right one clutches the steel handle of the knife. The cross-hatch grip is coarse against my palm. I walk into the octagonal room that I have to pass through but I stop. I look around and see myself reflected in the darkened mirrors that form the walls. From the side, from the back, from the front, I see how extraordinary I look: overcoat, high heels, skin. I am a prostitute again, back where I started. It doesn't feel that peculiar to me which upsets me. And then something snaps inside me. The pretence ends.

Since I agreed to kill Giler, the question has been gnawing away at me: can I really see it through? I have ignored it. My training has prepared me for this and I have somehow convinced myself that this act is a necessary evil that will permit me to move forwards in my quest for justice. What incredible nonsense. I look at my reflected identical sisters and I see the lie in every one of them. Proctor was a brave man who paid for his bravery with his life but I know that he would never have paid this price for justice. Repellent as Giler is, I cannot kill him in order to find out who killed my family. This isn't my world. It belongs to somebody else.

The thing that truly astonishes me is that I've come this far. Here I am, naked in New York, ready to gut my victim like a fish. Why didn't I stop this at the start? Some part of me must have known all along that I wouldn't be able to do this. Brazil was different. Ferreira was self-defence. Marin was not self-defence, but he was certainly 'heat of the moment'. Did I ever seriously believe I could graduate to 'cold blood'? Perhaps I just never thought it would come to this, that the situation would miraculously change somehow and that I wouldn't be forced to see it through.

I think of myself as I was when I was in Brewer Street. And I look at myself in the mirrors and see that I haven't come very far at all. I see that I could be back there very soon and very easily.

Leon Giler is safe from me and this failure of mine sets me free.

*   *   *

Fourteen hours later, Petra was back in London. She got off the District Line at Embankment, just a couple of minutes' walk from Magenta House. Since leaving Leon Giler's apartment, she'd expected somebody – anybody – to intervene at any moment. Even while she was dressing in the bathroom, she'd half-expected Giler to shout at her, telling her to hurry up. Once dressed, she'd slipped out of the flat silently and called the lift. The seconds elongated as she waited for it. In the entrance hall, Randall had looked surprised to see her again so soon and she'd pre-empted his question by pulling a mournful smile and say-ing, 'Not enough silicone.' He'd seemed to understand. Outside, she'd turned left, not right as Wilson had instructed her, and had then broken into a run. She lost the wig before returning to her suite at the Lowell, where she'd hurriedly gathered her things before checking out and catching a cab for JFK. Still no one came for her. At the airport, she was early for the check-in and feared that the wait would allow somebody to catch up with her. But they didn't. Once she was airborne, this fear began to recede and was replaced by a sense of euphoria. Her mind was too wired to allow her any sleep on the brief overnight flight. There were too many possibilities to consider, one of which was to simply disappear. In the end, however, she discarded this option. She decided she needed to confront Alexander face to face, to show him that his threats no longer scared her, to show him she was serious, to show him that if he didn't leave her alone she could bite back.

Now, just a short walk away, she felt the thrill of immi-nent release. She was exhausted but that only seemed to add to the slightly giddy sensation that her euphoria had provoked in her.

She used the Lower Robert Street entrance, punching her personalized code into the key-pad. The lock released and she pushed it open. She took the stairs and then marched down the corridor to Alexander's office. Margaret was startled to see her.

'Stephanie. What are you doing here? You can't go in there –'

Petra threw open the door. The office was empty. She stepped back outside. 'Where is he?'

'Downstairs. The conference room.'

Alexander was smoking. He sat at the far end of the oval table. There were no papers in front of him, just an ashtray and a remote control for the bank of nine televisions to his right. But they were switched off. There was no image on the large screen behind him. The lights were half-dimmed.

Petra had planned to march in and say her piece before he got a chance to say a word. But the environment unsettled her. She looked around, half-expecting someone to materialize behind her. But there was no one.

Alexander said, 'Why don't you close the door?'

'Because I'm not staying.'

He shrugged. 'Frankly, I'm surprised you bothered coming here at all. No one else thought you'd show up but I had a sneaking suspicion that you might.'

'I wanted you to hear this directly from me.'

'That's what I thought.'

Not wanting their conversation – or rather, her threats – to be overheard, Petra closed the door and then moved closer to the table. 'I assume you've heard what happened. I imagine Wilson's been in contact.'

'He has. And it seems congratulations are in order.'

Petra frowned. 'For what?'

Alexander took a long draw from his cigarette and exhaled slowly, blue strands of smoke forming a dancing veil in front of his face. 'A brutal job well done.'

He picked up the remote control and, with a casual flick of the wrist, pointed the device at the bank of nine TV monitors to his right. His eyes never strayed from Petra. The screens flickered to life but only one of them produced an image. The others turned blue.

Alexander muted the sound. The CNN logo appeared in

a corner of the screen. Behind it, firemen and paramedics were moving in and out of smoking wreckage. Stunned civilians wandered aimlessly among abandoned vehicles, their blank faces picked out by the flashing lights of the emergency services' vehicles. The TV cut away to a helicopter shot. There was a bridge beneath the camera. Plumes of black smoke were rising from its centre. As the helicopter banked and turned for another approach, the skyscrapers of Manhattan came into view. Then a 'Breaking News' caption occupied the screen and was followed by a concise headline: FIVE DEAD IN QUEENSBORO BRIDGE BOMB BLAST.

Petra turned to Alexander. 'I don't understand. What is this?'

'Can't you guess?'

'A bomb on the Queensboro Bridge? No.'

'What you're watching was recorded last night. This is what's happening now.'

Alexander pressed a button and another of the TV screens came to life. He released the sound. It was still CNN. This time, there were two news-anchors behind a desk in a studio in Atlanta. The woman spoke, her power-suited thinness severe on the eye, while the male mannequin to her left looked appropriately sombre.

'The FBI has joined the New York Police Department in the search for those responsible for the Queensboro Bridge bomb yesterday evening, which killed media tycoon Leon Giler and three of his five children. Giler's driver and bodyguard, former Cleveland Browns offensive lineman Ken Randall was also killed by the blast, which caused a multi-vehicle crash on the bridge, leaving thirteen people injured. Four of them are thought to be in a serious condition. Speaking earlier on CNN, Captain Richard Ross of the New York Police Department said it was a miracle that only five people had been killed.'

The TV showed Ross shouting into the microphone to make himself heard over the sirens and the close thud of

270

helicopter blades. 'We coulda easily had twenty or thirty dead people out here.'

Alexander muted the sound again, which was not something he had to do to Petra; for a while, she was too stunned to speak.

'What did you expect?' he asked her. 'That we'd just let this opportunity go? That we'd allow you to walk away and jeopardize everything?'

He picked up his Rothmans from the ashtray.

'How?' she whispered.

'The same way we did Grigory Ismailov. A car-bomb activated by a mercury tilt-switch. In this instance, combined with a timer.'

'Wilson?'

Alexander nodded. 'He suspected you might not be able to see it through so we devised a back-up plan, just in case.'

Andrew Wilson in his bad suit with his bad teeth. She had an image of his home in Surrey, of his plain wife and their three awkward children, of curtains that clashed with the sofa, of a family eating roast beef for Sunday lunch.

Petra's eyes were still drawn to the images on the screens. 'Three children . . .'

'I know.'

She turned to Alexander, aware of the bitterness that was starting to rise within her. 'What do you mean you know?'

'I mean they weren't supposed to be in the vehicle. Giler's wife was in New York with all five children. Giler was going out to the mansion on Long Island to see his mother. On the spur of the moment, he decided to take the three eldest children with him. We didn't even know about it until after it had happened.'

'And that's your excuse?'

'I'm not making an excuse. I'm telling you what happened. It was tragic timing. Bombs are messy. They suck the innocent in, so now we have five dead, not one.'

'Bastard.'

'Don't lay the blame at my feet.' Alexander's pale watery eyes were entirely without compassion. 'If you'd done your job, Giler would still be dead, but the three children would be alive. Think about it.'

'Fuck you.'

'Say what you like, it's the truth and you know it.'

Petra struggled to keep her anger bottled. 'I quit.'

Alexander rolled an inch of ash into the ashtray. 'You know you can't do that.'

'Oh, I see. You think your threats will keep me in line? Try it. See what happens. I don't care, I'll live with the risk. Maybe I'll even use some of that wonderful training you've given me against you. You can't threaten me. Not any more.'

'This isn't a golf club. You can't just resign because you don't want to play any more. You *are* Petra Reuter.'

'When I walk out of that door, you'll never see me again.'

Alexander looked up to meet her gaze fully. 'Like I said, bombs are so messy. Innocent people die, families are blown apart. You of all people should know that. After all, it's already happened to you once.'

That stung. Petra found it hard to understand how Alexander could be so callous yet sound so casual and look so calm. 'You really are a work of art.'

'It can happen again,' he said.

Petra felt the energy drain out of her. 'What?'

'Your brother. His wife. *Their* three children.'

It took her several seconds to absorb the threat completely. 'Not even you would stoop that low.'

Alexander extinguished his cigarette. 'You don't think so? You should watch more TV.'

20

Soaked to the skin as she was, the cold gnawed at her bones. Petra thumped a clenched fist against the sturdy wooden door several times. Again, there was no answer. She moved to the window on the right. She wiped frozen fingertips across the glass and peered through a crack in the curtains. The lamp on the table behind the armchair was on, casting a dull glow over the room, which appeared empty. The wash of light was the first hint of warmth she had encountered in hours. She began to tap on the window and tried to call out but the muscles in her jaw were stiff from the cold. The rain continued to pelt her back and the wind swallowed the feeble tapping of her knuckles on the glass.

She became aware of the presence behind her before she actually heard the crunch of boots on stone. Slowly, Petra turned around. She immediately recognized the pistol that was being pointed at her: a SIG-Sauer P210-6.

Iain Boyd said, 'I don't get visitors out here in the middle of the night.' Petra saw him squint at her through the rain. 'What are you doing here?'

Warm and dry, she was still shivering. The physical numbness had gone but, mentally, Petra remained frozen. An hour had passed. They were sitting in Boyd's kitchen. He was preparing another cup of sweet milky tea for her. Swathed in blankets, she stared vacantly at the temperature gauge on the front of the Rayburn.

Boyd set the mug on the table and sat down beside her. Steam rose into her face and she welcomed the wet heat.

'What happened?'

Petra met his gaze but was mute, a condition that endured for the rest of the night. He stopped questioning her but continued to talk, telling her how the summer season had been, how he continued to climb the rock faces on which she had excelled, how the recent weather had been colder and wetter than usual. She heard him but wasn't listening.

It was dark and cold when she awoke. She felt sick, the leaden cramps forcing her to stay in her foetal curl. She stared into the gloom, seeing nothing, feeling nothing.

The realization that she was the architect of her plight was what numbed her most. Alexander had been true to his word. He'd tried to dissuade her from following this path. He'd warned of the horrors ahead and of there being no escape. He'd actually pleaded with her to choose a real life over this. But, of course, she had known better. She was prepared for anything. How arrogant that now seemed. The bleakness that cloaked her was as inevitable and inescapable as the fate that awaited her. She was tied to Alexander until Khalil was dead and there was no way out.

For two days, she was adrift. Sometimes, she felt the crushing weight of depression in a quite physical way; it was hard to stand, hard to breathe, impossible to resist. She withdrew into herself, shutting out the world. The retreat to the comfort of the womb was a sensation she knew well. It was an act of desperation.

Daylight on the third morning brought more rain. Ferocious and icy, driven by wind, it was typical of the season and region. Petra dressed in the spare clothes that Boyd had left in her room on the first morning; old jeans that were slightly large for her – but that were definitely too small to be his – a T-shirt, a thick wool shirt and a bulky roll-neck jersey. Petra assumed the garments had belonged to Boyd's wife.

When she'd opened her eyes on the first morning, she'd been surprised by her surroundings. It took time for the details of the previous day to filter through the memory's sieve; the panic, the urge to run, the choice she'd made. Boyd. An odd choice, perhaps, since Boyd was one of them. And yet, at the same time, she'd felt she could trust him. She'd flown to Inverness and taken a train to Lairg, from where she'd caught a bus bound for Durness. The driver had been concerned when she insisted on being dropped at the roadside. He'd fretted about the weather and the darkness but she'd been adamant. She'd waited until the red tail lights had vanished into the night, before setting off down the rough track towards Boyd's loch. In her mind, these details, though fresh, were blurred.

Emotionally, she had been too scattered for reason or clarity. For the first two days that she spent in Boyd's care, this confusion persisted. Her ability to concentrate was non-existent. She found herself swinging between states of extreme agitation and complete lethargy. Boyd appeared to recognize the signs; he never pushed her with questions or instructions. Instead, he seemed content to be patient.

Now, on the third morning, they were in the kitchen again. Boyd was preparing the porridge that she had once found so repellent but for which she now had a nostalgic craving. His back was turned to her. She said, 'I thought I could live this way but I was wrong.'

He didn't turn around. 'What happened?'

'Do you know about New York?'

'No.'

'Have you contacted Alexander?'

'No.'

'Are you going to?'

'I don't know.'

She saw that her hands were trembling. 'I don't have the nerve for it. Not when it matters.'

Boyd turned around and set a bowl in front of her. 'Here. Eat this.'

She looked up at him. 'I've got to disappear.'

'Eat.'

As she always had, she obeyed Boyd, who watched her. He made tea for both of them and when she had finished her porridge, he said, 'Now tell me about New York.'

She described the operation in detail, starting with Serra, ending with Alexander. Boyd was silent throughout and, by the time Petra had finished, half an hour had elapsed.

'You can't just disappear, Stephanie.'

'Why not? The world's big enough.'

'You know why not. Your brother, his family.'

'But would Alexander really go that far?'

'It's not beyond him.'

Petra buried her face in her hands and muttered, 'Christ, what a mess.'

'You're not the first person to be in this position.'

'That doesn't make me feel any better.'

'It's not supposed to. I'm just saying that you're not alone. Losing your nerve was natural. Under those circumstances, it was the *right* thing to do. It shows you're human.'

'I didn't think I was supposed to be human.'

'You're not. But if I were you, I wouldn't regard that as a failure.'

Petra frowned. 'Whose side are you on?'

They were in Boyd's Land-Rover on the road between Durness and the Laxford Bridge. It was early afternoon, not long before dusk. Petra gazed out of the window at the rust and lead of the surrounding peaks and passes.

'My parents would have loved it up here.'

Boyd made a sound beside her that suggested doubt.

'What's that supposed to mean?' she demanded.

'That they might've liked it here, but only for a week or two a year. That's what people really mean when they say that.'

276

Petra was irritated. 'How would you know?'

'Because living here fifty-two weeks a year is not the same thing.'

'You worked that out all by yourself, did you?'

'I've heard it a thousand times – '

'But you never met my parents. I'm telling you, they could have lived up here all year, no problem. Just them, the land and the weather, perfect.'

A pause followed and then Boyd smiled, which didn't suit him. 'That's what we felt.'

'We?'

'Rachel and me.'

'Your wife?'

He nodded. 'We were selfish in that way. We couldn't have cared less about the rest of the world. We never wanted to be a part of it. We were perfectly matched.'

'What about now?'

'What about it?'

'Now that she's gone.'

He thought about it for a minute and then shrugged. 'Now it doesn't matter. Nothing does.' He suddenly appeared oblivious to her presence in the vehicle. 'When Rachel died, the best part of me died too. I'll never get that back. I don't even want to. So I'll just stay here – the place where we were happy – and it'll be enough.'

Petra felt his hurt in her chest. Watching Boyd bare his soul was distressing. Confession seemed to compound his pain and loss, not ease it. Then, as suddenly as this inner glimpse of him had occurred, it was gone.

'You're going to have to go back,' he told her.

'I know,' she whispered.

The following afternoon, Petra opened the door to her flat. Among the envelopes on the floor, there was a piece of folded paper with Marina written on it. She opened it up. *Marina, I don't know what happened last night. If it was something I did that upset you, then I apologize. If you feel you*

277

can, call me. Frank. She screwed the paper into her fist and kicked the front door shut with her heel.

Before taking a bath, she left a message for Marc Serra on the Heavens Above web-site, signing off, as usual, as V. Libensky. Serra replied three hours later, providing a Parisian phone number for her to call at midday. She left her flat at eleven, keen for a walk to clear her head.

She bought a BT Phonecard and called Paris from a phone-box.

'My client is very pleased at the way things have worked out. It sends out the right message.'

Petra closed her eyes. 'I'm glad he's happy.'

'The rest of your money will be transferred to the same account by the end of the week.'

'Fine.'

'He asked me to tell you that he is extremely anxious to work with you again. I was wondering whether we could meet to discuss it.'

'I don't form relationships. If we're going to do more business, I'm going to need to know more about him.'

'I think that could be possible now. I can't guarantee total disclosure but I feel he may be more responsive than before.'

'In that case, we can talk. Where and when?'

'I'll be in Amsterdam next week.'

'I wanted to say sorry. And I wanted to get you something as a token of that. But I couldn't think of anything appropriate. Then I saw these. I don't know how appropriate they are, but they were so beautiful, I thought they'd do.'

Frank looked down at the lilies Petra was holding in her arms and said, 'I don't think I've ever been bunched before.'

'Then at least it's original. That's good.'

She offered him the flowers and he accepted them. 'You're right, they are beautiful. Thank you. Do you want to come in?'

'No.'

Frank looked slightly taken aback. 'Okay.'

Petra managed a smile for him. 'Soon, but not now. I haven't forgiven myself yet.'

Cyril Bradfield was wearing fingerless gloves. He saw Petra staring at them and said, 'The central heating is broken. It's freezing in the attic.'

She handed him an envelope and followed him up the stairs. It grew colder as they rose. On a work-bench, there were three groups of documents, one for each identity. As Bradfield opened the envelope and began to count the cash, Petra picked up a Canadian passport belonging to Jennifer Sommers, a native of Toronto. She saw herself in the sealed photo and then flicked through the pages. There were stamps for Malaysia, Thailand, Australia, New Zealand and several European countries.

'I thought she might be a travel journalist,' Bradfield explained, answering Petra's question before she had asked it.

'Actually, she won't be. But thanks for the thought.'

Petra looked at the other two; Martha Connor, an Irish woman from Dublin and Claudia Neumann, a German. She sifted through identity cards, passports, driving licences, even a Dublin-registered library card.

'When will they be complete?'

'They are all at different stages.'

'Can you have one ready by next week?'

'Claudia Neumann, I think. Would she be all right?'

'She'll be fine. I'll call to arrange a time to pick her up.'

'By the way, you've paid me five hundred too much.'

'No I haven't.'

Bradfield smiled sincerely. 'My discretion comes with the work. You don't have to pay extra for it.'

'Then think of it as a gift. It's the season for it.'

* * *

On Christmas Eve, Petra found herself crossing Oxford Street at four in the afternoon. She marvelled at the crassness of the decorations and the sheer insanity of the congestion. There were roast chestnut vendors on the street corners. Department store doors were flung wide open like vast jaws, ready to feed on the shopping plankton that drifted through them. Slowly, Petra made her way through the mass of motion. Christmas. Since the crash, it had always been the worst time of the year. In the past, her regular clients had occasionally brought her a gift, usually one of the cheap perfumes that clogged TV commercial breaks in the run-up to Christmas. This year, though, there would be nothing, for which she was grateful because there was no mawkish sentimentality left in her.

Christmas Day was fine. She awoke early and followed her stretching routine before going out for a walk. London was empty. It was quite surreal; the only times she had seen the city so deserted was in films. She ate pasta for lunch and drank green tea. In the afternoon, she walked through Hyde Park, only returning to her flat as dusk descended.

Frank White was getting out of his car, as she turned into Clarges Street. She stopped and considered retreating before he saw her. But it was too late.

'Marina. How are you? Happy Christmas.'

She returned the greeting. 'So, where have you been?'

'I was with my parents, the same as every year.'

'Where?'

'Near Marlow. My sister and her family are staying there so I just went down for lunch.'

'That must've been nice.'

'It was. What about you? I thought maybe you'd gone back to Belgium, or wherever . . .'

Where indeed. 'Switzerland,' she corrected him. 'No. Not this year.'

'How come?'

Her reactions were a little rusty. 'Er, because . . . because I had meetings yesterday. And tomorrow.'

Frank raised an eyebrow. 'Tomorrow? On Boxing Day?'

'With some Japanese. It's very important. It can't wait.'

He slammed his car door shut and locked it. 'So what've you done today?'

'Oh, nothing much. A little work . . .'

'Working on Christmas Day?'

'It doesn't matter.'

They moved off the street and into the entrance hall. He said, 'Have you forgiven yourself yet?'

'What?'

'What you said the other day when you brought me those flowers.'

She was embarrassed. 'Oh, that.'

'Yes, that. Have you?'

'Well . . .'

'How about a drink? I haven't had one yet and I could use one.'

'You don't have to . . .'

'I'd like to.'

'In that case, yes.'

It felt strange to be in his flat again. She saw the samples of beryl and apatite that she had held. She ran her hand over the oak table at which they had sat. The lilies were in a green glass jug, their heavy heads drooping sadly. Frank peered into the fridge, its light bleaching his face in the kitchen's gloom.

'We're in luck,' he said, producing a chilled bottle of champagne. 'I got given two of these at work last week. I meant to take them to my parents today but forgot.'

Petra watched him peel the foil from the bottle. 'I haven't had champagne for ages. Not since my niece's christening, I don't think. That was when I was at university.'

'Have you got lots of nephews and nieces?'

'No. Only two. I mean, three. Actually . . .'

Petra's heart stuttered. Wrong life. Stephanie was the one with a niece, a nephew and an unknown. The blunder was a shock. When she looked at Frank, she saw that he was waiting for her to finish speaking.

Nieces. Nephews. She selected mental files and got Petra. But she was Marina, not Petra. She searched again, found Marina, and opened the file. It was blank. Like an actress forgetting her lines, Petra found she had nothing to say as Marina, her character for this play. So she improvised.

She waved it aside. 'It doesn't matter.'

'No, I'm interested.'

'It's really very boring. I don't keep in touch much. You know how it is.'

Frank appeared to recognize that he was straying into sensitive territory and changed tack. 'So, you were at university?'

She nodded and tried to remember whether that was the right thing to do.

'Which one?' he asked.

Durham. That was the Stephanie answer. But what was the Marina answer? It was getting worse. Everything was fading. Alberto and Francine were her parents but where did they live? How old were they? Had they provided brothers and sisters for her?

Petra knew the answers but couldn't retrieve them. She felt the panic in her stomach clawing its way up her throat.

'Rome,' she said, it being the first word that came to mind when the silence had become too awkward to endure. There had to be a university in Rome.

'That can't have been too bad.'

She would have sighed with relief but the next awkward question was already on its way. What course did she study there?

'How come you're so interested to know?'

'How come you're so reluctant to talk about yourself?'

'I'm not,' she protested.

'The other night, I didn't get anything out of you.'

'And I didn't get much out of you. As I remember it, we didn't talk about a lot of personal stuff.'

'True. But every time you asked me a question, I gave you an answer. Whereas every time I asked you a question, you skilfully avoided an answer.'

Petra looked hurt. 'You're exaggerating.'

Frank shook his head. 'You'd make a great politician. But look, if you don't want to talk about it, that's okay –'

'No,' Petra insisted. 'I do. Honestly, I really do. It's just . . .' A pause grew. 'I don't always find it easy, that's all. But you can ask me anything.'

So Frank put the questions to her and she invented the answers on the spur of the moment, not caring that she might forget them when questioned again. She found the dishonesty depressing, which in itself was something new for her. Lying had become so deeply ingrained that she never normally gave it a second thought and the lies themselves never troubled her conscience. Or what was left of it.

To compensate for this unhappiness she drank her champagne quickly. And when the conversation steered towards safer, neutral territory she drank more champagne out of relief. Between them, they emptied both bottles. By the time she left Frank's flat, Petra felt a little drunk. She awoke the next morning with a hangover and remembered something that had occurred to her the morning after her niece's christening: she'd never liked champagne.

On the morning after Boxing Day, Petra switched on the computer screen and visited each of her selected web-sites. There was nothing new for her on them so she merely refreshed two of her own messages. There was, however, some e-mail for Andrew Smith.

Andrew,
How are you? Haven't seen you for a while.
Give me a call a.s.a.p.
M.

283

Petra pulled on a coat and left her flat. She picked one of the phone-boxes on Curzon Street, near the corner with Berkeley Square. Through the Adelphi Travel receptionist, she ended up speaking to Margaret, who said, 'How are you, Stephanie?'

'If you must know, I've been better.'

'I know. I'm sorry for you, I really am. I feel terrible . . .'

'Don't worry about it, Margaret. I know it was nothing to do with you.'

'Well, you know where you can find me, if you need me.'

'Thanks. Is he in?'

'No. But he asked me to give you a message. The Empire cinema on Leicester Square. The eleven-fifty performance.'

'This evening?'

'This morning. Pick a seat at the very back, towards the right-hand side as you look at the screen.'

Petra arrived five minutes early. Alexander was already there, his overcoat draped over the seat in front of him, a briefcase on the seat to his left. The vast auditorium was almost empty. Petra sat beside him. After their previous encounter, there was plenty of scope for awkward small-talk but Alexander elected to bypass that.

'You're off to meet Serra in Amsterdam tomorrow, then?'

'Yes.'

'There's something else you need to know about Sons of Sabah. It was something that Kassir produced but which we've only just learned about.'

'What?'

'It's called the Fat Three List.'

'The Fat Three List? What does that mean?'

'I don't know. It may be a computer file. Or it could just be a list, memorized, or on paper, or recorded in some other way. What we do know is that it contains details of the crucial elements of Sons of Sabah.'

The house lights began to dim and the huge curtains

parted slowly. The screen came to life with commercials.

Petra said, 'Whoever put together the Giler file for me suggested that his support for the Israeli programme for building Jewish settlements in the Occupied Territories might be the reason for Khalil wanting him dead.'

'And?'

'And I know that's not it. I don't want to meet Serra not knowing the real reason, otherwise I'll look like an idiot. I need to know more about Giler's relationship with Khalil. You told me there was some history between them.'

'Why do you think you need to know?'

'It was something Serra said in passing. Talking about what happened in New York, he said it sent out the right message.'

Alexander considered this for a moment and then said, 'Yes, that makes sense.'

'How?'

'Well, it's hard to know the precise details without knowing who Khalil actually is, but his problem with Giler almost certainly centres on Sheikh Abdul Kamal Qassam. After the 1993 bombing of the World Trade Center, Qassam orchestrated a campaign of retribution against the United States for the conviction of those who were prosecuted for the bombing.'

'That was the blind Muslim cleric?'

'That's right. Sheikh Omar Abdel Rahman was one of them.'

'So who is Qassam?'

'A follower of Rahman's. At least, that's how he rose to prominence.'

'How does he fit into this?'

'As well as wanting revenge for Rahman's imprisonment, he also has direct links to Khalil; Khalil has acted on Qassam's behalf before. Anyway, there were attacks on US embassies in Madrid, Manila and Kuala Lumpur, and there were others planned that never actually happened. The biggest operation that Qassam sanctioned, however, was an attack on New York, where Rahman stood trial. The plan was relatively straightforward but would have been catastrophic had it succeeded and we are pretty sure that it was devised by Khalil himself. It was to start as a hijack. The aircraft would have belonged to Alitalia or Olympic, Rome and Athens having possibly the worst airport security in Europe. The destination was to have been New York. But this was not to have been a conventional hijack. It was a suicide mission, for which five men volunteered.'

'How were they going to do it?'

'They were going to wait until the aircraft was descending towards JFK, thereby giving the authorities on the ground no time to react. Two members of the terrorist team were former airline pilots with PIA. Having murdered the flight crew, they were going to assume control of the aircraft and crash it into the middle of Manhattan. As it turned out, one of the two pilots got cold feet about meeting his maker prematurely. In Athens, he deserted the team and turned up at the American embassy seeking sanctuary, which was provided in return for information.'

'Was Khalil supposed to have been one of the five?'

'No. Being part of a suicide team is not his style. But he devised the plan, which was scrapped after the pilot's defection. Back in the States, though, the FBI were very concerned that Khalil and Qassam would merely dream up an alternative horror of similar proportions. Not knowing who Khalil was, they elected to take Qassam out of the picture. So they decided to snatch him. Giler provided information to help the Americans pinpoint him.'

'How?'

Alexander shrugged. 'I don't know exactly, although it's not a secret that he was very well connected in Israel. There were no doors that were closed to him there. Also, Giler provided the Gulfstream that allowed the Americans to spirit Qassam out of Greece to a US airbase in Germany, where he was transferred to a military plane before being flown back to New York to stand trial.'

'Where Rahman also got sentenced?'

'Yes.'

'And where Giler was based.'

'Exactly.'

'I suppose that makes some kind of sense.'

'If anything we do does, yes.'

The commercials on the screen made way for a series of trailers for forthcoming films. Alexander prepared to leave, reaching forward for his overcoat.

'By the way, I understand you requested a Grade Two profile for someone the night before you went to New York.'

Petra's blood stopped flowing for a moment. She was relieved that they were in partial darkness and that he couldn't see her properly. 'I cancelled it.'

'The operator ran the check anyway. Frank White. That's his name, isn't it?' Petra shrugged. 'Who is he?'

'Nobody. Just someone I keep running into. He lives in the same building, that's all.'

'So why did you request the profile in the first place?'

'I made a mistake. I was tired. It was nothing.'

'Aren't you curious?' Alexander asked. 'Don't you want to know what we discovered?'

She wasn't sure. If there was something bad, part of her – most of her – wanted to remain ignorant of it. 'What?'

She could see Alexander smiling in the darkness. 'There was nothing. He's just some geologist who works for a firm of mining consultants. He's single but had a young daughter who died three years ago. That's about it.'

'See?'

'Steer clear of him. I don't want you forming relationships.'

'I'm not forming relationships. With him or with any-one. I told you, I just kept running into him and I thought it was beginning to stretch coincidence. That's all there was to it.'

Alexander pulled on his overcoat and withdrew an envelope from one of the pockets, which he handed to Petra. 'This is the full report, if you're interested.'

She sat on her bed with her knees hunched close to her body. The document was five pages long. Date of birth, place of birth, names, names of parents, a copy of the birth certificate, addresses, schools, university, working record, bank records, tax records, medical records, National Insurance number, passport number, driving licence number, criminal record – none, vehicle registration number, credit cards with both account numbers and PIN codes, five years' worth of travel details, marital status – single. So this was a Grade Two profile. Petra wondered what Grade One could possibly include that wasn't already here.

Making the request had been a mistake but she thought cancelling it had rectified that. In fact, it appeared to have compounded the error by arousing Alexander's suspicion, which was the last thing Petra wanted. She knew she should have felt too ashamed to flick through the document – to look was to cheat, like ransacking a private diary – but Petra's shame was exhausted.

She found herself looking at the details of his family. The parents with their address in Marlow. His sister, married to a stockbroker, with their four children. She pictured their Christmas Day lunch, a traditional scene. It seemed peculiar to have to verify the facts but that was what happened when everything you said was a lie. It became difficult – impossible, sometimes – to believe anything you heard. Which made it necessary, occasionally, to remind yourself that not everybody was the same, that there were still some honest people left.

It was ten-to-eleven. She left her flat and knocked on Frank's door. When he opened it, he made no attempt to conceal his surprise. 'Marina?'

'I know it's late. I'm sorry.'

'That's okay. I'm still up.'

'Can I come in?'

'Sure.' He stood aside to let her pass, closed the door and then followed her into the living room. When she turned round to face him, he said, 'Would you like a drink?'

She shook her head.

'Is something wrong?'

'Not exactly. But there's something on my mind which I need to sort out.'

'That sounds serious. What is it?'

'That kiss.'

'What kiss?'

'The kiss we never had.'

Justifiably, Frank looked suspicious. 'What about it?'

'I made a mistake.'

21

Frank lies beside me. *He is asleep. The electronic clock's red digits tell me that it is four-twenty-seven. I have not yet been to sleep and soon I shall have to get up. I listen to the sound of his breathing. It is slow and peaceful.*

I was nervous because I was Stephanie again. At least, I think I was. Certainly, I wasn't very much like the Marina that I am supposed to be. Or maybe I was Marina and the change that occurred was within her. Who can say? Who cares? Not me, that's for sure.

Frank is the first man I have kissed, apart from Proctor, since I was a university student – I never allowed my clients to kiss me – and he is the first man I've wanted to have sex with since then. It hurts me to admit that I can't recall who that last person was. Some student, for sure, but which one? I wonder what he's doing now. Armed with a degree, he probably works in the City as an investment banker, with a wife and children, a Mercedes and an alcohol problem.

The entire episode felt alien to me; there was no coercion, no money changed hands. There were no artificial catalysts of any sort. Just the two of us and the desire to make it happen. I cannot say we made love – we had sex – and I cannot say that I enjoyed it.

I was too anxious to feel pleasure. I've forgotten how to accept affection. For me, sex is an activity that I've learned to endure in a state of total emotional numbness. So when Frank's fingertips found my hardening nipples, the shock was almost painful, a surprise in the mind as much as a physical sensation. I am someone who is prepared to strip in front of a complete stranger yet I felt acutely shy as he undressed me. I found my fingers were trembling and that I was unable to cope with the buttons on his shirt. As we lowered ourselves on to his bed, the tension in my stomach tightened. When his hand slipped between my thighs and his skin brushed my pubic hair, I grabbed his wrist and held him still for a moment. He asked if everything was all right and I found myself at a familiar crossroads. It was sheer willpower that conquered the instinct to panic and flee. So I lied and said yes, and let go of his hand.

More than anything, I was terrified that I'd become a whore again. I didn't want to do anything to him that I did to those who paid me. I didn't want to feel anything similar at all. And as this insanity fed upon itself, I even began to worry that he might see through me, that I might do something which would reveal my past.

We had sex twice and, both times, I was cold and scared. I have never been quite so naked. He would have had a better time if he'd been a paying client. I thought I might have forgotten how to be human and I still don't know whether this is true or not. What I do know is that in a few hours' time, in Amsterdam, I will be a soulless robot.

It will be a relief to be normal once more.

She looked at the electronic clock again. Five past five. Petra slipped out of the bed and gathered her clothes in silence. She dressed in the hall and then returned to her flat where she had a quick shower and packed a small bag of hand-luggage. At five-forty, she caught a cab and was at Heathrow's Terminal Four just after six. Her flight left on time at seven and arrived at Schipol at ten past nine, from where she took a train to Centraal Station. By ten past ten, she had checked into the Hotel Ambassade on Herengracht. At five to eleven, five minutes ahead of schedule, she was sitting in a café, thanking a waiter for bringing her a cup of hot chocolate. Her table was next to a large window. She gazed at the Nieuwe Kerk across the square. A few drizzle-dampened tourists huddled beneath tangerine umbrellas outside the church's entrance.

Serra was ten minutes late. The café was crowded and it took him time to spot her. As he weaved his way through the tables, she noticed he was limping. And when he reached the table, he struggled to shed his black wool over-coat, his right shoulder the apparent area of trouble.

'What's wrong with you?'

'Have you ever been to Amman?'

'Maybe. Maybe not.'

This made Serra smile. 'Well, if you have, you'll know how easy a motor accident can be.'

He ordered coffee and sat down opposite her. The leaden skies opened fully and fat drops of rain began to splatter diagonally across the window. The grey square glistened.

'The balance of your fee should have reached your bank by now.'

'It has.'

'Good. That brings us to this, then. My client now wishes to discuss with you the possibility of further work.'

Talking about his client, Serra sounded like a lawyer, which was an impression that was reinforced by a cream cotton shirt with gold cufflinks, a Hermès tie, a double-breasted navy suit and polished black shoes. Petra, by contrast, wore old jeans, a pair of scuffed Chelsea boots, a ragged electric-pink T-shirt and a loose-necked, long-armed brownish-red jersey. Her leather jacket was folded on to the chair between them.

She ran a hand through her short black hair several times. 'What does he have in mind?'

'Something more – how shall we say it? – *significant*.'

'Do you want to be more specific?'

'Not until I have established that there is a genuine possi-bility that you'd consider working for him again. It is well known that you rarely work for, or with, the same people twice.'

'That's true. But I don't rule it out. In this instance, it'll depend.'

'On what?'

'On the money. On what I think about working for Khalil.'

292

Serra stiffened. When their eyes met, Petra goaded him, inviting him to tell her she was wrong. But he couldn't.

'And what do you know of Khalil?'

'I know he likes writing large cheques.'

The blood had drained from Serra's face. He plucked a cigarette from the pack and began tapping the tip on the table. Petra had hoped to provoke a reaction but had never imagined it would be quite so severe.

'Information is gold.'

'Always,' Petra agreed. 'In my position, how could it be anything else? I told you when we first met that I like to know who's paying me. Especially when they're paying too much. That arouses suspicion.'

'My client was very insistent.'

'Obviously. And it leads me to conclude – or at least, suspect – that he wanted me to discover his identity. To see whether I could. And if I could, to see whether I would see the contract through.'

Back at the Hotel Ambassade, Petra took a manila envelope from her suitcase and emptied it on to the bed. She checked the contents: Claudia Neumann's German passport, her driving licence, some credit cards, and a small plastic wallet containing cash – two thousand Deutschmarks and one thousand American dollars. She returned everything to the manila envelope and left the hotel immediately.

She took a taxi to the city centre and secured a safe deposit box at a branch of ABN-AMRO where she placed the envelope. Next, she found a pay-phone and, using a credit card issued in Marina Gaudenzi's name, called Magenta House in London to ask for information. Afterwards, she called Frank's number but got no answer.

She returned to her hotel and slept for several hours, awaking at dusk. She stretched, took a shower and then decided to take a walk before her second meeting with Serra. From the Oude Kerk, she found herself inexorably drawn towards the red-light district in the same way that a drunk is drawn towards the bottle. The whores were coming out for the night, displaying themselves in their windows. It seemed like a variation on the cards that Petra had once had displayed in London's phone-boxes. She remembered that one of those cards had brought Proctor to her room on Brewer Street. Without the card, there would have been no intervention, no Petra, no escape from her terminal decline.

Looking at the whores on the other side of the glass, Petra imagined herself as one of them, a not-so-fresh cut dangling on a butcher's hook. *Frank passes by in the street. He sees me and stops, allowing himself time to examine me from beyond the glass. Then he moves on and chooses the whore next door.*

'Can I ask you something about Mechelen?'

'What?'

'How did you plan that? I mean, how did you know the two who got killed?'

'Through Anna Gerets.'

Serra frowned. 'But she wasn't involved. I understood she was in the Far East.'

'She was. I met her in Bangkok.'

He raised an eyebrow and nodded. The answer apparently made some sense to him. 'There have been so many rumours about her. That she was in Malaysia, or the Philippines. Or that she was dead.'

'When I met her, she'd been in Thailand for a month and was about to head for New Zealand.'

'And she just decided to tell you about what she'd done in Belgium?'

'Not at first.'

'How, then?'

'It just took a little time, that's all.'

'Did you torture her?' Serra asked, playfully.

'Torture?'

'I wouldn't put it past you. Not with your reputation.'

'If you must know, I slept with her.' The answer tripped

Serra up. It was Petra's turn to tease. 'Does that shock you?'

He managed some indignant protest. 'Of course not.' And then he modified it when he realized he'd overplayed it. 'It's a little surprising, perhaps, but one does what one has to do, no?'

'Anna was tough. Force would have been pointless. But like everyone else, she had her weaknesses.'

'You said "was".'

'Yes.' When Serra opened his mouth for the next question, Petra cut him off. 'Don't ask.'

They were sitting at a table in Speciaal, an Indonesian restaurant on Nieuwe Liliestraat in the Jordaan district. Serra had ordered Tafel Speciaal for both of them, which was a mixture of typical Indonesian dishes. He looked more casual now, in Eurotrash fashion; a pale yellow Ralph Lauren shirt, a navy jacket, grey flannel trousers and black leather slip-ons. Petra was still wearing the same scruffy clothes she had put on in London.

'Why did you need the men anyway?' Serra asked.

'I knew about Marin's delivery and I felt Belgium would be the best place to intercept it. I wanted locals who knew how to pull off a job like this, who didn't mind being ordered around by a woman and who were expendable. They were perfect on all counts.'

The lies fell easily from Petra's lips – they always did – and that made them all the more convincing. When she asked him what Khalil's agenda was, the question appeared to bore Serra. He waved a hand through the air as if the enquiry were a pesky fly that needed to be swatted. 'Oh, you know, the usual militant Islamic thing. Hatred of Israel, hatred of the United States, particularly for supporting Israel, hatred of any nation that is friendly towards the United States, hatred of the West in general. And when it's convenient, hatred of anything at all that is un-Islamic. The usual shit that keeps that part of the world in chaos and me in business.'

Straight-faced, Petra said, 'What it is to be a banker.'

'I've diversified.'

'Haven't we all.'

'You more than most. A student anarchist in Stuttgart, then Berlin, and now what?'

'I found I'd become the anachronistic anarchist.'

'That doesn't answer the question.'

'It's as close as you're going to get. My agenda is private. What happens between us has no bearing on what I choose to do independently, no matter whose money pays for it.'

They spoke softly, leaning close to one another. Petra supposed that to an onlooker, they could have appeared as lovers. She imagined Serra looked like a wealthy married man with his young mistress, a single girl who probably considered herself wild and free-spirited but who had, nevertheless, allowed herself to be bought by his charm, sophistication and money. Particularly the money.

'Still,' he murmured, 'there seems to be some shared ground between you and my client.'

'Such as?'

'The assassination of Elaine Freemantle, the US ambassador to Uganda. We believe that was your work.'

The Kampala car-bomb came courtesy of an imagination at Magenta House. The murder had never been convincingly claimed. It was several months before rumours began to circulate through the intelligence community that Petra Reuter was the culprit. It was vigorously denied for the lie that it actually was but sometimes it was enough just to make the suggestion.

Petra was inscrutable. 'What of it?'

Serra wasn't finished. 'And then there was Bruno Kuhlman, the US diplomatic envoy to Bosnia, shot dead in his hotel room in Geneva by an unidentified woman.'

Kuhlman's death had been a bizarre accident. The intended target had been a Russian businessman staying in the neighbouring suite. The female killer had escaped but was herself killed less than a week later by her Muscovite bosses in an attempt to protect themselves from the truth. That truth, when reported, sounded more implausible with every genuine detail, so it had been relatively easy for Magenta House to quietly spread the word that it was nothing more than a second-rate cover story.

'What is your point?' Petra asked.

'My client proposes an alliance.'

'I've told you, I don't form alliances.'

But Serra had a pitch to make and he was determined to see it through, no matter how awkwardly. The information was scattered thinly across their muted conversation. Petra understood this. As Stephanie, she had encountered plenty of men who wished to unburden themselves in a sense that went beyond the mere physical. Most of these revelations had been unremarkable – typically, wives who no longer interested them sexually, or who had lost their sexual appetite – but to speak of such things always seemed to be such a tortuous process. So it was with Serra. He would have liked to have told her concisely but could not bring himself to allow it.

So Petra hunted among the scraps. There was a plan, part of a grand scheme, and Serra wanted Petra's assistance. Was she to be a part of this plan? Perhaps not. Maybe she could fulfil a role as some sort of consultant for . . . for whom? Khalil? Serra remained reluctant to whisper the name. Besides, it seemed Serra himself was in charge. In charge of what? It was hard to say. For all Serra's front there remained, throughout the dialogue, a hidden presence, a shadow over the shoulder. Petra felt an invisible hand guiding him. Khalil. She was sure of it.

Petra met vagueness with vagueness. Yes, she told Serra, she would think about it but she couldn't promise him anything. How could it be any other way? How could she be enthusiastic over such an amorphous proposal?

Dinner ended and they walked back along Nieuwe Liliestraat towards the centre of the city. They crossed canals and when they reached the junction with Herengracht, Petra said she was turning right to head back for her hotel.

'Why don't you come back to my house?' Serra asked her.

'You have a house here?'

'I've been coming here for twenty years. I have many friends in the city. The house is not mine. It's borrowed.'

'How convenient.' Petra realized she should accept, if only to discover the address so that Magenta House could trace the owner and engineer further information on Serra. But she said, 'I don't think so.'

'Not even for a drink?'

She smiled coldly. 'Especially not for a drink.'

Serra shrugged ruefully. 'We'll be in contact, then.'

Petra watched him turn away on the bridge and was unable to resist a little dig. 'By the way, I don't know anything about driving in Amman but I hear that Al Mafraq is a dangerous place these days.'

Serra froze and Petra knew that Magenta House's information was right. Her call to them earlier in the day had been productive. There had been a triple shooting near the Jordanian town, which lay roughly ten miles south of the border with Syria. It was the closest match the researchers had been able to make. Two miles outside the town a gun-fight had occurred, leaving three dead Syrians in a Mercedes and one dead Iraqi on the roadside. Unconfirmed reports told of a Toyota speeding away from the scene with four men inside, one of whom was reputed to have been slightly injured.

Serra turned round and when he spoke it was almost a hiss. 'What did you say?'

'Al Mafraq.'

He stared at her, either in horror or in anger. It was hard to tell which. Perhaps it was both.

Petra shrugged. 'Like you said, information is gold.'

* * *

On New Year's Eve, they went into the West End to meet some of his friends at an Italian restaurant. It felt extraordinary to Petra to be surrounded by normal people having a good time. She laughed with the strangers who were Frank's friends; a doctor, two journalists, a sculptor, three full-time mothers, a house-husband, an accountant, a college lecturer, a film editor and another geologist. In her mind, she had somehow contrived to create a universe that only she and Frank occupied but these interlopers were a delightful shock. She knew this was how other people lived and she was just astonished to discover that she fitted in. That she *could* fit in. In the end, she concluded that it was because she was with Frank. What other reason could there be?

They left the restaurant at eleven and stepped into the freezing night. But the wine in their bellies and the crowds in the streets insulated them against the cold. The group headed for Trafalgar Square where tens of thousands of people had gathered for midnight. But Frank and Petra peeled off from the party and he led her down to the Victoria Embankment, which was also congested but not quite so severely. They secured a place on the wall overlooking the Thames and stared at the glittering lights on the far bank. Frank put his arm around Petra and hugged her close to keep her warm. The gesture brought a lump to her throat. She tried to remember the last man to do that. Proctor? Not that she could recall. Some inconsequential boyfriend? Possibly, but not likely. Her father? Probably. She didn't want to guess how long ago that had been.

Midnight came and a new year began. Big Ben boomed and the crowds on the Embankment cheered. Car horns hooted. Fireworks soared into the sky and erupted over the Thames, their reflections brilliant in the choppy surface of the black water. Frank kissed Petra and she felt happy, which, almost inevitably, stirred a sadness within her. Frank saw it in her eyes and had the grace to say nothing.

A new year was a time for a new beginning. But every vision of the future was corrupted by Alexander. As her heart lifted, her stomach sank. It didn't appear that one could exist without the other.

They walked back to their building, past the drunks in kilts, past those unconscious on the pavement, past the overcrowded buses, past intoxicated streakers, past the invisible homeless, past the streamers that hung from tree branches like leaves of brightly coloured spaghetti, past those who were searching pointlessly for a taxi.

In the lift, Frank said, 'Do you want to come in?'

'No.' He looked disappointed. Petra said, 'I want you to come to me.'

It was only as they stepped over the threshold that Petra realized it was the first time Frank had entered her flat. She watched him absorb the living room, comparing it for size, searching for signs of her in the furniture or in personal items. But the furniture wasn't hers and there were no Gaudenzi photographs. Not any more. Getting rid of them had been an exorcism of sorts. Free from the ghosts of her manufactured history, Petra had been able to regard the flat as some sort of home, not a museum.

She took him by the hand and led him to her bedroom. He reached for a light but she stopped him and whispered that there was enough light coming through the window. The curtains were left open. Slowly, she shed her clothes while he watched. Neither of them spoke. And when she was naked, she undressed him before melting on to the sheets.

His touch was becoming more familiar to her. Where initially it had left her tense and cold, now she welcomed it. She allowed his fingers and mouth to move as they wished. She denied him nothing and, gradually, found her mind emptying. The rogue thoughts faded and what filled the vacuum was purely physical. Petra had lost count of the men who had been inside her. At the end of her first week of prostitution numbers had become meaningless

300

and that had been so long ago she now regarded it as an entirely different era. Now, however, it felt as though none of them had ever existed, as though she had imagined all of them. There were no rough hands running over her body, parting her, forcing her, bruising her. Her breasts were no longer sore from mouths and fingers that pinched for the pleasure of her pain. No slaps, no oily sweat, no gagging body-odour, no scouring beards, no halitosis. Sweetest of all, no money.

She felt the orgasm most intensely in her stomach. It was a gorgeous, volcanic tremble that left her so tender she couldn't decide whether it was exquisite or excruciating. That was where it started but it spread like a fever, the heat consuming her completely, and she offered no resistance to it.

For Stephanie, for Petra, for Marina, for everyone she was, the sensation was a revelation. To give without holding anything back. It ran contrary to who she was. But then Stephanie had always derived maximum pleasure from being contrary. It was her nature.

4

MARINA'S
WORLD

22

Petra examined her reflection in the bathroom mirror. Icy air brought goose-bumps to her skin. Her nipples contracted, hardened and darkened. She touched her right breast, fuller now than when she had been Stephanie but tauter since she'd begun to exercise. She ran the palm of her hand over her stomach muscles, the definition both tangible and visible. The puppy fat that had appeared during her days with Proctor was now long gone. Her fingers moved through her dark pubic hair and between her thighs, where it remained warm, tender and sticky. She gazed at her short black hair and could hardly imagine herself with Stephanie's long, bottled-blonde locks. This cut suited her face which had grown severer. She glanced at the cosmetic scar on her left shoulder. When Frank had asked her how she'd got it, she'd told him she'd been impaled by a piece of metal during a car crash as a teenager. The ruined skin felt like plastic beneath her fingertips. Then she looked into her eyes. Deep and dark, fathomless lagoons of oil, they offered nothing to the viewer. They were shark's eyes and, excepting her mouth, were still her best feature.

Petra returned to the bedroom where he was waiting for her. Knowing what he wanted, she climbed on to the bed, took two pillows, placing one on top of the other, and then lowered herself on to them so that they raised her hips, presenting him with an invitation. He moved behind her. She heard the tear of the condom wrapper and waited for his thighs to move between hers, forcing them further apart, for his hands to run over her buttocks and hips.

He entered her with a force that caused her to shudder involuntarily, sucking air into her lungs through clenched teeth. His left hand ran up her spine to her shoulder blades and he pressed her face into the crumpled sheets. Petra closed her eyes and pretended it was Frank.

Marc Serra vanished in January. Petra tried to contact him by phone but the numbers she had for Paris and Amsterdam had been disconnected. She posted messages on her web-sites but none of her e-mail addresses received a reply. Using contacts to tap into the networks of other intelligence agencies, Magenta House tried to locate him but without success. For Alexander, Serra's disappearance was a source of great concern. For Petra, it was a bonus. It left her in London and that allowed her as much time as she wanted with Frank.

All her life, Petra had fought against love. As a child, when she was loved unconditionally, she thought she could live without it. She poisoned love and infected those closest to her. Boyfriends were always a phase to her, she remembered. Those who'd tried to win her with sensitivity were cruelly scorned, while those who mistreated her were matched and then bettered, their unpleasantness repaid with interest. Love never came into it, preparing her perfectly for the loveless world she encountered in London. In that environment, there was no love. Love was the enemy. But not any more. She saw that now, yet remained unable to think about love in any context that related to her. Even the word itself seemed alienating.

Frank travelled to Namibia for ten days towards the end of January to conduct a series of tests at potential mining sites. Petra was astonished and then ashamed at how much she missed him. Nothing had prepared her for this brand-new sensation: the ache of longing. She found it hard to sleep and lost her appetite, and although Frank called her twice, it was, somehow, worse than not speaking to him at all, since it only served to underline the distance between them. She caught herself hoping that Frank was suffering in the same way; for the first time in her life it mattered to Petra that she was missed.

The feeling was worse than addiction. In the beginning, you told yourself it was just an experiment, something to be enjoyed casually, without complication. You told yourself you could control it. But it crept up on you. It began to colour every thought in your head. It created a craving and for Petra, a first time victim at twenty-three, the shock to the system was total.

Together, they began to establish little routines. An embryonic social life developed; they started to operate as a unit and not as two separate entities. Admittedly, this social life revolved entirely around friends of Frank's but that was okay. Marina was supposed to be a stranger to London so she wasn't expected to have friends or relatives in the city.

Petra hated being Marina. She disliked having to maintain the slight trace of a foreign accent just because English was Marina's third language. She hated having to get out of bed early every weekday morning so that she could pretend to go to work at Brillex-Martins in order to sustain her cover. Lying to Frank hurt her and she resented the fact that she found it so easy. Dishonesty had always served her well. As a prostitute, it had become second nature. Most of her clients were liars and she was a liar too; she faked everything. And now, as Petra, lying was as vital to her life as blood itself. It was the only guarantor of the possibility of a future. Lying to Frank, however, felt worse than infidelity. A lie, once established, had to be backed up by other lies which, themselves, had to be secured by yet more. Once started, the process never ended. Lies infected every part of the relationship. No conversation was spared, no thought was free to be idly thought; it had to be screened for security. More than once, Petra had come to the conclusion that what she felt for Frank didn't really exist. That it was just another lie. After all, if the

307

feeling was so stained by deception, what could it honestly be? Logic offered her no answer. All she knew was that there was no antidote to the rush she got when she thought about Frank. There was no remedy for his touch.

To her surprise, she found it was the small things she enjoyed most about Frank. She liked to watch him shave in the morning. Sometimes, he'd catch her reflection in the mirror and ask what she was doing and she'd shrug and say nothing. She noticed herself absorbing details, cataloguing the minutiae in the library of her mind. His watch was Swiss with a worn leather strap. He was right-handed. None of his clothes had a designer label and he tended towards the conservative in cut and colour. He wore circular glasses to read and she liked the way they sat on his large Roman nose. He was a slow eater. There was a small scar by his left eye, the legacy of a childhood fall. When he talked of his travels, which at Petra's instigation he often did, his eyes glazed over and she knew he was back in the place he was describing.

These were the things that made Frank three-dimensional to Petra. Each trivial fragment was a revelation, compounding all those that had gone before. And as the days melted into weeks, she found herself becoming increasingly enveloped by this private universe, to the exclusion of everything that existed outside it. Which made Serra's reappearance all the more unwelcome.

On the third of February, there was a response to V. Libensky on the Heavens Above site. Petra initiated the dialogue in the usual way and, forty-eight hours later, they met in Amsterdam. Petra noticed the difference immediately. Well tanned and slimmer, Serra was more subdued than before. There was no talk of imminent collaboration although he did raise the prospect of a longer-term arrangement. On the other hand, he seemed pleased to see her on a personal level so that when he said they should meet again to discuss the future, Petra wasn't sure what future he had in mind. For her own part, she was true to type and was indifferent towards him. Serra, too, was true to type and appeared to enjoy it.

Back in London, Alexander fretted. It had been a gamble to reveal to Serra that Petra knew that Khalil was his pay-master and it appeared to have back-fired. Rather than proving to be a pass to the inner circle, it seemed Serra had opted for caution and had excluded her altogether from whatever was forthcoming. Alexander insisted Petra remain in contact with him to see if there was any way he could be persuaded to reconsider. Serra's January tan concerned Alexander. Where had he got it? Discounting the holiday destinations of the southern hemisphere, Alex-ander focused on the Far and Middle East and on Africa. The list he created only fuelled his anxiety.

Petra and Serra met again in Amsterdam at the start of the third week of February. As before, she stayed at the Hotel Ambassade. They spent three days in the city, meet-ing between other appointments he had to keep. Serra seemed more relaxed and talked openly about an alliance where Khalil would select targets, where Serra himself would organize finance and where Petra would carry out operations. She agreed to consider it but promised him nothing. On their third and final evening in Holland, Serra made a pass at Petra. She rejected it but not too firmly, allowing the scent of possibility to linger. A date for Paris was fixed.

Petra had already considered that she might have to resort to something personal in order to get close to Serra. While she found the prospect distasteful, she was not worried about her ability to see it through. As a prostitute, she had learned how to compartmentalize her mind. In Scotland, Boyd had taught her techniques to reinforce this skill; picturing the mind as a house with many rooms, all separate, into any one of which a problem could be dispatched. The trick was learning how to shut doors. As Stephanie, it was a talent she had developed to perfection, divorcing herself from Lisa, so she was confident that if she had to have sex with Serra, it would have no influence on her relationship with Frank. It would not be infidelity. It would be business. Just like it used to be.

When Serra came, the sound that emerged from his throat was like a strangled cough. The next thing Petra knew, his body was pressing down on her, crushing her to the sheets. His skin was damp with perspiration, hers was dry. For several moments, neither of them moved. Their breathing was the only sound in the room. Petra felt her heart thumping inside her chest and tried to ignore the faint sense of nausea in her stomach. Serra withdrew from her slowly, leaving a sore heat in his wake. She watched him get off the bed and head for the bathroom to remove and dispose of the condom. When he returned, he said, 'Are you sure you have to leave tomorrow?'

She nodded. 'You're not the only one with other interests.'

'Where are you going?'

'You think that just because you've had sex with me, I'll tell you anything you want to know?'

'You never tell me anything I want to know.'

'Then we have something in common.'

'But you know where I live. This is Paris. This apartment is my home.'

'And you know where I live. In my computer. You'll always find me there.'

'I could have you followed.'

'You could try.'

They talked for twenty minutes before Serra turned out the light. It was eleven-forty-four. Petra waited until half-past-twelve, allowing him time to slip into a deep sleep. Then she got up.

In the bathroom, she opened her wash-bag and took out a small bottle of scent, a cellophane-wrapped tampon travel-pack and two sachets of 'Nu-Fresh Handy-Wipes', which were supposed to be disgusting moistened squares

310

of cleansing tissue, but which actually contained a small amount of anaesthetic gel. She opened the tampon container. Inside was one syringe and two needles. She freed one of the needles from its wrapper and attached it to the end of the syringe, before removing the suction-sealed lid from the top of the scent bottle. The scented masking agent, which was sweet, was neutral and harmless. The liquid in the bottle was Ketamine, which was what had been injected into Petra when she had been abducted by Magenta House. Ten milligrams per kilogram of body-weight would provide between twenty and twenty-five minutes of surgical anaesthesia but without the necessity for assisted breathing. Petra didn't want to send Serra so deeply under but she needed secure time to roam, so she altered the dose slightly. If necessary, there was plenty of Ketamine left for a second administration.

She returned to the bedroom with the syringe and one of the sachets. Gently, she moved on to the bed beside Serra, who had begun to snore. He was sleeping on his side, which was good. At first, she considered a buttock for the intramuscular injection but then opted for the knotted muscles at the back of the shoulders, which, in Serra's case, were fairly hairy. She tore a corner off the sachet and squeezed some of the gel on to her fingers. Serra shifted at her touch but the movement of her fingers was slow and rhythmic and his breathing soon settled. It took sixty seconds for the anaesthetic to work its way through the skin and into the muscle. Petra waited for two minutes just to be sure.

She was certain the needle would wake him but Serra never stirred when it pierced his skin by the edge of a large, dark mole. She depressed the plunger and sent the Ketamine into his system.

It was cold so she got dressed, pulling on a pair of jeans, a thick black jersey and her navy socks. She reached into her canvas rucksack and unfastened an inner pocket from which she took a small, portable document scanner. Then she moved from the bedroom into the hall, through the large living room that overlooked the rue de Rivoli, and into the office at the other end of the apartment. It had taken Petra three days to study Serra's routine, to identify those things she wished to investigate in private, to earn some partial trust from him. And during those three days – and the nights that divided them – she had denied him nothing. That was the price that had to be paid for this moment. As an act of prostitution, her performance was without equal.

Petra knew what she was to Serra: something rough and something dangerous. That was the thrill for him; he possessed a disdain for low culture and outsiders, yet he conducted business with the worst dregs from humanity's barrel and took pleasure in it. Petra was familiar with the type. Men who publicly conformed to a certain station in life, but who, privately, liked nothing better than to get dirty with the targets of their contempt. She had seen the hunger in his eyes as she traipsed through his magnificent apartment like a tramp he'd scraped from the street, her scruffy rucksack slung over her shoulder, her boots scuffing the floor. When they had sex he was coarse and indulgent, and Petra could easily imagine his other women; pale, fine-boned creatures to whom he had to 'make love'.

Now, she was alone. She drew the curtains in his office and switched on the light. His lap-top was on a mahogany desk. She raised the screen, switched it on and drew up a directory of the system files and the data files. In the system files, she examined the times and dates of file entries. Then she turned her attention to the data, starting with the names and numbers in his address books. Some were familiar, most were not, none startled her. After fifteen minutes, she came across a folder entitled 'FDS/12'. Inside, there were four files: FAT, FAT/1, FAT/2, FAT/3. And so a minor mystery was solved: the Fat Three List was FAT/3. Petra saw that there had been an original FAT list, followed by three revisions. The last recorded amendment to each of the files confirmed this. They had been emptied in order, at intervals of one week, three and a half months and six days. FAT/3 had been cleared at the beginning of December.

She opened the top drawer of his desk and found the plastic container full of paper clips. Her fingers clawed the key out of the bottom of it – she had watched him put it in there the previous morning when he thought she was out of sight – and used it to unlock the filing cabinet by the door. There was a mass of correspondence to and on behalf of Banque Henri Lauder. She found folders full of bank statements, some personal, some commercial. The French-Arab Scholarship Society, she noticed, had an account in Zurich with almost eight million Swiss Francs in it. It received a monthly income of one hundred thousand Swiss Francs from a Sliema-based branch of the Mid-Med Bank in Malta. Alexander had wondered how the Society was really funded, how it could afford to sponsor one hundred and thirty-five 'students' throughout the European Union. Now Petra knew the answer, and the truth was that one hundred and thirty-five seemed rather meagre.

She began to run the document scanner over the information she deemed valuable. Much of it would be of little use to Magenta House but she knew that Alexander would find a way to pass the information on to another, more appropriate intelligence agency if he thought it merited it. That in itself would make it valuable currency. It took two passes of the machine to record a sheet of A4, which would later be cut and reassembled side by side to form the page. Petra was meticulous when it came to replacing everything exactly as she found it.

In other drawers, she found other documents. In one folder, she came across receipts and invoices for imports and exports handled by a London-based firm called Anglo-Egyptian Cargo Company, which was based on the Earls Court Road. There was a travel agency – RJN Travel – in

Hogarth Road, which was also in Earls Court. She recalled that the al-Sharif Students Hostel was nearby, which seemed too close to be a coincidence. Petra made a mental note to have the connection investigated. Intriguingly, she found an invoice from a firm of west London electricians which contained FAT/3 in the box that should have contained the date. There were twelve entries on the list but they all appeared as product code references. Once she'd scanned the list, she closed the folder and moved on.

There were letters to and from Telegenex, the French firm who manufactured missile guidance systems. Serra was acting on behalf of a client who was, himself, a broker for an anonymous end-user. There were monthly payments to a private account from Murray-Gardyne, the small Canadian arms manufacturer. Interestingly, the payments came from an account in Mexico City and Petra knew that the firm owned an illegal land-mine production facility in Guadalajara.

Other files revealed a large amount of information and a surprising proportion of it was London-based: Arab newspapers, Middle-Eastern diplomatic officials, banks, restaurants, import-export companies, hotels, property firms, airlines, private individuals. Nearly every entry had a contact name to go with it but of all those she saw, only one stood out: Alexandria Clothing Company – garment importer/ Qadiq, I.

When Serra awoke, Petra pretended she was still asleep. He shuffled into the bathroom and she heard the shower. Half an hour later, she rose from the bed and pulled on his grey silk dressing-gown. She found him in the kitchen, fiddling with a chrome espresso machine. The hand holding the cup and saucer was trembling.

'Morning,' she said.

He jumped, spilling some of the scalding coffee on to his fingers. Petra leaned against a wall and folded her arms as Serra sat down at the zinc-topped table and lit a Marlboro.

His eyes were bleary, the whites stained a sickly yellow. There was a greyness to his skin that added ten years to him.

'You don't look too good.'

He glanced at the empty bottles of burgundy by the sink. 'I feel like shit.'

'A hangover?'

'Worse. Ill, maybe, I don't know . . .'

Petra shrugged unsympathetically. 'I hope it's not contagious.'

Serra's left arm reached across to rub the back of his right shoulder. 'I have an ache, too.'

Petra smiled. 'So it's true, then.'

'What?'

'That Parisians are the greatest hypochondriacs in the world.'

She filled the kettle, fired a gas ring and placed it on the blue flame.

'When are you going?' Serra asked.

'Half an hour.'

He scratched his jaw. 'There's something we need to discuss before you go.'

'Can't it wait? You don't look up to it.'

'No. It can't wait. It's Khalil.'

Petra hoped the lurch in her chest hadn't manifested itself in any way that Serra could notice – if, indeed, he was in a condition to notice anything. 'What about him?'

Serra sucked on his cigarette and looked thoughtful. 'Rightly or wrongly, Khalil believes the United States is leading a crusade against Islam.'

'Not an original idea.'

'No. But a sincere one.'

'Maybe even a correct one,' Petra said.

'Exactly.'

'Not being a Muslim, it's not something I feel personal about.'

'No. But American imperialism is, perhaps, something you feel personal about?'

'What I feel personal about is personal.'

They kissed, they hugged, then they kissed again. Then Frank said, 'How was it?'

Petra looked into his eyes. 'Tiring.'

He led her into the kitchen where he began to prepare green tea. She sat on a steel stool and watched. He asked her questions and she made up answers for him. Yes, the trip had been a success but Brussels had been damp and cold. No, she wasn't sure when her next trip would be.

The kitchen was the same. Frank was the same. Everything was as it had been before. It wasn't necessary to believe that she'd had sex with Serra.

Frank turned round and offered her a mug of green tea. Petra took it, placed it on the table and then took hold of his hand. She said, 'I missed you.'

It's five to six in the morning and I am in Frank's sitting room, a mug of coffee in my hands. I am wearing a thick black jersey of his that almost reaches my knees. The wool scratches my skin. I have been awake for hours.

Rosie, one of Magenta House's in-house operators, once told me about Greta Muller, an East German spy who worked undercover in Britain from 1981 until the fall of the Honecker regime in East Germany. Among those in the international intelligence community, Muller has become a minor legend. Posing as a Swede – she spoke Swedish fluently – she came into contact with a vulnerable GCHQ operative named Roger Bolton, whom she married the following year. Not only did she marry him, but she had three sons and a daughter by him. Her exposure only occurred when secret Stasi files were made public and her true identity was revealed. By the time MI5 was alerted – less than twenty-four hours after the discovery – Muller had vanished, abandoning her husband and four children. Bolton, it transpired during interrogation, had never suspected a thing. Why should he have?

She had never given him a reason to doubt her. They had even stayed with her parents – their children's grandparents – in Stockholm, he claimed. They were fakes too, it turned out, elaborate extras in an extravagant deceit. Today, nobody knows where Greta Muller is, or whether she is even alive. But her reputation is assured.

I take a sip from my coffee mug. Marriage, children and a decade of deception. How did she do it? Perhaps she avoided making the critical error that I have made. Perhaps she avoided the pernicious side-effects of love. Once the heart infiltrates, it subverts. I thought reason and willpower would protect me but I should have known better.

Last night, I made love with Frank and it was beautiful. When we kissed my soul flooded into his mouth and when I looked into his eyes, he was the world and everything in it. Nothing else mattered or even existed. But when I closed my eyes, I saw Serra. And the more I tried to banish him, the more persistent he became.

I want Frank but I cannot have him without Serra. Frank is the future but Serra is the key to the future. Or rather, he is the key to one future, one of many. I am trapped and I don't know what to do.

23

Alexandria Clothing Company. That was the name painted beside the door at the rear of the warehouse. Last time, she had followed Ismail Qadiq into the building through the front. Now, at five to midnight, the building was deserted and would remain so until morning.

Petra tested the small black rucksack, ensuring that it was fastened securely to her back, and then flexed her fingers inside thin black gloves. The palms and fingertips were coated in spray-fine rubber for extra grip. She checked the narrow alley for observers but saw no one. At the foot of the drain-pipe there were four cartons of discarded Chinese food. The aroma of sweet and sour stuck unpleasantly at the back of her throat. She began the ascent. Despite the wetness, the grip on her boots never faltered on the brick. A lesser climber might have made for the three small windows high to her right in the hope that one of them was unfastened. But Petra went straight for the flat warehouse roof. At the top of the drain-pipe, she tugged on the guttering. It wobbled so she turned her attention to the concrete overhang. She ran her fingers over the surface. The rain had made it slippery but Petra felt confident. One hand rose to the top of the ledge, her fingers splaying and then tensing. The second hand followed. When both were in place she gently released her thigh-grip on the drain-pipe.

For a second, she looked down into the alley below, a slice of blackness between the backs of two buildings. She steadied her hanging body and thought, momentarily, of Frank, alone in his bed, under the impression that there

318

was a panic at Brillex-Martins and that she was expecting to have to work through the night.

It was too risky to attempt any swing so she hauled her body upwards, bringing her chin level with her hands, aware of the heat generated in her biceps. She needed another eighteen inches. With a surge of power she pulled her body yet higher and reached for the back of the ledge. A secure grip attained, she scrambled over the overhang.

Easy. She was her mother's daughter, for sure. Boyd would have approved.

She patrolled the roof, aware of the cold trickle of rainwater that ran down the back of her neck. There was a large ventilation unit at the centre of the roof and there were four skylights, one towards each corner. She stepped over discarded pieces of scaffolding on the tarpaper and looked at the nearby tower-blocks, their upper floors fading into a wet and gloomy soft focus. The road below was illuminated by the orange light that fell from street lamps. A group of drunken men staggered out of a pub, laughing and swearing. One of them vomited over the bonnet of a parked Vectra. Somewhere in the distance, police sirens cut through the night.

Petra returned to one of the skylights and produced a jemmy from her rucksack. It opened easily, the rotten plastic frame offering little resistance. She opened the skylight and lowered herself on to the metal gantry that ran around the upper areas of the warehouse. A caged ladder led to the floor.

She saw wooden crates piled high along one wall, opposite three baby fork-lift trucks. Remembering where the office was she swung her Mag-Lite torch in its direction, the light reflecting back off the grease stains on the glass. Then she made her way to the warehouse entrance and laid two small black boxes on either side of the cargo door. There was a switch on the smaller unit which, when activated, started blinking. She played with the position of the box until a steady green light appeared; the beam between the two units was now established. She headed back towards the office and turned on the hand-held monitor; if the beam was broken, an alarm would sound.

She switched on the light in the office. Curiosity drew her to the wall at the back. A collection of receipts and invoices was pinned to it. She looked behind them and saw the hole. Someone had clawed the bullet out of the plaster but they hadn't bothered to repair the damage. Petra smiled. It was pure luck she hadn't killed Ismail Qadiq. Stephanie hadn't had a clue what she was doing and yet had managed to squeeze the name of Reza Mohammed from the Egyptian more easily than Petra could have. On the other hand, Stephanie could just as easily have killed him by mistake.

For five hours, Petra went through Qadiq's records. Some of the information she came across was in Arabic but most of it was in English. She saw Mustafa Sela's name several times. The Reza Mohammed-Mustafa Sela connection remained a mystery. She came across two references to the al-Sharif Students Hostel in Earls Court. One had the name Obaid by it, the other had Mirqas, which later pricked her attention when she discovered a piece of paper in an old notebook. Scribbled in biro, in one corner, was the name of Keith Proctor and his address. It was followed by a slash and the name of Mirqas. Also written in the same hand were some four-digit numbers. The way the information had been put down, Petra guessed that Qadiq had been having a conversation on the phone; it wasn't the primary material on the page. Perhaps the notebook had been the closest thing to hand.

Just after four, she found a photo-copy of a fax. Her eye was caught by an item near the top of the single page: **Re: FAT/3**. There were twelve incomprehensible lines beneath it. Each was a collection of numbers and letters. There appeared to be no coherent factor linking any of them. The sender's name and number had been removed and the space for the date was blank.

Petra left the building the same way she had entered it, just after six. She got into the white Volkswagen Golf that she had parked three streets away and drove back through the City. The first of the bankers and brokers were making their way from the Underground stations to their glass towers. She headed for the Embankment and then parked in Savoy Place. She left the keys in the glove compartment. The Magenta House courier would have keys of their own.

She was back at her flat by seven.

Midday. Petra trawled the aisles of the Europa supermarket. The fluorescent overheads compounded her headache. She tested bananas and oranges for ripeness but her mind paid no attention to what her fingertips were telling her. Keith Proctor consumed her thoughts. Seeing his name scribbled in Qadiq's notebook had soured her heart.

She had often assumed that Reza Mohammed had killed Proctor. Proctor had been in contact with Qadiq during his search for the NE027 bomber – Stephanie had got Qadiq's address from Proctor's computer diary – so it seemed reasonable that Qadiq might have alerted Mohammed to the fact that there was a journalist who was intending to expose him. But now it seemed that someone named Mirqas might have been responsible. It occurred to her that Mirqas and Mohammed were one and the same but then she dismissed the thought for being too convenient.

Proctor was the reason that Stephanie had become Petra. The goal might have been justice for her dead family but Proctor had proved to be the catalyst. Without him, Petra would still have been Stephanie masquerading as Lisa. Probably. Or maybe she would have been dead by now, a victim of a savage client, or of Dean West's expired patience, or of an overdose, perhaps intentional, perhaps not.

Petra spent the afternoon watching a black-and-white film on Channel Five. Dressed in a grey vest and black leggings, she lay on the sofa, her frame curled around the cushions she clutched to her ribs. At six, she checked her lap-top. There was a message on the Heavens Above site for V. Libensky. She replied using Andrew Smith's e-mail. It was Serra, suggesting a meeting. Could she be in Paris by mid-day tomorrow? She sent a return message to say that she could and then had a quick bath so that she wouldn't be late for Frank.

There are six of us around the table in this Italian restaurant in Marylebone. On my left is John Fletcher, an old friend of Frank's who works as an analyst for an investment bank in the City. Mary, his mousy wife, is sitting opposite me. Rick Donald sits to my right. He is an architect and used to work for Sir Norman Foster. His wife is Rachel and she is talking to Frank.

John Fletcher has come straight from work and is still wearing his pin-stripe suit. It is badly creased. So is he. Fletcher is not a public-school product who sailed into his job; he comes from a broken background of poverty, unemployment and divorce, and it is a past he is trying to leave behind for ever. And no matter how successful he becomes, he will never succeed. His drive never allows him to relax for fear of falling behind so that although this is essentially a social occasion, he cannot resist introducing a professional element to our conversation.

'Brillex-Martins,' he murmurs, as he scans the data in his memory. 'They're constructing that new chemical facility near Antwerp, right?'

This is heading towards dangerous waters for me. 'Actually, it's pharmaceutical,' I correct him, wondering whether the error was deliberate, 'but yes, it is close to Antwerp. About fifteen kilometres from the centre.'

'Have you worked for them long?'

'Nearly five years,' I say, hoping that this is what I told Frank.

My stomach tightens with each question. I sip some Barolo. As Petra, I would find this easy but I am trying to be Marina and I cannot simply transfer the attributes of one to the other. I wish I could.

'And how long have you lived in London?'

'For about three months.'

He begins to ask me about Brillex-Martins products. About research rumours. About patents. About impending lawsuits. About potential mergers with other companies. My pulse starts to accelerate. Even though Frank is talking to Rachel Donald, I am suddenly convinced that he is listening to me and that he will sense the trouble I am in. This cover is supposed to be effective for those in Khalil's world, for the kind of people Marc Serra knows, not for City analysts. They were never on the menu. I don't know the intimate details of my company's business practices, or even of the products they manufacture. I can see the doubt in Fletcher's eyes and hope that he construes my reticence as professional caution and not as total ignorance.

'And what exactly do you do for them?' he asks.

I use the same reply that I once gave to Frank. 'I'm a trouble-shooter.'

This raises an eyebrow and I feel it's time to kill the conversation, so before he can cross-examine my answer, I say, 'What about you? What exactly is it that you do?'

My food arrives. Spaghetti puttanesca. Naturally.

This is the way some people behave in this city. This is normal. They are in their mid-thirties, mostly. They are professionals, they are spouses, they are parents. I look around at the other diners in this restaurant and many of them are the same. Their normality only serves to heighten my sense of abnormality. It is true that I am younger than all those at this table. At twenty-three I should, perhaps, still be a student. Or maybe I should be embarking upon a career, underpaid but full of optimism. But I don't feel twenty-three and my optimism lies in fragments at the bottom of the Atlantic Ocean. Frank only succeeds in intensifying this feeling. If there was no Frank, I wouldn't have to worry about losing him. I would be alone and, therefore, unafraid.

Mary Fletcher and Rachel Donald begin to talk about babies. Mary has a boy of four and a girl of two, Rachel has a pair of boys, one of three and one of eighteen months. This conversation *persists for most of the rest of the evening. They reminisce about first steps and first words, about sleepless nights and cracked nipples. Occasionally, one of them finds it in herself to include me in the conversation.*

'Being Italian, I imagine you'll be wanting a large family,' Mary says at one point.

I smile and say that I'm not sure. Being Italian? Being a mother? I am neither, and neither would seem to suit the real me. The real *me. Now there's someone I'd like to meet one day.*

Rachel says, 'I'm sorry, Marina. This must be very boring for you, listening to the two of us going on like this. I'm afraid it happens to all of us. Once you've had them, you can't talk about anything else.'

Evidently.

When I was a teenager, I was adamant that I would never have children. I didn't mean it. I didn't even think about it. I just said it to provoke a negative reaction. Now, when I think about it, I find I'm not sure. For instance, I look across the table at Frank – who sees me out of the corner of his eye and manages to direct a smile at me even though he's listening to Mary – and I can picture us as parents. Frank and Marina (or Stephanie) and their one/two/three children. But this image is transmitted from a parallel universe where he has a perfect job, where I am a happy housewife and mother, where we have a house in the country.

Do I feel the maternal instinct deep within me? Not at the moment. Have I ever felt it? As a child, maybe, but I don't remember. Besides, bringing a baby into the world in which I have spent the last four years would surely constitute an act of criminality. Perhaps my maternal instinct was eradicated by the alcohol I drank, or by the drugs I took, or by the men who beat and fucked it out of me. Or perhaps it is alive. Perhaps it is dormant, waiting for a time when it will be safe to emerge from the darkness. Yes, perhaps this is what has happened to it.

I cup my glass with both hands, take another sip of wine and cling to this thought. My stomach now feels pleasantly warm. A tired smile creeps across my lips, which draws Rachel's attention.

'A penny for your thoughts,' she says.

And I reply smugly, 'Sorry. Money can't buy them.' Which, given my recent past, seems a peculiar thing to say.

Arm in arm, they crossed Oxford Street. The shoppers were gone, replaced by the homeless who made beds out of damp cardboard and bedrooms out of shop doorways. Two drunks were sitting on a bench, clutching cans of Red Stripe, arguing about nothing. A third drunk urinated on to a recently-planted sapling.

'What's wrong?' Petra asked.

'I was just thinking about something John said to me.'

'What?'

'He said he thought you were very defensive.'

Petra resisted the instant urge to deny it. 'Really?'

Frank nodded. 'He thought you were evasive when he was asking you things.'

'Well, maybe, but you know how it is. Perhaps I would've been less reluctant if he'd been a teacher or a doctor. But he's an analyst for a City firm and I don't really know him so I have to be careful what I say to him. Information is currency.'

'He seemed to think your caution extended to personal questions as well.'

'That might also be true. I don't know him well enough to be discussing things I consider deeply personal.'

They walked past the American embassy in Grosvenor Square and headed down South Audley Street. The silence jarred.

Eventually, Petra said, 'What is it? What's on your mind, Frank?'

'It doesn't matter.'

The answer irritated her. She stopped walking, forcing him to turn to face her. 'Of course it matters.'

'No,' he insisted. 'It doesn't.'

But Petra persisted. 'Let me guess. You agree with him. You think I am evasive and cautious.'

325

She watched Frank consider a denial and then dismiss it. 'To be honest, yes.'

Suddenly, there was nothing to say. Petra felt like an idiot for pressing him. He offered her a way out. 'But it's not a problem.'

A mixture of panic and anger flared within her. 'Well, it obviously is. You think I'm holding out on you.'

'I think you're taking your time to tell me stuff. That's all. And it's okay.'

She noticed she was shaking. 'Everybody has secrets, Frank.'

'I know.'

'Even you. You must have secrets.'

'Of course I do.'

Something snapped within her – a baby wishbone inside her head – and the words were suddenly spilling from her lips before she could censor them. 'Then don't be such a bloody hypocrite!'

'I'm not being anything.'

Frank's smile was supposed to be conciliatory and sympathetic. To Petra, it looked patronizing and it enraged her. 'God, do you really think this is funny?'

'I think you're over-reacting.'

'I don't have to tell you everything about me. I don't have to tell you anything!'

A couple passed by. They stared at Petra and, in return, she glared at them until they averted their eyes.

Frank said, 'Marina, what's the matter with you?'

The pause lasted long enough for Petra to lose the edge. Her anger waned just as suddenly as it had exploded. She was cold again. She took several deep breaths and then buried her face in her hands. She felt Frank's hands on her shoulders, felt the welcome weight of reassurance flooding out of them and into her. And this depressed her yet further.

'It's okay,' he told her. 'I meant it. It doesn't matter.'

* * *

Dawn was a steel sky leaking rain. When Petra entered the kitchen, Frank was standing by the window overlooking Clarges Street, a mug of coffee in his hand. She wondered how long he had been up; the bed had been empty when her eyes had opened.

'Morning,' she said.

He looked around. 'Marina, about last night –'

More through shame than anger, she said, 'Oh don't, Frank. Please.'

He raised a hand. 'Fine. But there's just one thing I've got to say. And then I'll give it a rest.'

'What?'

'I don't need to know everything about you. And perhaps it's better that I don't. I care about you, not your past, or your job, or anything else.'

They'd returned home in a charged silence and had made love in the darkness before drifting into sleep with hardly a word exchanged between them. On waking alone, Petra had winced at the replay in her mind and had read Frank's absence as a bad sign. She'd quickly pulled on a pair of old cargo pants and a thick black jersey, the sleeves of which extended beyond her outstretched fingertips. Then she'd crept through the flat, anxious to find Frank. And anxious about what kind of mood he'd be in.

He said, 'If you have reasons to be evasive, then that's okay. Let's leave it at that. Maybe you'll feel you can tell me things in the future, maybe not. But let's not make it a problem now. All right?'

Words failed her. Petra crossed the kitchen, put her arms around his neck and drew him into a full-blooded kiss. She could taste the coffee on his tongue.

They kissed and Petra tasted nicotine on his tongue.

Serra said, 'I've missed you.'

Petra swallowed her instinctive reaction. 'I've missed you, too.'

He kissed her again and she felt his fingers fumbling

with the buttons on her shirt and she wished she had worn something else.

'Is this what you brought me here for?' she asked, tersely.

'Would you be angry if it was?'

'Yes, I would.'

'Well, it isn't.'

He took her hand and led her through to the bedroom. Five hours ago, in London, she had made love with Frank. Now, in an apartment on the rue de Rivoli, it was Serra's mouth that was busy with her nipples, that traced a line over her stomach and pressed itself between her thighs. Petra closed her eyes and tried to remember how to play the part.

Half an hour later, they were in Serra's living room. He was drinking a glass of wine, Petra was having Coke. She hadn't bothered to shower – she'd been in a hurry to cover herself – and now she regretted it. She felt dirty. In both body and mind.

'Tell me about Khalil,' she said.

'What about him?'

'I'm curious. He's a name to everyone but nothing more.'

'Like you are.'

'But not to you. Who is he? What do you know about him?'

Serra shrugged. 'Only what I've been told myself and none of it came from him.'

'But you know him better than most, right?'

'Of course. But that doesn't mean it's all true.'

'I understand that.'

Serra lit a cigarette with a match. 'As far as I know, Khalil was probably born in Kuwait City in 1966. His father may have been Mohammed Khalid Mahmud, an engineer from the Baluchi tribe in Pakistan. His mother may have been Palestinian and still nobody knows Khalil's full name. If, however, these were his parents, then Khalil was raised in the Fuhayhil area of Kuwait City, which is a working-class district with a large Palestinian population. In 1986, Mohammed Khalid Mahmud returned to Pakistan, settling in Peshawar in the Northwest Frontier. By this time, as you know, Peshawar had become a strategic launching pad for the Mujahidin who were conducting their war against the Soviets just across the border in Afghanistan. So Khalil's experiences in Kuwait City and Peshawar probably provided the basis for what he has become.'

Petra drank from her can. 'I know that he took spiritual guidance from Sheikh Abdul Kamal Qassam and that like Sheikh Omar Abdel Rahman, Qassam was convicted by a New York Court. That would be enough to give Khalil motive, but without finance, there's no end-product.'

'True.'

'And you organize money on his behalf so what I'd like to know is this: where does it come from originally?'

'Kamal Ibrahim Karim.'

'I don't think I know him.'

'A follower of Osama bin Laden. Karim was trained in one of the Algerian camps financed by bin Laden. Where Karim differs from most of bin Laden's followers is in the fact that he is rich, like bin Laden himself. Karim's family have amassed hundreds of millions of dollars through oil, shipping, construction and banking. I don't know the true value of Karim's own fortune but it is certainly more than one hundred million dollars. He's not Khalil's only sponsor but he's the main one.'

'Are they ideologically aligned?'

'Only in the sense that the United States is the number one enemy. Karim may be a Pakistani but he follows the Wahhabi sect of Sunni Islam, which is predominant in Saudi Arabia. Saudi Arabia has a special status throughout the Islamic world because it is home to the two holiest shrines in Islam: *Haram al-Sharif*, the Noble Shrine, and *Masjed an-Nabi*, the Prophet's Mosque. For these two reasons alone, Kamal Karim finds it totally unacceptable

that there should be American soldiers – *Christian* soldiers
– on Saudi soil. They insult Islam by being there. That is
his primary motivation. But even if they withdrew
tomorrow, the United States would still be the number
one enemy because of its support of Israel and for being
a nation of Cross-worshippers. Until the enemies of Islam
are defeated, there can be no rest. For Khalil, though,
the matter is more personal. He craves revenge for the
imprisonment of Sheikh Abdul Kamal Qassam.'

'Khalil and Karim – how was their alliance made?'

'Karim is based in Peshawar, where Mohammed Khalid
Mahmud moved in 1986, so the chances are it had something to do with that. It would certainly lend credibility to
the theory that Mahmud is Khalil's father.'

'Unless that theory itself was floated as a piece of misin-
formation.'

'True.'

Petra sat cross-legged on the sofa but Serra was pacing.

'How long are you staying in Paris?' he asked.

Her lying response was automatic. 'I'm flying to Zurich
early this evening.'

Serra raised an eyebrow. 'Zurich?'

'Don't even think about it.'

'Of course,' he said, some slight mockery in his tone. 'I
should have known better.'

'Yes, you should've.'

'There's no chance of you staying tonight, then?'

'No chance.'

He smiled ruefully. 'That's a shame.' She reciprocated
the dumb smile. He said, 'Since you left, I've been thinking
about you. About us.'

Play the game. She dropped her gaze in an effort to look
coy, a look which had never been natural to her. 'So have
I. More than I should have.'

'What does that mean?'

She looked up. 'It means that it could be dangerous for
us.'

Serra nodded and then said, 'I have something to ask you that needs an immediate answer.'

'And for this, I had to come here?'

'There was no other way to discuss it. And there isn't much time. Depending on what you say, I'll need to make preparations straight away.'

'What is it?'

'Khalil wants you to be a sleeper.'

Petra took her time. 'A hostage situation, then?'

Serra nodded. 'A hijack.'

'On an aircraft?'

'Yes.'

During a hijack, it was a sleeper's job to masquerade as one of the hostages. From this position, they spied on the hijackers, the aircraft's crew and any on-board security. They did not participate in the hijack themselves, even in the event of the operation going wrong.

'The answer's no. Hijacks are too difficult to control.'

'Not this one.'

'Every hijacker thinks they have it worked out. Unless they want to die. And I'm not in that category.'

'Believe me, the outcome of this hijack is assured. The hostages will be released. You will be one of them.'

'Why me? Why not one of the hijack team?'

'Khalil wants an outsider, someone who did not train with them. A non-Muslim. Someone he can trust.'

She laughed at the irony. 'So much for faith within religion. He thinks he can trust me just because he's hired me?'

Petra knew as well as Stephanie that money was no guarantee of loyalty.

'No. He knows he cannot trust you. That's why he wants you to do it on the same basis as New York. For the money.'

'What's the angle?'

'He wants to meet you.'

'There are easier ways.'

'Not to meet Khalil. He is obsessive about security. He

avoids all conventional meetings. He is suspicious of everyone and constantly fearful of identification, or something even worse. In this case, though, he sees a way.'

'Let me guess. He's going to be in the seat next to me?'

'He won't be on the aircraft. But he will be waiting for you when you get off it.'

Petra had to concede that her curiosity was pricked. 'Go on.'

Serra stopped pacing and sat in the armchair nearest her. He leaned forward, his elbows on his thighs, his voice lowered as though they were in a public place and might be overheard.

'The aircraft will come down in Malta. It will be on the ground for a matter of hours – maybe twenty-four or so – and then the hostages will be released.'

'Why?'

'Because they will have served their purpose.'

'Which is what?'

'You don't need to know that.'

'Where's this flight supposed to be going?'

'That remains a secret, too.'

'Along with its place of departure, I suppose?'

'Of course.'

'And the timing?' He gave her a dismissive look, to which she said, 'You'll have to tell me sooner or later.'

'I know. And it'll be later. At the moment when it is necessary and not before.'

Petra found a smile from somewhere and said, 'I'm glad to see that despite our situation, you haven't lost your edge. We can share anything except trust.'

Serra leaned back and exhaled blue smoke. 'Unnecessary information should never be given out, not even to one's closest friends. The Prophet Mohammed said, "He who keeps secrets shall soon attain his objectives."'

'You're a regular reader of the Qur'an, are you?'

'I've found that in my line of work, it pays to have some knowledge of it.'

'Oh, I can imagine.'

'So, what do you think?'

'It's too sudden.'

'I know, I know. But I need an answer.'

She bit her lip. 'Why me?'

'I don't understand.'

'I assume this plan has been in development for some time. Khalil must have known that he was going to need a non-Muslim sleeper. Why did he leave it so late? That doesn't make sense.'

'There was a sleeper in place. But he is no longer available.'

'What happened to him?'

'He had a car accident.'

'Right.' Petra manufactured a knowing smile. 'What really happened?'

Serra gesticulated with his hands. 'It's the truth. It was the kind of thing that could happen to anyone. He broke both his legs.'

'He's not dead, then?'

'No. Just hospitalized.'

'When did this happen?'

'Three days ago. Right here, in Paris.'

'So I'm a substitute?'

'Exactly.'

'How does Khalil fit into all of this? Was he going to meet the man I'm replacing?'

'No. But when – how shall we say it? – this vacancy arose, he saw an opportunity. Khalil will be in Malta when the plane is on the ground. That was always his intention.'

Another jolt to the system.

'Along with a lot of security.'

Serra smiled. 'If you know Malta, it's an easy place to lose yourself. Khalil visits the island and moves around it as he pleases. He has always felt comfortable there. It's like a second home to him.'

'What does he have in mind for me?'

Serra shrugged. 'I don't know the details. But he'll find a way to contact you.'

Khalil on Malta. The idea crystallized. But to get there – to get the chance she needed – there was the hijack. And, for the moment, it was a hijack without details.

Serra was asking her what she thought about the proposal.

Petra tried to gather her scattered thoughts. 'I don't know yet.'

'I realize it is very quick. But I have to have a yes or no.'

'And I have to have some time. Not much, but some.'

'Is it a question of money?'

'It's always a question of money.' Serra opened his mouth – presumably to make a generous offer – but Petra cut him short. 'But I know that Khalil will pay whatever I ask, so in this case, it's a question of something else.'

'What?'

'The Prophet Mohammed said, "He who keeps secrets shall soon attain his objectives." Like me, you'll just have to wait and see.'

24

As instructed, Petra left the Eurostar Terminal at Waterloo by foot and headed for Waterloo Bridge. She had called Magenta House from Paris and had been told that she would be met. The rain was torrential, reducing the roads to a shimmer. She was passing the National Theatre on her right when a black Mercedes pulled to the kerb. Alexander was in the back. Petra climbed in beside him, glad to be out of the rain, if nothing else. She shook her head, spraying drops of water over the leather seats.

'Why the call?' Alexander asked.

'I know who the Sons of Sabah are.'

'Who?'

'Khalil has planned a hijack. They're the team who've been trained to carry it out.'

'Serra told you this?'

'Not exactly. But it all fits.'

'Why's he letting you in on it?'

'Because he wants me on board as a sleeper.'

'What kind of sleeper? What do you have to do?'

'He hasn't said. I'm supposed to be replacing the original sleeper who had an unfortunate accident in Paris a few days ago. A car crash. Both his legs were broken. The thing is, Serra needs an answer immediately. That's why I called. I need to know about the car crash.'

Alexander nodded. 'It shouldn't be a problem.'

They were halfway across Waterloo Bridge. To her left, Petra could see the large Adelphi building, monumental in the night. Magenta House, however, was invisible behind the black branches belonging to the trees in Victoria Embankment Gardens, although she caught fragments of light which might have been from its windows. Magenta House never slept. Nor, by reputation, did Alexander.

'A hijack,' he mused. 'As far as I know, it would be a first for Khalil.'

'There's something that doesn't feel right about this, don't you think?'

'Is Khalil part of the team?'

'No. But he'll be there at the end. That's the point of my inclusion, apparently.'

'And where will the end be?'

Petra opened her mouth and then shut it. She thought of Rio de Janeiro and New York, two straightforward operations that had gone wrong.

'I don't know. Serra wouldn't give me any details. No flight, no date, no places. But he's in a hurry so we can assume that it's imminent.'

'You don't even know where you will meet Khalil?'

She shook her head.

They drove across Trafalgar Square and headed along the Mall towards Buckingham Palace, where they veered right up Constitution Hill to Hyde Park. Alexander dropped her by the Inter-Continental. From there, it was a five-minute walk to her flat but she was drenched by the time she reached it.

She shed her damp clothes in the bedroom and took a hot shower. Afterwards, she wrapped herself in a towel and made herself hot chocolate flavoured with cinnamon. She flicked through her meagre collection of CDs and picked out 'OK Computer' by Radiohead. Then she called Frank.

'I'm back,' she told him before he'd had a chance to say anything.

'Do you want to come over?'

'No. I'm too knackered. I want you to come here.'

Forty seconds later, there was a knock on the door. They kissed. Petra led him into the kitchen, where she offered him the remains of the chocolate.

'No thanks. It looks like you could use it more than me.'

She rested her head on his shoulder. 'You've no idea.'

In the sitting room, they lay on the sofa in one another's arms and were largely silent until Frank asked her, 'What is this we're listening to?'

The song was 'Exit Music (For A Film)'.

'Do you like it?'

He grimaced. 'It's suicidal.'

'I know. But do you like it?'

'What's there to like? It's depressing.'

'That's the best kind of music there is. My idea of Hell is the Beach Boys.'

'You don't like to be uplifted?'

'This *is* uplifting.'

They went to bed and Petra remained awake despite her exhaustion. The phone rang at ten past one. Yes, they had found the man in question. There had been a seven-car collision the previous week on the Boulevard Périphérique, near the Porte de Bercy. One woman had been killed, four people had been injured, including Eduardo Montoya, an Argentinian tourist. Both Montoya's legs had been broken and, after initial treatment, he was now recovering in a private clinic. The voice on the other end of the phone told Petra that Montoya was really Hugo Pentoral, a Venezuelan national who had started out in the narcotics trade and who had spent the last three years operating in Europe as a lowly-paid, unskilled assassin, specializing in the Eastern bloc, where his targets tended to be unprotected government officials who had the nerve to be honest. Petra put the phone down quietly but Frank was awake.

'Trouble?'

'Nothing but,' replied Petra, slipping out of bed.

'Where are you going?'

'I've got send to send an e-mail to someone.'

'At this hour?'

*　　*　　*

It is cold in the sitting room, which is appropriate. I think of the people who are due to fly on the aircraft that Khalil intends to hijack. They are the same people who were on flight NE027. They are my family, they could even be me.

In the back of the minds of air travellers, those little questions linger. Will we be delayed? Will an engine fail? Will we crash and be killed? But how many people actually worry about being hijacked? We see it on the TV and imagine the horror but we console ourselves with the statistical improbability of suffering such a fate. But somewhere out there, right now, people are plotting to seize commercial airliners or blow them out of the sky. Like being involved in a car crash, being a victim of terrorism always happens to other people. Until it happens to you. And then it's too late to do anything about it.

I send an e-mail to Serra.

The sign on the basement door said the Anglo-Egyptian Cargo Company was closed. Beyond the rusted railings, weeds sprouted from cracks in the concrete. Pollution had turned the grass grey. Petra pushed the gate open and stepped off the Earls Court Road. Behind her, the evening rush-hour crawled towards the Thames. She went down the steps to the basement. The company sign was nailed above a door which had iron bars across a panel of frosted glass. She peered through the main window, which was similarly protected, but could see nothing. Beyond the grime, the curtains were drawn.

Magenta House research had revealed that the building was owned by Forest Property Services, which also owned the building occupied by the al-Sharif Students Hostel, as well as RJN Travel on Hogarth Road. Forest Property Services itself was owned by Marchand, a French investment firm based in Paris. Petra had not been surprised to learn that Marc Serra was on the board; the address had come from his private files in Paris.

There was a small, dark passage to the right of the door that led to an abandoned garden at the rear. Apart from the basement, the building was entirely residential, although not in quite the fashion its architect would have envisaged. Housing records from the Royal Borough of Kensington & Chelsea showed that each floor had been subdivided into two or three separate flats. The occupancy rate for the building varied. At the moment, for whatever reason, residents were few and far between.

Petra reached the other end of the passage, which opened on to the garden. The weeds had grown so tall in their ceaseless struggle for air and light that they had successfully concealed the wall at the far end. She retreated and stopped at the door halfway along the passage. She tried the handle. It was locked but loose; the surrounding wood was rotten. She took a step back and unleashed a sharp kick. Wood splintered as the lock fractured. Using her shoulder, she forced the door open. She winced at the smell that assaulted her nostrils. It was rank, as though something had died and disintegrated inside the airless space. She waited for several seconds, allowing her eyes to adjust to the darkness. She was in a store-room; wood-worm-infested chairs piled in one corner, a bicycle bereft of a wheel and chain in another, empty cardboard boxes that had once contained Hitachi TVs filling much of the remaining space. The door out of the store-room led into a short corridor that connected the two principal rooms of the Anglo-Egyptian Cargo Company.

The room at the front was an office; a pair of desks, half a dozen plastic chairs, two ancient computers, calendars on the wall and three notice-boards containing messages that were mostly in Arabic. There was a small bathroom to one side of the room and a cupboard-sized kitchen to the other. Petra spent half an hour sifting through office documents but found nothing revealing and so turned her attention to the room at the back. Most of the merchandise that passed through the company's hands never came close to Earls Court. It sat in warehouses at airports and docks, before being transferred by sea or by air to other warehouses at other airports and docks. She knew that Ismail Qadiq used the company for transporting his T-shirts from Cairo to London. But there were smaller consignments too and some of them had been stored in the second room, which had once been a sitting room. By the far wall, there was an old sofa. Two armchairs had been placed on top of it to create more floor-space.

Some of the boxes were open and some were sealed, but most bore labels detailing the contents and their transportation details. It was a strange collection of goods: one hundred cartons of Winfield cigarettes; a small package containing twenty cheap Casio wristwatches; a case of Greek olive oil; two boxes of blank Scotch three-hour VHS tapes; a box full of cashmere jerseys; five crates of Coca-Cola; twenty pairs of Nike running shoes; two cases containing bottles of cleaning fluid for contact-lenses; three black bin-bags crammed full of Levi 501s; four hundred Bic lighters; a case of Glenlivet; a bulk purchase of Duracell batteries; fifteen Gucci handbags; two thousand Mates condoms; one Bang & Olufsen TV.

'Import export,' Petra murmured to herself in a tone that was stranded between contempt and admiration.

Above the distant background murmur of the traffic, she heard a cough. Followed by metal on metal; a key searching for a lock. The door at the front, she realized. She headed for the corridor but it was too late. Someone – actually more than *someone* – had already entered. She would never make it to the store-room in time. She turned round. The window into the garden was barred and locked.

Think! What do you do now? What were you taught? What is it that is supposed to be instinctive but which you seem to have forgotten?

Different voices were talking in Arabic. They were getting closer, leaving the room in front and moving into the corridor. She tried to count them. Two, certainly, probably three. She retreated behind the sofa and fell into a crouch in the corner, behind the Bang & Olufsen packing case, before curling into a ball on her side. She tugged some moth-eaten curtain her way and pinned it to the back of the case with her knee. It would give her a little extra cover, she hoped. She pressed her left cheek to the carpet, which had once been a mass of purple and burgundy swirls but which age had reduced to a collage of dark stains. It reeked of accumulated filth, of abandonment, of the years themselves. Petra prayed the dust she was inhaling wouldn't make her sneeze.

Each beat of her frenzied heart made her dizzy. An image came to her. She remembered the rain, the mist, the conversation in the peat hag. Keep your breathing under control and your panic will be suppressed. She wondered where the man who had given her that advice was now. And then she focused on her lungs and heart. Gradually, her pulse began to slow.

She saw three – then four – pairs of feet through the sofa's legs. They all belonged to men. The conversation was loud and excitable. They began to move some of the goods around the room. Petra heard the tear of masking tape, the cough of cardboard lids being parted. Gradually, one voice assumed dominance. The other three spoke rarely. The feet remained still, apart from the occasional shuffle. A lecture, perhaps? There were other sounds which meant nothing to her, related to actions above her field of vision. Somebody was doing something with their hands.

She fought the panic, slowly recalling how Boyd had taught her to stay still and silent for hours, if necessary, no matter how close the threat. She focused her mind on each part of her body, pictured that part relaxing into a state of total inertia, provoking a slow-down throughout the system.

The men stayed for an hour and a half. Petra never moved, ignoring the pins-and-needles and one painful bout of cramp in her right calf. When they were gone, she waited a further ten minutes before emerging from her

341

fetid hiding place. She massaged her calf and examined the merchandise in the room. Nothing appeared to have been removed or added but then she hadn't had the time to examine everything in detail.

It is the afternoon and Frank has brought me to the National Gallery, which is a new experience for me. I don't know anything about art and, apart from one relatively recent visit to the Tate Gallery, I have never been to a proper art museum before, so I'm surprised at how moved I am as, hand in hand, we drift past the works of Titian, Rembrandt, Raphael and Velazquez. I like the coolness and quiet of the galleries themselves. They're calming. I gaze at the paintings and at the people looking at the paintings. Experts and amateurs alike, those in study and those in love. Like us, perhaps.

But then, in a single dagger moment, everything changes.

Of course, I don't recognize him at first. He's wearing a tatty tweed jacket with leather patches on the elbows. His trousers are corduroy, his shirt a pale blue button-down. His hair was a little longer back then and his glasses have changed from circular to oval, but the frames remain matt black. Until now, I have only ever seen him in a suit. What confuses me, though, are not the subtle changes in his appearance but the context in which I am seeing him.

Philip. Three o'clock on a Wednesday afternoon, as I recall. He used to be a regular. He was one of the bearable ones. He even used to give me small gifts from time to time. Cheap bottles of scent, or a pair of sunglasses, but nothing that cost more than his customary half-hour. He told me he worked in advertising. And he told me that he was unmarried which now looks like a lie because there is a woman standing next to him. They are talking and she's wearing a wedding ring. She's holding the hand of a young girl. An older boy – he might be eleven or twelve – is standing on Philip's right and looks bored out of his mind.

Philip. I wonder what his real name is. I wonder if he really works in advertising or whether he made up all those office-politics stories he used to tell me while he was getting dressed.

*He feels me watching him and turns his head. Our eyes meet
and his pupils dilate. I can't see this change occur but I can feel
it. He hasn't recognized me yet but he knows he's seen me somewhere before. I could just look away and the moment would pass
but I don't. I've earned this moment.*

*And then he gets it. I see his body tense to rigidity. The colour
drains from his face. His wife is still talking to him about the
picture in front of them but he doesn't hear a word. He can't
stop staring at me. He knows that I truly see him and that now
he is the naked, vulnerable one. I imagine the inside of his mouth
is as dry as sandpaper. He attempts a half-hearted smile, a peace
offering of some sort, which, naturally, I reject. I continue to glare
and I gently steer Frank in the direction of this unsuspecting
family.*

*The man formerly known as Philip urges his wife and children
towards the next gallery, turning his back on me. But I don't
mind because I know that he can feel my gaze drilling into him,
right between the shoulder blades. Frank is all that prevents me
from introducing myself to the wife.*

*For half an hour, I follow in his wake. I fill every half-glance
he steals and my only regret is that I cannot see the turmoil
inside his head.*

*Later, as Frank and I leave the museum, he turns to me and
asks if I've enjoyed the National Gallery. And I tell him that I
had no idea it could be so rewarding.*

Following her e-mail to Serra, Petra made two trips to Paris
over the following week, the first of which was a day-trip.
Serra greeted her at his apartment with lusty intent but
she denied him testily, claiming she only had a couple of
hours to spare. Serra had quipped that two hours was
surely enough, even for a tigress like her, to which Petra
had replied, 'Perhaps we should keep our relationship on
a purely professional basis until after this operation is completed.'

He took the rejection badly which pleased her. It was
a beautiful, frosty day and they took advantage of it by

walking along the banks of the Seine and around the Île de la Cité. Serra wore a cashmere overcoat over a Pierre Cardin suit, Petra wore a three-quarter-length leather coat over a sweatshirt with a fading print of Iggy Pop and the words LUST FOR LIFE on the front.

Serra said, 'Khalil is unhappy about your financial demands. He realizes that you know that he will pay you, but half a million dollars is too much for a sleeper, no matter what they do.'

'I thought Kamal Ibrahim Karim had more than one hundred million dollars.'

'He does. But for an investment of five hundred thousand, he expects a better return.'

'Well you haven't told me what I'm supposed to do yet.' Petra yawned. 'Besides, I don't really care whether he likes it or not. Being mercenary means I don't have to care. It's half a million or it's nothing.'

Serra put his arm around her shoulder and Petra flinched, a reaction she quickly tried to compensate for by moving closer to him and putting her own arm around his waist.

They walked past a group of ambling tourists in silence. Then Petra said, 'I know you're keeping secrets but can I ask you something anyway?'

'What?'

'I'm curious. Why Malta?'

'Khalil sees it as an Islamic issue.'

'Why?'

'At the heart of Islam is the concept of the City of War and the City of Faith.'

Petra shook her head. 'Which is what?'

'Any place where Islam rules supreme is Dar al-Imam, the City of Faith. Anywhere else is Dar al-Harb, the City of War. Islam is a constant struggle between the two. There can never be peace between the City of Faith and the City of War. One must prevail and it is the duty of every Muslim to ensure that it is the City of Faith. At least, this is Khalil's view of Islam. Malta's position in the middle of the Mediterranean, halfway between Africa and Europe, halfway between East and West, is more than a mere coincidence of geography. As well as being a practical crossroads, it is also deeply symbolic. We tend to view it within the loose group of Westernized countries, but Muslims consider Malta to be within the realm of Islam, which means it belongs to the City of Faith. However, despite that, ninety-eight percent of Malta's population is Roman Catholic.'

The significance of the location became clearer. 'So Khalil intends to make a statement?'

'He intends to do more than that. There are practical reasons for bringing the aircraft down in Malta. His people move among the Maltese freely which makes it safe for him to be there. But there is also the question of the statement. To complete a successful operation in a country that is regarded as Westernized and Roman Catholic would serve to underline the deeply-felt, historical claim that Islam has on the island. The island itself is not hugely significant, but its position is.'

Her second trip to Paris occurred five days later. She arrived in the late afternoon and took a taxi to the rue de Rivoli. Serra greeted her with caution, unsure of which Petra to expect. She played the harlot. Later, in the evening, he took her to a small restaurant in Le Marais. It was the kind of place she would have loved to have visited with Frank, huddled over a table, fingers entwined, faces illuminated by candlelight, eyes ablaze with signals, stomachs aglow, warmed by food, wine and anticipation. Faking it stung. Petra ate fish stew laced with wine and garlic. Serra chose thinly-sliced strips of lamb steak that were so rare the rosy flesh at their centre was cool.

They leaned close to one another, as lovers do, and spoke not of the future or of the heart, but of Khalil and the hideous schemes in his head.

'Khalil can call volunteers from anywhere,' Serra told her. 'The Philippines, Malaysia, Iran, Pakistan. The word

345

goes out and they come to him. His name is a magnet.'

'Where do they go to?'

'It depends on the mission.'

'This team?'

'The first base was in the Bekaa Valley in Lebanon at a camp run by Hizb'allah. Khalil has worked for Hizb'allah from time to time over the last ten years and, in return, gets to use their facilities. Like Malta, Lebanon falls within the realm of Islam and it has long been a desire of the fundamentalists to rid the country of its Christians. This is a view shared by Khalil.'

'Does Kamal Ibrahim Karim ever visit the camps?'

Serra shook his head. 'He lives nomadically on the border between Pakistan and Afghanistan and never leaves the region. Not any more. But he likes to spread his influence as far as possible.'

Serra told Petra how each volunteer was screened for security before moving on to the next camp.

'Which was where?' Petra asked.

'Libya.'

'How did they get there?'

'Libyan military aircraft, a direct flight to Tripoli – it's a routine procedure – and from the airport, the recruits were transferred by truck to the base in the desert. LV241, a new camp paid for by Kamal Ibrahim Karim. That's where the real training took place.'

'And what's it like?'

'To begin with, it's physical. Fitness and discipline are considered crucial. Then there is ideological and religious conditioning. Later, they are instructed on weaponry and, finally, they receive technical training. There is an old hangar there. Inside, using fragments of retired aircraft – Tupolevs, Boeings, Lockheeds, Ilyushins and so on – they recreated the interior of the aircraft that will be hijacked so that the team could practise in "real space". Khalil says they're a good unit now.'

'They'll need to be. What do you think?'

'I don't know. I haven't seen them.'

Petra wasn't buying that. 'But you were there, weren't you? Or is your January tan merely the result of a month on a sun-bed?'

The days between her two trips to Paris had been difficult. She found it easy to lie to Serra, to say to him the things she wanted to say to Frank. That frustrated her and when she was with Frank, it began to show. Never being able to say what was on her mind to the one person she wanted to tell became a pressure. How was it, she asked herself, that she could fake so perfectly for Serra and then have such difficulty in telling Frank that she enjoyed being with him, that she liked him more than anyone she had ever known, that he was the first and only man she had ever felt she could trust?

Now, lying in Serra's bed, she found she was able to roll over on to one elbow and whisper into his ear, 'You know, under the right circumstances, Marc, I could fall in love with you.'

That word. The word she could not force from her throat in Frank's presence. And yet with Serra, she managed it without thinking. Serra, who was still trying to catch his post-coital breath, looked momentarily startled. Petra chose to qualify her declaration. 'But unfortunately, these aren't the right circumstances.'

'In two days' time, I will introduce you to the hijack team.'

'Where? Here?'

'No. In London.'

'London?'

Her reaction was too quick, too jittery. Serra had noticed it. 'Is that a problem for you?'

She tried to sound dismissive. 'Of course not. London will be fine.'

'Once you're in London, you stay there until the mission begins.'

'The flight leaves from there?'

He grinned. 'Not necessarily. Most of you will be catching connecting flights from other destinations, to reduce the chance of something going wrong. But you start from London.'

'How long will I have to be there?'

'Let us just say that in about a week from now, you will be with Khalil.'

It was morning. Petra was preparing to leave. They were in the entrance hall when Serra said, 'I have something for you.'

'What?'

'A present.' From behind his back he produced a plastic carrier bag containing a box. 'I'm sorry that it's not beautifully wrapped.'

Petra took the box out of the bag. It was a Sony Walkman. Between other people, it might have seemed a normal gift, but not between the two of them. Petra's surprise made way for some sense of embarrassment, which, in itself, irritated her.

'Do you like music?' Serra asked.

She knew he was toying with her. 'Sure. Some types.'

'Well, now you can listen to whatever you want.' He let the sentence hang in the air before making a casual addition. 'One thing, though. Don't push fast-forward and reverse at the same time. At least, not when you're on an aircraft.'

Petra's skin tingled. 'Why not?'

'You never know what might go off in the cargo hold.'

Despite herself, her eyes widened. 'Are you serious?'

Serra looked it. 'You wanted to know what your role as sleeper will be. Well, now you do.'

Petra played it coolly. 'I'm not blowing myself to pieces for half a million dollars.'

'I've already told you, you and most of the passengers and crew will be released in Malta.'

'*Most?*'

348

'There may be some who stay on board.' He pointed at the Walkman. 'This trigger has a range of one thousand metres but, to be sure, you should use it at no more than eight hundred metres from the aircraft.'

'What about Khalil's men?'

'They have all volunteered to be martyrs, to die for the glory of Allah the Avenger. Your job is to make sure that they do.'

25

The electric iron hissed, steam rising from the scalding plate. Petra spread a crumpled grey T-shirt across the ironing board. She felt clumsy with the iron in her hand. The drone of the washing machine competed with the banality of daytime TV; cookery shows, make-over programmes and those game shows too feeble to make prime time. Earlier, she had wrestled with the vacuum cleaner while trying to change the bag and had only succeeded in splitting it, spilling dust and dirt across the sitting room carpet. Domestic chores were new to her; when she was a child, her mother had done them all, hardly ever asking her to help, whilst as a student, domesticity had been an optional extra that she and most others had chosen to bypass. And as a prostitute, it was never even an issue. The places she worked in were beyond redemption, although Joan, one of her maids, had occasionally run a vacuum cleaner across a carpet. Stephanie had never cared about the filth or about clean clothes because she hadn't cared that she was dirty herself. What was the point of cleaning the outside when everything on the inside was so sordid?

Now, she found these trivial acts of domesticity were strangely cathartic. In collaboration with the TV, they numbed the mind, which was a partial freedom. The tedious routines allowed her to pretend that her life was tediously routine, which was what she now craved. Frank had eroded her cutting edge, blunting her instinct for revenge and justice.

There was a knock on the door and he walked out of her thoughts and into her presence. He'd been naked in his bed when she'd last seen him at seven-thirty in the morning. Now he was wearing a black suit, a very dark blue shirt with no tie, and black brogues. Petra didn't think she had ever seen him look so good.

'I was walking past your door and I heard the TV,' he explained. 'So I knocked.'

'Do you want to come in?'

'No, I've got a couple of urgent calls I need to make.'

'Okay.'

'I thought maybe you'd left it on when you'd gone out.'

'Gone out?'

'To work.' Petra felt winded. He'd caught her off-guard. Not deliberately, of course, but that hardly mattered. He tilted his head to one side. 'That was where you were going when you got up this morning, wasn't it?'

'Of course,' she replied, almost bristling at the suggestion that it might not be true.

In the early days as Marina, Petra had made more of an effort. During working hours, she had gone out to libraries, museums, cinemas, shops. Sometimes, she had even gone to Magenta House. But recently, her discipline had slackened. She no longer possessed the determination to maintain the most tedious aspects of Marina's life. Instead of going out to 'work', she frequently hid in her flat. Instead of dressing in suits and applying the make-up that made her look so severe, she resorted to worn jeans and faded sweatshirts. The façade of Marina was cracking and Petra didn't care.

Frank looked around. 'So ... how come you're not there?'

Her initial instinct was to employ aggression as defence. That was what was natural to her and had it been anyone else, she would have resorted to it. But not with Frank. She saw the look in his eyes. He didn't just want an explanation, he wanted to believe it too.

'I was on the Underground going in and I began to feel ill. I was hot and had a splitting headache. I thought I was going to throw up. So I got off at Holborn and waited on the platform for about ten minutes, hoping it would pass.

351

But it didn't. So I went up to the street to catch some air and then took a cab home.'

Frank picked up the Sony Walkman that Serra had given Petra and began to turn it over in his hands. Petra wanted to shout at him to put it down but knew that she couldn't. He wasn't really examining it. He was just fiddling with it. The drum began to spin inside the washing machine.

'You okay now?' he asked.

'I feel a little better. I went to bed for an hour.'

'You should've called me,' he said, before pressing the 'open' button.

'Where?'

'What?'

'Where should I have called you? I thought you were going out too.'

For a moment, Frank looked as stranded as she had been, which she found strange. Certainly, he was dressed for a meeting of some kind.

'Yes, I ... er ... you could have left a message on my machine.'

'I suppose I could have, yes.'

He looked inside the Walkman, which was empty. 'No Radiohead, no suicide. What a relief.'

Petra entered the Hilton on Park Lane, walked through the lobby and ground floor, and exited out of a staff entrance. The Ford Transit van was waiting for her in Pitt's Head Mews. She climbed into the back, hauled the door shut and the driver pulled away. As far as she was concerned, Alexander's insistence on such measures was excessive and childish but he had been adamant that if she wanted to come to Magenta House this was the way it had to be. It took half an hour to reach Lower Robert Street, Petra being required to use the lower and more concealed of the two entrances.

Margaret was drinking tea at her desk. 'How are you, Stephanie?'

'Surviving. Just. You?'

'I'm well, as usual.'

Petra nodded towards Alexander's closed office door. 'And our man Beria?'

'I think "agitated" is the word.'

'A first, surely.'

Petra found Alexander peeling the wrapper off a pack of Rothmans. 'I've arranged for Rosie to help you with your computer enquiry.'

'So that she can report back to you all the stuff I'm interested in?'

'There's no need to be facetious.'

'Oh, you'd be surprised.'

'How was your visit to Paris?'

'I went through some of his personal files but I didn't find much hard stuff.' She placed a manila folder on Alexander's desk. 'This is other material that you or somebody else might find useful or interesting.'

Alexander's nod of appreciation was grudging. 'What about this hijack? Any development there?'

'No.'

'You still don't know what he requires of you as a sleeper?'

'No,' lied Petra. 'He hasn't said a thing yet.'

Petra had elected to keep Alexander in the dark for her own protection. After Rio and New York, what little trust she had ever had in him had evaporated. She knew that she would have to feed him occasional scraps of information to prevent arousing his suspicion but that could be managed.

Rosie met Petra in the basement. An Indian, she was the only non-white person Petra had ever seen inside Magenta House. They were the only two inside the sealed computer room. Petra made coffee for both of them before they sat side by side in front of the screen. Rosie operated the keyboard.

'Okay, what's first?'

353

'I'm looking for a military training camp.'

'Where?'

'In Libya. It's new.'

'Does it have a name?'

'LV241 is all I know.'

Rosie scanned files but came up empty-handed. So then she tried Algeria, Tunisia and Sudan. Again, nothing. She broadened the search to include Lebanon, Iran, Syria, Turkey, Afghanistan, Pakistan, Indonesia, the Philippines, Thailand and Malaysia. Still there was no match for LV241.

'I could try some foreign agency records,' Rosie suggested. 'The CIA, perhaps?'

'How about cross-referencing with Kamal Ibrahim Karim? He paid for it.'

This approach was also unproductive. Next, Petra asked Rosie to run the Khalil file. He was rumoured to have been trained at Niaravan, the first revolutionary camp to be established in the Islamic Republic, where the Party of Allah's Volunteers for Martyrdom were trained to kill and die in the name of the Imam and in the service of the Party of Allah. Established in 1980, Niaravan was set in beautiful parkland in the suburbs of Tehran. Khalil was supposed to have gone to the camp in 1988. The most promising students were selected for special combat training to transform them into lethal instruments for Allah the Avenger. These special units were known as *goruh zarbat* – literally, strike unit – and were specifically intended to operate abroad. Khalil had been part of such a group, operating under Sheikh Abdul Kamal Qassam, until Khalil had decided that he could operate more effectively by himself.

And now the Sons of Sabah existed, which forced Petra to wonder whether they were Khalil's own *goruh zarbat*?

There was a sign in the window of RJN Travel on Hogarth Road. It listed air-fares to over twenty destinations around the world. The amounts had been written in red felt-tip pen but sunlight had faded the ink to pink. Petra stepped inside. Behind three desks sat three operators in front of three computers. Each terminal was a museum piece; an abacus to the modern calculator. One of the operators was dozing, one was busy smoking a cigarette, one was on the phone. They ignored Petra, who sat down opposite the one who was smoking. 'I'd like to buy a ticket.'

He looked at her through filthy tinted glasses. 'To where?'

'Tokyo and Bremen.'

His spine stiffened. 'Wait a moment.'

He picked up a phone and muttered something into it. A few seconds later, the door behind him opened and Serra appeared. Dressed in jeans, a red and black check shirt and a charcoal grey jacket, he looked American to Petra, which was a style she would never have associated with him.

From Earls Court, they took the Underground to West-bourne Park, from where they walked. The building was dilapidated, the plaster and paint crumbling from the façade, the steps to the front door cracked and uneven. The plastic intercom panel had a dozen buttons. To the right of it, there were twelve mail-boxes, four of which had been prised apart. Serra pressed one of the buttons. There was a clunk as the lock released. The hall had been partitioned lengthwise so that it was absurdly narrow. Climbing the stairs, they moved through different zones; the smell of onions frying, a small dog yapping, black damp patches on the wall, Pulp on a sound-system, a man and woman arguing in a language that sounded like Russian.

The flat was on the third floor. Suspicious eyes peered at them through the partially opened door. Once Serra was recognized, the door opened fully and they entered. There was graffiti on the walls – some of it in pen, some of it sprayed, some of it English, some of it Arabic. They passed a small bedroom on the right. The door had been replaced by a thin purple curtain that was partly open. A woman sat on a mattress breast-feeding a baby. In a tiny kitchen, three old men argued in Arabic while a kettle whistled on a Sixties stove.

They moved into the cramped sitting room, which overlooked the street. There were more drapes suspended from the curtain rails above the windows. Some had been tied to one side, others hung limply, filtering the daylight in orange and green. Petra counted eight men and two women in the airless room. The man who had let them into the flat retreated and shut the door.

Serra turned to Petra. 'These are the ten who will perform the hijack. For reasons of security, they know each other only by the names they used during their training. The reason you are here is so that they can see your face and recognize you. You will not have a name. Okay?'

'Fine.'

'Good. Then let me tell you who they are.' Starting on the left, Serra went through them one by one. 'Yousef, Ali, Mouna, Markoa, Mirqas, Zyed, Khan, Fatima, Basit, Obaid.' They were young and conservatively dressed. Generally, they wore dark trousers, plain shirts – mostly buttoned to the throat – and six of them wore jackets. Their clothes were tatty but they were neat, hair cut short and beards – five of the eight men had them – tidily trimmed. Both women were dressed in black trousers and black jerseys. The one called Mouna had her hair drawn back from the face, the other, Fatima, wore her hair as short as the men. Petra felt excluded by the suspicion coming from the eyes of all ten. Serra said, 'Basit will lead the team.'

At the mention of his name, Basit rose from a chair, his face emerging from the gloom.

I am speechless. My breath has been stolen. Serra is saying something to me but I don't hear him. Instead, I stare at Basit because Basit is Reza Mohammed. I cannot tear my eyes from him. The last time we were this close I had a gun in my hand and I was pointing it at him through a pane of glass. His hair is a little shorter now, his beard a little fuller, but there's no mistaking those hooded eyes or that aquiline nose, which is a similar shape to Frank's but not quite so large. A cold energy surges through me. If we were alone, I would . . . to be honest, I don't know what I would do. I'd like to think I might tear him to pieces but I doubt that I would. I force myself to look away before my stare attracts attention. Now I turn to look at Mirqas, who is a sinewy man, about the same height as Reza Mohammed. He has a lazy eye. He's sitting on the arm of a sofa and I am wondering if he's the one who killed Keith Proctor. Mirqas was the name scribbled by Ismail Qadiq next to Proctor's address.

Serra said to Petra, 'You will have no contact with any of the people in this room unless there is some kind of problem and, in such a circumstance, they will come to get you. If they do, there is a procedure in order to protect your true identity.' He turned to Reza Mohammed. 'Basit?'

Mohammed said, 'If we need to speak to you, we will come into your section of the aircraft cabin and ask if there is a doctor who speaks French. All you have to do is raise your hand.'

'And if there's more than one, you'll just pick me anyway?'

'Yes.'

Serra told Mohammed to tell the others to memorize Petra's face because this was the only chance they would get. Serra then explained to her that only four of them spoke English. Two of the others spoke French, but there were four who spoke only Arabic.

Mohammed offered Petra a piece of paper with a foreign phone number on it. 'Call me tomorrow and I will tell you where and when to pick up your ticket.'

Petra took the scrap of paper from Reza Mohammed and brushed his fingertips with hers.

They walked, after leaving the building, and had reached Notting Hill Gate when the first drops of rain began to fall.

Daylight was fading fast. Serra turned up the collar of his coat and looked at his watch.

'In about an hour, they will have dispersed,' he told her.

'To where?'

'Anywhere and everywhere. By train, by aircraft, by ferry, they will spread out across Europe until it is time for them to come together again.'

'And where will you be in an hour?'

'On the Eurostar.'

'So this is it, then?'

'Until afterwards, yes.'

'Where will we meet?'

Serra shrugged. 'I don't know where you and Khalil will go. Or how long you will be there. But you know where you can find me.'

They kissed by the entrance to the Underground station. Serra said, 'You and I are different, Petra. We are not shaped by the world, we are the ones who shape it. Our future can be anything we choose.'

Petra wore a small smile for him. 'Or anything Khalil chooses.'

'No. Not even Khalil can control us. Nobody can.'

Some perverse nostalgic instinct persuaded Petra to take a cab to the Edgware Road. From there, she walked to Bell Street, pausing outside the building in which Keith Proctor had lived. She looked up at the windows. There were no lights on. By the entrance to the building, an estate agent's placard announced a flat for sale. She crossed the street and entered Bell's Café and bought a cup of milky tea. She sat at the table nearest the entrance, the one she had always preferred. Her view of the street was still obscured by the net curtain that hung over the lower half of the window.

She had somehow hoped that in the run-up to the hijack, she would learn enough about Khalil to track him down independently of the atrocity but all she had learned was that he would be in Malta. That wasn't enough. Serra had been cautious and now there was no way to proceed. When the time was right, she would ensure that the targeted flight never left the ground and that would be the end of it. Khalil would be as out of reach as ever. The prospect of being back where she started was more than bleak. It was impossible.

Frank kisses the cosmetic scar on my left shoulder and I flinch. We are on the floor of my sitting room. Our clothes are all around us – but not on us – and we are trying to catch our breath. I close my eyes and imagine us together in a house somewhere far away. The Isle of Skye, perhaps, or even Islay. We went on a family holiday there once and the beauty of it has stayed with me ever since. I imagine Frank and me leading a life of spartan simplicity. I think it would suit us both. We would take pleasure in the daily routines, in the gorgeous inconvenience of living in such a place.

'This must have hurt,' he says, running a fingertip over the disk of ruined skin.

'More than you can imagine,' I tell him, praying he won't ask for details, that he won't force me into yet another spree of lies.

We are silent for a while and begin to drape our discarded clothes around ourselves without actually getting dressed. Perhaps this is because we know we will make love again. I feel that Frank has something to say and I am soon proved right.

'Do you think of the future much?' he asks.

What a question to put. To me, of all people. 'I'm starting to,' I admit.

'Me too.'

Not for the same reason, I'm thinking.

'It's been a long time since I've looked ahead,' he tells me. 'After Karen left me and after Rosa died I just didn't see the point. Especially after Rosa. Even after the grief had settled down, I couldn't bring myself to make plans. It seemed cheap at first,

and then it just seemed like a waste of time. I went from day to day, then week to week. And since then, that's always been enough.' He turns to face me fully. 'But not any more.'

I am petrified that he is going to do something crazy like tell me that he loves me or, even worse, propose to me. If he does, part of me will melt. But another part will be apoplectic, or miserable, or something equally inappropriate. That's the trouble with falling for me: you get all of me and all the different versions of me. Love me, love my secret family. The question is, who would be the object of that love? Stephanie? Petra? Marina? Or a blend of all three, perhaps?

Frank says, 'You're bringing me back, Marina.'

Which is exactly the way I feel about him. He's hit the perfect note. I nod in agreement, which appears to surprise him.

'It's true,' I tell him. 'Ever since I was young, there's been something missing. And as time has moved on, I feel, somehow, that I've been drifting further and further away from it. But now I feel I'm getting closer, getting warmer.'

Frank takes my hands in his. 'I'm falling in love with you, Marina. I can't help it.'

I don't know what to do. Verbally, I want to reciprocate but I know that I will never succeed in forcing that word past my lips. Frank's tearing me apart and doesn't even know it.

I say, 'No one has ever felt like that about me.'

'That you know of.'

'No,' I insist. 'There's been no one. How could there have been? The boys I knew when I was young and the men I've known since then . . .'

I run out of steam.

'There must have been one.'

I think of Keith Proctor. 'There might have been. But nothing came of it.'

'Why not?'

'He went away. He had no choice.'

Frank kisses me and I think about what he's said. I am drifting back towards the shore. He's right. I am losing my appetite for revenge because it cannot compete with love. Frank is resurrecting

360

me. If I am not careful, there may be a danger that he could create a complete human being out of me.

I smile ruefully and say, 'It's strange but I've always resisted moments like this. In my mind, that is. In practice, they never occurred. I never let them. I never let anyone get close because it was easier and safer not to. Not my parents, not even my brothers or my sister. I was scared to open myself up to anybody. I only saw it in terms of becoming vulnerable. But it's different now.'

Frank looks a little perplexed. Perhaps this is because he is unused to any form of outpouring of emotion from me.

'What's wrong?' I ask him, when the pause stretches beyond reason.

'I thought you were an only child.'

'What?'

'You told me that you were an only child. But just now you mentioned brothers and a sister.'

I feel my cheeks flushing. As the words of denial form in my throat, I stop them. I cannot lie to Frank now. Not at a moment like this when we are confessing truths. I've lied so much already but I will not corrupt the feelings that I am expressing to him. And yet I cannot tell him the whole truth. Frank sees something in my face and we both know that this moment is pivotal.

I take a deep breath. 'I had two brothers and one sister. Now, I only have one brother left and I never see him. My parents are dead, too.'

This takes a moment to absorb. 'Why didn't you say so before?'

'Because I couldn't. And I still can't. I shouldn't even be telling you this.'

'Why not?'

'Because it could be dangerous for both of us.'

He squints at me. 'What are you involved in, Marina?'

I bite my lip to buy some time. Then: 'Did you mean those things you were saying?'

'Yes, of course.'

'Well, I meant all the things I was saying, too. No matter what happens, I want you to remember that.'

'What's going to happen?' Franks asks.

361

'I don't know yet.'

'Look, I . . .'

I place a finger on his lips to silence him. 'Don't ask. I don't want to lie to you. Not now.'

Frank isn't sure what to do or say. He looks away from me.

'I want to be with you,' I tell him. 'And that's why I've got to make this right. And if you want to be with me, you're going to have to let me.'

He doesn't respond and I don't expect him to.

I venture one last question. 'If we had to disappear, could you live with that?'

A saxophonist was playing 'In The Mood' at the foot of the escalator at Piccadilly Circus. Passengers tossed coins on to a grubby grey blanket that he had spread on the ground at his feet. The acoustics flattered his meagre talent. Petra looked at her watch. She was five minutes ahead of the four o'clock schedule. At the top of the escalator, she passed through the exit barrier and headed for the phones, as Basit – Reza Mohammed – had instructed her. Both men were already there. Mirqas and Yousef. They exchanged nods with her but neither of them said a word.

They walked along Shaftesbury Avenue and turned into Wardour Street. Petra tried her best to ignore the proximity to her past. The building they entered had been under development when she had been Lisa and when Keith Proctor had come to visit her. Now it was open. The façade had tones of Art Deco running through it, but the inside was just a collection of unimaginative office units. A restaurant and bar occupied the ground floor; zinc tables, white walls, lots of glass, lots of hard edges and empty spaces. The entrance to the upper floors was a door to the left of the restaurant. According to the copper board just inside, the building was home to a catering firm, a film production company called Unicorn Films, a travel agency specializing in long-haul discounts, the administrative office of a clothing firm and a secretarial agency. The travel agency was located on the top floor. Petra wondered why they hadn't picked up their tickets from RJN and assumed it was part of Serra's rigorous security procedure. Keep everything separate. Divide and rule. Don't let any one part of the plan be in a position to compromise any other part and, therefore, by extension, the plan in its entirety.

The office was L-shaped. There were pictures of Bermudan golf courses and Mexican ruins pinned to the walls behind the operators. Yousef spoke with a skinny woman in a tatty turquoise cardigan. A cigarette was wedged into the corner of her mouth. She sorted through a drawer full of paper and found the package – a bulging envelope secured by a rubber band – which she handed to Yousef, who put it into the inner pocket of his ill-fitting grey jacket.

They were halfway down the stairs from the second floor when two men emerged from the offices of Unicorn Films on the first floor. They moved on to the landing and turned to look at the three strangers coming down the stairs towards them. Petra found her attention drawn to the smaller of the two. As she got closer, she recognized the sickly skin, the bulging eyes, the crooked yellow teeth. And she saw recognition in the same instant that she gave it out herself.

Surprise reduced his voice to a rasp. 'I don't fucking believe it!'

Dean West.

26

West was wearing a burgundy knee-length leather coat that Petra remembered from her past. Beneath it was a black polo-neck – another favourite – camouflage combat trousers and Caterpillar boots. The protection standing behind him was new but he belonged to a general category that was familiar; six foot five, stubble for hair, a dark green Armani suit, a diamond ear stud.

'Well fucking well,' West muttered. 'What a fucking surprise. How you been, Steph?'

Her own name paralysed her.

'You've scrubbed up nice, I must say. Got rid of that dye job and put some meat on your bones. Betcha charging twice as much these days.'

Petra glanced at Mirqas and Yousef, who were looking at each other in confusion.

'What's the fucking matter, Steph? Not allowed to speak unless your friends say so? Bet the bastards make you walk behind them in the street, too. Barry said he thought you'd started shagging the towel-heads in Mayfair but I said, "Leave off. There's no fucking way those tossers are gonna start shelling out five hundred upwards for some fucked-up slut like Steph." Looks like I was wrong.'

When she spoke, still employing the slightly Germanic accent that had become second nature to her, Petra's stare glinted with hardness. 'I'm sorry. You've made a mistake.'

'What's with the Eva Braun? Anyhow, you're the one who's made the fucking mistake. That twat you laid out with the bottle cost me large. The filth shut down Brewer Street for about three months on account of what you done.'

Mirqas and Yousef's anxiety had bloomed into alarm. Petra turned to them and saw in their eyes that she had already lost them. Yousef began to move down the stairs. West pointed at him. 'Oi, Noddy! Stay there!'

People always underestimated West because he was slightly built but his rage was more than adequate compensation for his lack of physical presence. Petra recognized the signs; the pursing of the bloodless lips, the wildness in the eyes. The minder was familiar with the routine too. He reached inside his Armani jacket and produced a 9mm Heckler & Koch from the waistband of his trousers.

Petra felt numb. Everything was disintegrating. She thought of the journey she had taken from Brewer Street. Around the world, through a procession of months, through a slew of identity changes, she had arrived at this moment just a few yards from where she had started. Was all she had endured to count for nothing?

Suddenly, Yousef was holding a gun too. A Walther P88. Petra had assumed neither he nor Mirqas would be armed. West's frog-like eyes bulged in their sockets. 'Who the fuck are these two jokers, Steph?'

'My name isn't Steph.'

'Stop messing around and answer the bloody . . .'

Something snapped inside her.

It happened in a fraction of a second, but the effect was colossal. For the first time in months, she felt no pressure. In an instant, it evaporated. The burden of lying to Frank – and the burden of being Petra for Serra – was suddenly gone. And the fury that replaced it was pure and liberating.

West's jaw was still pumping, his mouth opening and closing, but she didn't hear a word he was saying. Hand on the rail, she leapt over the banister and lashed out with her left foot, catching the protection on the side of his face. Large as he was, he still spun like a top. The Heckler & Koch went off once before slipping from his grasp. The bullet hit Yousef in the neck. West and Mirqas were stunned to stillness and silence. The protection was quick and reached for the weapon, despite the blow. But Petra beat him to it. Nevertheless, he grabbed her ankle and yanked it, pulling her off-balance. Automatically, Petra twisted round and shot him through the top of the head.

The second crack of gunfire filled the stairwell and left a ringing in her ears. She shook the dead hand from her foot. By now, Mirqas had pushed past West and was descending towards the ground floor. West grabbed Yousef's Walther P88 and turned to aim at Petra, but she was quicker. The first shot knocked him down. As he tumbled, she remembered him at his worst. She thought of the rapes and how the pain in her mind had lingered long after the bruises and grazes had healed. By the time she had rescued herself from these memories, the Heckler & Koch was empty.

Petra inhaled the gun's smoke deep into her lungs.

Out of the corner of her left eye, she saw Mirqas at the foot of the stairs. Yousef was dead. She reached inside his jacket pocket and removed the envelope containing the air-tickets, stuffing them into her own coat pocket along with the Heckler & Koch. Then she was down the stairs and out on the street.

Petra knew the shots would buy her time, particularly since there had been so many of them; she had fired eight or nine into West himself. That noise would compound the first thirty seconds of confusion for those who were nearby. She looked left and right. Half the people on Wardour Street were standing still, looking at one another, which made it easier to spot Mirqas. He'd turned right.

Past the amusement arcade, past the stalled lorry blocking the traffic, past St Anne's Church, Petra kept Mirqas in her sight. He turned left on to Shaftesbury Avenue and looked back for a moment. Petra assumed that he'd seen her. He cut across the traffic without looking. There was a screech of rubber on tarmac. A black taxi swerved to avoid him and clattered a dispatch-rider, knocking him from his bike. Petra wove in and out of stationary vehicles.

She saw Mirqas turn into Gerrard Street and Chinatown – he was turning back on himself – and saw him exit at the bottom of Wardour Street, where he turned left.

Petra needed him to slow down so she slowed herself and watched him turn left into Leicester Square. She took Lisle Street, sprinting past the back of the Empire cinema. She caught a glimpse of him down Leicester Place. He was still running, but not as fast as before, half-turning to see if he was still being followed and appearing somewhat perplexed to find that it didn't seem he was. Petra knew he would keep moving and that it would probably be in the same direction; that is, away from his pursuer the last time he had seen her. Petra accelerated into the short stretch of Newport Street. By the time she had turned right on to Charing Cross Road, she had slowed to a walk.

She glimpsed him for a moment. Head spinning, almost colliding with several passers-by, he was frantically checking every face for hers. Then he ducked into Leicester Square Underground station. Petra followed but couldn't see him once she was inside. She bought a ticket, passed through the barrier and was presented with a choice. Piccadilly Line or Northern Line?

She chose Piccadilly. She heard the rumble of an approaching train while she was halfway down the escalator. She hurried her descent, taking three steps at a time. Then there was another choice to be made. Eastbound or westbound? An eastbound train hurtled into the station, carriages grinding, metal wheels shrieking. The platform was crowded. She couldn't see Mirqas so she rushed across to the westbound platform, which was virtually empty, a train having just departed. He wasn't there. She returned to the eastbound platform. Those disembarking were heading for the escalators while those who had been waiting were now boarding. The mass of movement was hopeless. Perhaps she should have chosen the Northern Line after all. The doors began to close.

Petra just made it, squeezing through the narrowing gap.

The train began to pull out of the station. That was when she saw him. On the platform. She pressed her face to the glass and he turned round. Their eyes met. No! It wasn't him. Similar, but not the same. She pressed the palm of her hand to her chest and closed her eyes. When she opened them, several passengers were staring at her.

Leicester Square to Covent Garden is one of the shortest stops on the entire Underground network. The train began to decelerate almost as soon as it was in the tunnel. What now?

The doors opened. Only four people from her carriage were getting off. She leaned out to look along the platform and that was when she saw Mirqas again. There was no mistake this time. Two carriages ahead, his back was turned to her. Petra let more passengers get between them and was about to step on to the platform herself when she saw Mirqas re-board the train at the next carriage.

She stayed where she was.

He got out at Holborn. So did many other travellers, which gave Petra some reasonable cover. But Mirqas didn't leave the station. Instead, he transferred to the Central Line, heading west. Petra watched him meander towards the far end of the platform. There weren't enough people on it to allow her to follow him. A train came in two minutes.

Where are you going? What will you do now?

He only stayed on for one stop, disembarking at Tottenham Court Road. Petra glanced at the electronic notice-board overhead. Another train was due in a minute. Mirqas was still going through the process of ensuring his safety but Petra could tell that his senses were dulling. The initial panic over, he would now be trying to think, trying to absorb and comprehend what had happened on the stairs, trying to figure out a plan. Just as she was.

She reached the foot of the steps and saw that he was not rising towards the exit, but was ambling on to the eastbound platform. She stepped back out of his field of vision for a moment. A breeze began, teasing a piece of paper into a dance. Petra felt the vibrations from deep within the tunnel. A group of people hurried down the steps towards the platform, anxious not to miss the train. Petra allowed herself to be absorbed by them and moved on to the platform, which was not crowded. She saw Mirqas just ten yards away.

He glanced at the group as a single unit, not scanning the individual faces within it, and thought nothing of it. They drifted down the platform, getting closer to him. Light began to emerge from the darkness of the tunnel, reflecting off the gleaming steel of the rails.

She was behind him now, just five feet away. The group had moved on, their backs turned to them. The train roared out of the tunnel to their left and into the station. She looked right and saw that no one was watching so she stepped forwards until her mouth was just inches behind his right ear.

'This is for Proctor,' she whispered.

Mirqas began to turn his head but both her hands were already ramming into his back. He didn't even have time to scream. Clawing at the air, he tumbled. Petra had turned away by the time the train hit him and she was already at the foot of the steps when she heard the first scream.

Emotions suspended, Petra walked along Oxford Street. The rush-hour was beginning, for which she was grateful; the pavements were filling. Above, daylight was fading. Another plus. Behind her, sirens made themselves heard over the grumble of traffic.

Analysis, analysis. She saw now that some subconscious part of her had known that it would end this way the moment Dean West had identified her as Stephanie. There were no alternatives. She'd been careless, emptying the gun into West when one clean shot would have brought down Mirqas before he was out of the door. Three months ago, she would never have made such an error. A year ago, however, she would not have coped at all. She didn't know whether that was good or bad.

Walking helped her to stay calm, allowing her to process her thoughts. Gradually, a strategy formed. She found a vacant phone-box and dialled a number, hoping she could remember the sequence correctly. A recorded message greeted her. 'You have reached the offices of Adelphi Travel. We are sorry that there is no one available to take your call. If would like to leave a message, please speak clearly after the tone.'

'Market-East-one-one-six-four-R-P.'

There was a five-second wait. 'Go ahead. You're clear.'

'I need to speak to Mr Alexander.'

'Where are you?'

'Oxford Street. A pay-phone.'

'Please hold.'

She extracted the envelope from her pocket, removed the rubber band and opened it. Three air-tickets. She found her own. Elizabeth Shepherd, as she had been in New York. British Airways flight BA283 to Los Angeles, leaving the day after tomorrow from Heathrow's Terminal Four at quarter-past-midday. There were no connections. She checked the envelope. Mirqas and Yousef had been booked on to the same flight. Neither of their tickets displayed any connections, either.

Alexander was as blunt as usual. 'Yes?'

'I've got a serious problem.'

'How serious?'

'Four dead. Three in Wardour Street, one on the Underground at Tottenham Court Road.'

For once, Petra had robbed Alexander of breath. Eventually, he asked, 'Are you hurt?'

'No.'

'Under threat?'

'I'm fine. But I need some damage control.'

'What kind of control?'

Despite every instinct within her, Petra found herself

admiring Alexander's composure. He listened to her revised version of events and to her request, and then said he'd see what he could do, before asking Petra what she intended to do.

'I don't know. I'll contact Serra and see what happens.'

She heard him light a Rothmans, heard the deep sigh of the first inhale. 'Perhaps it's time we brought you out,' he suggested. 'Perhaps it's time to look at another angle.'

'No.'

'This is messy enough already and it's liable to get worse.'

'I know. But I'll go with it for as long as I can.'

Another pregnant pause ended with: 'All right. But I want you to keep me fully informed.'

Petra moved to another phone-box to make her call to Serra. There was no reply. She continued walking. At Marble Arch, she tried again and, this time, got an answer.

'Yousef is dead and Mirqas has disappeared.'

'What happened?'

'I met them as planned. We went to get the tickets. As we were leaving, we were intercepted by two men. One of them started arguing with Mirqas – they seemed to know each other – and then the other one pulled a gun. He shot Yousef and then turned it on me, but I disarmed him. And by the time I'd dealt with him and the other man, Mirqas was gone.'

'Were you seen?'

'Not properly. We were still inside the building.'

'Where are the tickets?'

'Yousef was carrying them but I have them now.'

'Did any of you look at them before this happened?'

'No. He put them in his pocket straight away.'

'Have *you* looked at them yet?'

'I have now.'

'You said that Mirqas seemed to know the man who shot Yousef?'

'No. It was the other man who shot Yousef. The smaller man was the one who seemed to know Mirqas. He started

371

asking Mirqas where he had been, saying that it was a long time since they had seen each other. Mirqas tried to look blank but Yousef and I could see that he knew who this man was. But it never got further than that.'

'And where are you now?'

'On the street.'

'Are you safe?'

'Safe enough.'

'I'm going to come over.'

'When? Tonight?'

'No. I can't come now. But I'll be there tomorrow.'

It was Petra's turn to pause. 'So what happens now?'

'Nothing.'

'Meaning?'

'Meaning we wait to see if anything develops. But even if it does, we still proceed. It's too late to stop anything now. The others have dispersed. Not even I know where they are.'

'But the team is reduced by two. Can they cope with that?'

'They'll have to.'

I am back in my flat. I am in the bathroom. The door is locked. It's two hours since I pushed Mirqas beneath the train. I stand naked in front of the mirror and watch myself shaking. I can barely bring myself to look at the monster in the glass and yet I cannot tear my gaze away.

Who am I?

I feel like a schizophrenic. I am one person and then another. The ice is thawing and those things that were instinctive and automatic are now subject to scrutiny. The part of me that is Stephanie sits in judgement on the part of me that is Petra.

I cannot live like this. I killed three people today.

I whisper it to myself. Hello, darling, how was your day? How was the office? I killed three people today. What shall we eat for dinner? Shall we get pizza? I pushed a man beneath a train and shot one through the top of the head. Let's watch TV. Perhaps we should get out of London this weekend. Just another day at the office, I killed three people today.

The person who is staring at me volunteered for this. It was an informed choice. The consequences lie here and I will have to accept them for as long – or as short? – as I live. How will I end this? How will I end? Where is Stephanie? Does she even exist any more or has Petra killed her too? And who is Marina now? I am constantly evolving. I am never one thing, I'm always a compound.

Frank is knocking on the door and trying the handle. He's asking me if I'm all right. My clothes are on the floor. My black jeans are splattered with Dean West's blood.

There were fresh flowers at the centre of the table in a clear glass vase. Also on the table there were wine glasses, bottles that were mostly empty, plates, a board of cheeses that had been attacked with relish, a bowl of fruit, candle-holders and candle-wax, two ashtrays, cutlery, elbows. Around the table, they sat eight. Frank and Petra, and six others. A social occasion to celebrate a thirty-ninth birthday. Frank had cooked and now everyone was purring in appreciation. A bottle of brandy appeared. Murmurs of approval all round. The lamps were dimmed allowing the candles to cast their liquid light over the gathered faces. There were tired smiles and sleepy eyes. It was half-past-midnight.

Petra remained as taut as a violin string. She smiled when required and was as welcoming as her state of mind allowed. She managed an occasional laugh and hoped it didn't sound too much like a cough. Internally, there was no turmoil. There was no activity at all. Everything was frozen solid, trapped in the ice, and she could feel how brittle she was. One tiny chip and she would shatter, she was sure of it. Even once the last of their guests had left, there was no release.

They began to clear glasses and plates into the kitchen. She sensed Frank behind her but when his hand touched her shoulder, she jumped. It was a reflex she couldn't prevent. Frank withdrew the hand.

'Are you okay?'

'I'm fine.'

'You seem a little tense. In fact, you've seemed tense all night.'

'I told you, I'm fine.'

'And I'm telling you that you're not.'

The tone of his voice startled her. She turned round. 'What do you mean?'

'I mean, there's something wrong.'

'What is it?'

'Why don't you tell me?'

Petra looked as confused as she felt. The killings in Wardour Street had been on the news. It had been a topic of conversation during dinner. Had he somehow discovered that she was involved? It seemed so improbable. 'What is it, Frank?'

'John Fletcher called me today.'

The name came out of nowhere. 'Who?'

'John Fletcher. Who's married to Mary.'

Petra pictured mousy Mary. And then John. 'So?'

'You remember when we went out to dinner with them and he thought you were evasive?'

Petra did, without fondness. 'Yes.'

'Well, yesterday, he's at work and has to look into something or other and the name Brillex-Martins comes up. He recalls that you work for them and so he decides to give you a call to see if you can help him out. And guess what?'

Petra knew what, but shrugged ignorance. 'You tell me.'

'No one in their London office knows you. They've heard of you but none of them have met you.'

Frank offered her an opportunity to say something but she stayed silent because she couldn't form a coherent sentence. At least, not one that was going to be an answer.

'Anyway, if nothing else, John's tenacious. He remembers that you told him that you were something of a trouble-shooter for the company, so he thinks that perhaps you're more of a roving employee, going from one office to the next, sorting out trouble wherever trouble occurs, in which case maybe you're registered at the head office in Brussels. He checks with them and discovers that your name does indeed appear on the company pay-roll. So the mystery is partly solved. Or so he thinks. But then it turns out that it isn't because further enquiries with Brussels reveal that no one there has ever met you either, and that although you're on the pay-roll, you're not being paid. Not only that, but recorded information about you is non-existent; there are no photographs of you, no one knows your address, or your age, or how long your name has been on that list.'

Somewhere deep within Petra, there was a hint of relief. Closer to the surface, there was anger. *I can't deal with this now. Not after today.* She held open her hands. 'So what do you want me to say?'

'Look, you know that I know there's been some strange stuff going on and I've never pushed it. But don't you think now might be a good time to come clean?'

'You have no idea what you're talking about.'

'I know. That's exactly the point. I can't help you if I don't know what's –'

'You can't help me anyway.'

'How do you know?'

'Because if I thought you could, I'd have already let you in.'

'I thought maybe after last night, a little more openness –'

'Then you thought wrong.'

'For God's sake, Marina, I'm trying to help!'

'Aren't you listening? *You can't!*'

'Well, we can't go on like this.'

Petra felt her spine stiffening. 'What are you saying?'

'I'm saying that this is absurd. You're not telling me

375

anything and I'm going crazy trying to decide what's a lie and what isn't.'

She didn't want to resort to attack as a means of defence but felt herself being dragged in that direction by some invisible and familiar force. 'Do you think I enjoy having to be like this?'

'I don't know. I mean, if you say you don't, how do I know if you're telling the truth?'

'That's hilarious, Frank,' Petra retorted, unhappy at being reduced to sarcasm. 'Really bloody funny. Brilliant.'

'Actually, it's the truth.'

The reason in his tone only made it worse.

'Then this whole thing between us is completely pointless. I mean, if you can't trust me –'

'For Christ's sake, Marina! Listen to yourself. How am I supposed to trust you when I know you're lying to me?'

Ten past six on a cold grey morning and I'm on the verge of a nervous breakdown. At least, that's what it feels like but how can I tell? In the past, I never reached moments like this. Drugs and drink replaced the decline with chemical oblivion. What I face now, however, is naked oblivion. Everything has been stripped to the bone.

Marina versus Petra versus Stephanie.

I wonder now whether storming out of Frank's flat was the right thing to do. We needed to talk. I wanted to talk. But I would still have been forced to lie to him. So perhaps it was for the best. I wonder whether he's awake and find myself hoping that he is, hoping that it matters too much to him to allow him to sleep. And then I'm disgusted with myself for being so selfish and hope that he's asleep. This was my doing. There's no reason he should suffer any more than he already has.

No longer able to care about avenging the dead, no longer motivated to seek justice and retribution for an unpunished crime, I just want to sleep now. I am twenty-three years old and tired of life.

27

At half-past-eight, Petra knocked on Frank's door but there was no answer. She returned to her flat and dialled his number. The answer-machine asked her to leave a message but she couldn't find the right words to express what she felt, so she replaced the receiver without speaking. She tried again at nine and there was still no answer. Then she went out and bought an identical Sony Walkman to the one that Serra had given her.

Later, she had a cup of coffee in a café. She watched the rain slither down the window and thought about tomorrow and the day after tomorrow. Tomorrow, she would try to foil the Sons of Sabah and ruin the plan devised by Khalil and organized by Serra. She didn't yet know how she might achieve this or if it was even possible, but she knew that she had to try. So far, Petra had kept Alexander in the dark and in order to retain control and protect herself, she intended to keep it that way until the moment of her choosing. But what of the day after tomorrow? Khalil would remain as elusive as ever and she would remain bound to Alexander and Magenta House. Had it not been for Christopher and Jane, and their children, she would have taken a chance and gone on the run, with or without Frank. Petra didn't actually believe that Alexander would harm the remains of her family but she also knew that she couldn't take the risk. And she knew that Alexander knew that too. Every time she was inclined to dismiss the threat and disappear, she thought about Leon Giler and his family, and saw the smoking remains of his car on the Queensboro Bridge. Tomorrow there would be chaos. But what would the day after tomorrow bring?

At eleven, she called Serra on his mobile and they agreed to meet at midday.

The Clarendon on Jermyn Street would have been easy to miss. There was no sign outside the entrance, which was a door between a tailor and a shop selling over-priced shirts. Petra entered a narrow corridor that led to a small lobby towards the rear of the building. Behind her, the door closed slowly, shutting out the noise of the street, shutting out modernity. There were armchairs and a sofa in the lobby. Years of wear had polished the leather to a sheen. Wooden panels formed the walls and from them hung prints of hand-drawn maps on paper that had turned yellow. Behind the reception desk sat a man who was at one with his surroundings; dressed like an Edwardian butler, he creaked with age and manners.

'May I help you?'

'I'm here to meet one of your guests. Preben Olsen.'

'Is he expecting you?'

'Yes.'

He consulted the register. 'Room nine. It's on the second floor.'

Petra was alone in the cage-lift, which rattled as it rose. She smelt polish coming off the wood and saw herself reflected in the brass. The tension she felt was not visible. The same could not be said for Serra, whose anxiety existed on the surface, in the greyness of his skin, in the smudges beneath his eyes, in the restlessness of his hands.

'Sleepless night?' Petra asked.

He nodded. 'You?'

'Of course.'

She shut the door and surveyed the room, which was not a bedroom, but a small reception room. The bedroom was through a door on the right. In front of her, there was an oval table with a china vase at its centre. There were lilies in it. A silver tray of sandwiches sat next to the vase. By the window, there was a sofa and a pair of armchairs.

On a small lacquered side-table sat Serra's constant companion, his lap-top. The oil paintings on the walls were mostly country landscapes and stately homes, their parklands peppered with horses and cattle.

'Nice place,' she said.

Serra pointed at the tray of sandwiches. 'I ordered those for us.'

'I haven't got much of an appetite at the moment.'

They sat down and Serra asked Petra to repeat her version of the previous day's events. He cross-examined every detail and when Petra had finished he asked her to relay it to him once more. He referred to the *Evening Standard* coverage of the Wardour Street killings, pointing out that one of the victims – a man called Dean West – had been a notorious local criminal. What kind of connection would such a man have had with someone like Mirqas? Petra said she had no idea, since she knew neither of them. The report told of two people fleeing from the scene and said that the police were anxious to trace both of them. Petra said she didn't know which direction Mirqas had taken; by the time she'd reached the street, he'd vanished.

Several pages on, a smaller article reported the unfortunate suicide of a Kuwaiti student who had thrown himself in front of a Central Line train at Tottenham Court Road. There had been a witness to the tragedy, a middle-aged woman on her way home after shopping in Oxford Street. She explained how the young man had walked to the edge of the platform and how she had thought that he was too close but had not called out to him because, as she said, 'I never thought he'd jump.' Petra recognized Magenta House's handiwork.

She looked up from the paper at Serra. 'A suicide?'

'I know. It's impossible to believe.'

'Except that this woman saw him.'

'She saw something but it wasn't suicide. Mirqas wouldn't have killed himself. It is expressly forbidden in the Qur'an.'

'What about suicide-bombers?'

'There is a distinction between those who die in the name of Allah and those who just elect to die.'

Serra lit a cigarette and stood up, arching his back. He ambled over to the window, parted the net curtains and gazed at the damp street below.

'What happens now?' Petra asked.

'Nothing and everything. It's too late for me to alter the plans that have been set in motion. They have a momentum of their own. As for me, I'll just have to wait.'

'Then why are you here?'

He looked back at her from across the room. 'Because you are the only part of the plan that can change. The hijack will go ahead with or without you. I'm here to discover what you intend to do.'

'And what do you want me to do?'

He shrugged. 'The plan can succeed without a sleeper. But there are still two reasons for you to go: to ensure the aircraft is destroyed and to meet Khalil in Malta. What I need to know is whether what happened yesterday has changed your mind about tomorrow.'

He was watching her, trying to read the answer in her eyes before he heard it from her mouth. Petra sensed the magnitude of the moment. Supposing she conceded to doubt, what would the consequences be?

'No,' she said. She thought she saw the smallest wince, a flicker of sadness in the eyes. Or maybe she'd just imagined it. 'What are you thinking?'

Serra wandered over from the window to the table and began to examine the sandwiches on the tray. 'I'm thinking about Mirqas. About what happened to him.'

'You think he was killed?'

'Yes.'

'By?'

Serra turned round to face her. 'I don't know.'

*   *   *

This is what Serra says to me but it isn't what he's thinking. I see the truthful answer in his eyes, which meet mine and then look away almost immediately. He believes I killed Mirqas.

We talk some more before Serra says he wants to make love to me. It is only in this moment that I really understand the type of man that Serra is. He is no different to the men who used to pay to have sex with me in Brewer Street and I know what is happening as we go through to the bedroom.

I scan the room quickly; a large double bed, two bedside tables made of oak, a dressing table with a large gilded mirror on it, a tall mahogany wardrobe with a matching chest of drawers. I wonder where the threat will come from.

Serra asks me to strip in front of him. Of course. He wants to know that I am unarmed. There is always the possibility that I am wrong so I am compelled to continue this act, this long and painful performance. I shed my clothes slowly for him. Does he really imagine that I am unarmed when I am naked?

On the bed, he wants it all and I give everything, consoled by the fact that whatever happens, this will be the last time that I have to have sex with Marc Serra. I vow to myself he is the last man I shall ever trade for. He presses his fingers inside me, he sucks me and I suck him, and eventually he enters me with his customary lack of finesse. When I am flat on my back his whole body presses down on me, pinning me to the mattress. His fingers dig into the hard muscles of my thighs. He means to leave bruises. When I sit astride him, he holds me tightly around the waist so that he can pull me down as he thrusts up. And when he persuades me to move on to all fours – his favourite position by far; he likes to press my face down into the pillows – I become nervous because I can no longer see him. I rotate slightly, so that my head is nowhere near the pillows and so that I can catch a partial glimpse of him in the mirror on the dressing table. I resist his attempts to push my head down into the crumpled sheets. Eventually, he gives up as he becomes increasingly selfish, his grip tightening around my hips, his movement growing deeper and quicker until, finally, he comes with a shudder and groan. He sounds like he's been winded.

We lie next to one another, not speaking. I think of Falstone and the house in which I was raised. I can see the view now, the fields of rough wind-worn grass falling away from me, the hawthorn trees on the hill that grow with their branches bent to the east courtesy of the continual winds from the west. I see Anne Mitchell in her high-rise block in Chalk Farm. She cries when she's by herself because of her husband's infidelity, because of the life in which she's trapped. She once told me that she wanted to be a flight attendant so that she could see the world. All she sees now is Telecom Tower in the murky distance. I remember my first kiss, a tentative experience that left me queasy. I see a black-and-white picture of my parents. They're standing on top of the Matterhorn. The photo used to sit on a heavy stone mantelpiece in the kitchen, above the stove. Then I think of Anne again and of the disappointment that her life has become. I try not to draw parallels for fear of coming off worse.

'I'm hungry,' Serra says. 'Do you want one of the sandwiches?'

I make a sound that is neither yes nor no. Serra rises from the bed and pulls on one of the thick, white towelling dressing-gowns that the hotel provides for its guests. He leaves the room. I stay still. He returns carrying the silver tray. I feel tense but hope that I still look relaxed. He sets the tray on the bed beside me. This may be the moment. But it isn't. He walks over to the dresser and takes a cigarette from the pack that lies on top of it. He lights it and takes a long appreciative drag from it.

He starts to stroll back towards me. I begin to think that I might have been wrong.

'We should start to consider the future,' he tells me. 'What we should do after you and Khalil . . .'

The knife appears to come out of nowhere. I have to admit, he's craftier than I thought. It's a switch-blade and seems to slip down his sleeve and into his right hand as an extension of the movement which propels him towards me. The cigarette discarded, Serra is lunging. The rapidity of my reaction is caught in his expression; a photo-flash of surprise. I am quick, but not quick enough. The blade slices through my left biceps. It is so sharp, I barely feel the initial contact.

382

I continue my roll and slither out from beneath the bulk of his body. Already, I am trailing scarlet across the white cotton sheets. Serra is rising from the bed but I am on my feet. I want to unleash an early strike but he knows this and the tip of the blade is already pointing at me. He steadies himself and we have a stand-off.

I see fear in his eyes. He knows about me. My reputation scares him. He might have the weapon but he realizes that he doesn't have the speed. He knows — we both know — that if he doesn't make his next move count, he will have lost all the advantage he ever had.

He tries a feint. A duck to the left and a surge to the right. It is a manoeuvre I know well. When he goes to his left, I should go to mine to avoid him, but I don't. I go to my right and stay there. He is already committed to the thrust and, as he moves forward, I slip further right, spinning away from him. All this happens in a second. Now, he is off-balance and I am already preying on his weakness. He tries to correct the stumble and to turn left in the same instant. It's a mistake. He needed to distance himself from me first. I spin on my left foot. My right foot is carving a broad and perfect arc through the air. Then it clatters into the side of his face, jarring the jawbone. A tremor runs through his entire body. The blow leaves him momentarily dazed but he doesn't fall and he still clutches the switch-blade. Nevertheless, he is stunned and this brief moment of confusion is critical. I spin round again and, this time, I unleash a strike to the throat with a clenched fist.

Petra rinsed the cut with cold water, the blood reappearing from the fine line across her biceps as soon as it had been wiped clean. By the sink, there were several strips of the cotton sheet that she had torn apart. She wrapped one of them around the wound, making sure it was tight.

Back in the bedroom, Serra was alert and was struggling against his bindings. Petra had placed him in a chair and tied his hands behind it with a leather belt. She was confident that he would be unable to loosen it. But even if he did, each leg was bound to a chair-leg by torn sheets. They were not the strongest shackles but they were quite sufficient. At the very least, they would buy time and that was all Petra needed; they both knew his struggle was more symbolic than practical.

She pulled on her underwear and the plain white T-shirt that she had been wearing beneath her sweatshirt. The cotton binding around her biceps protruded from below the truncated sleeve. A scarlet smudge was beginning to form on it.

'You should have killed me as soon as you had the chance.'

'I know,' Serra said, his voice reduced to a hoarse whisper that was almost as painful to listen to as it was to produce.

'Did you know it was me before I even arrived?'

Serra shook his head.

'But you suspected . . .'

He nodded.

'And then, being the man that you are, you thought you could have it all. How typical. I've known men like you before. Too many, too often.' Petra's anger was coloured by disappointment. 'If you'd been half the man you think you are, I'd be dead by now. But people like you, once you get a sniff of it, you can't help yourself. You're like a dog. Or a junkie. You knew this would be your last opportunity – I expect you knew I was going to die – so you thought you'd enjoy yourself one more time. One for the road, you might say. Hence the hotel. I mean, there's no need for you to be in London tonight, is there?'

Serra's silence was all the answer she needed.

'Sex,' sighed Petra. 'It's undone more men than anything else.'

It never ceased to amaze her how the bright could be so dim, how the strong could be so weak.

'How did you know?' she asked him.

'It wasn't just one thing. It was several.'

384

'Like?'

'It didn't make sense – Mirqas and some London criminal.'

'Mirqas was a criminal himself. In this city.' When Serra frowned at this assertion, Petra said, 'He murdered a journalist here last year.'

Serra said, 'Mirqas didn't speak English.'

'What?'

A fragile flame of victory flickered in Serra's eyes. 'He only spoke Arabic and French.'

Petra was about to refute it but then stopped. She tried to remember Mirqas talking and found she couldn't. She'd never heard him. Not once. 'I didn't know that.'

'So unless this London criminal was fluent in French or Arabic . . .'

'Is that it?' Petra snapped. 'Or was there something else?'

'No. There was also LV241.'

'What about it?'

'It doesn't exist.' Of course. That made sense. A morsel of information tossed to her as bait. She guessed what was coming next. 'I have paid sources who provide me with information. Like if there's anybody making enquiries about a new camp called LV241 operating in Libya. There was somebody who was interested in it, but nobody knew who it was.'

'It could've been me.'

'Possibly. But I didn't believe that.'

'Why not?'

Serra shrugged a little. 'Intuition.'

'Intuition's a gift. You should have used it more. What else?'

'Your decision to proceed.'

'What about it?'

'It doesn't make sense. Not for someone like you. To be honest, I was suspicious as soon as you accepted the role of sleeper.'

'Why did you offer it to me, then? Simply as a test?'

'No. Because Kamal Ibrahim Karim insisted upon it. And he is the one with the money. He has always insisted upon you. As soon as I informed him that I had made contact with you, he was determined that you should work on his behalf, no matter what the cost.'

'Why?'

'Because of your reputation.'

'You don't sound convinced.'

'To me, his behaviour was more like an adolescent crush.'

'What about Khalil? What does he think?'

'Karim is the one with the money.'

'I know. But what about Khalil?'

A weary smile spread slowly across his face. 'That's what this is all about, isn't it?'

Petra said nothing.

'That is the reason you accepted the role of sleeper in the first place. A woman like you – the great Petra Reuter – acting as a sleeper with only the promise of a rendezvous at the end? No. Not unless there was an agenda. And for someone like you – a terrorist turned highly-paid assassin – what other agenda could there realistically be?'

'If that's what you thought, why didn't you warn Khalil? Or Karim? Why risk involving me at all?'

'Firstly, because there is no risk. The hijack will succeed. You cannot prevent it. Secondly, because I have no personal interest in this business. Clients come and go. It doesn't matter to me who they are, just that they pay me.'

'I don't believe that.'

'And I don't care what you believe.' Serra coughed and each contraction of his bruised throat expressed itself in his face. There were tears in his eyes. He swallowed gingerly before speaking again. 'It is now clear to me that your interest was in Khalil right from the start and not in the money that he was offering you. I expect somebody else is paying you even more to terminate him. I imagine Giler was merely a sacrificial pawn. A pawn worth a million dollars to you, for sure, but a pawn nevertheless. How much are you getting for Khalil? Two million dollars? Five? Ten? I believe the American government has let it be known that they'll pay up to five for Khalil.'

'As you say, clients come and go. It doesn't matter to me who they are, just that they pay me.' Petra picked up the switch-blade from the bed. 'And if you have no personal interest in this business, you might as well tell me where I can find Khalil.'

Serra's half-smile persisted. 'I thought so.'

'Where is he?'

'I don't know.'

'You'll tell me sooner or later.'

'I may tell you something but it won't be where you can find Khalil. Or what he looks like. Or who knows him. Or anything about him. And do you want to know why?'

'Why?'

'Because Khalil doesn't exist. He's not real. He is – how would you say it? – a flag of convenience. A ghost, a legend without substance.'

Had she been someone else – *anyone* else – Petra supposed she would have dismissed Serra's answer with contempt. But she was the one person who could not do that. She stared at Serra and he realized that there was more to her reaction than simple incredulity.

'What about the Sons of Sabah? Are they ghosts too?'

The name sent a jolt through Serra and his response was too feeble and too slow. 'Who?'

'The Sons of Sabah, Marc. The ones who are going to hijack fight BA283. Are they ghosts?'

'Who are you? BKA?'

'Come on.'

'CIA? Mossad?'

'What does it matter? We know about the Sons of Sabah.'

'You know nothing.'

387

'You're forgetting that I've seen them.'

'You've seen *some* of them. That's all.'

Petra was dismissive. 'Right.'

'Do you think I would have let you near the hijack if that's all there was?'

'I'm wondering why you let me near it at all.'

'Because I had to have something to offer you. Something legitimate.'

'Keep your friends close, keep your enemies closer?'

'Something like that.'

The coldness spread through her. 'I'm not buying this.'

Petra saw panic forming when Serra said, 'Whether BA283 leaves the ground or not, the Sons of Sabah will not be denied. You can't stop them. *I* can't stop them.'

'So why the hijack?'

'To create an impression.'

'What impression?'

'You'll see.'

Petra held the switch-blade in her right hand and began to tap the tip on the edge of the silver tray. Serra's eyes were glued to the steel, not to her. She said, 'Are the Sons of Sabah a creation of Karim's?'

'Does it matter?'

'To me? Yes.'

'Yes, they are.'

'And this hijack – is that also his idea?'

'He paid me to organize it but the concept was his.'

'And was it his idea to place a bomb on board North Eastern flight NE027?'

For Serra, the question came out of nowhere. He stopped looking at the blade and turned to Petra. '*What?*'

She repeated the question for him. 'Was it his idea?'

Serra was trying to calculate where this line of questioning was leading. The anxiety on his face told Petra what he tried to avoid saying directly. 'It was ... something different.'

'Was Karim behind it?'

'Yes, he was.'

A sharp pain ran through her. Sadness quickly followed by anger, then exhaustion. The circle was complete. She wished Proctor was at her side to hear the answers. She said, 'And the man who carried it out was Basit. Am I right?'

Each question was a secret exposed and with each revelation, Petra watched a man whose world was collapsing. He struggled pathetically against the leather belt. *'Who are you?'*

'Do you remember how you once told me that you thought Khalil and I were similar?'

'Yes.'

'Well you were right.'

'What?'

'Except that we're not similar. We're the *same*.'

Serra was sweating. 'I don't understand.'

'There is no Petra Reuter, Marc.'

'What are you talking about?'

Petra milked the moment, taking her time, allowing his confusion to feed upon itself. 'How would *you* say it? Petra Reuter is a flag of convenience. A ghost. She doesn't exist.'

'But you're here!' he protested.

'I know. But you don't know who I am.'

When he next spoke, the aggression of defiance was replaced by caution and curiosity. 'Who are you working for?'

'I'm working for myself.'

He shook his head slowly. 'I don't believe you.'

'I never thought you would. But it's true.'

'Who are you?'

'I'm a whore. That's who I am, Marc. A cheap whore. Actually, not so cheap any more, but a whore all the same.'

She could see that Serra supposed she was being cryptic. 'I don't understand.'

'Despite all your reservations about me, you thought we had something good together, didn't you? That we made a good team. You at forty-four and me at twenty-three.'

'*Twenty-three?*'

'And what was this based on? Sex. That's what. We never had anything in common but you liked the look of me and the idea of me. You liked the fact that I was dangerous. It made me more exciting. But more than all these things, you liked the sex, didn't you? Even better, you saw that I liked the sex. You liked the way that I'd do anything you wanted, you liked the way you tamed me.'

'You're crazy.'

'No.' She waved an admonishing finger at him. 'I know men like you. You bring a woman to orgasm and you think that a little part of her is for ever yours. But it never happened, Marc. There was no orgasm. There was no cry of pleasure. It was all faked.'

'Bullshit!'

She laughed but there was no humour in it. 'How typical, how arrogant. How *you*. You can't believe it, can you? You think you're so good and now this? I don't blame you for being shocked. In fact, I'd be astonished if a man with your ego reacted in any other way. But the truth is this: I *was* a prostitute, Marc. Day in, day out, I faked it for people like you. And every time I did, I learned a little more. I'm a professional. Deceit is my only practical qualification.'

'You're lying.'

'For once, I'm not. You're nothing to me. You were just work.'

She had hoped there might be catharsis in the truth, but there wasn't; it merely fuelled her hatred. Her grip on the blade was tighter than ever. She closed her eyes and pictured herself driving it into his chest.

Keep it together.

She took a deep breath, which she let out gradually. Then she went through to the reception room and returned with Serra's lap-top, which she set upon the bed. She drew

390

up a list of the data files but didn't notice any obvious difference; there was virtually no data stored on the unit.

It was back to business. 'Do you want to tell me what FAT/3 is?'

Silence.

'It looks to me as though you keep your data elsewhere. On a disk, maybe. Or do you down-load it to somewhere secure? No, I don't think so. Phone-lines are vulnerable. I imagine you'd prefer a disk or a ZIP drive. Now, I wonder where I'd find such a thing. In your clothes, perhaps?'

Petra sorted through every garment Serra had brought with him, searching pockets and slicing linings apart, but she found nothing. Then she checked every other item that belonged to him before conducting a thorough search of the bedroom, bathroom and reception room.

Eventually, she returned to Serra himself. 'What's the data stored on?'

He shook his head. Her anger was under control, but only just. She could feel it simmering beneath the surface. She ran the tip of the blade down Serra's right thigh towards the knee-cap. 'I'm not going to ask you politely next time.'

Growing paler by the second, he shook his head again.

Boyd had once told Petra that the most important element of physical terror was not the act itself but in persuading the victim that you had the will to see it through.

Petra leaned close to Serra and whispered. 'If you scream, I'll kill you.'

She thrust the blade through the skin and soft tissue until it crunched against gritty bone inside the knee. Serra squealed, his teeth clamping down on his tongue, his body jolting as though the chair was electric. Eyes wide open, he tossed his head from side to side, the veins bulging in his neck. The beads of sweat that had formed on his fore-head began to run. Petra reversed the blade with a slow twist, compounding his agony. Having been utterly drained of colour, the effort of stifling a scream had left his face beetroot. Tears blurred his vision.

Petra felt nothing. No pleasure, no disgust, just the numbness she was so used to. Slowly, very slowly, she steered the bloody blade towards Serra's right eye, halting the steel tip an inch from the pupil. When she spoke, her voice was soft and slow, little more than a murmur. 'What is the information on?'

His resistance was broken. 'A disk,' he wailed. His voice quivered, his pretence at courage crushed. 'It's on a disk.'

The speed at which he offered up the answer disturbed her. 'Where is it?'

'I don't have it.'

'Who has it?'

'Basit.'

'I don't believe you.'

'I swear it's the truth!'

Reza Mohammed, she thought. 'And where is he?'

'I don't know.'

Petra moved the tip closer to the soft centre of the eyeball. Serra screeched. *'I swear to God! I don't know!'*

'I thought you'd organized the Sons of Sabah.'

'They made individual arrangements. It was safer that way.' The words were coming out in an undignified rush now. 'So that if anyone was caught they would not be in a position to betray the others. Including me.'

'Crap.'

'It's true. I promise you! I was the one who arranged the training and the schedule. But the other details were left to them. I don't even know which country Basit is in. I don't know his real name or the name on the passport he's using.'

'But at twelve-fifteen tomorrow he'll be on BA283 bound for Los Angeles?'

'Yes.'

* * *

392

I circle Serra, checking that his hands are still tightly bound. An hour has passed. I have gone through the files on the computer and questioned him but, in truth, there is little of substance in them. I know there is a fourteen-letter password – LESFILSDU-SABAH – to activate or deactivate the encrypted material on the disk but since the password is so obvious, I am assuming that the un-encrypted material may still be incomprehensible. Serra is exhausted. His head lolls to one side. I peer through the window. The sky is beginning to darken.

My rage is spent. Earlier, I could have killed Marc Serra in a blind fury. That would have been easy. This is going to be much harder. I have to kill him anyway. There is no alternative. I cannot leave him alive in this hotel room. He will escape and raise the alarm and the consequences of that are too chaotic to calculate. And I cannot leave him to Magenta House because they will find out from him as much as he knows and that means that Alexander will be in a position to ruin everything, and I cannot let that happen.

Serra's throat is badly swollen and bruised. When he talks it's hard to understand what he's saying. 'Who are you, Petra?'

I get to my feet, leaving the knife on the bed where he can see it. 'My name is Stephanie Patrick.'

'Who are you working for?'

'I've told you. Myself.'

'Why?'

What a question. It hurts just to consider the possible answers. My parents, Sarah, David, Keith Proctor – they are the first five reasons to spring to mind. I think of the pain I have caused Christopher and I think of the way my life disintegrated in the aftermath of the tragedy.

I look into his bleary eyes. 'Most of my family were on the North Eastern flight. I'm doing this for them and for an architect from Uniondale, New York called Martin Douglas.'

'Who?'

'He was the passenger in seat 49C. The passenger in my seat.'

Serra looks astonished and then mortified, as though he cannot

believe that all this trouble has its roots in something so trivial.
'It's personal?'

'Increasingly,' I reply. 'And when I see Reza Mohammed, I'm
going to get the disk and then I'm going to kill him.'

'Who?'

Interesting. 'Reza Mohammed,' I say. There is still no reaction.
Perhaps Serra is a good actor, perhaps he is for real. It makes
no difference to me. 'Basit,' I tell him. 'Basit's real name is Reza
Mohammed.' Or is it Mustafa Sela? 'He was the one who placed
the bomb on the aircraft at JFK.'

Serra nods a little. 'It won't matter.'

I walk behind him and remove the lampshade from the brass
lamp on the table by the window. 'What won't matter?'

'Killing Basit.'

I pull the plug from the socket. 'Well, in that case, all the more
reason to do it.'

'If that flight fails to leave tomorrow, nearly four thousand
people will die.'

Something occurs within me when he tells me this. It's in his
eyes as he turns to look at me. It's in his voice as the words take
to the air. I try to ignore what I am feeling and step out of his
line of vision. My grip tightens on the lamp. 'What?'

'Four thousand people will die.'

'How?'

'It doesn't matter how. You can't stop it. I can't stop it.'

'You're lying.'

'Maybe. Maybe not. Only time will tell.'

And if Marc Serra lives, Alexander will learn of the hijack
and the flight will never leave. Serra does not know it but he's
condemned himself. Either way, he loses. I swing the lamp and
hit him over the back of the head, knocking him unconscious.
Then I go to the bed and pick up the switch-blade.

Petra stepped out of the shower and dried herself with a
large, white hotel towel. She dressed quickly, gathering
her own things and then sorting through Serra's to see
which she would take with her. On the computer, the

folder that had contained the files FAT, FAT/1, FAT/2 and FAT/3 was called FDS/12. Fils Du Sabah/12. There were ten hijackers, originally. Now there were eight. There had been an invoice from a firm of west London electricians among Serra's papers in Paris, she remembered. FAT/3 had appeared in the date-box. There had been twelve items on the list. And somewhere else – she couldn't quite remember where – she had seen another reference to FAT/3. That had also contained twelve mixtures of letters and numbers. She grabbed Serra's mobile phone, switched off his computer, placed it in its padded carrying-case and reached for her coat.

28

Petra stepped into the rain on Jermyn Street. She found a pay-phone on Church Place and called the Adelphi Travel number, where she was greeted by the recorded message that ran twenty-four hours a day. She relayed the identification routine that she had used the day before and, within a minute, she was speaking to Alexander.

'The Clarendon on Jermyn Street. Room nine. It's a mess.'

'How many?'

'One.'

'Anyone I know?'

'Serra.'

The silence was as predictable as it was long. '*Serra?*'

'Yes.'

'What happened?'

The question annoyed her. 'Oh, for God's sake, he cut his throat while shaving. Does it matter what happened? He's dead. I can't explain it right now. There isn't time.' Lying to Alexander had always been easy. Sometimes, even pleasurable.

'Are you under observation?'

'I'm not sure, but I don't think it's safe for me to come in. Everything's going to proceed even though Serra's dead so I need to stay clean. If I can, I'll call you tomorrow.'

'Fine. But if there's a problem, don't bother with protocol.'

She made her second call from a different pay-phone.

A cab took her to George Street and Dr Brian Rutherford greeted her personally. 'Mrs Morgan's already gone home,' he explained. 'And you only just managed to catch me in time.'

'So I see. That's a very fancy outfit you're wearing.'

Rutherford was dressed in black tie. 'I've got to go to a dinner at Grosvenor House.'

'I'm sorry to have held you up.'

'Don't be. You've done me a favour. It's one of those corporate things. A pharmaceutical firm trying to sweet-talk us into their products.'

He led her through to his surgery and shed his jacket. Beneath sharp white lights, he cleaned and disinfected the cut before stitching it and applying a dressing. As he was washing his hands, he said to her, 'You know, you should take better care of yourself, Stephanie. I don't know how you accumulate these little injuries – and I don't want to know – but you're collecting too many, too young.'

'I know.'

'I'd hate to think that one day you might get seriously hurt.'

Petra pulled on her T-shirt. 'I'll bear that in mind. And thanks for your concern.'

'At your age, you think you'll live for ever. But when you get to my age, you'll realize just how short for ever can be.'

Petra couldn't help herself and smiled. 'What is this? Any wound requiring five stitches or more and you get pearls of wisdom for free?'

There was a sadness in his gaze. 'If it's for free, you should take it, don't you think?'

'Maybe. By the way, I was wondering if you could lend me some paper, an envelope and a pen?'

'I expect I could manage that.'

'I also need a torch.'

'A torch?'

'You know. Hand-held, runs on batteries, emits light from one end.'

Rutherford nodded and began to rummage through one

of the drawers in his desk. 'I like you, Stephanie. You're a nice girl. But that doesn't mean I want to keep seeing you here. Think about it.'

From Rutherford's surgery, she walked to Bond Street Underground, took the Jubilee Line to Green Park, changed on to the Victoria Line and got off at Victoria. From there, she walked to the corner of Wilton Road and Longmoore Street. On a cold, damp evening Gallagher & Sons was an oasis of cosy warmth. She remembered the place now; the wooden panels and the mustard yellow paint, the mirror on the wall, Cyril Bradfield sitting beneath it nursing a pint of Guinness. She stopped in front of his table.

'Can I buy you a drink?'

He looked up at her. 'What are you doing in here?'

'I needed to see you.'

'You've got my number. You could've called.'

'I couldn't wait.' She glanced at his glass which was two-thirds empty. 'Another one?'

'Shouldn't we . . . ?'

'It's not that type of business.'

'In that case, why not?'

This was the first occasion she had been in contact with Bradfield since collecting the last of the three identities he had prepared for her. The first was lodged with a branch of ABN-AMRO in Amsterdam, the second was in a safe deposit box in Paris. The third was in London. By the time Petra returned to the table with a freshly poured pint of Guinness, Bradfield had rolled himself another perfect, thin cigarette despite having three bandaged fingers on his right hand and two on his left.

'What happened to you?'

'Acid burns. An occasional occupational hazard, I'm afraid.'

Petra took a sip from her Coke and then passed Bradfield the envelope she had taken from Rutherford. He looked uncomfortable accepting it. Another occupational hazard of his particular profession, she supposed.

'What's this?' he asked, lowering his voice, even though there was no one within earshot.

'Instructions.'

'For what?'

'Everything's written down. There's a telephone number in there and a series of words and phrases. It explains how to make contact and what to say.'

'Make contact with . . . ?'

'Never you mind. The voice on the other end of the phone. You just follow those instructions and everything will be all right.'

'When?'

'Tomorrow. Maybe.'

'Maybe?'

'From midday onwards, keep your radio on, or the TV. Listen to the news.'

'What am I listening for?'

'An aircraft hijack. A flight out of Heathrow.'

Bradfield sucked on his cigarette and whatever he was thinking, he chose to remain silent.

Petra leaned forward. 'You only open the envelope if the hijack goes ahead. If you don't hear anything after twenty-four hours, burn it without opening it. Is that clear?'

He nodded and then took his first sip from the pint of Guinness. 'What I'd like to know is why you think you can trust me.'

'Because the first time I came to you, you saw straight through me. You told me I shouldn't carry a gun unless I was prepared to use it. Do you remember?'

He nodded slowly. 'I do.'

'Despite that, you didn't kick me out.'

'And that's your reason for trusting me now, is it?'

'Partly.'

'And the other part?'

'You know the other part.'

* * *

399

Brewer Street. She promised herself this was the very last time and then wondered how many times she had made exactly the same vow. The rain had eased off to a persistent drizzle. She walked past the door which was closed but, she was sure, not locked. It never used to be. A gentle nudge would reveal the dark hall she knew too well. She looked up at the windows on the floors above, their light blocked out by drawn curtains, and then moved on.

Two minutes later, she was on the fire-escape at the rear of the building next to the one in which she used to work. The iron ladder felt as unsafe as ever, dust crumbling from the brick to which it was attached. She reached the top and checked the superfluous padlock; the bolt still had nowhere to slide to. One heave of the shoulder forced the door open. Once she was inside and had closed it behind her, she turned on the plastic torch that Rutherford had found for her. The beam was feeble but sufficient. She cast it over the attic.

The place was still a museum, a perfectly preserved piece of the past. The twine-bound papers and magazines were just where they had always been. So were the discarded packing cases. Petra went over to the empty water-tank and shone her light into it. Proctor's computer was still there. Then she went back to the front door so that she could count the floorboards forwards before moving the correct distance to the left. She got on to her knees and lifted the board. The plastic pouch containing Proctor's seven disks was still where it was supposed to be, next to a small blue wash-bag that had originally been the property of Varig Airlines. Petra had placed the bag next to the disks in the week between Christmas and New Year. Inside it was a roll of banknotes containing sterling, dollars, francs and Deutschmarks, as well as the third identity that Cyril Bradfield had created for her.

Serra's lap-top was on the table in her sitting room next to the two Sony Walkmans – the one she had been given and the one she had bought. The glare from the screen provided the only light in the room. The files she examined reinforced the unpleasant truth: without the data disk, she had nothing significant. Yet who was to say that what was on the disk would necessarily provide a solution?

Petra placed her face in her hands and took a deep breath.

If that flight fails to leave tomorrow, nearly four thousand people will die.

Those were the words he had used. She turned them over in her mind. What did they constitute? The bluff of a man who knows his fate, or a last-ditch attempt at self-preservation by a man too scared to die? Nearly four thousand people. Why that number, specifically? Perhaps there was no reason. No matter how hard she tried, Petra could not see how these people would die if the aircraft stayed on the ground. Once it was in the air, there might be a way. Once it was in the air, there was no telling what kind of damage could be created. Except that Serra had assured her that the hijack was due to come down in Malta and that the passengers and crew – most of them, anyway – were going to be released. Then again, Khalil had been a lie – *apparently* – so why shouldn't Malta be a lie too?

Thinking about the possibilities wasn't helping. The more she considered them, the more confused she became. So she concentrated on the things she knew. Alexander would never sanction her participation in the hijack. If the hijack was halted, nearly four thousand people *might* be at risk. If the hijack proceeded, three hundred or more passengers would *definitely* be at risk. And most importantly of all, Alexander would never believe that Khalil didn't exist, despite the fact that he was the one who had created Petra Reuter. Coming from her, of all people, he'd find the suggestion absurd, perhaps comic, and, no doubt, painfully predictable.

Unsure of anything any more, she switched off the laptop and called Frank.

'Marina?'

'Mmm.'

'I've been thinking about you all day. Can I come over?'

'No. I need to get out of here. I'll come to you.'

We kiss and he leads me by the hand into his sitting room. He offers me some wine. There is a bottle of Rioja open. I accept gratefully. The wine warms me. He takes hold of my arm to gently steer me towards the sofa and his fingers press into my freshly-sutured knife wound. I flinch – it's a reflex – and spill some of the wine on to the coffee table and the carpet. Frank isn't bothered about that, though. He's looking at me and he's worried.

'Are you all right?'

I'm not going to lie so I just stand there.

'What's wrong with your arm?' *he asks.*

I just shake my head. It's not that I'm choosing to stay silent. It's that I can't speak. Not at this particular moment. He seems to sense this. I am wearing a thick black shirt over a grey vest. His fingers unfasten the shirt's buttons until it is open. Then he pulls the material to one side and sees the dressing around my left biceps.

'What happened?'

'I got cut.'

'How?'

'By a knife.'

Naturally, Frank's eyes widen. 'Who did it?'

'Sit down,' *I tell him.*

'Marina . . .'

'Sit down.'

He does. Then I sit beside him on the sofa.

I say, 'Frank, I've got something to say to you – actually, I've got a lot to say to you – and I want you to hear it all before you say anything in reply. Okay?'

'Okay.'

'My name is not Marina Gaudenzi.' *Already, his expression is* changing because I've dropped my accent. 'My name is Stephanie Patrick. I'm English and I'm twenty-three years old.'

He gets my family history and discovers what a poisonous child and adolescent I was. He shudders when I tell him about flight NE027 and my involvement with it. After that, he is shocked and then disgusted by the story that follows. I know he is. Of course, he tries to pretend that he isn't but the truth has a way of making it to the surface. In my story, Keith Proctor comes and goes and is then followed by vagueness. I cannot tell Frank about Alexander, or Magenta House, or Serra, or the ghost called Khalil because I fear that this information may put him at risk. I tell him this and he accepts it. He asks how I got the cut and I refuse to give him details. When he asks what happened to the person who did it to me, I tell him the truth. He nods grimly and, after a reflective pause, says, 'I had a feeling you'd say that.'

It is after one in the morning by the time I have finished. Three hours have elapsed. Last night is forgotten, rendered meaningless by what I have just told him. We are both exhausted. I don't ask Frank what he thinks because he hasn't had time to absorb anything, and any answer he gives me is going to be something diplomatic and I don't need that now. I've never needed that. He says we can talk some more tomorrow and I say that would be good.

Although Frank has had some time to get over the initial shock of my confession, I am surprised at how composed he seems. Surprised and grateful, since I need his support now in a way that I have never needed support from anyone before. I want to be held. I want to be comforted. I want to know that everything is going to be all right.

We make love.

It feels different. Not better, not worse, but different. Perhaps it's because it's Stephanie who makes love with Frank tonight, not Petra or Marina. The feeling goes deeper than the name. In a sense, I am losing my virginity. Not physically, but emotionally. As a rebellious teenager, Stephanie had sex, but she never made love with anyone.

Later, in the darkness, I feel wetness on my face. Tears. I can

403

hardly believe it. They do not make me angry which I find surprising. In fact, I can feel my face is smiling.

I am Stephanie. Tomorrow, I will be Petra again. But tonight, lying next to Frank, I am Stephanie and I recognize this feeling that consumes my heart.

Quietly, so quietly that I am sure he cannot hear me, I whisper the forbidden phrase.

'I love you.'

And I mean it.

5

THE
RHYTHM
SECTION

29

Eighty minutes after leaving Heathrow, flight BA283 was hijacked. The plan Petra had devised to prevent the hijack had been simple enough. She had intended to phone Alexander from Heathrow and tell him that the flight was due to leave the airport around midday and that he should alert the appropriate authorities. She was then to have insisted that no action should be taken until her second call. Naturally, she'd expected he would resist such a proposal but she'd decided to withhold the flight number, thus presenting him with an awkward dilemma. He could either play it her way or he could get the entire airport shut down. But, as she would have pointed out to him, if he chose to close the airport, incoming flights would be diverted and those terrorists who were connecting to BA283 would slip through the net. Indeed, it now seemed likely that *all* of them were going to connect to the flight and that she, Yousef and Mirqas had been the only three who were supposed to depart from Heathrow. On balance, she'd felt that Alexander would be forced to concede to her.

The hijack occurred during lunch, when most passengers were confined to their seats by the trays on their lowered tables. Being at the rear of the aircraft, Petra's cabin was the last to be secured.

It began with a series of shrill cries that came from the forward sections of the 747. Around Petra, initial confusion quickly made way for fear as the pleas and shrieks in front persisted. Faces froze with fright and a deathly hush fell over the passengers until Zyed appeared, clutching an MP5 carbine in one hand and a female flight attendant in the other. A muscular forearm was wrapped around her throat while the muzzle of the weapon was pressed against her right cheek. The sight provoked gasps of astonishment and horror. As the panic spread, the noise level rose; cries of outrage blended with squeals of fear. A few prayed for deliverance while a few more were too stunned to make any noise at all. Mouna appeared at the head of the other aisle and began to shout instructions that Petra couldn't hear. On the far side, a man in a navy fleece began to rise from his seat. Zyed swung the MP5 carbine at him. The flight attendant screeched at him, begging him to stay down. He paused halfway between sitting and standing, and then sank back into his seat.

Zyed and Mouna waited for the din to diminish before Mouna repeated her two instructions; no one was to leave their seat, everyone was to do as they were told. Providing these rules were obeyed, she assured them, no one would be hurt. The flight attendant reinforced the message in a high-pitched voice that trembled with fear. Shock began to subdue the passengers into silence; soon, an occasional whimper aside, nobody was making a sound.

Later, Mouna, who was carrying a Beretta 40-calibre pistol, began a slow trawl down both aisles, scanning the passengers. Petra was sitting near the back in seat 45K. As the number of unchecked faces decreased, she saw something close to panic in Mouna's expression. Where was Yousef? Where was Mirqas? Mouna's eyes met Petra's eyes. Not a flicker was exchanged. Her failed search complete, she returned to the front of the cabin, whispered something to Zyed and then vanished from view.

Ten minutes later, the aircraft began a broad turn to the left.

Petra had never planned to board the flight. She *had* intended to check in for it because she needed to be beyond passport control when she made her second call, but that was as close as she had expected to get to the aircraft itself.

Her visit to Cyril Bradfield, for instance, had been entirely precautionary. An insurance policy against something unforeseen. When she'd kissed Frank goodbye and told him that she was already looking forward to that evening, she'd meant it. In her mind, she had been sure that, one way or the other, it would all be over by the end of the day. After all, if her plan worked perfectly, nobody would be hurt and all the terrorists would be apprehended. And if it only worked partially, at least the aircraft would never leave the ground and its three hundred and eighteen passengers, sixteen cabin crew and three flight crew would be spared.

That was how it should have been. This was how Petra had intended it to be. But by the time she reached Heathrow Airport, she knew that was not how it was going to be.

If that flight fails to leave tomorrow, nearly four thousand people will die.

Petra knew about liars and lying. She was a professional. As Stephanie, and then Lisa, and now as Petra – or as Elizabeth Shepherd, Marina Gaudenzi or Susan Branch – deceit was entirely natural to her. She understood it and recognized it in others, saw how and why they used it, and the different ways in which they used it. Dishonesty had kept her alive. It had protected her. She regarded it not in terms of right or wrong, but in terms of practical choice.

In her heart, she knew that Marc Serra had not been lying. It was pure instinct and, once she'd submitted to it, her conviction strengthened and she saw that she had known it all along, and that she had tried to resist it because she didn't want to believe it.

Petra had understood Serra. She understood men like him and she had understood him in particular. His claim was made out of a genuine desire for her to know what was going to happen so that when it did, Petra would know that she'd had advance warning of it and might have prevented it. Serra had known he was going to die so it hadn't been some feeble attempt to buy clemency. On the contrary, it was a last stand, a moment of bittersweet defiance. That was to be his legacy to her. And that was the kind of man Serra had been. The challenge made, he'd died assuming victory.

Where was the evidence to support her theory? There was none. And supposing she was wrong? After all, nobody in their right mind was going to risk three hundred and eighteen passengers, a cabin crew, a flight crew and a Boeing 747 to allow Petra to pursue an instinct based purely upon her self-professed understanding of liars and lying. She accepted that, which was why the only course of action left open to her was to deny them the chance to make that decision.

Four and a half hours after the aircraft had been seized, the British Airways 747–400 began its descent for Malta. The initial eruption of panic now over, fear lingered in the crushing silence that surrounded Petra. Although she could no longer hear the anxiety of the passengers, she could see it in the faces drained of colour, in the unblinking eyes, in the white knuckles of hands that clutched arm-rests too tightly. Too scared for coherent thought – almost too scared to breathe – they existed on the narrow border between enforced self-control and hysterical breakdown. For her own part, Petra existed in the numbness she knew so well, and was content with the divorce of body and mind.

It was just before eight in the evening local time when the aircraft touched down at Luqa Airport, landing on runway three-two, before taxiing to runway zero-nine. The captain instructed the passengers to close all the window blinds as the aircraft rolled to a halt as far from the airport terminal buildings as possible.

It took half an hour to merge the three hundred and eighteen passengers, the First Class and Club World passengers being ushered into the economy cabins, a manoeuvre that left a mere handful of economy seats unoccupied. Petra understood the thinking behind it. With the hijack team reduced by two, concentrating the passengers in one area of the aircraft prevented the terrorists from being spread too thinly.

'I am looking for a doctor who speaks French. *Je cherche un médecin.*'

The terrorist named Markoa was at the front of the cabin, searching for volunteers. He was tall and skinny, all bones and angles. Petra raised her hand slowly. Markoa came down the aisle.

'You're a doctor?'

'Yes.'

'Bring your things and come with me.'

Petra's seat was by the window. The two passengers on her left had to move into the aisle to allow her out. She took her bag from the overhead locker and followed Markoa forward. There were two terrorists at the very back of the aircraft, one on either aisle, each commanding a clear line of view up the aisle to the front of the forward economy cabin. They passed another terrorist – Obaid – stationed in the galley between rows thirty-eight and thirty-nine. There were a further two at the front of the forward economy cabin – Fatima and Zyed – standing in front of drawn aisle-curtains. That left Markoa as a roving extra, one upstairs on the flight deck, and the leader himself, Basit. Or rather, Reza Mohammed.

Dressed in a black suit with an open-necked plain white shirt, he was standing in the First Class section, in the nose of the aircraft.

'Yousef and Mirqas are not here.'

The statement came as a question.

'They're dead,' she told him. 'The British security services killed both of them.'

She saw a flash of fear in Markoa's eyes but Reza

411

Mohammed remained calm and focused himself on her. 'When?'

'Yesterday.'

'What happened?'

'I don't know. Serra didn't know either. And he wasn't going to wait around to find out.'

'You saw him?'

Petra nodded. 'He came to London to see me yesterday evening.'

Mohammed was staring at her, waiting for the betraying signal that she refused to give him. 'If the British security services had killed Yousef and Mirqas already, surely he would have kept as far away as possible.'

'I was the only one he could contact. The rest of you were out of reach.'

She wondered if that was true. It was what Serra had said to her, but what did that count for? Mohammed was inscrutable. 'What did he say?'

'That everything should proceed as planned. And that I should assist if necessary. He also gave me his computer.' As casually as she could, Petra reached into her shoulder bag, pulled out Serra's lap-top and said, 'He told me that you had the disk.'

For a moment, Reza Mohammed said nothing and Petra feared she had made a mistake. Then he patted his jacket pocket and said, 'Yes, I have it.'

'Could I have a look at it?'

'There is no need for you to look at it. There is nothing on the disk of any importance. I've checked.'

Petra wanted to protest but restrained herself. She forced herself to shrug, as though it made no difference to her.

Reza Mohammed said, 'Did Serra say what he was going to do?'

'Only that he was planning to disappear.'

Mohammed nodded. 'Then he will. What time is it?'

Petra looked at her watch. 'It's almost nine-thirty here, eight-thirty Greenwich Mean Time.'

'And so . . . three-thirty in New York. I think it's time to make our demands. You can come.'

They walked back through the lower Club World cabin, up the stairs and through the deserted upper Club World cabin to the flight deck, where Ali was standing in the open doorway, a Ruger 9mm in his right hand. Ali, who was the eldest of the hijack team, had been a pilot for Saudia. He exchanged words with Reza Mohammed and then made way for both of them.

Reza Mohammed told the captain that he wanted to make his demands. Petra glanced at the two co-pilots. The strain was evident in both their faces but they appeared outwardly calm. She looked through the window and saw the brilliant glare from the airport arc lights in the distance. Mohammed took the co-pilot's headset and waited for a signal from the captain.

The instructions, which were written on a piece of paper, were precise and concise.

'I have a statement to make. We demand the freedom of Sheikh Abdul Kamal Qassam. He is to be released from his illegal imprisonment in the United States of America. By midday Greenwich Mean Time tomorrow, he must have left the maximum-security facility in Colorado where he is currently being held captive and he must be airborne. By nineteen hundred hours Greenwich Mean Time tomorrow, he must be clear of United States airspace. On account of the distance he will eventually travel, his flight will be permitted to stop once on the eastern seaboard to take on fuel. Once Qassam is confirmed over the Atlantic, a phased release of hostages will begin, culminating in the release of all the remaining hostages and crew once Qassam has reached his eventual destination. If either of these deadlines is missed, retribution will be swift and merciless. Similarly, any attempt at sabotaging our demands will be punished severely. There will be no further communication from this aircraft until shortly before the first deadline. These demands are not open to

413

negotiation. They are final and absolute. We are the Sons of Sabah.'

As Petra followed him back along the upper deck, she said to him, 'The United States government will never agree to it.'

Reza Mohammed nodded. 'I know.'

I am alone in the forward galley. I perform a small series of stretches to ease the stiffness in my back. The aircraft is eerily quiet. Where I am, it is easy to believe that it is empty and I'm glad that I'm not stuck in seat 45K. I look at my watch. It's three-forty-six GMT. In another quarter of an hour, the terrorists will rotate their positions in the economy cabin, two of them being replaced by Zyed, who is currently roving, and by Mouna, who is taking her shift up on the flight deck. Only Reza Mohammed and I are excluded from this duty loop.

I should feel some pity for all the people at the other end of this aircraft because I put them there but I don't. I look forwards because I cannot afford to look back.

I try not to think about Frank but he fills my head. What can he be thinking now? That I have disappeared for good? Somewhere in the deeper, darker recesses of my mind lurks the fear that I will never see Frank again. I could die or, worse, I could survive and return to him only to discover that he cannot overlook the landslide of deception. Why should he? He fell for a woman named Marina Gaudenzi. He has no idea who I am. Nor do I.

I am on an aircraft that has been hijacked. I feel like a hostage, a victim, but I am a perpetrator; I feel like Stephanie but I am Petra. Or am I?

There was a time when I thought the divisions were clear. I felt confident as I changed from Petra to Marina to Susan Branch and then back to Petra. It was as easy as flicking through the channels on TV. But now the signals are confused and the picture has become blurred beyond recognition. I am none of the above and, at the same time, all of the above. Petra has been compromised by Marina, while Elizabeth Shepherd, Susan Branch and

the others have merged into one amorphous being. And as for
Stephanie Patrick, I have no idea who she is any more.

Reza Mohammed was sitting by the window in the front row of the Club World cabin, his seat fully reclined. His jacket was draped over the back of the neighbouring seat. He looked exhausted. Petra perched on the arm-rest of the chair across the aisle. He opened a blind by a couple of inches before closing it again.

'The sun is coming up.'

'Are you going to talk to the authorities again?' she asked him.

'Maybe an hour before the first deadline, just to remind them that they have an hour left.'

'And they'll say that they need more time.'

'Of course. And I'll say they've had plenty of time and that they still have sixty minutes.'

'Can I ask you a question?'

He shrugged. 'If you want.'

'How did you do that North Eastern flight?'

She watched the change from disinterest to alertness.

Petra said, 'Serra told me about it.'

She could see that he wasn't sure whether to believe her. But she stayed relaxed, as though it didn't matter to her whether he told her or not. 'I'm just curious,' she added. 'From a professional point of view, you understand.'

Gradually, his initial suspicion waned. 'It wasn't difficult.'

'Serra said it was a shaped Semtex charge. Is that right?'

'Yes.'

'How did you get it in place at JFK?'

'Ground crew.'

Petra glanced at his jacket, which was across the aisle from her, only a yard away. 'That can't have been easy, not with the security and everything.'

'It wasn't as difficult as you might imagine. To begin

415

with, we chose not to try to infiltrate. Instead, we recruited from those already on the staff. I was only involved at the end. But overall, it wasn't satisfactory.'

Petra frowned. 'Why not? The outcome was what you wanted.'

'But the process was too inflexible. It involved too many people, which meant too many risks. We were looking for something else.'

'We?'

His response was typically enigmatic. 'I am just one person in a chain.'

With Reza Mohammed at one end, Petra saw the chain extending to the mountainous border between Afghanistan and Pakistan's Northwest Frontier, and to Kamal Ibrahim Karim himself.

'Aren't we all?'

'Not you,' he sniped. 'Money is the only master you have.'

'It's still a line of command.' Reza Mohammed shrugged again. Petra said, 'I don't see that money is necessarily a worse master than religion.'

'Perhaps not. But what does religion have to do with anything?'

'Isn't that what this is all about for you? Slaying the enemies of Islam?'

When Reza Mohammed looked at her she was unable to interpret his expression. 'You would like to think that, wouldn't you?' he said. 'It would make it easier for you if that was true.'

'It doesn't matter to me one way or the other.'

'I've lived in Europe. I know what it's like to be a Muslim in Europe. I've encountered the inherent racism of Europeans, I understand the stereotypes, the demonizing. We're barbaric savages. We're fanatics. We're animals from the Third World.'

'You're paranoid.'

'You think so?' Petra didn't reply. 'The Cold War is

finished but the West still needs an enemy. Israel needs an enemy outside its borders so that it doesn't have to confront the threat inside its borders. Europe needs a common enemy to prevent fragmentation. Powerful American arms manufacturers need an enemy to keep profits high. Fear works. That is why Islam is inaccurately portrayed as a religion of intolerance and aggression. Because it *needs* to be seen like that.'

'I thought you said this wasn't a matter of religion.'

'It isn't. But that doesn't mean that Muslims aren't portrayed as monsters.'

'Well if it isn't religion that's brought you here, what is it?'

He paused for several seconds before finding an answer. 'If I die, it will not be in the name of Islam. It will not be for the glory of Allah the Avenger.'

'What will it be in the name of, then?'

The question was met with silence. Reza Mohammed stared into Petra's eyes. The anger she had expected to see was not there. Nothing was there.

Eventually, she said, 'You said you were looking for something else.'

He frowned. 'What?'

'NE027.'

'Ah, yes.'

'So the North Eastern flight wasn't a success, then?'

'It was a success but it also showed weaknesses. If I had not placed the device myself – if it had been placed in another part of the aircraft – it might have failed to destroy it. And infiltrating ground crews – or recruiting from them – was never considered a realistic proposition for the future. It's not something that can be easily repeated. Indeed, it's not easily achieved in the first place.'

Petra thought about Reza Mohammed's course at Imperial College and of the course taken by Mustafa Sela. She wondered whether she was now looking at both of them. Sitting in front of him inside a 747, it was easy to

417

picture him in a lecture theatre studying aircraft structure, seeking out the points of greatest vulnerability.

She said, 'I don't see how you can get around that.'

'Around what?'

'The difficulty of recruiting from ground crews. Or infiltrating them.'

'Actually, it's easy, although it's not something you could ever do,' he told her, the scorn in his voice quite evident. 'You have to have volunteers who are prepared to die for something they believe in. I know that as a mercenary, you believe in money, but would you die for it?'

'Of course not. To a mercenary, Heaven is here on earth and it's paid for in cash.'

'Well, that is the difference, then.'

'A suicide bomber still has to get the device on board.'

Reza Mohammed was dismissive. 'That's the easy part. Did you know that I walked on to an Alitalia flight from Rome with a gun in my hand-luggage once? It's true. About two years ago. I was astonished when I got to London to find it sitting in the bottom of the bag. I don't know who put it there. I think it was a careless mistake probably. Having said that, I was not astonished that I managed to get through Rome's security with it. And a bomb is so much easier. You take it in parts. A trigger housed in a personal stereo, perhaps. The timer – if you even need a timer – could be a cheap watch. After that, some batteries. And then the explosive itself, of course. If it's liquid, you could take it in any kind of container. A bottle of contact-lens cleansing solution, for instance.'

'Then you go into the toilet, put the pieces together, put them in a bag and . . .'

'And then place it. That is the important thing. On an aircraft like this, in some parts of the cabin, you're sitting just eighteen inches above the fuel tanks. And do you know how strong the cabin floor is? Not very. It's tested to take the pressure from a woman's stiletto heel and not much more. The North Eastern flight was an experiment. A starting point. It was a one-off that could not be multiplied or repeated, but it pointed the way forward.'

'To what?'

'Everything that is happening now.'

It's as though I've been winded; I've forgotten how to breathe. I remember something Anne Mitchell once said to me, just as I was making the transformation from Stephanie to Lisa. She said, 'You don't know what true degradation is until you have to discount yourself, only to find out it makes no difference.' I feel something similar now. This is a new low.

That my parents – that any of those on board NE027 – should have died in the way that they did is too dreadful to forgive or forget. But that they should have died in what was, essentially, a partially successful experiment makes it even worse. I never thought that was possible. And, in a sense, it shouldn't be. After all, they're dead. What does it matter now? Nothing will bring them back.

But the feeling will not be denied. The emptiness inside me now seems, somehow, deeper than before, in the same way that as a child, when I tried to envisage outer space, I could not cope with the concept of infinity. Space had to come to an end somewhere, it seemed to me. But if it did, what kind of barrier would bring it to an end and what would exist beyond the barrier? Perhaps this is the equation that best expresses how I feel right now: sorrowful and hollow multiplied by infinity plus one.

The shock of Reza Mohammed's revelation plunges me into turmoil. I hope that it doesn't make its way to the surface. I try to gather my scattered emotions and focus on the task ahead.

I tell him that I'll be in the First Class cabin if he wants me. I rise from the arm-rest on which I have been perched. I stretch and carelessly brush his jacket with my hip. It slips to the floor. I pick it up and replace it. He never sees the sleight of hand as I pluck the disk from the inner pocket he patted earlier. This is a skill that Magenta House never taught me. This is a skill I inherited from Lisa. The last time I used it, I stole wallets from two drunken Bulgarian businessmen in a seedy hotel in King's Cross.

This is easier.

Alone in the First Class cabin, Petra sat in one of the seats and opened the lap-top. The need to know basis. That was how Serra had dispensed information. Reza Mohammed was correct. The data contained on the disk had no obvious value. But Petra knew that the files were hosts for a series of hidden programmes, including one for implementing encryption and one for reversing encryption. Serra had designed the system so that the lap-top and the disk operated in tandem. Without engaging with its counterpart, neither functioned fully. Together, they formed a perfectly self-contained system. It had been Rosie who had explained to Petra how to search for the hidden components.

She stumbled from one error to the next, as she slowly made herself familiar with the host directories and the sub-directories contained within them. She examined the FDS/12 folder on the lap-top. FAT, FAT/1 and FAT/2 were empty, as they had first appeared when she had seen them in Serra's apartment, but FAT/3 was not. She tried to open the file and was asked for a password. She remembered the very basic fourteen-letter code: LES-FILSDUSABAH. Sure enough, the screen cleared and was replaced by a page headed FAT/3. Beneath it were twelve lines and fifty columns of jumbled numbers and letters. At the bottom of the page she was offered a choice: Proceed or Cancel. She pressed 'Proceed'. The screen asked for another password. She entered LESFILSDUSABAH again but was rejected. She tried SONSOFSABAH, then SER-RAMARC and various other versions of his name, before moving on to the names of the terrorists. For half an hour, she fed guesses into the machine but was constantly denied.

Her concentration was fragmented. The lingering aftertaste of Reza Mohammed's revelation combined with the fear of discovery undermined her ability to focus. Every few seconds, she looked over her shoulder to see if anyone was watching, and the longer she remained unobserved, the tenser she became.

She turned her attention to the twelve lines of the FAT/ 3 file to see if she could detect any kind of pattern among them. Again, she came up with nothing. An image of her parents came to her. Standing in the field that ran down from the house to the stream, they were smiling at her. It was a cold bright day, the wind blowing the grass into a shimmering sea. She returned to the password and entered NE027. The two letters and three digits waited in the box for her confirmation. She looked at the twelve rows and fifty columns above, the senseless grid of six hundred. She pressed the button to proceed.

A mass of letters and numbers – more than half, Petra estimated – were suddenly highlighted in blue. Then they vanished. Those that remained moved around the screen, sorting themselves, assuming new positions. When the screen settled, there were still twelve lines, but the columns had been reduced to nineteen in number. Petra looked at the first line. BA117LHR0845JFK1125. British Airways flight BA117, departing Heathrow at eight forty five, due in to New York's Kennedy Airport at eleven twenty five. She looked down the list. Two flights from Frankfurt, three from Amsterdam, one from Paris, one from Zurich, one from Gatwick, four from Heathrow. Three of the flights belonged to British Airways, three belonged to American Airlines, two to United, two to Delta, one to Lufthansa, one to KLM. Ten of the dozen were due to be airborne by midday GMT, all twelve were scheduled to be in the air an hour later. Beneath the FAT/3 heading there was a date. Today.

Contact-lens cleansing solution and the Anglo-Egyptian Cargo Company on the Earls Court Road. She remembered now that in the room at the back, among the rest of the stored merchandise, there had been two cases of bottles of contact-lens cleansing solution. She also remembered cheap Casio wristwatches and batteries in bulk, and although she couldn't recall personal stereos for triggers, they could easily have been concealed within another product. Or perhaps they were merely stored elsewhere. The point was, Reza Mohammed couldn't have known that she had been inside the Anglo-Egyptian Cargo Company. When he talked of bomb assembly, he made it sound theoretical, whereas Petra now knew that he was being specific.

The Sons of Sabah. Serra had not been lying when he'd told her that she had only seen some of them. She should have known; the signs were there. There had only ever been ten hijackers but the FAT/3 list had always run to twelve.

Whether it was Serra or Kamal Ibrahim Karim, the architect of the plan had understood what was really important about terrorism: striking disproportionate fear into the hearts of the innocent. Reza Mohammed had almost laughed when Petra had stated the obvious; that there was no possibility that the American government would release Sheikh Abdul Kamal Qassam. That was the whole point. The objective of the Sons of Sabah was not to get Qassam released. The objective was to terrorize.

At midday, Reza Mohammed would make contact with the authorities once again and ask if Qassam was free. They would say that the request was impossible, or they would stall, at which point, Mohammed would presumably break off communications and wait for events to unfold. The dozen destroyed aircraft and the four thousand dead would be seen as punishment. High in the mountain passes that form the Afghanistan-Pakistan border, the reclusive and nomadic Kamal Ibrahim Karim would have his victory.

In truth, he was the man who had murdered Petra's parents, her sister and a brother. But she no longer cared about that. Karim was faceless and remote, an anonymous monster in another part of the world. But the faces of the passengers on the twelve flights due to leave Europe later in the morning were real. She knew them all. In their homes and hotels, they would be waking up now, having breakfast, packing. The businessmen would be trying to shave minutes from their busy schedules. The tourists would be looking forward to holidays that were about to start, or enjoying the warm embers of holidays that were about to end. There would be those who were excited at the prospect of reunion and those who were leaden-hearted at the prospect of separation. For the flight crews and cabin crews, today was supposed to be nothing more than another day at the office. These people were her family, they were Martin Douglas, they were her.

As I sit here in the nose of this aircraft, it feels as though all my life has been poured into some vast funnel which has narrowed everything down to this point of a moment. I cannot wait any longer. Flight BA117 is the first of the targeted twelve due to take off. I have less than sixty minutes. And since I have to assume that the passengers will start boarding the aircraft some time before departure, it means I have less than that. Effectively, I have no time at all. I have to act now.

I have tried to think of some way to get a message out. A mobile phone, perhaps. Except that Reza Mohammed had one of the terrorists clear all First Class and Club World hand-luggage to the rear of the economy cabin. I have even considered writing a message on a piece of paper and sticking it to the window in the hope that some powerful lens or scope might seize upon it and be able to identify what I have written. But that is such a long-shot that I cannot afford to take the chance. There is no time left and I need to be sure.

I know that I can't get off the aircraft, which leaves the flight deck as the only viable means of communicating with the outside world. But the flight deck is under constant armed guard. It's possible that I can overcome the terrorist on duty without drawing

*attention from downstairs but, even if I do, I know that the
victory will only be temporary. Sooner or later, what I have done
will be discovered and that will be the end of it. But there are
no alternatives, so there is no choice to make.*

*I pick up the piece of paper on which I have written down the
details of the targeted flights. From my bag, I take out the asthma
inhaler, replacing the Salbutamol canister with the CS gas canister. I am ready.*

*Back in London, Alexander once expressed his opinion on
Islamic fundamentalist terrorists and it has stuck with me ever
since. He said, 'These people do not speak for Muslims around
the world. What they are doing is overlooking the Islamic experience of fourteen centuries. They are reducing all of that knowledge
to one embryonic form of Islam that may or may not have existed
in Medina when the Prophet Mohammed ruled. And do you
know why they are doing this?'*

*At the time, I doubt I even cared. I think I shrugged in ignor-
ance. 'Why?'*

*'Because they are terrified of the modern world. They cannot
adapt to it and it scares them senseless. So instead, they seek
sanctuary in a past that never actually existed in the way that
they interpret it today. They have a fear of life – of modern life
– and this fear of life makes them worship death. And this is
the reason they yearn to crawl back into the womb of history.
They want to feel safe and protected. They want to feel warm in
a cold world.'*

424

30

I step on to *the upper deck. There is no turning back now. I move down the central aisle. Ahead, the door to the flight deck is ajar. My eyes scan everything and miss nothing. A shape pushes through the gloom by the two forward toilets. I recognize the squat, muscular build. It is Fatima. Her hair is cropped short in a masculine style. She holds a Beretta 9mm in her left hand. I am two rows of seats away from her, then one. I don't know whether she speaks English or not so I say nothing. Instead, I hand her the piece of paper in my left hand and smile.*

She has no reason to expect any danger from me and the hours of tension have taken their toll. Her reflexes are jaded. As she bows her head and peers at the numbers and letters on the paper, she does not notice my right hand coming up. I fire the inhaler into her face. A blast of CS gas hits her in the eyes but she cannot cry out because I have already winded her.

One strike to the stomach, then two, from shoulder to fist, my flesh tenses to steel. Each blow helps to release the anxiety within me. Temporarily blinded and gasping for air, she instinctively wants to crumple into a curl but I don't let her. I keep her straight and then head-butt her. Her nose pops. As she slumps, I catch her beneath the armpits; I don't want her landing with a thump. I let her down gently and prise the Beretta from her fingers. She groans softly.

I pistol-whip her twice and she is unconscious.

Petra picked up the piece of paper and checked the Beretta. There were ten rounds left, nine in the clip and one ready to go. She entered the flight deck. The captain and two co-pilots could not have looked more confused but their expressions contained hope. They would have listened to an explanation if it had been offered but there wasn't time. Petra knew that all airline pilots were under instruction to comply with the demands of hijackers.

She pointed the Beretta at the captain. 'I need to get a message out of here right now.'

As English as theirs, her accent shocked them all.

'Do you want to speak to the control tower?' he asked.

'No.' She handed him the piece of paper. 'These twelve flights are all due to leave Europe for the United States. There will be a suicide-bomber on each one. None of these aircraft can leave the ground. Do you understand?'

'Yes. Of course.'

'What can you do?'

The captain exchanged glances with his crew and then said to Petra, 'We could use ACARS.'

'What is that?'

He pointed to a small screen and key-pad on the instrument board dividing his seat and the co-pilot's. 'It's like a radio. It works on VHF. I type a message into it and send it. The moment it leaves here, it arrives there.'

'Where?'

'Wherever you send it to.'

'And where would you send this message to for the quickest action?'

'Heathrow.' Petra looked sceptical so the captain added: 'They already know we're hijacked so the message will automatically be transferred to the crisis centre.'

'Which crisis centre?'

'The one at the airport. It's situated beneath the Queen's Building.'

'Then do it now. Be quick but tell me before you send it.'

The captain began to type. Petra sat in the jump-seat behind him with the second co-pilot in the jump-seat to her right. She peered through the windows, looking for signs of a security presence, but saw nothing. Then she glanced over her shoulder to check the aisle.

426

'Okay. It's ready to go.'

She looked at the message on the screen. EMERGENCY. STOP TAKE-OFF OF FOLLOWING. The captain had then listed the flights in chronological order of departure. BOMBS ON ALL, CARRIED BY PAX.

She said, 'Now add this: call sign: Market-East-one-one-six-four-R-P.'

Once it was done, the captain hit the 'summary' button and pressed 'send'. A moment later, MSGXMIT appeared on the screen.

'It's gone,' he told her. 'What now?'

'I don't know,' she admitted.

'Who are you?'

'Believe me, you don't want to know.'

Petra hauled Fatima's unconscious body off the floor and pushed her into one of the two toilets at the front of the upper deck. The second co-pilot showed her how to lock the door from the outside.

Back in the jump-seat, Petra was unable to prevent herself from looking at the second hand on her watch. Each flick seemed to take longer than the last. There was an edgy silence on the flight deck until the captain said, 'Looks like we've got a reply.'

He was examining the central main screen at the front. By the engine indicators, it read: ACARS MSG. The in-built printer began to spew paper. The captain activated the ACARS screen for Petra to look at.

TO: MARKET-EAST-ONE-ONE-SIX-FOUR-R-P.
MSG RECEIVED, UNDERSTOOD. 12
GROUNDED.
YOU: SECURITY FORCES READY.
ON YOUR COMMAND.
I.B./RHYTHM SECTION.

I am amazed at how quickly the reply has come and it forces me to conclude that Alexander is at the nerve centre. That makes sense if Cyril Bradfield followed the instructions that I gave him. His anonymous call would have alerted Magenta House to the unsavoury truth: if the hijack has happened, Petra Reuter is on board. That would have given Alexander his reason to be at the heart of the security services response. I imagine that he is beneath the Queen's Building at this very moment.

I look at the screen again. I.B./RHYTHM SECTION. I quickly understand the easy part: I.B. is Iain Boyd. For RHYTHM SEC-TION, I find I am back in Scotland. I am on a hill as the mist descends. My running companion and I are forced to sit it out. The wind is blowing rain at us so we drop below the ridge and take cover behind a collection of jagged stones at the edge of a peat hag. He won't tell me his name so I tell him to make one up. Geordie, he says. It matches his accent. He has buzz-cropped blond hair and a face that is creased by a permanent scowl, even when he smiles. As we wait for the mist to lift, I ask him how it's possible to kill in cold blood. At first, he is reluctant to answer but eventually he tells me that the secret is in self-control. If you panic, you lose. Breathing is the key. If your breathing is under control, it's impossible to fall to panic. The lungs and the heart, the bass and the drums, the rhythm section.

'Keep the rhythm section tight and the rest of the song plays itself.'

That was what he said to me. I remember now. Geordie was a soldier. The type of soldier who comes out of nowhere and returns to nowhere. The type of soldier who is not permitted to have a name.

I hear a male voice behind me on the upper deck. 'Fatima?'

Petra kept her back to the door and murmured to the captain, 'Send another message immediately. Tell them to proceed. The passengers are in the rear economy cabin. Sign it Rhythm Section and replace I.B. with P.R.'

The voice was more insistent second time around. 'Fatima?'

'Do it now!' she hissed at the captain.

Petra turned round and walked out of the flight deck.

Reza Mohammed was standing at the far end of the upper deck. He was wearing his jacket. He stepped forward. To watch him emerge from shadow was to watch him emerge from Stephanie's past into Petra's present. In his right hand, there was a gun. The part of her mind that still belonged to Magenta House made the analysis: a Smith & Wesson 645, employing powerful .45 ACP bullets in an eight-round single-column box magazine, with a double-action trigger system. The other part of her mind was suspended in confusion.

Reza Mohammed frowned at her. 'Where is Fatima?'

'Downstairs.'

For a second, he almost bought it. Then he began to shake his head. 'No. She was up here.'

'She went down.'

His eyes began to deaden. Petra recognized the signs.

'Where is she?' he demanded.

'I've told you . . .'

He raised the Smith & Wesson. Petra raised her Beretta.

'Put the gun down,' he said.

'You first.'

'Put down your gun,' he told her, 'or I will destroy the aircraft and kill everyone on it.'

Now she understood. In his left hand, he held a Sony Walkman. His thumb was over the 'reverse' and 'fast-forward' buttons.

'If I press my thumb down, I will detonate a bomb in the cargo hold close to the fuel tanks.'

Was it her Sony Walkman? Certainly, it looked like the same model from this distance. He could have taken it from her bag in the First Class cabin. In which case, it was useless. But it was not inconceivable that Reza Mohammed would be equipped with a trigger of his own. And if he was, would it be housed in the same brand and model of machine that Serra had given her? More than likely, Petra thought, when she considered the bulk purchases she had seen in the store-room at the Anglo-Egyptian Cargo

Company. Mohammed had even mentioned personal stereos passing as hosts for triggers when they had talked earlier.

'I won't put down my gun,' she said. 'And if your trigger finger flinches, I'll take my chances and shoot you dead.'

Reza Mohammed said, 'That is the difference between us. I am not afraid to die.'

'Then you underestimate me.'

They looked at one another. Again, Petra expected to see fanatical hatred on his face. But she didn't. Their eyes and guns locked together, there seemed to be no way out.

Eventually, he said, 'Are you married?'

'*What?*'

'Are you married?'

'No.'

'I was. Once. But she was killed.' Petra felt a kick in her chest. 'Five years ago, in Jerusalem.' He paused to swallow and seemed to have difficulty doing it. 'A group of Palestinian youths were throwing rocks at Israeli soldiers. In return, the soldiers opened fire with automatic weapons. They killed a teenager and a boy aged nine. They injured another five. And they killed my wife. She was crouched in a doorway, trying to hide.'

Petra's attention remained focused on the line that led from her eye past the tip of the Beretta to the centre of Reza Mohammed's chest.

He said, 'The baby inside her – it would have been our first child – was killed instantly but she clung to life for three days. I was at her bedside until she died.'

'You're not the only one who's suffered.'

'Three times, the Israelis have murdered my family.'

Petra tried not to let herself be distracted. 'What are you talking about?'

'I was sixteen in June 1982 when Israel invaded South Lebanon. Israeli aircraft dropped leaflets on Tyre, which was where we lived. They said that the Israeli army would blow up any home that was suspected of sheltering PLO terrorists. They ordered all citizens to hang white flags on their windows and balconies but that didn't stop their tanks from firing into the buildings anyway. My family escaped shortly before the city was cut off. With hundreds of others, they fled north to Sidon, where they hoped to be safe. But they weren't. Sidon was subjected to intense bombardment from aircraft and artillery. And when the troops arrived in the city, they showed no restraint at all. Buildings were destroyed, civilians were killed. My grandparents and my father were executed in the street. My mother was forced to watch my sister being raped by Israeli soldiers before being raped by them herself. Then she was shot. My sister escaped but it was nearly two years before I saw her again and another three before she was able to bring herself to tell me what had happened.'

Petra found that she had lifted her head. Reza Mohammed had lowered the hand holding the Sony Walkman. He noticed that she had noticed, but he made no attempt to reverse the movement.

'I was in Egypt when the invasion happened. Later, I was sent to live in Paris with one of my uncles. He was a wise man. He understood that our future could only be secured through compassion and tolerance. He realized that we would have to give in order to get. In Paris, he earned a good reputation for helping destitute Palestinian refugees find accommodation and work. He established a small foundation which paid for their clothes, for their food. It helped their children get into schools. He was a man who used his wealth to assist others. He taught me not to hate the Israelis for what they did to us, but to try to understand *why* they did it to us. He preached and practised forgiveness. And in 1991, they killed him.'

'The Israelis?' she asked. Reza Mohammed nodded. Petra frowned. 'Why?'

'Mossad were acting on intelligence passed to them by the CIA. They believed my uncle was using the foundation as a cover to assist terrorists to move throughout Europe.

But they were wrong. Not for the first time, the CIA's information was corrupted.'

Something passed between them. Unspoken yet undeniable, the dynamic changed. Petra watched Reza Mohammed lower the Smith & Wesson to his side.

'First my parents and my grandparents, then my uncle. Finally, my wife. I wish I could forgive them but they have done too much to me to permit that.'

Petra was still pointing the Beretta at him. 'You think this is going to make it stop?'

'Israel behaves in the way that it does because it is bankrolled by the United States. It doesn't feel it has to make an effort because it can always rely upon America to support it.'

'So you punish America to put pressure on Israel?'

Reza Mohammed nodded. 'The Americans have no business interfering in our part of the world. They have to learn that they must stop. They do not understand us so they should leave us alone. I don't hate Israelis. I don't hate Americans. I just hate the people who keep destroying me.'

'And what about the innocent? Is it okay for you to destroy them to make your point?'

Reza Mohammed opened his mouth but no sound emerged; the automatic answer stalled in his throat. Petra was familiar with 'acceptable sacrifices' and 'the ends justifying the means' because Magenta House traded in such phrases all the time but the two of them had moved beyond resorting to such cheap dishonesty. So Reza Mohammed allowed his silence to speak for him. *There is no defending the indefensible.* Petra recognized a man whose beliefs and grievances were as legitimate and sincere as ever but who, deep within his heart, knew the bitterness of the truth.

She said, 'Because I don't understand how that would solve anything.'

'I'm not trying to solve anything. I'm just trying to get

them to stop.' He looked pensive for a moment, and then confused. 'Who are you?'

'Who are *you*?' she countered.

His expression changed again. Instead of looking at her, he was now looking at something beyond the confines of the aircraft. Another time, perhaps, another world.

'My name is Mustafa Sela. I am a Palestinian. My country has been stolen from me, my family has been torn apart. My people are regarded as dogs by the West.' The focus returned to his gaze. 'You wanted to know what brought me to this point. Well it isn't religion and it isn't politics. Think about the things I have told you and then tell me that if you were in my position, you wouldn't be the same as me.'

I'm already the same as you; fate has cost us our families.

Petra said nothing and he nodded slowly. 'You can't, can you? It's rage that has brought me here. I tried to control it but what chance did I have? None. That is what it is to be Palestinian.'

Petra lowered the Beretta to her side. 'Whatever happens to us, the Sons of Sabah have failed. I've identified the twelve flights from the disk that I took from your jacket. They've been grounded. And when they check in for those flights, the rest of the Sons of Sabah are going to be caught.'

'You're lying,' he said, but she could tell that his heart wasn't in the denial.

She smiled sadly. 'You haven't even checked your jacket pocket. You already know that I know about the flights, don't you? And you know that I've been on to the flight deck. So what other conclusion can there be? I've got my message out.'

'And what of the people on this aircraft? Do you care what happens to them?'

Petra said, 'It's over.'

He cocked his head to one side. 'The message will be the same. It will be enough for the world to know that it *could* have happened. The margin of the escape will still be narrow enough to chill hearts. In the end, that's what really matters.' They gazed at each other without hostility and then Reza Mohammed added: 'So this is, in fact, better. This is perfect.'

The lights go out. Outside the 747, somebody has shut down the Auxiliary Power Unit. It's started. With the blinds pulled down and the flight deck door now closed, we are in total darkness. We cannot see each other. My training and my natural instinct for self-preservation kick in at the same time. I raise the Beretta and point it into nowhere. I release the safety-catch and start to squeeze the trigger. But I do not fire. I can't.

Reza Mohammed – or Mustafa Sela, perhaps – doesn't fire either. I imagine him in front of me as a mirror-image of myself; I cannot shoot him because I cannot shoot myself. That is what I would be doing if I fired now. I ease the safety-catch back on and lower the gun again. What will be will be and I am resigned to it.

Neither of us says a word. We hear the screams below us. We hear the triple crump of explosives. We hear the pop of gunfire. We hear shouts, we hear an accent that is familiar to me; it belongs to the anonymous soldier. We hear the heavy tread of boots on the stairs leading up from the main part of the aircraft to the upper deck. Red lasers cut through the darkness. A pinpoint of brilliant scarlet dances across my face and then settles on the centre of my chest.

The aircraft has not exploded. Mustafa Sela has not pressed the buttons on the Sony Walkman. He has not fired his Smith & Wesson 645. We are the same, this man and I. Neither of us were volunteers. Both of us were driven to this point on the earth at this point in time.

There is a cough of gunfire from the rear of the upper deck. In the inky blackness, I see nothing except a brief muzzle flash. Then there is a thump in front of me as a dead weight hits the floor. It could have been me. But it isn't.

I am still standing so I must be alive.

434

0617 GMT

Alexander lit a Rothmans and stared at the cassette on his desk.

Of the eight terrorists who had seized British Airways flight BA283, seven were dead. The other had been discovered locked in a toilet. Under any other set of circumstances, that might have seemed comic. Two passengers had been killed during the SAS storming of the aircraft and another fourteen had been injured, of whom three were in a serious condition. As regrettable as the losses were, Alexander considered the casualty figure extraordinarily low. Within the confined environment of a commercial aircraft, a far higher toll could reasonably have been expected.

How had it come to this? It was now clear to Alexander that Petra had developed an agenda of her own and had run it independently of him. The anonymous caller who had phoned Magenta House using her security clearance had not yet been traced and Alexander very much doubted that he ever would be. Petra would have made sure of that. At least it had alerted Alexander to her presence on board, thus giving him time to contact Boyd who had connections with the SAS hierarchy at Hereford; he had arranged for Alexander to masquerade as a 'technical liaison' for the operation.

Petra. Where was she?

In the immediate chaos that followed the end of the hijack, she had slipped through the net and vanished. Alexander recognized that for someone with her training, it would have been absurdly easy. None of her identities had been used in the three days since Malta and no money

435

had been withdrawn from any of the bank accounts in those names. Alexander was forced to conclude that she had developed at least one identity of her own, independently of Magenta House.

There was a knock on the door. It was Rosie.

'Is he ready?' Alexander asked.

'Yes, sir. He's downstairs. But there's something else.'

'What?'

'I've just had confirmation that she was in Zurich the day before yesterday. At Banque Henri Lauder. She left their office at three-thirty in the afternoon.'

The numbered account at that bank had been established to handle Serra's payments to Petra. It had not been one of her personalized accounts.

'So, she went from Malta to Zurich,' Alexander said. 'And we know she was in Paris last night. But where does that leave us this morning?'

'Sir, the money's gone.'

'What?'

'The money for the Leon Giler termination. It's gone. She closed the account and walked away with the cash in a leather shoulder bag.'

The colour drained from Alexander's cheeks. 'A million dollars?'

'A bit more, actually. She'd also already received the first tranche of the half-million she'd negotiated for the hijack. Minus deductions, it comes to roughly one million and eighty thousand.'

Alexander poured himself a mug of coffee from the pot. It was a small room with no windows. There was a circular table at the centre with six leather-clad swivel chairs around it. Tiny tungsten bulbs embedded in the ceiling dropped a dozen cones of light into the room. The walls were grey. So was the carpet.

'I apologize for asking you to come here at this hour.'

Frank White said, 'I'm not interested in your apologies.'

'Then let me get straight to the point. This woman – Marina Gaudenzi – you had an affair with her, yes?'

'That's right.'

'That must have been convenient for you. With her living in the same building, I mean.'

'What exactly is your point?'

'My point is this: you were supposed to keep an eye on her. Not sleep with her.'

Frank sat back in his chair, folded his arms and didn't reply.

'What happened?' Alexander demanded.

'Look, if you'd wanted someone to spy on her, you should have sent her somewhere else. Not to my building. You never even said what I was supposed to be looking out for.'

'I should have thought that was obvious.'

'Not to me. Our arrangement was never like that. Remember? I used to do the occasional favour for you when I was abroad and when our spheres of interest coincided. I'd trade a piece of information, make a low-level contact, keep my eyes open in some of the more politically sensitive areas in which we were testing. But that was as far as it went. You know that as well as I do. So don't try to rewrite the rules now. It's too late for that.'

Alexander sat down opposite Frank. 'So what do *you* think you were supposed to do?'

'Keep my eyes open, see who she saw, that sort of thing. Look at her envelopes in the hall . . .'

'And who did she see?'

'Apart from me, no one, as far as I know. I never saw her with anyone else. As for checking her post, I never bothered. And to be honest, by the time I'd spoken to her once or twice, I'd lost interest in whatever it was that you wanted.'

Alexander's posture stiffened. 'Ah. A romantic. How nice.'

'Well, you don't strike me as the sort of man who'd understand something like that.'

'Where do you suppose she is now?'

'I have no idea. She never said that she was going anywhere. The last thing she said to me was "see you tonight".'

'Do you think you'll see her again?'

Frank shook his head. 'No, I don't.'

'Why not? I thought the two of you were –'

'She won't risk making contact with me because of you.'

'You don't know that.'

'Actually, I do. I know who she really is. Her name is Stephanie Patrick. She told me everything. Except about you which, I imagine, was an attempt to protect me. She had no idea that I already knew who you were. And *what* you were.'

Alexander considered this for a while. 'Then you've lost her, I'm afraid.'

'And so have you. The difference is, I can feel good about it because, at last, she's free.'

A black cab dropped Frank at Curzon Street and he went into the Europa supermarket to pick up some milk and bread. He remembered meeting Marina – no, Stephanie – in one of the shop's aisles. She had been hostile towards him and the thought of it now made him smile. In fact, it was a sweet miracle that he had fallen for her at all. He paid for his groceries and stepped out of the supermarket. The rain had become torrential. Beside him, a man stood in the doorway, trying to avoid the worst of the downpour. He was expertly rolling himself a thin cigarette, despite having plasters around three fingertips on his right hand and two on the left. He lit it and then said, 'I've got a message for you.'

Frank wasn't sure he'd heard correctly. 'What?'

'She called me last night. From Paris. She's moving on this morning but she asked me to find you.' A flash of lightning illuminated Curzon Street and was accompanied by a thunder-clap; the rumble ran through both of them. There were too many questions Frank wanted to ask. Instead, he just stared at the man, who seemed to understand, and who smiled at him and said, 'So, do you want to hear the message or not?'

Back in his office, Alexander was standing by the window when the lightning shot everything into photo-negative. Rain streaked the glass. He returned to his desk and picked up the cassette, which was a recording of the message left on the Adelphi Travel answer-service just after ten the previous night. The call had been traced to a Parisian pay-phone. He pushed the cassette into the machine and pressed 'play'.

Khalil is dead. Whatever you might hear to the contrary, Khalil is dead. I killed him. And no matter what you think, the contract between us is now terminated. Don't bother trying to find me. You won't succeed – you've trained me too well for that. The world's a big place so there's no need for us to run into each other. But you should be clear about one thing: I will be watching you and what is left of my family. If any harm comes to any of them, I will step out of the darkness once more and then I will vanish for ever. Do you understand? I hope so, for your sake. If you ever see me again, I'll be the last thing you ever see.

CPSIA information can be obtained
at www.ICGtesting.com
Printed in the USA
LVOW08s1943141217
559738LV00008B/55/P